The Golden Queen

The Golden Queen

Dave Wolverton

TOR®
A Tom Doherty Associates Book / New York

THE GOLDEN QUEEN

This book is printed on acid-free paper.

A Tor Book
Published by Tom Doherty Associates, Inc.
175 Fifth Avenue
New York, N.Y. 10010

Book design by Richard Oriolo

Library of Congress Cataloging-in-Publication Data

Wolverton, Dave.
The Golden Queen / Dave Wolverton.
p. cm.
"A Tom Doherty Associates Book."
ISBN 0-312-85656-3
I. Title.
PS3573.0572G65 1994
813'.54—dc20 94-7146
CIP

First edition: August 1994

Printed in the United States of America

0 9 8 7 6 5 4 3 2 1

For Mary, who makes it all possible

One

Veriasse could taste the scent of vanquishers in the crisp mountain air. Beneath the sweaty odor of the horses, lying deep below the aroma of pine needles and leaf mold, he could barely detect the acrid scent of a dronon vanquisher's stomach acids. This was the third time he had caught that scent in as many days, but this time it was closer than in the past.

He reined in his mare at the crest of the mountain, raised his right hand as a sign for those behind to halt. His big mare whinnied and stamped its feet, eager to forge ahead. Obviously, the horse tasted the strange scent, too.

On the muddy road behind him, the Lady Everynne reined in her stallion, and Veriasse just sat a moment, looking back at her. She had the hood of her blue cloak pulled up, and she hunched wearily in her saddle, too tired to remain alert any longer. The wind was blowing at his back in wild bursts, rushing through trees with the sound of an ocean, gusting first from the east, then from the south. In such weather, one could seldom tell where a scent originated. A vast forest spread below them, and Veriasse could see little of the road they had just traversed—only a thinning of the pines in the valley. Overhead, thunderclouds rolled across the evening sky. In minutes, full dark would fall upon them, with the storm.

Veriasse raised his hands. The olfactory nerves running up his wrists could detect the subtlest smells. He could taste a person's nervousness from across a room, detect the scent of an enemy across a valley. Now, he could smell a man's fear behind him, along with the acrid odor of a vanquisher.

"Calt?" Veriasse called softly. The big warrior was supposed to be trailing them as a rear guard. With Calt's sharp ears, he should have heard the call even at half a mile. But he didn't answer. Veriasse waited for a count of four.

Downhill, far behind them, Calt whistled like a thrush, three short calls. It was a code: "Our enemy is upon us in force! I will engage!"

Everynne gouged her stallion's flanks, and the horse jumped forward. In a heartbeat she was beside Veriasse, looking back down the trail in confusion, as if to wait for Calt.

"Flee!" Veriasse hissed, slapping her stallion's rump.

"Calt!" Everynne cried, trying to slow and turn her horse. Only her ineptitude as a rider kept her from rushing headlong back down the mountain.

"We can do nothing for him! He has chosen his fate!" Veriasse growled. He spurred his own mare, grabbed Everynne's reins as the horses surged forward, struggling to match pace.

Everynne looked at him, her pale face flashing beneath her hood. Briefly, Veriasse saw the tears moistening her dark blue eyes, saw her struggling to fight off her confusion and grief. She hunched low and clung to her saddle horn as Veriasse pulled her horse over the rise, and soon their horses were fluidly running downhill, side by side, over muddy roads where one misstep would throw a rider headlong to his death.

Veriasse pulled his incendiary rifle from its holster, gripped it with a cold hand. A wailing sound echoed over the mountains, freezing Veriasse's bones, a keen death cry that could not have issued from the mouth of anything human. Calt had confronted his vanquishers. Veriasse held his breath, listening for more such cries, hoping Calt would be able to fell more than one of the monsters. But no more cries reverberated over the hills.

Everynne gasped, and a wracking sob escaped her as the horses raced through the oncoming darkness between the boles of tall black pines.

Five days. They had known Calt only five days, and already he had sacrificed his life in Everynne's service. Yet of all the places the vanquishers could have attacked, this is where Veriasse least expected it, on a quiet mountain road in a backward place like Tihrglas. This should have been a pleasant ride through the woods, but instead Veriasse found himself hunkering down on his horse, thundering over a muddy road, numbed by cold and grief.

Veriasse was weary to the bone, yet he dared not close his eyes. For an hour they rushed through the darkness and pelting rain until the horses could no longer see well enough to run. Even then, Veriasse pushed the horses as fast as he could, sensing that the vanquishers would soon overtake them, until at last the woods opened up and they clattered over a long, sturdy wooden bridge.

The river below them was a swollen flood. Veriasse shouted, drove the horses forward mercilessly till they reached the far side of the river, then halted.

He leapt from his horse, studied the bridge. It was constructed from heavy logs with planks laid over the top. He could see no easy way to topple it, so he fired his incendiary rifle into the planks. Stark white flames erupted for fifty meters across the bridge. The mare jumped and bucked beneath him in fright. She had never seen the chemical fire of an incendiary rifle.

The cold rain had soaked through his robes, and Veriasse longed to stay a moment, warm himself beside those flames. Instead, he took Everynne's reins and pulled her stallion forward.

"Let's stop here," Everynne said. "I'm so tired."

"There is bound to be another settlement just up the road. We can't stop now, my child. We're so close to the gate!"

He urged the horses on, and Everynne did not answer him, just sat stiffly in her saddle. Ten minutes later, they climbed another small hill. Veriasse looked back to see his handiwork. The bridge was an inferno across its entire length, lighting the muddy river in a dull red, firelit smoke billowing overhead.

Yet on the far banks of the river, Veriasse saw the giant form of a green-skinned vanquisher in battle armor, staring at the swollen river in dismay.

When Gallen O' Day was five years old, his father took him to the Widow Ryan with the notion of getting the boy a kitten, and on that day, the Widow Ryan said something that saved Gallen's life a dozen times over.

It was a cold morning in Clere, with a dusting of new-fallen snow on the autumn ground. Gallen's father wore a badly stained brown leather greatcoat and a pair of green woollen gloves that had no fingers, and Gallen clenched his father's hand as they went to knock at the widow's door. The Widow Ryan was so old that many of the children in town told stories on her, naming her a witch and saying that the priest had drowned all her babies for being leprechauns.

The widow's house was grown from an ancient, gnarled pine tree, thirty feet in diameter and two stories tall, with assorted black branches poking out like ruined hands. Many houses in town had grown from seeds taken from its cones, but none of the other houses were quite so vast. Often, crows would fly up from the rocky bay and caw in its branches. The widow's husband had been a tinker, and when he'd found a pot that was not worth mending, he had brought it home to use as a planter. Many a blackened iron kettle still hung from branches on that ancient tree, and Gallen imagined they were suitable vessels for a witch to boil children in.

Gallen's father rapped on the heavy door. Moss grew up the wrinkled bark of the tree, and a large brown snail oozed near Gallen's foot. The widow opened the door, hunched beneath a heavy blue shawl. She ushered them into the warm house—a fire crackled in the stone fireplace—and took them to a box by a faded couch. The widow's cat had seven kittens in a variety of colors—one with orange-and-white stripes, two calicos, and four that were black with white faces and boots. Gallen hardly knew which to choose, so the widow allowed that he could sit and watch while she and his father talked.

Gallen looked the kittens over, and he half listened as the widow told stories from her youth. Her father had been a merchant and once bought seven olive presses down in Ireland, thinking to retire. He'd taken the whole family with him, but a storm blew them into uncivilized lands where wild Owens roamed—hairy men who had lost their Christianity and now wore only brass rings piercing their nipples. The wild Owens ate her family, but held the widow prisoner on a rocky isle where they brought their dead along with gifts of food every full moon, leaving the corpses for her blessing. She'd have to feast for days before the food rotted, then she'd starve afterward for weeks. The island's soil was white with the bones of dead Owens. The widow survived for a summer in a haphazard shelter under a leaning slab of marble, teaching herself to swim until she could finally brave the vast waters.

Once she escaped, she traveled the world. She'd gazed on the statue where Saint Kelly had carved the face of God after seeing his vision at Gort Ard, and as she described the statue, neither male nor female, old nor young, she cried at the remembered beauty of it.

She told how she had wandered for days at the Palace of the Conqueror near Droichead Bo, never twice entering the same room, and there she found a small hoard of emeralds that had been overlooked by treasure hunters for two hundred years.

Gallen quit listening, turned back to the kittens. Between his breathing on them and poking them, the kittens soon woke. He watched them stretch and search for their mother's nipples; then he began playing with them, hoping that since he could not make a choice, perhaps one of the kittens would choose him. But the kittens were not used to small boys, so they ran about the house frolicking with one another.

One kitten in particular caught Gallen's eye: the orange-and-white one would glance into a shadowed nook and hiss as if it had seen a ghost, then it would leap up the couch, climbing as if a wolf nipped at its tail, then it would prance along the spine of the couch with all of its hackles raised, its back arched. When Gallen wiggled his finger, the kitten became all eyes and crouched to stalk for the attack.

Despite the kitten's playfulness, Gallen wasn't sure he wanted it: the widow had fed the cats a fish, and its breath smelled bad. A bright calico with blue eyes caught Gallen's fancy. When it became clear that he'd never be able to choose, the widow bent her wrinkled face close and said the thing that saved Gallen's life, "Take the orange one that plays so much. He'll live longest."

"How do you know?" Gallen asked, frightened, wondering if the widow really was a witch and somehow knew the future.

"Clere is a big town," she said, "with tough old tomcats living on the wharf, and hounds on every corner, and many a horse riding through that could crush a cat. But that orange tom can handle life in a dangerous town. Look at the way he practices the skills he'll need in life. He'll do well."

Gallen grabbed the orange kitten in his stubby fingers. The kitten nuzzled into his woollen jacket, and the Widow Ryan continued, "You can learn a lot from that kitten, child. There are many kinds of people in this world. Some live only in the present—moving through life from day to day without a thought for tomorrow or a backward glance. They live only one life. For these people, life is a dream.

"Another kind of person lives in the moment but has a long memory, too. These people often fester under the weight of old slights or bask in triumphs so time-worn that no one wants to hear of them. For these people, the walking dream is spiced with a past that they can't escape.

"Then there is a third kind of person, a person like your cat. This person lives three lives. Such people don't just muck about in the past or drift through the present, they dream of tomorrows and prepare for the worst and struggle to make the world better.

"This orange kitten, he'll likely never get crushed by a wagon or be eaten by a dog, because he's faced all those dangers here." She pointed a crooked finger to her head.

Gallen took the orange kitten. Sure enough, within six months the others in the litter had been tragically massacred by dogs or crushed under carts or thrown into the ocean by mean-spirited boys. But not Gallen's orange tom. It died of old age years later, and by that time Gallen had learned all that the cat could teach.

As a boy, Gallen lived three lives, but by far the life of his imagination was the fullest. Like the cat, he imagined every possible danger and worked to avert it, and like his cat, he was a rangy lad.

So one summer night when he was seventeen, he surprised himself when he and a neighbor named Mack O'Mally were accosted by two highwaymen on a dark road. Both robbers wore loose black flour sacks to cover their faces. The robbers attacked from behind, and just as one was about to plunge a knife into Mack, a screech owl called out. This distracted the felon, making him turn his head. Gallen noticed the small peepholes the robbers had burned into the sack, and realized the sacks must be mighty inconvenient to see out of. So he snatched both flour sacks, turning them so that the robbers were blinded, then he pulled Mack from their grasp. Within five seconds, he had both highwaymen gutted on the ground.

Gallen and Mack made five pounds and three shillings when they rifled the murderers' pockets, and when they got back to Clere, they went straight to the alehouse and bought everyone a round and gave the change to an undertaker to dig a hole for the dead robbers.

In a sense, that was the beginning of the legendary "fantasist" Gallen O'Day, but that's a far cry from the end of his tale.

No, I suppose that if one were to tell it right—and it's a tale that demands to be told in whole—one would have to continue the story two years later. Gallen had been down south for a year building a name for himself. He had taken up a friendship with a black bear named Orick, and together the two worked as bodyguards for wealthy travelers. In those days, the family clans were strong, and it was hard for a merchant to make a living when the O'Briens hated the Hennesseys and the Hennesseys hated the Greens. An unarmed traveler could hardly ride a dozen miles without someone trying to bloody his nose. But there were worse things in the land.

Rumor said that Gallen himself had rid the countryside of two dozen assorted highwaymen, cutthroats, and roadside bandits. In fact, every highwayman in six counties had learned better than to accost the dreamy-eyed lad with the long golden hair. He was building a grand reputation.

But that fall, Gallen got word that his father had died, and he returned home to Clere to care for his aging mother.

So it was, that one night . . .

An autumn storm kept the rain rapping at the windows like an anxious neighbor as Gallen sat in Mahoney's alehouse with his friend Orick the bear, and as Gallen listened to the rain knocking the glass, he had the unsettling feeling that *something* was trying to get in, something as vast and dark as the storm.

Gallen had come to the inn tonight hoping to ply his trade as a bodyguard, but even though the inn was full of travelers and the roads around Clere were rumored to be thick with robbers, no one had approached him. Not until Gallen caught the eye of a fellow at another table, a prosperous sheep farmer he knew from An Cochan named Seamus O'Connor.

Seamus raised a bushy brow from across the room, as if asking Gallen for permission to sit at his table. Gallen nodded, and Seamus got up and tamped some tobacco into a rosewood pipe, went to the fire and removed a coal with some tongs, then lit his pipe. Father Heany, the local priest, came over to borrow use of the coal.

Seamus sat across from Gallen, leaned back in the old hickory chair, set his black boots on the table and sucked at his pipe, with his full stomach bulging up over his belt. He smiled, and at that moment Gallen thought Seamus looked like nothing more than a pleasant fat gut with a couple of limbs and a head attached. Father Heany came over in his severe black frock, all gaunt and starved looking, and sat down next to Seamus with his own pipe, sucking hard to nurse some damp tobacco into flame. Father Heany was such a tidy and proper man that folks in town often joked of him, "Why the man is so clean, if you took a bath with him, you could use him for soap."

Together, the two old men blew the pleasant smell of their tobacco all about until they were wreathed like a pair of old dragons in their own smoke.

"So, Gallen," Seamus said, "rumor has it that you'll be staying here in Clere now." He didn't finish the sentence, *now that your father has died, leaving your frail mother a widow.*

"Aye," Gallen said. "I'll not be roaming far from home, nowadays."

"How will you keep yourself, then?" Seamus asked. "Have you thought about it?"

Gallen shrugged. "I've been looking about, and I've got a bit in savings. It should last awhile. I've thought about taking up fishing, but I can't imagine any woman ever learning to love the smell of a fisherman."

"Sure, the blacksmith is looking for an apprentice," Father Heany offered.

"I saw him just today," Gallen said, remembering how the smith would pick up the horse's back foot, leaning his shoulders up against the horse's sweaty rump, "and to tell the truth, I'd rather *be* a horse's ass than work with my head so close to a horse's fertilizing region." Seamus and Orick the bear laughed, and Father Heany nodded wisely.

"Sure," Heany admitted, "a smart man can always find a job that will let him keep himself unsoiled." He frowned as if thinking furiously, then said, "There's the priesthood."

"A fine vocation," Orick cut in with his deep voice. The bear was sitting on the floor, paws on the table, licking out of a bowl. Some milk still stuck to his muzzle. "I've been thinking of joining myself, but Gallen here makes light of God and his servants."

"I'll not make light of God," Gallen responded, "but I've no respect for some who call themselves his servants. I've been thinking on it. Your Bible says God created man in his own image, and it says God is perfect, but then he only made man 'Good,' as in good enough? Like maybe he was lazing about. It seems to me that God could have done better with us, considering that we're his crowning creation: for instance, a day-old fawn can jump a four-foot fence—so why can't a day-old child?"

"Ah, and to be sure, Gallen O'Day—" Father Heany said with a fiery twinkle in his eye "—if God had had you looking over his shoulder on the day of creation to give him a little advice, we would have all been better off!"

Orick lapped at the bowl of milk on the table, and the bear had a reflective look in his dark eyes. "You know, Gallen," Orick grumbled soberly, "God only gave man weaknesses to keep him humble. The Bible says 'man is just a little lower than the angels.' Surely you see that it's true. You may not live as long as a tortoise, but you'll live longer than me. Your mind is far quicker than any bear's. And with your houses and ships and dreams, your people are richer than us bears will ever be."

Spoken like a true priest, Gallen thought. Few bears ever entered the priesthood, but Gallen wondered if perhaps Orick wasn't a natural for it.

"I'm not one for the priesthood," Gallen assured Father Heany. "I still love the road too much. I'm looking to buy some property, then lease it out. Other than that, I plan to continue my work as an escort. There are plenty of short routes hereabouts. I can take some work and still care for my mother." He said it mildly, but it was not the short roads Gallen wanted to travel. He wanted to someday head south to Gort Ard and look on Saint Kelly's likeness of the face of God, or head east to the Palace of the Conqueror at Droichead Bo and search for hidden treasures. But now he would be stuck here in County Morgan, never more than a couple of days from home.

"Heavens, boy!" Father Heany said. "Why, your reputation has already traveled farther than your foot ever wandered. Every highwayman in the county will clear out in a week, and no one will *need* escorts anymore! Why, you're your own worst enemy!"

Seamus nudged the priest with an elbow, cleared his throat. "Ah, don't give the boy a fat head. He's not that good!" He turned to Gallen. "But, to tell the truth, Gallen, I do want to contract your services. My son's gone ahead to tell Biddy that I'll be home later, but I'm not half as drunk right now as I want to be in an hour, and I'll pay you two shillings if you get me home alive."

"Two shillings?" Gallen asked. It was a low price for a bodyguard, but then it was late of the night—too late and too rainy for robbers to be about. Gallen would only have to escort Seamus over the hills from Clere to the village of An Cochan, a distance of four miles, making certain that Seamus didn't fall off his horse. "Give me four and it's a deal."

Seamus grimaced as if he were passing a kidney stone. "What? Why you've got an inflated notion of your own worth! I've nothing against you, lad, but there's little room in the world for such a fantasist. You're so hot to become a landlord, you're already evicting imaginary tenants!"

"Five shillings," Gallen said. "Four for my services, and one for insulting me."

"Three!" Seamus said with finality.

Gallen held his eye a moment, nodded agreement. The only sound was the wind howling outside and the paddles in the butter churn. The scullery maid, a sweet sixteen-year-old girl named Maggie Flynn, normally churned fresh butter every dawn, but with the stormy night and so many travelers passing through town, she was trying to get a head start. She had dark red hair and darker eyes, a patina of perspiration on her brow. She caught Gallen looking at her and shot him a fetching smile.

Seamus winked at Father Heany and said, "Ah, Father, it doesn't get any better than this, does it? Lazing about after a fine dinner."

"No," Father Heany agreed. "Not much."

"No, not much better at all—unless," Seamus said, exhaling a cloud of blue smoke, "you were in your own house with your own sweet wife sitting on your lap while you were smoking your pipe, and your dear wee children all tucked into bed." Seamus cocked an eye at the priest, as if daring him to disagree—what with the priest being celibate—but Father Heany just sucked on his pipe thoughtfully, seemed to take a cue from Seamus.

"Ah yes, a wife." Father Heany sighed. "'Tis a fine thing, I'm sure."

"Now, if I were a young man like Gallen," Seamus said, "just moving back to town, getting ready to settle down, I'd be looking for a wife. In fact, I'd almost think it my duty to find some fine County Morgan girl and marry her." Gallen wondered what Seamus was hinting at. Seamus had a couple of young daughters out on his farm, but the oldest was only fourteen. And while it wasn't unheard of for a girl to marry so young, Gallen couldn't imagine that Seamus would be talking about "duty"—unless some boy had filled one of his daughters with a child and then run off into the yonder and now Seamus was desperate to find the girl a husband.

Father Heany must also have been trying to fathom where Seamus was leading, for he said, "Now that you speak of it, there's that Mary Gill down in Gort Obhiann whose husband got kicked by a horse last summer, leaving her with three strapping little boys, all of them fatherless. If I were looking for a wife, I'd certainly pay a visit to Mary. A beautiful girl! Beautiful! And she's guaranteed not to leave you childless."

"Ah, she's pretty enough all right," Seamus agreed. "But dumb as a pine cone, I hear. Like as not, she'll fall in a well or catch a cold from standing in the rain too much, then leave her husband a widower."

"Hmmm?" Father Heany asked, cocking a brow.

"Now, there is Gwen Alice O'Rourke—smart as a bee's sting, and a hard-working girl, too."

"Nooo, no!" Father Heany threw up his hands as if to ward off a blow. "You can't go trying to unload your ugly niece onto the boy," the priest said. "That would be a sin. She's a nice enough girl, but with those buck teeth—"

"You don't say!" Seamus frowned in mock horror. "You daren't talk about my niece that way!"

"I will," the priest said. "God agrees with me on this point, I'm sure. The girl has tusks as dangerous as any wild boar's. Now, if Gallen is looking for a nice young woman, I'm sure others could be found."

Maggie got up from her churn. The cream had hardened to butter, and she could no longer turn the crank. Her face and arms were covered with perspiration. Gallen figured it must be midnight, yet she'd been working since before sunrise. She stood wearily, put a heavy log into the fire, then sat at a nearby table with a sigh that said, "Ah, to hell with it."

"Well, there is Maggie here," Seamus said with a wink, and Gallen saw that he'd been planning this all along. With Gallen and Maggie sitting so close together, it was a perfect opportunity to torment them both. No one in town could have missed the glances they exchanged, and Gallen had just about decided that Maggie was the one for him. "Now, Maggie has it all—she has her wit, she's a charmer, and she works as hard as three people."

"True, true," Father Heany agreed.

"And looks!" Seamus said. "More men come here to look at Maggie than ever came in for a drink! Why, if some boy were to marry her, it would deal a horrible blow to John Mahoney's business. Sure, you'll not find a better catch in all of County Morgan than Maggie Flynn."

"But . . ." Father Heany said with a sigh, "she's too young. The poor girl is only sixteen." He said it with such finality, Gallen knew it was more than a casual thought, it was a verdict. Father Heany was only repeating aloud in front of Gallen the things that others in town had decided in private.

"Too young?" Seamus argued. "Why, she's but two months away from her birthday!"

The priest held up his hands. "Sixteen—even an old sixteen—is marginal, very marginal. Marrying a girl so young borders on sin, and I'd never perform the ceremony!" he declared. "Now, if you ask me—and I'm sure the scriptures would back me up on it—eighteen is far more respectable! But if you make a woman wait until she's twenty, then it seems to me you're sinning the other way and ought to be roundly chastised for making the lady wait."

Seamus raised his brow, gave Gallen a look that said, "You can't argue with a priest," then drained his glass. Maggie got up to refill it, but Seamus shooed her away with a wave. "So, that's how you feel about it, Father Heany," Seamus said as he hitched his pants and strolled to the bar. "Well, all I can say is that it's growing mighty cold in this corner of the room, so I think I'll sit me by the fire and leave the young ones be."

Seamus filled his mug, then sat at a table nearer to the fire. Father Heany and Orick followed, leaving Gallen alone. Father Heany took up a fiddle and began playing a mournful tune appropriate for a cold night. Maggie sat down next to Gallen. He put his arm around her shoulders, and as soon as Seamus had his back turned, she glanced around the room quickly to make sure no one was looking, then nipped Gallen's ear.

"Gallen O'Day," she whispered fiercely, "why don't you come up to my room? I'll let you play on my feather bolster, and you can undress me with your teeth."

"What?" he whispered, feeling blood rush to his ears. "You've got to be joking! You could have a baby from that. You wouldn't want to get tied down with children so young."

"I'm old enough to cook and clean from sunrise to sunset for a bunch of dirty beggars who give me no consideration and don't know enough to take off their muddy boots before they flop onto a bed. Taking care of a husband and a couple of sweet young ones would be a holiday after this."

"Ah, Maggie," Gallen said, "you heard Father Heany. Give yourself another year or two to grow up."

"I'll have you know, Gallen O'Day," Maggie said, "that most men in these parts think I'm old enough already. You should see my backside: I've been pinched so many times that it looks like I've been sitting in a bowlful of black currants!"

Gallen knew a threat when he heard one. She was saying, either you pay more attention to me, or I'll find someone who will. And she wouldn't have to look far. Gallen took a thick oak stick from his pocket and began simultaneously twisting and squeezing it, an exercise he used to strengthen his wrists. "Hmmm . . ." he said, "maybe I should take a look at your backside." He felt her warm breath on his neck.

"You're not a religious man, are you?" she asked. "I wouldn't want you to think I'm just after fornicating with you. If you would rather have a priest and some vows first—"

"No, it's not that," Gallen assured her, yet marriage was exactly the problem. She was so young that no honorable man would propose to her, yet she couldn't bear the thought of working here for another two years. So, if she happened to turn up with a child in her belly, the whole town would just wink at it and hurry the wedding. It was an odd turn of events, Gallen thought, when the town would view a shameful wedding as somehow being more noble than an honorable proposal.

"If I were to propose right now," Gallen said, "it would hurt us in the long run."

"In what way?"

"I want to have a political career," Gallen said. "Father Heany is right. I'll never make a living by selling my escort services around here.

I've killed too many highwaymen. Next year, I plan to run for county sheriff. But I can't do that and go tumbling in bed with you. It would bring shame on us both. I beg of you, give yourself time to grow up."

"Is that a promise you're making me," Maggie asked, her shoulder muscles going stiff in his arms, "or are you just trying to brush me off like a gentleman?"

Gallen looked into her dark eyes, eyes such a deep brown that they were almost black. She smelled of good honest sweat and lilac perfume. Outside, a fierce guest of wind howled and sleety rain spattered against the windows with such startling ferocity that Gallen and Maggie turned to glance at it. The window rattled so loud, Gallen had been sure that someone had pushed against it. He turned back to Maggie. "You're a sweet girl, Maggie Flynn. I beg you, be patient with me."

Maggie pulled away, disappointed, perhaps hurt. He still hadn't promised himself to her, and she wanted a commitment, even if it was informal.

The inn door swung open, and a sheet of rain whipped into the room. At first Gallen thought the wind had finally succeeded in blowing the door open, but after a moment, in walked a stranger in traveling clothes—a tall fellow in riding boots and a brown wool greatcloak with a hood. He wore two swords strapped over his cloak—one oddly straight saber with a strange finger guard on its hilt, and another equally long curved blade. By wearing the swords over the cloak in such a downpour, the stranger risked that his blades would rust but kept his swords handy.

Only a man who made a living with his weapons ever wore them so.

Everyone in the alehouse stopped to stare: the stranger must have been riding in the dark for at least five hours, a sign that he had urgent business. Furthermore, he stood at the door without removing his hood, then silently inspected each person in the room. Gallen wondered if he might be an outlaw. He didn't seem to want his face to be seen in town, yet his roving eyes appraised each person in the room as if he were a hunter, rather than hunted.

At last, he stepped aside from the door so that a slender waif of a woman could enter the room. She stood in the doorway for a moment, erect, head held high with her hood still covering her face. Gallen saw by his tense posture that the man was her servant, her guard. She wore a bright blue traveling robe trimmed with golden rabbits and foxes. Under her arm she carried a small harp case made of rosewood. She hesitated for a moment, then started forward and her hood fell back.

She was the most beautiful woman Gallen had ever seen. Not the most voluptuous or seductive—just the most perfect. She held herself with a regal air and looked to be about twenty. Her hair was as dark as a starless night. The line of her jaw was strong and firm. Her skin was creamy in complexion and her face looked worn, tired, but her dark blue eyes were alive and brilliant. Gallen recalled the words to an old song: "Her eyes kindle a fire for a lonely man to warm himself by."

Maggie boxed Gallen's jaw playfully and said, "Gallen O'Day, if your tongue hangs out any farther, all you will have to do is wag it to clean the mud off your boots."

Maggie got up and greeted the strangers. "Come in and get out of the weather, sit by the fire and dry those soggy cloaks. Would you poor folks like some dinner, a room?"

The tall man spoke with an odd speech impediment, loud enough so that the entire room could hear, "It is said that there is a place near here, an ancient arch with strange symbols carved on it—Geata na Chruinne. Do you know of it?"

Until that moment, everyone in the room had been listening but pretending not to. Now, they cocked their ears and became conspicuous about it.

Gallen wondered if these strangers might not be adventurers, out to see the sights of the world. Geata na Chruinne sometimes attracted such people.

"I know of the place," Maggie said suspiciously, studying the stranger's face, "as does everyone around here."

"Is it easy to reach?" the stranger asked in a thick voice. "Could we make it tonight, after a brief rest and dinner?"

"No one goes to the arch after dark," Maggie said uneasily. "People say it's haunted. You can stand beneath it on a hot day and feel cold air blowing off it like a sheet of ice. Besides, it's deep in the forest, in Coille Sidhe. You can't go there in the night."

"I could pay for a guide," the stranger offered.

"Well," Maggie said, "there are a couple boys in town who know the way, if you're willing to wait till morning."

"No—they can't be boys," the stranger said, standing over Maggie. "I want a man, a seasoned soldier. Someone who can defend himself."

Maggie glanced toward Gallen, lines of worry in her face. Few people in town had actually been to the ancient ruins called Geata Na Chruinne, "Gate of the World." And only one had any kind of fighting skills.

Gallen wasn't sure that he trusted these well-armed, secretive people. But he didn't want to miss the chance to make some money. He nodded.

"Gallen O'Day could take you there in the morning," Maggie told them as she jerked her chin toward Gallen.

The hooded stranger glanced at Gallen, said, "Are you a soldier?"

He advanced on Gallen, the hood shielding his face. "He's an armed escort," Maggie boasted, "and he's killed over twenty robbers. He's the best there's ever been."

As the stranger got close, Gallen could see that the tall man had vivid blue eyes, tawny hair going silver. He regarded Gallen with a distant expression.

Without flinching an eye, the stranger drew his sword and swung at Gallen's head. Gallen leapt from his chair and grabbed the stranger's wrist, pinching the nerves between the radius and the ulna, then twisting. It was a painful grip, Gallen knew, and made the victim's fingers spasm open. The stranger's sword stroke went wide, then the sword itself clattered to the table. Gallen twisted the man's wrist painfully in a come-along so that the stranger soon found himself at arm's length, standing on his tiptoes.

The stranger nodded, and said, "Well done. You've the reflexes of a cat, and you must have studied a bit of anatomy to have figured out that trick."

Gallen let the man go, surprised that the fellow had wanted to test him. Gallen's reputation had grown so wide that few employers ever bothered to test his skills anymore.

The young woman in blue looked Gallen over, shook her head. "Not him, he's too small."

"Size is an illusion," Gallen said, catching her eyes. "A man is what he thinks."

"And *I* think that if a foe who outweighed you by a hundred pounds swung a sword at you, you would never be able to parry his blows."

Gallen listened to her words with difficulty, realized that like the man, she too spoke oddly, as if she had a mouthful of syrup. Yet her accent wasn't as thick. He said, "I've been strengthening my wrists since I was six years old, knowing that I'd have to parry blows from bigger men. I believe a man can become anything he puts his mind to. And I assert that by thought, I have made myself bigger than I seem."

"He'll do," the guard said, picking up his sword and shaking the pain from his hand. "He's got a hell of a grip—better than mine."

The woman in blue opened her mouth in mild surprise, then smiled.

"I've already contracted a job for tonight," Gallen said. "But I can pick you up at dawn. The hike to the gate makes for a short trip, only five miles."

The stranger spoke to Maggie briefly. Once he'd purchased rooms for the night and ordered dinner inside, the two began walking up the staircase, and then stopped. The old man said, "We just came from the south, from Baile Sean. There's a large bridge over the river there. Lightning struck it just after we crossed. I suppose you'll want to inform the town." Several people cried out in dismay. By law, the two towns would have to come together and repair the bridge, an onerous task.

Gallen knew that he could not let the young woman, his new employer, go without introducing himself.

For a split second, he wondered, if I were the boldest lover in the world, what would I say to this woman now? She was halfway up the stairs, and he didn't have time to think. But he knew that the greatest lover in the world would not hesitate.

He stood and said in a loud voice, "My lady?" The two stopped in their tracks, and the woman glanced over her shoulder at him. Gallen continued, "When you walked in the room just now, and your hood fell back to expose your face, it was as if the morning sun had just climbed over the mountains after a dreary night of rain. We're curious folks hereabout, and I think I speak for many when I ask: may I beg to know your name?" The little speech came out sounding so sweet that Gallen could almost taste the honey dripping from his tongue, and he stood with his heart pounding, waiting for the woman's reply.

She smiled down at him and seemed to think for a moment. Her guard waited cautiously just above her on the stairs, but he did not look back. After a few seconds she said, "No."

They continued upstairs, turned the corner of the hall, and were gone. Gallen O'Day sat down in his chair, staring after them, feeling as if his heart had just turned sideways or he'd died a small death. The last few patrons in the inn looked at Gallen and chuckled. Gallen's face was hot with embarrassment.

Maggie quickly made up two plates and readied them to take upstairs, then came back to Gallen and set the plates on his table a moment and said, "Oh, you poor abused child! To think that she'd mistreat you so." She leaned over and kissed him heavily on the mouth.

Gallen suspected that she was both hurt and angry. He also reminded himself that, wisely, he'd made her no promises. He held her gently as she kissed him, then she slapped his face, grabbed her trays, and danced off, smiling at him over her back.

Gallen put his chin on his knuckles and sat alone, feeling stupid until Seamus O'Connor began to sing and the rain outside quit splattering the windows, then Gallen knew it was time to be off. He helped Seamus to his feet, Seamus snagged the whiskey bottle with his left hand, and they headed out the door.

Amazingly, the storm clouds were scudding by fast instead of lingering like they usually did. Gallen could see pretty well by the slivered moons that shone down like twin sets of eyes, gazing from heaven. Seamus's old mare was across the street, tied in the livery stable with plenty of sweet grass piled before it. Gallen saddled the horse and helped Seamus climb atop, then led the horse out of the stables north toward An Cochan. The mare's hooves clattered over the paving stones. At the back of the inn, in the dim starlight Gallen saw two bears feeding in the rubbish bin and stopped the horse, asking, "Orick, is that you?"

One of the bears grunted in a deep voice, "Hello, Gallen."

"What are you mucking in the slop for?" Gallen asked, surprised that he hadn't seen Orick leave through the back door of the common room. "I've plenty of money. I can have Maggie fix you up a platter." Gallen felt nervous to make the offer. Bears eat so much that they're notorious for always being broke.

"Don't bother," Orick said. "Maggie saved a nice plate of leftovers for me. When I finish here, I'm going up the hill to hunt for a few slugs. It will be a grand feast, I assure you."

"Well, to each his own," Gallen said, appalled as ever at his friend's eating habits. "I'll be back at dawn."

"Do you want me to come along?" Orick asked.

"No, go get some dinner in you."

"God be with you then, for I shall not," the bear said. Seamus hunched over in his saddle and began singing. Gallen shivered at the sound of Orick's cryptic farewell, but pulled the mare's reins, urging her forward.

That night in Mahoney's Inn, the Lady Everynne paced at the foot of her rough bed. The smell of its thick down tick and the soft texture of its heavy red quilts called to her, but even though she was weary, she could not rest. A single dim candle lit the room. She had taken two rooms for appearance's sake. Her guardian, Veriasse, sat at the foot of the bed, head bent in a forlorn attitude.

"Get some sleep, my daughter," Veriasse said. He had slept little in two days, yet she knew he would stay awake at the foot of her bed and keep wide-eyed until they reached safety. His brown hood was pulled back, revealing his weathered face.

"I can't, Father," she said honestly. "Who could sleep? Can you still taste their scent?"

The aging man stood up, shook his head so that his long silver-gold hair spilled down over his shoulders, and went to a basin in the corner of the room. There he poured a pitcher of cool drinking water over his wrists and hands, then toweled them dry. He opened a small window, raised his hands and held them out, long thin fingers curled like claws, and stood for a time with his piercing blue eyes closed as if in meditation. Though the old man could catch a scent with his hands, Everynne could see no sign that he was testing the air. "Yes," he said at last. "I can still taste the scent of a vanquisher. He is distant, perhaps no closer than twenty kilometers away, but I am sure he's here. We can only hope that when we destroyed the bridge, the vanquisher got trapped on the other side."

"Perhaps vanquishers have another reason for coming to this world?" Everynne asked in a tone that was part argument, part plea. "Just because you taste the scent of a vanquisher, it does not mean he has come for us."

"Don't fool yourself," Veriasse said at last. "Tlitkani has sent her warriors to kill us. With only one gate to watch, this world is the perfect spot for an ambush." He said it as one who knows. The Golden Queen Tlitkani had enslaved Veriasse for four years, had forced him to become her advisor. Veriasse was gifted at reading personalities, at studying motives and moods. He could anticipate an adversary's actions so well that many thought him a psychic. No one understood Tlitkani better than Veriasse did.

"The young man downstairs said that the gate is only five miles distant. Could the vanquishers have already found it?"

"It's hard to say—" Veriasse answered. "I feel certain that vanquishers are following, but they could be ahead of us, too. On such a windy night, I cannot even be sure that the vanquisher I smell is twenty kilometers off. It might be ten, or only two."

"Perhaps the vanquishers are searching for the gate, even as we are," Everynne offered.

"Or perhaps Tlitkani wants us to believe that her servants are only searching for the gate—hoping that we will foolishly rush into another trap. I think it best to wait here for the night." Veriasse yawned and rolled his shoulders to keep the muscles loose, clearly uncomfortable. "We should proceed to the gate cautiously. We may have to fight our way through."

Without Calt, Everynne thought, that will not be easy. She felt a pang of grief, hoped that Calt had died painlessly.

Veriasse said nothing for a moment, then asked, "And what of our guide, this Gallen O'Day? Shall we convert him to our cause? He reacts quickly, and he is marvelously strong."

"I won't do it!" Everynne said, perhaps too forcefully. She knew all of the arguments. She needed protectors, she needed an army of men like Gallen O'Day, but what could he know of her world, the weapons that her people used? You could hardly expect a man to battle vanquishers with nothing more than knives, and Veriasse had no weapons to spare. Even if she did choose to persuade the young man to come along, it would be the same as murdering him.

Veriasse sat down cross-legged on the floor, but gazed up at Everynne past heavy lashes. He looked at her knowingly. It was as if he read her mind as she considered the arguments, almost as if he were placing the thoughts in her head. "Then you are decided?" Veriasse said. He smiled secretively.

"What?" Everynne said. "What do you know?"

"I know nothing," Veriasse said. "I can only guess at probable outcomes based on what I know of my associates."

"What do you guess?"

Veriasse hesitated. "I've seen men like Gallen before. He will want to follow you. Regardless of your good intentions, you must allow him to follow you, to fight at your side—if necessary, to die at your feet. So many people depend on you! I would advise you to use this man as your tool. He is only one, but his sacrifice might save many others."

Yet Everynne could not bear the thought of watching another guardian die. Especially not one so ignorant as Gallen O'Day, one so innocent.

"Let's get some rest," she said. Everynne crossed the room, blew out the candle. She closed the window and stood for a moment looking out into the dark streets of Clere. There was a little starlight shining on the town. From this height, she could see over several house-trees and buildings, down to the quay. Small fishing boats lay on the rocky shore, dark, like beached pilot whales. Poles in the sand held twisted coils of fishermen's nets, hung out to dry. Everynne could almost smell the kelp and the sea rime upon them. She had passed those nets only an hour before, as she made her way into town, and the memory of that smell came strong to her.

High on the beach, the seagulls had huddled under folded wings, eyeing her darkly, ominously. Almost, it felt as if they were watching now, through the window.

Everynne shivered, moved away from the window quickly and lay on the bed. Veriasse's heavy, uneven breathing came to her, and she listened to it as she drifted off. Veriasse—with his unwavering devotion, his strong back—seemed somehow more than human. Certainly, by the standards of this world, he would not be judged human at all. Her teacher, her friend. He had guarded Everynne's mother for six thousand years. And during the course of Everynne's short life, he had been a solid presence, always at her side. Sometimes she tried to distance herself from him, think of him only as a warrior, the only one of her guardians to survive this journey. But she could tell that he was weary to the bone, worn through. She could not ask that he continue fighting alone.

The old man sat in the dark at the foot of her bed, wrapped in dark robes—ever faithful, ever determined in the face of overwhelming foes.

With a pang that tore at her heart, Everynne realized what she must do. She needed another guardian, someone to fight beside Veriasse. She knew that men like Gallen O'Day could not resist her. Something in them responded to something in her. It was biological, inevitable. When she had first walked into the inn, she could tell from Gallen's eyes that he believed he had fallen in love. Given an hour in her presence, he would be sure of that love, and within a few days he would become ensnared. Another slave.

Yet there was nothing Everynne could do to dissuade the unyielding devotion of men like Gallen and Veriasse. So Veriasse sat at her feet, waiting to die. Everynne hated her lot in life. But it was her fate. For she had been born a queen among the Tharrin.

Two

Gallen and Seamus had no warning before the attack. The road from Clere to An Cochan was usually well empty by that time of night. Both moons were down. The heavy rains had dampened the dirt road, leaving a thin glaze of water so that the stars reflected off the mud, making the road a trail of silver between columns of dark pine and oak.

They were near the edge of Coille Sidhe, so Gallen moved cautiously. Once, he caught sight of a flickering blue light deep in the wood. Wights, he realized, and he hurried his pace, eager to be away from the guardians of the place. The wights never attacked travelers who kept to the road, but those who wandered into the forest couldn't count on such luck.

Just over the mountain, the land flattened out into drumlins, small hills where the shepherds of An Cochan kept their flocks. Gallen was eager to reach the relative safety of human settlements.

One moment Gallen was walking the muddy silver road, leading Seamus's old nag through a ravine while Seamus hunched in the saddle, singing random songs as a man will when he's had too much whisky, when suddenly half a dozen voices shouted in unison, "Stand! Stand! Hold!"

A man leapt up from the margin of the road in front of them and waved a woman's white slip in their faces. The horse whinnied and reared in fear, pulling the reins from Gallen's hand, dumping Seamus off backward. Seamus landed with a thud, shouting, "Ruffians, blackguards!"

The nag leapt off up the side of the ravine, her hooves churning up dirt as she galloped through the hazel.

Gallen was wearing his deep-hooded woolen greatcoat to keep out the night chill, but the coat had slits at his waist that let him get to his knife belt quickly. He palmed two daggers, not wanting to show his weapons until the robbers got in close, then spun to get a better view. The robbers surrounded him, swirling up out of the brush. He counted nine: three up the road toward An Cochan, four coming behind on the road from Clere, and one more on each side of the ravine.

Seamus sputtered and tried to find his way up off the ground. The old man was nearly blind drunk, and he yelled in a deep brogue, "Off with you thieves! Off with you varmints," and the robbers all swirled toward him shouting, "Stand and deliver!"

In the starlight, Gallen could hardly make out the soot-blackened faces of the robbers; one of them had curly red hair. They were big men mostly, down-on-the-luck farmers sporting beards and armed with knives, the kind of aimless rogues you often saw sloughing around alehouses in the past two years. Drought one year and rot the next had thrown many a farmer out of work. Gallen made out the gleam of a longsword. Another young boy held a shield and a grim-looking war club.

Old Seamus began cursing and fumbled at his belt in an effort to pull his knife, but Gallen grabbed Seamus's shoulder, restraining him. "Don't be a fool!" Gallen warned. "There's too many of them. Give them your money!"

"I'll not be giving them my money!" Seamus shouted, pulling his dagger, and Gallen's heart sunk. Seamus was the father of seven. He could either let the ruffians have his purse and watch his family suffer, or he could fight and probably die. He was choosing to die. "Now back me, will you! Back me!"

Dutifully, Gallen stood back to back with Seamus as the robbers closed in. That is what Seamus had paid him for. Three shillings, Gallen realized. I'm going to get killed this night for three shillings.

The tall man brandished his sword. "I'll be thanking you to drop your purses, lads." From his accent and curly red hair, Gallen estimated that he was a Flaherty, from County Obhiann.

"I beg you sirs," Gallen said, "not to go making free with our money. I've got none to spare, and my friend here has a wife and seven innocent children."

One robber laughed. "We know! And Seamus O'Connor just made forty pounds while hawking his wool at the fair. Now out with the loot!" he shouted angrily, waving his knife. "An' if you give it to us casual, we won't hurt you so bad." Gallen watched the men close. One of their number must have seen Seamus's money at the fair and waited until the old man got on this desolate stretch of road before setting the ambush.

The robbers had them circled now, but held off a pace. Gallen thought of running. It was only a mile over the hill to An Cochan. A bead of sweat rolled down Gallen's cheek, and his heart was hammering. He glanced around at the circling men in their dark tunics. Seamus was growling like a cornered badger at Gallen's back, and Gallen could feel the old man's muscles, hard as cords, straining beneath his coat. Gallen wanted to stall, hoping that even with his mind all clouded by whiskey, Seamus might see that it made no sense to leave his family orphaned. An owl soared over the ravine.

Seamus began swearing and shouting, "Why do you have your faces blacked, you ugly bastards? I'm not a child to be frightened by a sooty face! Off with you! Off with you!"

Gallen half-closed his eyes and wondered, If I were the greatest knife fighter in the world, what would I do?

In an instant, it was as if a familiar mantle began to fall over him. Gallen's muscles tightened into coils and the world moved into sharper focus. Gallen felt the blood pounding hot in his veins, and his nostrils flared wide, tasting the night air. He sized up the ruffians before him, and though it was dark, subtle shades of light began to reveal details about each man. They were breathing hard, the way men will when they're afraid.

Nine men. Gallen had never fought nine men, but at that moment it didn't matter. He was, after all, the greatest knife fighter in the world.

Gallen tossed his head back so that his hood fell away, letting his golden hair gleam in the starlight. He chuckled softly and said, "I must offer you men fair warning. If you don't back away and give us the road, I'll have to kill you."

One robber gasped, "It's Gallen O'Day! Watch him boys!" The men swarmed around Gallen and Seamus faster, moving warily, but none dared venture in too close. The tallest robber shouted, "Take him, boys!"

Gallen didn't worry about the robbers at his back. Seamus had his knife out, and even though he was drunk, no sane man would try to tangle with him. Instead, Gallen sized up the five men to his front and sides. Two of them hung back half a pace—cowards who didn't want to look it. Another man stood close in, but he was tossing his knife back and forth between his left and right hand, hoping that the sight of it would strike fear into Gallen. Another robber was stocky, with an unsightly bulge under his cloak, and Gallen realized it was a breastplate; this robber breathed heavily and bent low to the ground on legs that were tense, ready to spring. The last of the five closest was their leader—a tall man with a longsword who likely would avoid joining the fray with such a weapon for fear of lopping the head off one of his own men.

Gallen heard the scuffling feet of a robber lunge behind. The robber grabbed Seamus's arm and tried to throw him to the ground, but Seamus twisted away at the last moment and made a stab. The robber yelped in pain, and hot blood splattered across the back of Gallen's neck.

"Take that for your trouble!" Seamus jeered, as if he'd won something, and then more robbers surged behind. A sharp blow from a club sent Seamus to the ground.

Gallen had been watching the man who tossed his knife from hand to hand. The knife was in the air, and Gallen leapt up and kicked it away, disarming the robber. He whirled and kicked an attacker off Seamus, slashed another across the throat. The lad with a club raised his shield to protect his face, and Gallen could have dropped beneath the boy's guard and lunged past, run to win his freedom. But Gallen knew he had keep the highwaymen from slitting Seamus's throat.

Gallen dodged and came up behind the young robber, grabbed the boy's hair and put a knife to his throat. "Hold where you are," Gallen shouted. "I don't want to have to murder this lad!" The boy struggled, but Gallen was ready for any move he tried. Gallen wrestled him still. "Now, off with you! Give me a clear road."

The highwaymen moved around them, keeping a safe distance. Gallen could see from their determined faces that they didn't value the lad's life. It wasn't worth forty pounds.

The boy cried, "For Christ's sake, Paddy, tell them to back off!" The boy was panting hard, and he began to cry. The sweat pouring off of his neck made him slippery.

Gallen looked up at the tall one with the sword, Paddy. Since it seemed that the boy was a worthless hostage, Gallen decided that Paddy might value his own hide more.

Gallen tossed the boy to the ground. The robber who wore the breastplate leaned forward, dagger at the ready. Gallen had already slipped beneath one attacker's guard, and the men held their weapons low, preventing any similar moves. One man lunged at Gallen from behind; Gallen sidestepped, slashed the attacker's knife arm nearly in half, then Gallen leapt at the man in the breastplate. He put his toe at the top of the man's throat and let it slide down till it hit the armor, then stepped up and used his momentum to somersault over the robber's head.

He hit ground, swung around and put his knife to Paddy's throat. It all happened so fast that the robbers could barely react. Paddy swore and threw down his sword.

The boy with the club sat on the ground for a moment, crying. Other than the boy, one of the robbers was dead, another was knocked unconscious, and two were nursing serious wounds. Paddy was disarmed. The last three robbers hesitated, not knowing what to do. Paddy said to his men, "All right lads, listen to him! Drop your weapons and give the man the road! Now!"

The three robbers all dropped their weapons and backed away.

"Paddy, you're a lousy bastard!" the boy shouted, still sitting on the ground. "You were going to let him slit my gullet, but you'll save your own? So you think you're worth forty pounds, but I'm not worth a bob?"

The boy got up and held his shield down low like a veteran, and he raised his nasty war club; its metal studs gleamed in the starlight. He advanced slowly, and the other robbers suddenly leered like the greedy thieves they were. As one they reached down and retrieved their weapons.

Seamus moaned and began coughing. Gallen saw that he would have to fight these last four. The men quickly circled him.

Gallen listened for the sound of a scuffing foot behind him, tried watching all directions at once. His senses were overwhelmed: he could smell the wool and sweat and scent of wet humus and ash on Paddy and the other robbers. He could smell the hot blood on his knife. A cool breeze washed through the trees, hissing like the sea. Somewhere over the hill a sheep bawled out, and Gallen wished he was there, safely over the hill, out of the dark Sidhe Forest and into the village of An Cochan.

Gallen slit Paddy's throat and stepped aside to meet these four robbers, hoping that a bold challenge would shake their confidence.

Gallen knew that he stood a good chance of getting killed if he let the men circle him, so he ran head-on into a robber, stabbed the man in the chest, then tried to throw the man behind him as a shield. But the dying robber grabbed Gallen's greatcloak and swung him back into the circle.

For one brief moment, Gallen realized he was in trouble, and then he heard the whirring sound of a club. Every instinct in him, every fantasy he'd ever concocted about such a situation, warned him to duck. He dropped his head to the right as the club smashed into him.

Dozens of brilliant lights flashed before his eyes. There was a roaring in his ears, and the ground seemed to leap up to meet him. Suddenly, the robbers were on him, kicking, and one man shouted, "This will teach you! Never again will you begrudge a man for a friendly knock on the head or for borrowing your purse!"

He looked up and saw a man ready to fall on him with a knife, and Gallen tried to roll away, but his muscles wouldn't cooperate, and he knew he was going to die.

"Hold!" a commanding voice shouted nearby, and Gallen's attackers stopped. As one they looked up the hill to gauge this new threat. The wind was still hissing in the trees, and the muddy road was cold against Gallen's back. He tried to roll over, look up to see his rescuer. The newcomer said evenly in a voice hot with warning, "Those who commit murder in Coille Sidhe shall never escape alive."

One of Gallen's attackers choked in fear, and the others stood up cautiously and stepped back. Gallen heard one robber mutter, "Sidhe."

Gallen's head was spinning so badly, he could only roll over. He'd lived on the edge of Coille Sidhe all his life, and never had he heard rumors that netherworlders might really inhabit the forest. It was said that the sidhe were lesser demons, servants of the devil, and that Satan often sent the sidhe to herald his approach.

"There's only one of them," a robber said, trying to bolster the courage of his fellows. Gallen rolled to his elbows and looked up: above him at the top of the ridge stood a man in the darkness, the starlit sky at his back. He wore garments of solid black, all darker than the night, and his head was covered with a hood. Even his hands were covered with fine gloves. Starlight reflected dully from a longsword in one hand and a twisted dagger in the other. For a moment, Gallen thought it was just a man standing in the darkness, but his eyes focused on the creature's face: its face shone like pale lavender starlight, as if it were a liquid mirror. Gallen's heart pounded in terror, and the sidhe leaned back and laughed grimly at the highwaymen. In that one horrifying moment, Gallen expected the ground to split open and the devil and his legions to crawl forth.

The robbers fled. Gallen urged his leaden arms to move, flailed about while trying to lift himself up, but his head spun and he faltered to the ground. Blackness swallowed him.

Sometime later he woke in a daze. The sidhe was hoisting him into the saddle of Seamus O'Connor's mare. Gallen lurched away from the sidhe's touch, as if it were a serpent, and bumped into something behind him. Seamus was slung over the mare's back, and the wounded man breathed raspily. Seamus's head had been bandaged, and the sidhe whispered, "Hurry, Gallen O'Day. Save your friend if you can."

Gallen's head still spun like leaves in a whirlwind, and he could barely grip the horse's mane to keep from falling off.

The sidhe took Gallen's chin, and Gallen looked into the creature's eyes. The thing looked human in nearly every way—Gallen could make out the fiery yellow hairs of its eyebrows. It was very much a human face, if not for the fact that it glowed like molten metal. "Remember, Gallen," the creature said with great heaviness, "I will hold you accountable for any oaths you make this day."

Gallen had only a moment to wonder at this portentous threat when the sidhe whistled and slapped the mare's rear. She leapt downhill, heading for An Cochan. Gallen dug his heels into her flank and gave her her head.

The night that Gallen O'Day fought off the nine robbers, Orick had been thinking about leaving Gallen forever. A dozen conflicting urges were moving Orick in ways that he did not wish to go.

His love of mankind and his desire to serve God by ministering to others was leading Orick toward the priesthood. Yet Orick knew that he and Gallen were not of the same heart on such matters. While Orick revered the Tome and its companion book the Bible, hungering for the wisdom of the ancient Christ and his disciples, Gallen's attitude toward the books was disappointing. The young man vacillated between grudging admiration for some of the Bible's teachings and open contempt for the Tome. Obviously, Gallen did not have faith in the holy books. Although Orick genuinely liked Gallen, their sharply divergent views on religion were troubling, and Orick believed that soon he would have to leave Gallen, if only to retain some peace of mind.

Furthermore, Orick found other urges beckoning him. He had been spending a great deal of time in the company of humans lately. But such a state of affairs could not long continue. He needed a female bear's company.

So, that night as the two said their good-byes at the back of the inn and Orick watched as Gallen led Seamus away on the mare, Orick's own words rang in his ears, "God be with you then, for I shall not."

The young female bear next to him, named Dara, pawed demurely through the garbage. "Have you decided then? Will you be coming to the Salmon Fest next week?"

Orick imagined the hundreds of bears that would be gathered at the fest, fishing in the day, sitting around campfires and singing all night on the rocky beach on the banks of the cold river. He imagined the smell of wet fur, the pine trees, whole salmon skewered on stakes as they leaned against the fire pits to broil. Though Orick didn't particularly relish the idea of wading in the icy waters of Obhiann Fiain all day trying to catch fish in his teeth, he was nearly four, and certain primal urges were getting hard to ignore. Orick saw that becoming a father would confer upon him a type of immortality, for he would live on through his progeny, and he hungered for that particular blessing.

Yet if he entered the priesthood, he would have to take a vow of chastity, and so he considered that this year he would need to go to the Salmon Fest. At the Salmon Fest many a fair young female bear would be hunting for more than a slimy morsel of fish for dinner, and frankly, as the bears say, "A she-bear in heat is the best kind to meet."

Sure, there would be games at the festival—competitions where the males would go at it tooth and claw, tree-climbing races, the log pull, the pig toss. Orick would have to win the right to breed, but he was becoming rather large, and he'd learned a few wrestling tricks by watching Gallen.

Who knows, he mused, perhaps I'll unseat old Mangan as the Primal Bear. He imagined how envious the other bears would be as he chose the best and brightest females to breed with, then Orick gobbled some cold cabbage and deep-fried clams from the garbage.

"I'm not sure if I'll come or not," Orick growled in response to Dara's question. "I'll think about it." It was possible to find a mate without going to the Salmon Fest, but a saying rang through Orick's mind: "While the common bear shivers in his wet fur, the superior bear builds a fire." So, Orick knew that if he really wanted a quality mate, he would need to make the journey to the Salmon Fest, leaving Gallen O'Day behind.

"I saw some deer up the hill in Covey's apple orchard," Dara said coyly. "I really like venison. How about if we go up there and see if we can kill us a deer?"

Orick grumbled, looked at her askance. He didn't like hunting for deer. The bucks had antlers, and even the females had sharp little hooves to kick with. Orick didn't like undertaking unnecessary dangers. Besides, he was hungry, and being hungry made him grumpy.

"Nah, I never developed a taste for venison," Orick lied. "I know where some squirrels have a midden. Do you like acorns?"

"Well," Dara said, "I'll go catch one myself." She left the garbage to Orick and headed up the north road. Orick watched her longingly. He knew that she expected him to follow. The chances were slim that she'd be able to sneak up on a deer herself. But deer usually ran uphill when frightened, so if Orick were to go uphill and wait for Dara to scare the deer up to him, the chances were pretty good that he could catch one.

Orick imagined a huge six-point buck charging uphill, antlers lowered like pikes, hooves slashing, and decided not to risk it.

He crept beneath the shadows of the pine boughs that sprouted from the inn, then lay down. The clouds were quickly blowing away and stars dusted the sky in a fiery powder while the moons sank lower, staring down like the eyes of God. For awhile Orick watched for falling stars and thought about Dara. She was a flirtatious young thing. Orick suspected that she had no idea how strongly her charms affected him, and he felt as he laid there that he was making a momentous decision: should I follow her to the Salmon Fest and see if I could win the right to mate with her, or should I stay with Gallen for one more season?

Above Orick's head, someone blew out a candle in one window of the inn. Orick suddenly noticed how dark it was. Nearly all the lights in town were out, and only the pale fires of heaven shone in the streets. The shushing whisper of waves breaking on the beach a quarter of a mile away lulled the bear.

Orick closed his eyes and rested his muzzle on the ground. He slept lightly for some time, but a dog's yelp interrupted his dreams. It was an odd bark, the noise a startled dog makes, but it was cut short, as if someone had kicked the dog in the ribs. Orick would have gone back to sleep if he had not noticed a faint, peculiar scent barely distinguishable above the salt tang of the sea air—blood. He blinked and looked down the road south of town, and for a moment thought he was dreaming.

Something was walking up the road. It resembled a human creeping on all fours, but its spindly legs could have been no less than eight feet long, as were its arms, while its torso was very short, perhaps only two feet. It moved jerkily, wary as a mantis, its tiny round head pivoting as it tried to gaze in all directions at once.

It carried something in one hand—the mangled body of a whippet. The creature got to a crossroad and hesitated in the shadows, then dropped the dead dog and bent its elbows so that its forehead nearly touched ground. Orick could hear the creature sniffing. It crept toward Mahoney's stables, keeping its nose to the ground, then suddenly seemed to catch a scent. It swerved back toward the inn.

The monster sneaked to the darkened windows of the inn, not twelve feet from Orick. It stopped, sniffed at Orick and regarded him a moment. The monster had large eyes that showed orange in the moonlight, and Orick saw that its marvelously long hands looked very powerful. Orick didn't move, and the creature must have decided that Orick was asleep and therefore didn't matter. Let sleeping bears lie.

It began inhaling near the small round windows of the inn, tasting the scents. The head was indeed human in shape, but the monster really did not move at all like a human. Its jaunty twitches reminded him more and more of an insect.

The thing reached up sixteen feet to a small window, grabbed the sill in one hand, and pulled itself up to sniff at the crack under the window. In performing this maneuver, it seemed to defy gravity, as if it were a mosquito clinging to its victim.

It reached one long arm sideways eight feet to the next small window, swung over to it, tasted the scent there.

Mahoney's Inn, like most structures in town, had grown from a house-pine seed. As with many such homes, the owners were of course obliged to put in windows and doors only where openings for such grew naturally, and new windows and doors had to be fitted every few years as the openings grew larger. So it happened that sometimes the window didn't fit snugly.

The creature must have known this, for it stuck its long fingers into the lintel, scrabbling with heavy claws to pull the window free. Orick heard wood splinter under the force of its assault, and though Orick had never before seen anything like this monster, he knew that this thing was intent on mayhem.

The monster pulled the window free and tossed it away with a flick of the wrist. Its hand shot into the dark cubbyhole of the room.

Orick roared in warning, then lurched from his hiding place, jaws snapping. Though the monster was incredibly long of limb, it looked to be rather flimsy. Orick grabbed a leg and shook his head, pulling the creature down, ripping its sinews.

For its part, the creature slashed at Orick with its long fingers, raking open wounds across the bear's face. In the heat of battle, Orick hardly noticed. He bit into an arm and found it to be much tougher than he'd imagined—indeed, Orick had once bitten into the haunches of a running horse, and the horse was not nearly as tough as this monster. Orick growled in his fury, clamped his jaws down and rolled, then finally managed to snap a bone.

The monster struggled up on three limbs to run. Orick heard shouts of dismay and screaming from the inn, and he worried that if he let the beast escape, it would return to town with murder on its mind.

Orick seized a foot in his teeth, pulled the monster to the ground, then dragged it backward like a sack of onions. Orick's teeth gouged through the thing's flesh, ripping its leg wide open, yet Orick felt as if his own teeth might be yanked out.

The beast raised its head, and Orick saw in the starlight that it had fierce-looking fangs. It blinked its orange eyes and screamed, an odd howling that rang through the city and out over the surrounding mountains like a war horn.

There were words in that cry, and Orick sat in astonishment as he recognized them—"I have found her! Come, fellow vanquishers!" Orick lunged for the creature's throat, trying to silence that call for aid, and with a vicious wrench he tore the beast's windpipes out.

Bloodlust hit Orick then, some primal instinct. He roared and tore at the dying creature, swatting it with his claws, ripping it with his teeth, dancing around it in a red fury until he became aware that a dozen people had poured from the inn.

John Mahoney rushed out with a lantern, and he shone it on the beast, a look of stricken horror on his face. For the first time, Orick saw that the thing had green skin, like that of a toad. "Get the priest! Get the priest!" John Mahoney began shouting. "Och, God, it's a monster!"

And most of the others from town were running around, shouting in dismay and disbelief. But among those who issued from the inn were a beautiful young woman and a hooded man who wielded a sword.

They stood for a moment, gazing at the dead monster, and though fear shone in their eyes, there was not the look of total incomprehension and shock that Orick saw in the faces of his townsmen. Instinctively, Orick knew that these two had battled such monsters before.

Indeed, the man leaned close to the woman, and Orick caught his words. "It called for other vanquishers. We must hurry into the woods. We can't stay."

"What of our horses?" she asked.

"They will do us no good in the forest, in the dark. Better to leave them."

The woman nodded. Her companion rushed back into the inn, came out with two packs. He gave the woman a pack and she immediately headed north up the road.

But for one moment, the warrior stood, pulled out his naked sword gleaming in the starlight. He looked right at Orick, as if to thank him, and raised the sword in a silent salute. Then he spun and rushed into the night.

A crowd gathered around Orick, congratulating him, and men brought out their torches. Orick warned that other such monsters might be about, and soon the men formed up into a militia and set to guarding the edges of town. A boy ran to the parsonage to wake Father Heany, who took one look at the creature and pronounced that it must be some unrepentant sinner, transmogrified by God in retaliation for its unholy deeds.

Many of the townspeople stood by, congratulating Orick, yet Orick himself wondered at what he had done. Who had he helped? What evil plans had the monster harbored? Orick knew so little about the creature—only that the beast's flesh was made of tougher stuff than anything he had ever sunk his teeth into. As townspeople brought their lanterns close to look at the beast, Orick smelled its torn flesh. It had an oily scent, not like any land beast, but more like a fish, yet without the putrid fishy flavor.

When he looked at the ropey coils of torn muscle, he saw that each fiber was like a tiny thread of white. Yet when he looked into the creature's face, aside from the heavy jaws and sharp teeth, it looked to be human, a young boy perhaps.

Orick did not know what the monster was, but others knew. Orick stared up the north road that led to the deep forest of Coile Sidhe, the direction that the two strangers had run. The vanquishers would be there, hunting the strangers, and Orick knew they would need help. He decided to leave as soon as Gallen returned.

Orick looked up at the moonlit sky, wondering what had taken Gallen so long.

Three

An hour before dawn, Gallen urged the mare under the canopy of Seamus O'Connor's house. His home had grown from a great oak, and at this time of the year the dead leaves in the canopy rustled in the wind under the starlight. Other oak houses, planted generations ago, grew near in a cluster, so the O'Connor farm—inhabited by several families of O'Connors—was more like a grove of houses. Here in the wilds, such groves gave one a sense of security, with people all around—though they were really little more than firetraps. Eventually, if the family didn't leave, they'd get burned out.

As Gallen neared the house, a watch owl swooped near his head, shouting "Who are you?" Gallen gave his name, fearing that the raptor might rake him with its talons. A candle burning in the O'Connor window bore testimony that Seamus's wife Biddy had waited up for him.

Seamus was in a bad way. He kept crying out at visions and couldn't answer a simple question.

Gallen slid from the saddle and shouted for help, then lugged Seamus to the house. Biddy unbolted the front door, and soon Gallen had him laid out on the sturdy kitchen table and all seven of Seamus's children got up. Brothers and aunts and cousins poured in from the other houses in the grove. Soon the house bustled with crying children. They gathered around Seamus and hugged his hand, wiping their snotty noses on his sleeve.

Biddy sent her oldest daughter Claire for the priest while her son Patrick fetched the doctor. Gallen watched Patrick make ready to leave. The boy didn't hurry—instead he just skulked away, lazy to go out. Patrick had a likeness to his father, but was still just a gangrel of a boy with long arms and a slouching posture. Word around the county said he was a rowdy and a drunkard that his mother wouldn't be sorry after once he left home.

Seamus woke and called for Biddy but didn't know her when she answered him. The doctor arrived and checked Seamus' wounds—a shallow cut to the ribs and a cracked head that was swollen and feverish.

The priest, a Father Brian who was a second cousin of Gallen's on his mother's side, gave Seamus the last rites even as the doctor drew cold well water to bathe Seamus's head.

Gallen told them the story of the attack, saying only that a stranger had intervened, frightening off the robbers. He was afraid to admit that the stranger was a sidhe. How could he explain that one of Satan's minions had rescued him?

Afterward, Gallen sat on a stool, holding his head in his hands, afraid Seamus would die. He kept replaying the whole fight in his mind, wondering if somehow he couldn't have made it come out better. He recalled one moment, when one of the blackguards had first jumped up from the roadside, waving the white slip to spook the horse, when he had thought to pull his knife. Yet he'd held still, wanting first to gauge his enemies, estimate his chances of winning.

But if he'd only pulled his knives from the start, attacked before the robbers consolidated their forces, Gallen would have stood a better chance. Gallen relived the incident over and over, and within an hour he was sure he could have won. He could have killed all nine bandits and gotten Seamus home safely.

And Gallen wondered about the sidhe. There, in the mountains at night with a spinning head, Gallen had been sure of what he'd seen, but now that he was back in a warm home, with people bustling around, those swirling images of the glowing lavender face seemed—astonishing, impossible. He could not have seen such a thing.

Just before dawn, Seamus lapsed into a deep, uneasy sleep, the kind of sleep that men seldom wake from. Gallen's eyes became gritty and his eyelids heavy. He was in that state where his skin felt as if it slept, as if he were losing the sensations of touch and heat and cold.

Biddy brewed some rose hip tea, sweetening it with honey, and the doctor forced it down Seamus's throat. Gallen watched from a distance, yawning.

Father Brian turned, his black robes swaying grandly, saw Gallen's face, and appeared startled. Brian crossed the room and in a hushed voice said, "You look like hell, my son. What's the matter, did you get all of the heart knocked out of you?" Gallen didn't answer. "Why don't you come outside with me for a walk? The stretch will do your muscles good."

"No," Gallen said, shaking his head. He felt as if leaving Seamus's bedside would be some form of betrayal. He needed to see this through, be there if Seamus died.

"You'll do no one any good here," Father Brian said. "Whether Seamus lives or dies or wakes up an idiot, there's nothing you can do for him."

Father Brian pulled at Gallen's hand, and led him out into the dawn. The sun was rising pink over the green grass of the drumlins. Morning fog burning off the downs crawled up the hillsides in some places like pale spiders of smoke. The raucous calls of crows echoed over the fields. Father Brian took Gallen out behind the O'Connors' barn, to a reedy pond. At their approach, several snipe got up and flew about Gallen's head, uttering sharp cries. A pair of mallards rose from the glassy water, and Father Brian sat with Gallen on a sun-bleached log.

"All right," Father Brian said, folding his hands. "Out with it. Give me your confession."

Gallen felt odd giving his confession to a cousin. Father Brian was only twenty-five, and the man was so fresh that he couldn't grow a beard to save his soul. Still, he was a priest.

"Forgive me, Father, for I have sinned," Gallen said.

"How long has it been since your last confession?" Father Brian asked, folding his hands like a steeple.

"A year."

Father Brian raised his eyebrows, looked at Gallen askance. "So long? How many men have you killed in that time?"

Gallen thought a moment, added his kills from last night. "Thirteen."

"Business sounds a bit slow," Father Brian mused. "Killing is a grievous thing—a mortal sin under some conditions. I assume that all of them were highwaymen and scoundrels?"

"Yes."

Father Brian folded his hands again. "Hmmm. And how much booty did you find on the corpses?"

Gallen had to think. He hadn't kept a running tally. "Well, if you consider the boots and clothes and weapons I sold, not more than a hundred pounds."

Father Brian whistled in surprise. "That much, eh? A good haul." After a bit of thought, he said, "Say a Hail Mary for each man you killed. That ought to suffice. And of course, I'd thank you to pay a tithe to the church."

"Ten pounds?" Gallen asked, his heart beating hard. He'd spent the money long ago. Sure, he made a lot of money as an escort, but he had to buy his food at the inn, pay lodging—his expenses were equally high.

"Well, you wouldn't want to risk dying with any kind of stain on your soul," Father Brian said. "God delivered these evil-doers into your hand. It's only fair that you offer something to show your gratitude."

"But ten pounds—"

"Och," Father Brian interrupted, "think nothing of it. You'll take more than that off your next couple of jobs."

Gallen nodded reluctantly, wondering how much Paddy and the other thieves might have had in their pockets. Father Brian stared hard at him. "So, what else have you got to confess?"

"About last night. I keep thinking, and I'm pretty sure I could have saved Seamus that knock on the head."

"Ohhh," Father Brian said thoughtfully. "So that's why you look so wrung out. I figured as much. You've never lost a client before. So what makes you think you could have saved him? You said there were, what, nine robbers? You're sure you could have taken so many?"

"I stood fast when they first came at us," Gallen said. "I knew what they wanted, but I advised Seamus to throw them his purse. But—"

"And why did you do that?" Father Brian interrupted. "You're not a coward, are you? I've never heard such talk about you. Think close, and give me the truth."

Gallen considered closely, remembered the men circling him in the dark, big men sporting beards, men who looked soft and flabby from lack of work, men armed with kitchen knives and a relic of a sword that had showed a faint patina of rust even in the dark. "I didn't want to have to fight them," Gallen said at last. "They looked like farmers, soft, down on their luck—not killers. A couple of them were just boys."

Gallen thought back, remembered the two strangers that had hired him last night at Mahoney's Inn. Now, the man who had worn two swords on the outside of his cloak—that man had been a trained warrior. Gallen had seen it in his stride, in the clean way the man had maneuvered through the common room without letting his weapons knock against the stools. His cautious demeanor showed that he'd been a man who lived with battle. Gallen had fought such men before—trained swordsmen out of Darnot who turned to butchery after the war. Gallen didn't mind fighting such men, though they could be more dangerous than a wounded boar.

"So, you took a little pity on some robbers," Brian said. "Christ advocated the same, that we have mercy on our brothers—but only if they are penitent. The men who were robbing you last night didn't merit mercy. They gave you no quarter and asked none in return. Now, if the survivors repent and turn to Christ and ask your forgiveness, then it would be appropriate for you to forgive them, welcome them back as brothers in Christ. In such circumstances, your feelings would do you merit."

"I know," Gallen said. Father Brian sounded as if he were trying his best not to chastise Gallen, make him see things in their proper light. In truth, Gallen was too tired to argue or think on his own. He only wanted to sleep.

"So, perhaps your hesitation did cause Seamus some hurt, and perhaps not. You can't know anything for certain," Father Brian said. "So I'll tell you what. I want you to take a vow before me now. I want you to promise God that when your heart is hot to come to the aid of another, you will never again hesitate."

Gallen glanced over at Father Brian, and in his mind the words of the sidhe echoed: "I will hold you accountable for any oaths you make this day." The morning sun seemed to go cold, and Gallen stood up and looked out over the drumlins at the white spiders of fog climbing the hills. Sheep were bawling in the distance, but otherwise the world seemed quiet, desolate. Gallen felt almost as if the sidhe stood nearby, with his hand cupped to his ear to hear the enunciation of the oath. Somehow, Gallen felt sure, the sidhe had known that Gallen would be asked to take this oath, so the sidhe had warned him that this was a solemn business. But would Gallen be speaking the oath to God, or to the sidhe? To speak an oath to a magical creature would be a sin. "Thou shalt not suffer a witch to live," the Bible said, so how much more wicked was a sidhe, a creature of pure magic? Gallen could not make a vow to the sidhe.

"Well," Father Brian asked innocently, unaware of Gallen's dilemma. "Will you speak the oath?"

"I will," Gallen said. "I'll speak it to God: If ever again my heart is hot to come to the aid of another, I will not hesitate." Gallen said the words, and out over the fields a crow began cawing and flew up into the hills as if to carry the message. Gallen wondered if the sidhe had taken animal form.

"Now," Father Brian said, "before the sun gets any farther up the sky, how about if you and I hike up the road and search those robbers? Maybe we could get a handle on some of that tithe you owe the church."

Gallen agreed reluctantly. He didn't expect much from these bodies, and it seemed rather ghoulish to be searching them in the company of a priest. Still, if they didn't hurry, some early traveler would get there first.

They headed up the road, over the mountain. When they got to the site of the ambush, Seamus's son Patrick was there. He already had the bodies laid out side by side like partridges. He hunched over them, hurrying to get their purses and anything else of value. When he saw Gallen and the priest, he hurried even faster, as if he would take the loot and run.

Gallen stood back and surveyed the scene. He knew he had killed three last night, but there were four corpses. One of the wounded men had bled to death on the spot. All four men looked small and harmless when displayed here on the ground. Their clothes were rough-sewn wool, worn through.

Patrick and Father Brian retrieved the purses and other valuables while Gallen scouted around the ambush site, checking the prints in the soft mud. Eight of the attackers had been from County Obhiann. Gallen could tell by the rounded toes of the boots, a northern style, but the ninth robber was probably a local, for his boots were pointed and soft of sole. Both outer soles on the boots had holes worn through, so that they left distinctive prints. Gallen found where the local had come down out of the brush beside the road, and Gallen tried to recall a face. The prints showed that this local robber had never really come into the fray. He'd hung back.

As for the sidhe, Gallen found his prints, too. The sidhe had worn a boot with heavy heels that cut the shapes of crescent moons into the soft mud.

Gallen went back to Father Brian and Patrick. They were just finishing up, checking to make sure that the thieves didn't have any silver coins in their boots. Gallen watched the priest grunt, struggling to pull a worn leather boot off of Paddy. Patrick—who was economical with effort but not with other people's property—took out his knife and tried to slice open the other boot. Father Brian scolded the boy, saying that the boots still had plenty of wear and could be given to the poor.

As he watched, Gallen saw that Patrick's boots were pointed, with distinctive holes worn in the outer soles. He had a drop of blood spattered on one toe. Now, in the light of day, Gallen could see that Patrick's sparse red beard had a streak of chimney soot on it, smeared down below the right ear.

As Father Brian wrestled Paddy's boot off, two silver coins fell out.

"Well, you old crows." Gallen smiled. "How much did you find on the pitiable corpses? Any meat on them bones?"

"Three pounds, two shillings," Father Brian answered. "Not much of a haul."

"Oh, I don't know about that," Gallen answered. "It sounds like plenty to me. Three pounds? Why, for that much money, I'd sit out all night in the cold with a gang of robbers so that I could point out my own father when he came down the road. Three pounds would be enough to betray my own kin for. Don't you think so, Patrick?"

The gangrelly boy looked up, uncertain. He startled back at the threatening tone in Gallen's voice. He didn't answer.

"You've got your father's blood on your boot, and you've still got a robber's soot to hide your shameful face," Gallen said. Father Brian looked at the boy darkly, saw the betraying marks. The priest bit his lip.

Patrick glanced longingly down the road to Clere, set his muscles as if to run. He wasn't an agile sort. Gallen judged that he could catch the boy in fifty paces.

"The likes of you," Father Brian grumbled at Patrick, "would be only a burden to your widowed mother even if you hung around."

"I didn't mean for anyone to get hurt," Patrick whispered. His face had turned red, and now hot tears poured down over his freckles.

"You thought you could steal from your brothers and sisters, and no one would suffer?" Father Brian asked, shocked. "What were you thinking? Aren't times hard enough with poachers stealing your sheep and wolves in the flocks? You wanted to add another burden to your father's shoulders, all for a few pounds to spend on whiskey?" Father Brian was known to be an occasional whiskey drinker, so he added, "or worse—beer?"

"Get yourself gone, now!" Father Brian shouted at the boy in disgust. "And never return to County Morgan. You're outlawed from here. I'll give you till sundown, and then I'll spread the word. If anyone in County Morgan ever finds you walking the road again, your life is forfeit. Go and make a living for yourself elsewhere if you can, but we won't tolerate you here again!"

"Let me stay a bit," Patrick begged, reaching for the hem of Father Brian's robe. "My father's hurt bad, and my heart is sore for it. Let me stay to see if he makes it through the week!"

"What?" Father Brian asked. "You beg to stay in striking range of a sick man's purse? Aw, to hell with you! I'd rather trust a weasel to guard the chicken coop. Get out of here before I have Gallen O'Day slit your throat."

Father Brian picked up a large stone and hurled it at Patrick as a sign that he'd been outlawed. The stone struck the boy on the shoulder, and Patrick hissed painfully but still looked at Father Brian with pleading eyes, begging to stay.

Gallen picked up a stone of his own and threw it hard, slamming it into the boy's thigh. "Get out of here, outlaw!" Gallen shouted.

Father Brian reached for another stone. If the lad didn't leave, then according to custom, Gallen and Father Brian had no recourse but to stone him to death.

Patrick jumped away up the road and began limping toward Clere, shooting angry glances back at the two. He seemed to be in the throes of trying to conjure some devastating curse, and finally he shouted, "You don't fool me, Gallen O'Day! You consort with the sidhe and creatures of the netherworld, and you're no better than a demon yourself! I saw him, Father Brian! I saw Gallen O'Day with a sidhe last night! He prayed to Satan for help, and a sidhe came to his aid!"

"I'd be pleased," Father Brian shouted, "if you wouldn't make such accusations about my cousin, you damned misbegotten purveyor of patricide! Get, now!" He hurled another rock, and Patrick dodged and hurried up the road.

They watched Patrick climb the winding mountain path, between the blue pine trees and the gloam of the wood. Father Brian kept his eyes on Patrick and asked with clenched teeth, "Was there any truth to his words? About the sidhe?"

A shiver ran through Gallen. He couldn't lie to a priest, even if that priest was only his cousin. "I've never prayed to the devil," Gallen said, "but last night, when those Flahertys knocked me in the head and were hot to skin me alive, some creature came out of the woods. It looked like a man, all dressed in black and carrying swords, but its face shone like molten glass. It warned them that anyone who committed murder in Coille Sidhe would never make it out of the woods alive."

Father Brian caught his breath and looked at Gallen askance. "You're sure it wasn't just a wight or some spirit of the woods?"

"It was flesh, like you or me," Gallen said. "It put Seamus up on the horse, and I looked into its face. It . . . I've never seen or heard of anything like it."

"But it warned men against murder," Father Brian whispered in a tone hinting at something between confusion and awe. "It couldn't have been in league with the devil. Therefore, it must have come from God. The thing that you saw last night," he whispered with desperation, "could it have been an angel?"

"I don't think so. It was dressed in black," Gallen said.

"Then it was an angel—" Father Brian said with finality, "it was the Angel of Death, walking at the right hand of Gallen O'Day and keeping guard over him. That's what we'll tell people. That's what we'll say."

"I'm not so sure—" Gallen started to argue, but Brian spun and grabbed Gallen's collar at the throat. "Don't dispute me on this! I'll not have it said that a cousin of mine consorts with demons. Only you and the robbers saw what happened last night. No one can contradict your testimony! It was God who sent the Angel of Death to stand guard over you—do you understand me? And I'll excommunicate anyone who begs to differ!"

"Yes," Gallen said, confused and frightened. Father Brian's argument made sense, but in his heart Gallen knew that he would not live this down easily. Five other men had seen the sidhe, and they could not but tell what they had witnessed. Somehow, Gallen felt sure, this would come back to haunt him.

Four

At dawn, the townspeople in Clere dragged the dead monster from the inn and dumped its body into the bay. Father Heany said that no creature damned to be so ugly should be buried on hallowed ground, and the ocean seemed the only place big enough to hide such a fiend.

The town militia guarded the roads but still hadn't seen more monsters. Yet Maggie knew they were coming. All over town, dogs sniffed the air and barked, sending up keening wails that troubled Maggie's soul.

"Can you smell them?" Maggie asked Orick just after dawn.

"Aye," Orick grumbled, standing on his hind legs to catch the scent. "There's an oily stench on the wind, not from anything human."

Everywhere, townspeople were rushing about frantically, spreading rumors. But Maggie Flynn just stood, watching longingly up the north road to An Cochan. Gallen still hadn't returned. He was hours overdue.

"I'm going to An Cochan," Maggie said at last to Orick, her voice quavering. "If Gallen doesn't know what's afoot, he'd better be warned." She glanced up the road again. There was a tightness in her stomach, a certain knowledge that Gallen had already found trouble. He would never willingly keep a client waiting, and Maggie suspected that his body lay somewhere on the road to An Cochan. If she was lucky, he might still be alive.

"You're as likely to meet one of those monsters on the road as he is," Orick said. "And he's better prepared to defend himself. Just sit tight."

Orick paced in a circle, rose up on his hind legs and tasted the air again.

Cries of dismay rose from the south end of town. Crowds of people began shouting. Maggie and Orick rushed to the crossroads, looked down the lane: between the shading pine trees, up the cobbled streets lined with picket fences, an ungodly array of giants marched three abreast. Some of them, green-skinned ogres, looked like huge men, eight feet tall. At their head was one of the monsters Orick had slain last night, its too-human head down low, sniffing the ground, blinking at the townspeople with orange eyes.

There were thirty or more of the monsters, and in their center, well protected, walked a creature straight from the bowels of hell. It stood seven feet tall and had a chitinous black carapace. It walked on four extraordinarily long legs, and it held two huge arms before it. One clublike arm seemed to end only in a vicious claw, while the other revealed a small, spidery hand that held a black rod.

The beast's head was enormous, with three clusters of multifaceted eyes in various sizes—two sets of eyes in front, one in back. A long, whiplike whisker was attached to each side of its lower jaw, beneath teeth that looked like something that might have belonged to a skinned horse. Its main body was only about a foot wide across the front, but across the sides it would have measured three feet. From its shoulders sprouted two enormous pairs of translucent wings, the color of urine. Its bloated abdomen, which was carried between its front and back pair of legs, nearly dragged the ground.

People shouted and ran for their houses, dogs barked and leapt about insanely. Some women and an old man fainted outright, falling to the ground.

Father Heany in his vestments rushed to the street and confronted the black beast. He swung a crucifix overhead and shouted, "Beelzebub, I command you in the name of all that is holy to turn back! Turn back now, or suffer the wrath of God!"

Beneath the black devil's mouth, dozens of tiny fingers drummed over a patch of tight skin.

The ogre guardians stepped aside, and for one moment the devil faced Father Heany. It pointed the short black staff at the priest. Flames brighter than lightning fanned out, catching Father Heany in the chest. For a moment, Father Heany stood, blazing like a torch, and then the flesh dropped from his bones and his skeleton fell in the middle of the road, amidst a puddle of burning skin and flesh. Maggie felt as if her blood froze in her veins.

The ogres walked over Father Heany's body and just kept advancing toward the inn.

Maggie backed away, retreating between two house-trees toward the edge of town, and Orick padded quietly beside her.

When the menagerie of creatures reached Mahoney's inn they stopped, and the doglike leader crouched to sniff the bloody ground.

He turned to Beelzebub and cried, "Master, a vanquisher died here!"

The giants stopped. Beelzebub strode forward and let the whiplike tendrils at his mouth feel the ground, twisting from side to side.

Orick circled behind a tree to hide. Maggie had seen enough. Her heart was pounding, and she struggled to breathe. Every instinct told her to run.

"Let's get out of here!" she said.

"Wait," Orick whispered. "Let's see what they want."

One ogre kicked down the door to Mahoney's Inn and rushed inside. A moment later, it dragged out John Mahoney. The innkeeper screamed, gibbering for mercy.

Beelzebub made clicking noises, and one of the giants translated, shouting, "Where did they go? When did you last see them?"

Mahoney fell to his knees, "I don't know who you mean. Who do you want?"

"You are the owner of this inn?" an ogre shouted. "Two strangers came here last night. A man and a woman."

"I didn't see them," Mahoney begged, crying. And Maggie realized he was telling the truth. He'd already been abed when the strangers came.

But the ogres thought he was lying. One of them growled, and Beelzebub flapped his wings suddenly and leapt into the air. He landed on John Mahoney, teeth first. Maggie saw red blood spurt from John's head, like the spray of a sea wave as it washes over a rock, then she turned and ran for her life, Orick barreling along beside her.

They hit the woods, rushing through the trees, leaping over logs. Maggie ran until her lungs burned and she could hardly tell which way to go. Still, no matter how far or fast she ran, it did not seem that she was moving far or fast enough to get away. Always she would look behind her, and the town seemed too close, the monsters seemed too close. She probably would have kept running forever, run like a maddened beast to her death, but Orick growled and caught her by the cloak, pulling her to a stop. She screamed and kicked at him, but the bear only growled, "Stop! The strangers went this way! I can follow their trail. We must warn them!"

The two strangers rushed ahead through the forest, and Orick sniffed at their trail in the early morning, forepaws digging into the thick humus while his hind paws kicked forward in a rolling gallop. Maggie struggled to keep up. Between the towering black trees, the forest was wreathed in mist, with the early morning smell of fog that has risen from the sea. Sometimes Orick would spot a juicy slug as he ran. He would dodge aside and grab it from the mossy ground, flicking it into his mouth with his tongue. Yet mostly as he ran, he dreamed, and not all of those dreams were his own: snippets of racial memories stirred in him, visions from the Time of Bears, glimpses of forests from ages past. As he ran among the silent woods, he remembered being a bear cub, tearing at a log for sweet-tasting grubs and termites. Winged termites fluttered above him in a shaft of sunlight, glittering like bits of amber or droplets of honey. Sunlight shone on the emerald leaves of a salmon berry bush. In the memory he felt a vague longing for his mother, as if she were lost, and he heard something large crashing through the forest before him. A trumpet sounded, and a great shaggy beast suddenly towered over him, curved tusks thrusting out impossibly long. It shook its head, and the tusks slashed through the air, casually scattering the flying termites. The cub turned and ran.

Orick relived tales told by his mother, tales so familiar that he could not separate them from his own memory: how she had loved the taste of squirrel meat until she discovered the squirrel's midden and found that eating its cache of food was wiser than eating the squirrel. He listened to his mother describe tactics for catching salmon—how an old bear should slap the fish from the water with his massive paws while a smaller bear should use his teeth, stretching his head down under the water to gaze open-eyed into the stream. In Orick's waking vision, he dreamed of bright silver fish slicing through the icy foam. He tasted the small scales in his mouth, the juicy salmon wriggling as it tried to swim free of his grasp.

So it was that as Orick ran through the forest, chasing the strangers, he felt as if he were running backward through time, to the heart of wonder. Surely this morning had already been magic. In solitary battle Orick had defeated a monster, and now he was galloping away from others of its kind, grunting under the weight of his store of winter fat, barreling into the primordial forest of his dreams, into the unknown.

Once, as he passed through a shadowed valley, Orick glimpsed a wight—the flickering green soulfire of someone long dead, a woman with long hair and a frown. She glanced at Orick, and then the wight gazed heavenward. She seemed to recognize that morning had come, and she sank into the hollow of a log.

Orick tracked the strangers' scent. After two hours, the strangers had marched into a bog of briny water and were forced to veer up a mountain and intersect the north road to An Cochan. Orick and Maggie crept to the edge of the road, Orick padding on heavy feet, sniffing the sour mud of the strangers' footprints.

He stopped. The morning sun had nearly cleared the hills now, shining on the road, and it seemed strange that the sun could be so warm and inviting on a day so filled with fear. Orick listened. Kiss-me-quick birds were jumping in the bushes, calling out for kisses.

Maggie was panting from the long run. Orick glanced at the road, inviting her to climb up.

She shook her head violently. "I think I heard something."

Orick tasted the scent of the strangers, looked uphill. They had crossed the road shortly before, heading up under the old pines, into a patch of chest-deep ferns on a knoll. Orick saw the bole of a young house-pine up there, grown from a seed gone wild. Though the house had only open holes for doors and windows, it was the kind of place that made a good temporary shelter for travelers. Orick could not see the strangers, but their scent was strong. He suspected they were hiding inside, resting where they could watch the road.

On both sides of them, the road curved sharply into the deeper woods. The trees provided heavy cover. Orick started to climb, but suddenly heard the shuffling of heavy feet on the muddy road to the south.

Both he and Maggie faded back, crawled into the shadow of a twisted pine. From under the heavy cover, Orick watched the road above.

Orick's snout quivered in fear, but the scuffling footsteps had halted a hundred yards off, and everything became silent. Orick wondered if the monster had stopped to wait for passersby, or perhaps quietly slipped off into the woods, or if it had turned around and headed back toward Clere. For ten minutes, he and Maggie waited in silence, and Orick was just imagining that the danger had passed when Gallen O'Day came ambling up the road, heading toward Clere, whistling an old tavern song. Orick moved a bit so he could see Gallen clearly. Gallen looked worn, and his head was wrapped in a bandage. Orick wanted to call to him, warn him of the strangers in town, but at that very moment a deep voice shouted, "Stop, citizen!"

Gallen stopped and stood looking up the road, his mouth hanging open. An ogre hurried down the road to meet him. The ogre's chest and lower extremities moved into view, and Orick got a close look at the thing. Its long arms—covered with bristly hair and strange, knobby growths—nearly reached the ground, and in one hand it held an enormous black rod, like a shepherd's crook. Its fingers could not have been less than a foot long, and they ended in claws that were like nothing Orick had ever seen on a human or bear. The ogre wore a forest-green leine, belted at the middle, and wore enormous brown boots. As Orick watched, the ogre clenched its fists rhythmically, in and out, in and out, flexing those claws threateningly. For a moment, Orick thought it would lash out, catch Gallen by the throat.

"Citizen," the ogre growled in a heavy voice Orick could understand only by listening intently. "I am searching for a man and a woman, strangers to your land, thieves. Have you seen them?"

"Thieves?" Gallen hesitated. "Well now, sir, with the great fair just ending at Baille Sean, the road is heavy with strangers. I saw several pass by an hour ago. Yet I must admit that in all my days, I have never seen anyone stranger than yourself. Would you mind if I be asking: do these strangers present as much of a spectacle as you?"

"No," the ogre answered softly, hunkering closer to Gallen. "The two I seek are more of your size, citizen. One man is a warrior, skilled in all arms, and he is a scholar. Yet if you saw the pair, your eye would catch only on the woman: she is of unequaled grace and beauty, and at first you would watch her distractedly, almost unaware of anything or anyone else.

But the more you watched her movements, the more entrancing she would become. Her every step is like a dance, every soft word a song, and soon you would fall under her spell. If you stood in her presence for an hour, you would think you loved her. If you were with her for a day, you would become lost, and you would find yourself helplessly worshipping her forever—such is her power."

Gallen's mouth had fallen open again, and he stared at the ogre. Orick bent lower so that he could try to see the ogre's face, but the trees were in the way. Orick was tempted to come out of hiding, if only to see this curious beast, but fear made him stay hidden. Finally, softly, Gallen asked. "What is this woman's name?"

"Everynne," the giant answered.

"I saw her," Gallen said, "late last night, at the inn in Clere. She had dark hair, and a face so sweet and perfect that she seemed then to steal my heart." Orick wanted to shout, dismayed that Gallen would betray the strangers, but Gallen went on. "And I saw her with her companion again this morning, only an hour ago. They stopped in An Cochan to buy fresh horses, and they hurried off north."

Gallen pointed up the road toward An Cochan, and Orick felt his muscles ease in relief. He could always tell when Gallen was lying, and right now the young man was sending the ogre off on a mad quest.

The ogre tensed and rose on his tiptoes, anxious to head off down the road. Gallen said, "Sir, may I ask what they have stolen? Can you offer a reward if I regain the merchandise?"

The ogre hesitated. "She stole a key made of crystal, a key which opens gateways to other worlds. If you recover the key, my master will pay a generous reward."

"How much of a reward?" Gallen breathed.

"Eternal life," the ogre said. The creature straightened its back and shouted, "Vanquishers, all north!" Its voice rang out with such amazing power that the ground seemed to shake beneath Orick's paws. In the distant woods, dozens of other voices bellowed the message, "Vanquishers, all north!"

Orick could stand it no more. He knew that if he did not get a good look at the ogre now, he might never get another chance. He edged lower in his hiding spot, and his heart began pounding and he wished he'd never seen the thing: The ogre's head was enormous, and its hideous face was deeply creased, while a massive chin hung down like the arm on a sofa. Its lips were reddish brown, the color of burnished wood, and its large teeth were as yellow as pears. Its eyes were as huge as a stallion's testicles, and they were a bright orange. Scraggly brown hair hung limp from its head. All in all, the ogre was like no creature he had ever dreamed.

The ogre seemed to realize he had urgent business elsewhere. It loped toward An Cochan, back bent, head held peculiarly low, as if that enormous head were some great burden that it carried.

Gallen stood watching after it for several moments, an astonished expression on his face. He licked his lips and shook his head in wonder. He muttered to himself, "Eternal life, is it? What if I want a bonus? How about eternal life and a pair of laying hens? Or maybe eternal life and a sack of potatoes thrown into the bargain? Would your penurious master go so high?"

Gallen stared down the road. The sunlight still shone on the road, birds were hopping in the brush. A light morning breezed sifted through the trees, and Gallen shook his bandaged head, then stood with his mouth open as if he could not believe what he'd just seen.

Maggie stepped forward from the brush and whispered, "Gallen?" Orick followed.

Gallen saw her, then looked back up the road where the ogre had gone. He began jumping up and down and pointing, "Ah, Christ, you missed it!" Gallen said. "I just saw the most incredible giant! Come here! Hurry! I'll show you its tracks! I swear to God, it had green skin and teeth as big as shingles!"

"I know," Maggie said. "We saw it, too. Gallen, there's a bunch of those things in the wood. They came through town and murdered Father Heany. It was terrible!"

Maggie was on the road by now, shaking her head and grabbing Gallen's arm as if to make sure he was alive. Up here on the road, Orick could smell the strangers more strongly—Everynne and her guard—but he didn't want to say anything, afraid that somehow perhaps one of the giants might hear.

"Father Heany is dead?" Gallen stepped back in shock. "But . . ." He searched for something to say.

"Father Heany tried to drive the monsters out of town. And they burned him up. Then they went to the inn, looking for those travelers.

They knew John Mahoney had let them stay in his inn. They killed him for it."

"But, he's an innkeeper, for Christ's sake!" Gallen shouted, looking angrily back up the road. "That's what he does for a living! Ah, hell, where is Everynne and her guard now?"

"They ran off into the forest before dawn," Orick said. "I've been trying to track them."

"You wouldn't turn them in, would you?" Maggie asked. "That beast may sound like he's offering some grand reward, but those creatures are devils! Beelzebub himself walked at the head of their procession!"

Gallen looked sober. "Even if I didn't know that they'd killed a priest, I wouldn't turn anyone over to that thing. I have my honor to think about. I promised to take Everynne to Geata Na Chruinne, and I'll do it, even if the woods are full of sidhe. Orick, can you still follow their trail?"

Orick shivered. He had not thought about it, but here they were in Coille Sidhe. The humans told stories of the sidhe—strange and brutal beings from the otherworld. Orick had always thought them to be only tales for children, but suddenly the otherworlders were walking about in the daylight, looking for an enchantress with a key. "I can sniff them out."

"Wait!" Maggie said. "Gallen, we've no cause to get involved in the affairs of the sidhe. Let the devils squabble among themselves. If this woman has stolen something, maybe she deserves to be punished!"

Gallen half-closed his eyes in thought, and his long golden hair shone in the sunlight, the bandage holding it like a bloody headband. Orick wondered why his head was bandaged. Gallen looked down at Maggie and Orick, the sun catching his powder-blue eyes. "I don't believe this Everynne is a thief. Her guard was loyal to her. Thieves are never so devoted to their own. Greed wrings all the devotion right out of them."

"Perhaps he was under a spell—" Orick said, "as the ogre warned."

"Perhaps," Gallen agreed. "But only an hour ago, I swore to Father Brian that if my heart was ever hot to give someone aid, I would do it. And this morning my heart is hot to give aid to Lady Everynne."

"Well spoken," a gravelly voice said from the knoll above them. As one, Gallen, Maggie and Orick glanced up. The hill was covered with pines near the top, but the voice had come from close by, from the fern beds not twenty yards away. Suddenly there was movement, and Orick saw a man standing in the ferns, wearing a deep-hooded robe painted in greens and browns. Images of ferns were painted on it so precisely that if the man had remained still, Orick would never have seen him. Yet as the stranger walked downhill toward them, the robe shimmered and turned a soft brown. The man wore two swords at his hip.

The stranger halted in front of Gallen, and his scent was muted—hard to catch even at ten feet. Of all the wondrous things that had happened today, to Orick this was the most wondrous, the man's lack of scent.

The stranger pulled back his hood. He appeared to be in his late forties, but he was well-muscled, and his skin was ruddy tan. His hair had once been a golden brown, but now was turning silver. "I am Veriasse Dussogge," he said, "Everynne's counselor and protector. Will you guide us to the gate now? We are in great need. It will not take long for the vanquishers to discover your ruse and return in greater numbers."

"I can take you," Gallen said, "but we have not yet agreed to a price."

The stranger licked his lips. "You said only a moment ago that your heart was hot to give aid to the Lady Everynne."

"True," Gallen admitted, "but I didn't say that my heart was hot to give it to her for free!"

Orick looked from Gallen to Veriasse. Veriasse seemed to be weighing his options. Obviously, he could not afford to spend hours searching for either the gate or a new guide.

"You have me at a disadvantage," Veriasse said. "What is your price?"

"Well, that depends," Gallen answered. "Finding the gate is easy enough, but I'm not eager to tangle with one of those ogres. I assume you knew they were following you? That's why you wanted a man-at-arms?"

Veriasse nodded. "The vanquishers are very dangerous. I should warn you that they carry weapons more powerful than any on your world. The vanquishers can easily kill you at a hundred yards."

"Hmmm. . . . Then my price needs to reflect the risk I'll be taking. How about eternal life?" Gallen raised a brow.

"It is not in the Lady Everynne's power to grant that to you now," Veriasse said, "but if she reaches her destination . . ."

"Then she can give it to me if she reaches Geata Na Chruinne?" Gallen asked.

"She has other gates to pass through," Veriasse answered. "She must face many dangers. But if she wins through, then, yes, she would return and pay your fee."

Uphill, a whippoorwill called. "Quickly!" Veriasse hissed, urging them off the road. "Vanquishers!"

He grabbed Gallen's arm and leapt downhill into the brush. Orick plunged after them, and Veriasse led them a few hundred feet off the road, into the shadows under a pine.

"Don't stir," Veriasse warned. Orick waited motionless for a moment. A trio of ogres passed on the road, marching quietly, heads swiveling as they searched the forest. Maggie was breathing so heavily, Orick feared the ogres would hear her. But they passed quickly.

After another two minutes, Veriasse whistled once like a thrush. Lady Everynne bounded downhill over the edge of the road, wearing her blue robes and a headdress made of triangular silver bangles fastened with a metal mesh. She bore her rosewood harp case under one arm; a pack was strapped to her shoulder.

Veriasse stood, and Orick saw that his robes were taking on the colors of the wood—deep grays and greens with splashes of yellow sunlight. Veriasse pulled his hood low over his eyes. "Everynne," he said, "this young man asks eternal life as his reward for leading you to the gate. Will you accept his price?"

Everynne looked at Gallen. "He doesn't know what he is asking. How could he? He doesn't know who I am, nor can he understand the limits of our power." She looked into Gallen's eyes. "When you ask for 'eternal life,' it is not what you think. I could change you—make you so that you will not grow old, cure you of all ills and injuries. Perhaps by doing this, I could extend your life—for a thousand or ten thousand years. I can give you new bodies, keep you so that you are reborn at each death. But you could still be killed. Your life will still end, someday."

"You can do this?" Gallen asked. Maggie was looking at Everynne in astonishment, and the young girl backed away as if afraid.

"Perhaps," Everynne said. "At the moment, I am as helpless as you. But I promise: if you take me to the gate and I survive the next few weeks, then it will be in my power to pay your fee."

Gallen offered his hand, and Maggie said, "Gallen, no!"

"Why not?" Gallen asked.

"It's a trick—" Orick cut in. "There's things she's not telling you. If you help her, you might not die of old age, but those giant vanquishers can come back and knock your head in! Listen to Maggie. You've no cause to be concerning yourself in her affairs." Orick's heart pounded, and he stared at his friend. Orick was a practical bear, and Gallen's bargain here just didn't make bear sense. Obviously these were magical creatures, and by bargaining with them, Gallen might win eternal life, but would he have a soul when he finished?

Gallen raised an eyebrow, questioned Everynne without saying a word.

"If I live, the vanquishers will become my servants," Everynne said, "and to my knowledge they will never return to this world to harm you or your family. Gallen, I cannot promise you that all dangers will fade from your life. There are worse things than vanquishers. If I die, I suspect that you and your people will learn more about what lies beyond the Gate of the World than any of you ever wanted to know."

"What do you mean by that?" Maggie demanded.

"We are at war," Veriasse cut in.

Orick looked hard at Gallen, and it was plain that the young man was wrestling with his thoughts. "Then," Gallen said, "I think I know what price I must ask."

"Which is?" Everynne asked.

Orick's nose was dry from fear, so he licked his snout. He waited for Gallen to ask for eternal life, but Gallen said, "I want to come with you beyond the gate into the realm of the sidhe and make sure that you reach your destination."

"No!" Everynne said. "You cannot even guess the kinds of dangers we will face. I cannot take you. You would not be a help—only a hindrance."

"You are a traveler and you need guards," Gallen said. "That is what I do."

Orick thought the man crazy, but Gallen had eyes only for Everynne. It was a case of lust, sure and through. And when Gallen got that set look in his eye, you could more easily pull a badger from his den than deter Gallen from his goal.

"Last night," Gallen said, "you would not tell me your name because you knew that these vanquishers would be following you."

"Yes," Everynne answered. "I didn't want to hurt you."

"Yet the vanquishers came. Inadvertently, perhaps, you have touched our world. Now I want to touch yours."

"It's not that simple," Everynne said. "I could let you come through the gate, but it does not lead to one world, it leads to a maze of worlds, and you are not prepared to enter. Even if you did, you would only want to come home again. In these last few days, I have grown to appreciate this world immensely for its simplicity, its ease of life."

"I don't know about other worlds," Gallen said. "But I suspect that this one is damned boring."

"A boring world is a valuable commodity," Everynne said. "I would that all worlds were so innocent."

Gallen thought a long moment, shrugged. "Then I'll take nothing in return for my aid. Only a scoundrel would extort money from a woman in need."

Orick shook his head, confused by Gallen's sudden turnabout. He wondered if he'd ever understand humans. The Lady Everynne smiled gratefully, raised her brow as if her opinion of Gallen had just raised dramatically.

In the distance was a sound Orick could just barely make out, though none of the others could have heard it. Voices shouting, "Vanquishers, to the south!"

"They're coming back!" Orick said. "Hurry!"

Gallen leapt into the woods, and the others followed.

Five

Everynne raced through the forest, following Gallen and Veriasse while Maggie and Orick brought up the rear. Everynne found it hard to toil through the thick undergrowth of Coille Sidhe. Everywhere, trees grew in a riot: dark pine brooded over the wrinkled hills and valleys. Tangled vine maple and ironwood climbed high to capture the dappled sunlight, their limbs twisted like snakes. Dense undergrowth covered the forest floor. Everywhere, ancient fallen pine trees lay molding.

Everynne wished she could hear the vanquishers' calls in the woods, but the pine needles and leaves of lesser trees muffled all sound. If the vanquishers fell upon them, there would be no advance notice.

Veriasse and Gallen ran side by side, Veriasse carrying his incendiary gun in both hands. Gallen kept glancing at it, but did not immediately ask what it was.

Veriasse hung his shoulders as he ran, weary. Everynne herself felt weary to the core of her soul, and she knew she needed more help. She needed a man like Gallen, and she considered taking him for a servant. She studied him as she ran.

After thirty minutes, Gallen reached a hill where a trio of tall stones hid them. Inside this natural fortress, he called a halt. He stood panting and asked Veriasse, "Those vanquishers, will they try to follow our tracks or are there enough of them so that they can beat the brush and force us out of cover?"

Veriasse heaved for air, said, "They will hunt us both by scent and by track. Gallen, we must take great care. If they have already found the gate, they will be guarding it. We will need to sneak up to it. Yet with vanquishers at our heels, we cannot afford to be timid."

Gallen considered. "You said that the vanquishers can kill from a distance, and they carried rods like the one you have. Is this the weapon they use?"

"It's called an incendiary rifle," Veriasse said. "When you discharge the weapon, it fires chemicals that burn very hot."

"So it's something like a flaming arrow?" Gallen asked.

"Yes, only far hotter. Where we come from, some creatures can only be killed with such a weapon. It has become our weapon of choice."

"How does it work?" Gallen asked. Everynne was surprised at how casually he asked it. She imagined that the young man, being a Backward from such a low-tech world, would find such weapons to be somehow shocking. But Gallen asked in a brusque, businesslike manner.

Veriasse held the weapon up for Gallen to examine. "Down here under the guard is a trigger. When I pull it once, the weapon becomes active and a red beam of light shoots from this lens above the barrel." He pointed the rifle at a stone, and the red dot of a laser shone on the rock. "You will also feel a vibration in the weapon when it's active. Whatever the red dot shines on, that is what you will hit if you pull the trigger a second time."

Veriasse flipped the weapon on its side, pointed to a little indicator light. "These lights show how many more shots you can take with the weapon." His indicator showed ten shots.

"How far can it shoot?" Gallen asked.

"Officially, it can fire about a hundred and fifty yards," Veriasse answered. "But the flames can carry farther if you aim high. You must never fire at an opponent who is too close—unless you want to burn with him. Once the weapon sits without firing for three minutes, it deactivates."

Gallen touched the rifle's stock. "This can kill an ogre?"

"Yes," Veriasse said.

"How tough are they?" Gallen asked.

"There are three main types of vanquisher," Veriasse answered. "Orick here killed a tracker last night—a creature with long legs and arms that walks on all fours. The 'ogre' that you saw is one of their infantry. They are tough warriors, and I would not advise you to fight them in hand-to-hand combat. They are very strong. Still, their vital organs are much the same as ours.

"In days gone by, my people created these creatures as guardians, to keep the peace on many worlds. But things have changed. The dronon warriors conquered our people and enslaved our guardians. The dronon are the third kind of vanquisher, and the most dangerous."

"Dronon?" Maggie asked, panting. Her face was pale, frightened.

"You saw one back in town," Veriasse said. "You called him Beelzebub, Lord of the Flies. He is really a dronon, a Lord Vanquisher from another world. Sixty years ago, his people came among us, and they were wise in the ways of war. At first, we tried to help them. But they envied our technology and sought to take it. They captured many worlds. Now, any guardians who were not slain all serve the dronon vanquishers. On some worlds, even humans serve the dronon's Golden Queen and her empire."

Gallen stood up, seeming to have caught his wind. "We'll need to keep to the trees so that they can't shoot us, and I'll lead them on some trails that will be hard to follow. If we can shake them off our track, we won't have to rush to the gate."

Gallen took off running. He set a path that the vanquishers would be hard-pressed to follow. He zigzagged between growths of jack pine, where the trees grew so close together that their branches formed a nearly impenetrable wall. Twice he made great circles so that his scent would be strong, then led the others over dry logs where no footprints would show, where even their scent would not hold.

When he had done all he could to obscure his trail, Gallen led them to a cave at the base of a mountain. He took the group to the largest opening, then at the black mouth of the cave he hesitated to enter.

"What's wrong?" Everynne asked.

"This cave," Gallen said, "has narrow passages and five openings. If we want to lose the vanquishers, we could go in here. But the cave is haunted by wights. We'll need to light a fire and take torches in to hold them at bay."

"We shouldn't go in," Maggie said. "It's too dangerous."

"Wights?" Veriasse asked. "What is a wight?"

"A spirit. If someone is too curious and breaks the laws of the Tome, the priests give the person to the wights."

"Surely you don't believe in ghosts?" Veriasse said. "There's no such thing. Have you ever seen such a thing?"

"Not ghosts," Gallen said. "These are wights. I've seen them more than once: there was an old woman in our town, Cally O'Brien, who experimented with herbs. One night the wights came and dragged her off screaming, down the road to An Cochan. No one ever saw her again."

Neither Veriasse nor Everynne looked as if they believed Gallen.

"What he says is true," Maggie offered. "Wights are real. At night you can see their soulfires glowing blue and green in the forest."

Everynne and Veriasse looked at each other and spoke simultaneously, "Artefs!"

But Veriasse asked, incredulous. "What would an artef be doing here?"

"Guarding this world," Everynne said. "Keeping its people in enforced ignorance. That is what their ancestors wanted, a world where their children could hide from the problems of a universe too large to control. I'll bet the original settlers downloaded their intelligences into artefs."

"So you're knowing the wights by another name, are you?" Orick asked. "You have them in the realm of the sidhe?"

"Yes," Everynne said. "We *make* them in the realm of the sidhe. They are simply machines that store human thought. We can travel through your cave safely."

"I'm warning you—the sunlight does not penetrate these caverns," Gallen said. "Inside, it is as dark as night."

"Sunlight weakens artefs," Veriasse said, "because the radio waves cast by your sun confuse them, leave them unable to think. But an artef can't withstand an incendiary rifle."

Gallen gulped, obviously still afraid. He led them in through a narrow chasm. He took Everynne's slim hand and pulled her through the dark. She could feel him trembling. She did not know if he feared this place still, or if he simply trembled at her touch. Often, men reacted that way to her. It was a mistake to let him touch her.

Gallen felt his way along a wall until he bumped his head on a rock outcropping, then took a side tunnel. After several hundred feet, he reached a narrow passage, then took another left where the cavern branched; they began climbing a steep slope filled with rubble. Dripping water smacked loud as it dropped to unseen puddles. Everynne struggled to keep from slipping on wet rock. The air had a faintly metallic smell, and Everynne hurried to get out. In the distance, she thought she saw sunlight shining through an exit, but instead a ghostly green apparition began leaping toward them through a large chamber.

It was an old man with muttonchop sideburns and a bushy mustache. He wore a leine without a greatcloak, and short boots. The wight stood quietly, gazing at them in the dark. Its phosphorescent skin let Everynne see the walls of the cave immediately around them, and she was surprised at the jumbles of stone, the numerous stalactites and stalagmites.

The wight asked cordially, "What are you doing in my cave? Don't you know that this forest is haunted?"

"Off with you!" Gallen said. "I'll not have you barring our way!"

"Och, why it's Gallen O'Day," the wight said merrily. "It's been a long time since I've seen you in these woods." But the wight studied Everynne, looking at the silver net she wore in her hair. It made a tsking noise and shook its head. "You're in a tight spot, Gallen—consorting with strangers from another world. Didn't your mother ever warn you against such things? Didn't she ever tell you what happens to curious boys?"

"Get back!" Gallen hissed. "We only want to pass."

The wight studied Veriasse's incendiary rifle. "Oh, I'll leave for now, Gallen O'Day. But it's sure that you can't shake me off so easily." The wight backed into a side tunnel, and ducked around a corner.

They hurried through the cave, climbing treacherous outcroppings, dropping down into crevices. The wight paced along behind them, crawling through the rocks. Soon another joined, and another, until Everynne counted a dozen of the creatures shadowing them through the cave. For a long way, their dim glow provided the only light for Everynne to see by.

The group reached the sunlight, and Gallen fell down to the forest floor, gasping. His face was pale, and Everynne realized that entering the cave must have been a great ordeal for the man, being a Backward who believed the wights to be invincible spirits. Soon Orick and Maggie rushed out behind them. Maggie's eyes were wide. Gallen looked up at Maggie, and he burst out laughing.

"What's so funny?" Maggie asked.

"Nothing is funny," Gallen said. "I just feel good."

Gallen got up and led them south a half mile to a steep slope that descended into a valley. A fire had recently burned the ridge, and large boulders dotted the ground. The soil around the stones had eroded away so that often the slightest touch could send a boulder tumbling downhill, and Everynne saw that Gallen was thinking ahead. A vanquisher, with its enormous feet, would be tempted to step on the boulders, and she imagined how it would go tumbling down in the resulting landslide.

At the bottom of the ravine, Gallen headed west, marching his followers down the channel of a rocky creek. Mosquitoes buzzed around their faces, and often mallards would fly up from the water. In one place where the channel narrowed and the water deepened, Gallen pulled up a small tree, sharpened it into a stake, and pushed it down into the mud where no one could see. It took only a moment. So far, they had traveled a little over five miles in eight hours. Everynne hoped that his tactics would give them more time in the long run.

They reached the shelter of the forest again at the valley floor, and there they rested for a few moments. Maggie was gasping, sweat pouring from her brow. They were all dirty and thoroughly worn. They had to rest.

From the mountain above them nearly half a mile back, a deep voice boomed: "Vanquishers, to me!"

The vanquishers had already found their exit from the caves. Gallen cursed under his breath and looked helplessly to Veriasse.

Veriasse studied Gallen's face. "You've done well," he said at last, and Gallen furrowed his brow, as if struggling to understand Veriasse's accent. "You've set as difficult a trail for the vanquishers as they could possibly hope to follow, but we must run now. We cannot afford more delays."

Up on the mountain, there was a rumbling roar and a scream as a vanquisher learned just how treacherous the trail was. Gallen stepped into a clearing where a tree had fallen. Everynne followed and looked up the mountain. Two humanoid infantrymen were helping a tracker to his feet.

"Veriasse," Gallen asked, "may I try your weapon?"

Veriasse handed Gallen the incendiary rifle. Gallen raised it. The barrel bounced a bit until he held his breath, relaxed his muscles, pulled the trigger. He frowned a second, obviously having expected the gun to discharge, then raised the gun a second time. Everynne could not see the red dot from the laser scope, but up on the hill, the ogres must have seen it. They suddenly released the tracker and leapt aside. Gallen pulled the trigger. A plume of white-hot chemical fire soared through the air, splashed over the tracker. The creature screamed briefly and burst into flame, then dropped in a pile of melting bones.

Gallen handed the rifle back to Veriasse. "That might keep them off our trail for a bit."

Gallen raced northwest. He led them on a clear path through deep woods, yet Everynne knew that the vanquishers would be able to run here just as easily. With their long legs, they would run even faster.

At last he reached a grove of pine-houses. Centuries before, perhaps, a town had nestled in this river valley, but it had been abandoned. Seeds from pine-houses had dropped to the ground, and a veritable city of hollow trees grew so close to one another that their trunks had fused.

No one could hope to walk through this section of wood. It was virtually impenetrable.

"We'll go through here," Gallen said.

"We'll never make it through that mess," Veriasse objected.

"I used to play here when I was a child," Gallen answered. "There are paths through the trees, if you're willing to climb a bit. This grove is eight miles long and two or three miles wide in most places, but up here a ways, it's only a quarter of a mile across. We'll go through there."

Like all homes grown from pine-house seeds, the houses naturally formed holes for doors. Always the seeds grew at least one door at the front of the house, and one at the back. In addition, at odd spots on each side, various openings grew for windows.

Everynne knew that the vanquishers would not be able to follow. Gallen skirted the trees till he reached a steep canyon, then walked to that impenetrable wall and entered a door hole.

They moved through the grove of pine-houses with great effort, grunting and struggling from window to window, often climbing up and down.

Perhaps as a child, Gallen had played here as a game, but windows he had squeezed through as a boy were now too narrow to permit an adult, much less a bear like Orick with his winter fat. Everynne was perspiring heavily. When they were halfway through the grove, Gallen suddenly halted, looking at a narrow window. Obviously, they could not squeeze through it, and Gallen furrowed his brow, deep in thought.

"What's wrong?" Veriasse asked.

"We're stuck here," Gallen said. "I used to fit through that hole nicely, and there is a narrow path ahead that we could follow, but we can't make it through here. There's no way to go forward."

"What will we do?" Maggie asked.

"I'll have to go out and scout another way."

"Do you need help?" Veriasse asked, yet obviously the older man was worn through.

"I'll find a way," Gallen said, and he went out the door. Everynne could hear him scrabbling around outside, climbing up a branch. The pine-house was dusty, full of needles and cones, the leavings of squirrels. A soft afternoon breeze blew through the little valley, stirring the treetops, even though down here on the ground it felt hot, sultry.

For the first few minutes, Everynne was glad of the chance to rest. Veriasse reached into his pack, pulled out a small flask and gave it to her to drink. She was terribly hungry—had gone all day without food—but they had nothing left to eat in the packs.

When Gallen had been gone for nearly an hour, Maggie said, "I think I'd better go look for Gallen. Maybe he's lost us."

She headed outside through a window and scuffled about in the tree, climbing limbs. The sunlight filtering through the open doorway had grown dimmer. Night was coming on, and Everynne could hear pigeons cooing from their roosts. It was very quiet, and Everynne began to feel nervous. They had been sitting for a long time, and the vanquishers could not be far behind. She began to wonder if one of the vanquishers might have already killed the young man, but dared not say it. The bear snuffled, looked out a window.

"Do you think Gallen could be lost?" Everynne asked Veriasse.

Veriasse shook his head. "No. As he's said, he played here as a child. I suspect he knows exactly where we are. I've been impressed by his competence. For a Backward, he seems to have grasped our predicament well, and he's led the vanquishers on a marvelous chase. He'll come back soon."

Veriasse said it with such certainty, that Everynne suddenly felt more at ease. Yet the older man also seemed to need to fill up the silence. "As a warrior, I find him . . . intriguing."

"In what way?" Everynne asked.

Veriasse smiled, contemplating. "He carries himself with a deadly grace. If I had seen him on any planet, I would have known he was a killer. He moves with caution, a type of confident wariness that one learns to spot quickly. Yet he is different from warriors on most worlds. Our ancestors relied heavily upon armor until the incendiary guns made it useless. Now, we rely upon our guns and upon tactics downloaded from personal intelligences. We fight battles at long distances and seldom look into the faces of our victims. Even more seldom do we purposely expose ourselves to risk. We have, in effect, become chess masters who've memorized too many classic moves. But this young man relies on quick wits for his survival, and his weapon of choice is the knife. It seems an odd choice."

In the corner of the room, the bear stirred in the shadows under the window. "Oh, Gallen would love a sword," the bear said, "but they're so expensive. You have to pay taxes on the damned things every time you travel through a new county."

Veriasse smiled at the bear, his eyes glittering. "So, even on your backward world," he said, "you practice arms control?"

The bear shrugged.

Veriasse sighed. "I feel fortunate. I have not met a man like him in many thousands of years." He stared at Everynne as if to say, "We need him. You could make him follow you." And a chill went through her. She remembered how Gallen had quivered when he touched her hand in the cave, the way he laughed off his fear of the wights. She, too, found herself intrigued.

"He is taking an awfully long time. . . ." Everynne said.

The bear was watching them intently, and he cleared his throat. "Is there anything you can do to help us find our way out of this wood? Do you know some magic?"

Everynne laughed. "We aren't magic, Orick, any more than you are magic."

"Oh," the bear said, disappointed.

A vanquisher bellowed in frustration. It sounded quite close. The creature had made it partway through the woods. Veriasse stood up, fingering his incendiary rifle, listening.

Ten seconds later, there was a swishing sound as someone leapt down through some upper branches of the tree.

Gallen's shadow darkened the doorway. "Come on. I found a new trail."

"What about Maggie?" Everynne asked.

"She's up ahead, waiting for us."

Gallen climbed up the tree, leading them through limbs with the grace of a marten. Yet the trail was very difficult.

Soon, Veriasse called for a halt and stood in the shadows under a limb. The sun was setting. He rubbed the backs of his hands against his shirt. "Stop a moment, stop," he said. He raised his hands. "I smell fire. The vanquishers have set these woods aflame. How much farther?"

"Not far," Gallen panted. "Not more than fifty yards."

Everynne was nearly senseless with exhaustion. They climbed ahead, and she found herself blindly grasping for limbs. Smoke crept through the forest like a thin fog. Just before they left the grove, Gallen pulled off his sweaty, soiled greatcoat and threw it into a crevice between two trees. Veriasse watched him and did likewise, and Everynne realized the value of leaving behind something strong of scent. She pulled off her own blue cloak, tossed it back. Everynne looked down, caught Gallen staring at her as she perched on a branch. He did not look away guiltily as some men might have. Instead, he just seemed to admire her. She wondered what he saw—a woman in a blue tunic, perched in a tree, silver ringlets in her dark hair. She realized that she was sitting in the last rays of the dying sun, and perhaps so lit, she looked resplendent. She had been bred to look that way to common humans.

She leapt to the ground and raced into the forest, under the tall pines.

Night was falling. Gallen seemed bone weary and had no more tricks in him. Now it was only a race to the gate, and the young man led them over the shortest route.

They reached an old forest at the fork of a canyon just at sunset. Behind them in the distance, Everynne heard an exultant howl. The vanquishers must have picked up their trail. In moments they would be here.

Everynne rushed to the gate and opened her harp case, throwing it to the ground. Gallen stood panting beside Maggie and the bear while Veriasse stepped up behind them. Everynne pulled out her key, a crystal shaped like a horseshoe, then held it up and thumbed a switch that transmitted an electronic code to power up the gate. Her crystal began glowing as the gate transmitted its acceptance signal.

The gate on this world was perhaps the oldest Everynne had ever seen. It was a small thing—taller than a man and two yards wide. It looked like a simple arch made of polished gray stone. On the posts of the arch were carved designs—flowers and vines, images that Everynne could not decipher.

As Everynne held her crystal aloft, the air under the arch began to glow pale lavender.

"My lady," Gallen said, "will you be safe in this next world?"

Everynne looked at him. Gallen obviously wanted to follow, and Everynne had to decide whether to take him. But the vanquishers were coming. The young man would need to guard Maggie and Orick. If Everynne let him follow, the others might die.

"I'll be safe enough for the moment," Everynne answered. "I have the only key to the gate. The vanquishers will have to hunt me in their sky ships. I should get a good lead on them. But for now, you and your friends need to leave here at once. The vanquishers want only me."

Everynne took one last look at this world—tasted the scent of the pine trees, the freshness of the air under the dark forest. On the first part of her journey here, she had seen the clean brooks full of trout, slept under stars where no one worried about dronon. She doubted that Gallen and Maggie understood what they had here, and she hoped that by leaving, the vanquishers would follow. Perhaps in ten years, people here would forget that vanquishers had once passed through a town. And in a hundred years, the account of Everynne's race through these woods would only become a fairy tale, the story of the time that the sidhe were seen walking alive.

Everynne looked at Gallen over her shoulder. The young man was tense, and Everynne could read his intent simply by looking into his eyes. He planned to leap through the gate when she did. She said quickly, "Eternal life, if I reach my destination. I promise. Gallen, will you pick up my harp case for me?"

Gallen bent over, and before he could react, she grabbed Veriasse's arm and pulled him through the gate.

Gallen had not known what to expect. He planned to wait until Everynne was ready to leave, then jump through the gate with her, but he'd wanted to say good-bye to Maggie and Orick first.

Instead, Everynne had taken Veriasse's arm and leapt forward. There was a flash of white, and suddenly the lights under the arch snuffed out like a candle. A freezing chill hit the air. The arch itself turned white with frost, and Gallen walked under it, stood a moment looking up at the ancient runes of flowers and animals carved into the stone. As a child he had brought a hammer and chisel to the gate, but had not been able to chip off any of that stone. Instead, his chisel got blunted and bent, and finally the handle to his hammer splintered. It was like no stone in the world. He looked at Maggie, took her hand.

Gallen felt as if his heart had been pulled from him, and he just stood, staring. He heard a shout from the forest behind, and Maggie tugged on his hand, urging, "Come away from here. Take your legs into your shoes. Run!"

Gallen found that he was shaking, and he ducked beneath the arch, felt a thrill of cold air, but nothing more. For him, the gate led nowhere. It had closed.

"Come!" Orick growled. The bear stood up, sniffed the air nervously.

They ran up a small hill. Gallen stopped near the crest and took cover behind a fallen log. Maggie and Orick lay down beside him. There was shouting below in the glen, and Gallen peeked over the log, the rotting black bark pungent under his nose.

Vanquishers rushed under the dark trees. Two ogres. They were battered, dirty. One ogre cursed and kicked at the arch. "They made it through," he said.

The ogre looked up while the other threw himself to the ground to rest. He spoke to the air. "Lord Hitkani, we've found the gate, but Everynne and her escorts have escaped." He listened for a moment, then answered. "Yes, we'll wait."

Gallen sat watching them for several minutes and heard a rumbling noise over the trees. A black creature with enormous wings dove below the treetops, settled on the ground beside the gate. It walked in circles around the gate, touching it with long feelers beneath its mouth. Gallen watched the dronon and could only name it to himself silently—Beelzebub.

The dronon reached into a pouch at its side, pulled out a crystal shaped like a horseshoe. It held the crystal in the air, watching it change colors to a soft lavender. In an odd, guttural voice it said, "They have gone to Fale. When the others arrive, we will renew the chase. You there," he said to one ogre, "see if you can get this key working."

The dronon sat on a thick carpet of pine needles, beating his wings softly, while one vanquisher fumbled with the key. The shadows under the trees were thickening. Gallen wanted nothing more than a bath and something to put in his shrinking belly. This seemed to have been the longest day of his life. He had not slept in over thirty-six hours. Yet he dared not move for fear of making some noise that would alert the vanquishers, and he dared not sleep.

Beside him, Orick and Maggie quietly watched the vanquisher work as the shadows deepened under the trees. An evening wind began blowing in from the sea, hissing through the treetops, making limbs creak.

Orick stuck his muzzle into Gallen's ribs, then looked off behind them to the north. Gallen followed the bear's eyes. In the woods, flitting through the trees, was a pale blue light.

It was said that a man's best defense against a wight was to lie low, hide. Yet Gallen knew the wights would be searching for him this night.

His mouth suddenly felt dry; he licked his lips. He spotted other lights flickering in the forest, pale blues and greens flowing between the trees as fluidly as a deer leaping a fence. By staying where he was, Gallen risked that the wights would catch him. Yet if he tried to make it out of Coille Sidhe now, the vanquishers would take him.

"Got it," the vanquisher muttered, a weary note of triumph in his voice. Gallen turned, saw that the arch glowed brighter. The ogre set the flaming crystal back into its pouch, then sat with the others a couple yards away.

The wind hissed through the trees, and a woodpecker began tapping above them. Gallen toyed with the idea of rushing the giants, grabbing the key and leaping through to another world. Everynne had seemed secure in the knowledge that she had the only key to the gate. She would not expect the vanquishers to follow her so quickly. But Gallen suspected that if he tried to attack, his little knives would hardly trouble the vanquishers.

Gallen put an arm around Maggie's shoulder and whispered, "Lie low and make your way home in the morning," then tapped Orick on the muzzle, stood up and leapt over the log quietly and began running downhill on the soft humus, letting the pine needles cushion the sound. Orick leapt over the log and ran beside him, glancing at Gallen fearfully. Gallen poured on the speed, thinking, by God, they won't see my heels for the dust.

But at that moment, the dronon lifted its head and hissed, making some spitting noise. Gallen had been running up behind the creature, but now he saw that it had a clump of eyes on the back of its head. The dronon pulled out its incendiary gun, but Gallen was too close for the creature to use it.

Gallen whipped out his knives, screaming, "Hold or you die!" and the ogres were so stricken with surprise that they scuttled backward a step.

Gallen was almost to the arch, and he snatched the pouch in one smooth move.

Fast as a striking serpent, one of the ogres grabbed Gallen's wrist, spinning him around. Gallen concentrated on holding onto the key as he slashed the giant's corded wrist. Huge gobbets of blood shot out, drenching Gallen's hand, but the giant held on. Gallen slashed again, jerked backward and fell to the ground, still holding the key.

He looked up. All three vanquishers had recovered from their surprise. In unison they lunged.

A piercing shriek rose behind them. They halted for half a second, and Maggie rushed between one ogre's legs. Gallen felt Orick's teeth biting into his collar as the bear tried to drag him under the arch.

Gallen scrabbled to his feet enough to kick backward a step, faintly aware of the ghostly lavender light radiating from the arch.

Orick roared in fear and Gallen kicked again and Maggie was with them, dragging Gallen backward. He saw the giants' faces twist in rage, yet suddenly Gallen was swept away through a cold, brilliant light.

Six

When Gallen and Orick took off down the hill toward the vanquishers, Maggie had felt a thrill of fear as she realized they planned to leave her. She buried her face in the dirt, trying to make herself as small as possible, then heard Gallen's shout.

Below her in the woods, she saw the green and blue lights of wights rushing uphill toward her, and she realized she was in the thick of it.

Her fear suddenly turned to anger. She got up, saw Gallen and Orick struggling to get the bag with the key from a vanquisher. She rushed down the hill, screaming, and bowled into Gallen and Orick, pushing them through the gate.

Any icy white light took her, and she had a strange sensation of gliding, as if she were a leaf fluttering through the wind.

Maggie fell back and hit the ground rolling, tumbling against Orick's warm fur. Gallen landed on top of her. She was furious, wanted to hit someone. Maggie shouted, "Gallen O'Day, you. . . ." Then she just sat and stared, her mouth open in wonder.

They sat in a meadow surrounded by a lush forest, thick with undergrowth. It felt like summer. A warm evening breeze rushed across her back, ruffling her hair, and in the distance a tiny oblong lavender moon hung on the horizon behind a swirl of clouds.

There was no sign of a gate from this side. Maggie looked all around, just to be sure. All around them, broad-leaved trees whispered and rippled in waves under the wind. Locusts sang in the darkness. Overhead was a sky filled with more stars than Maggie had ever imagined.

Gallen got up, folded his arms and stood staring. "What?" he asked, absently. Orick sniffed the air.

"Gallen, is your head filled with nothing but blubber?" Maggie shouted. "You've done it to us bad! I don't like the looks of this place."

"Fale," Gallen whispered under his breath. "The vanquishers called it Fale."

Suddenly, carried on the wind, there were screeching sounds from above. A flock of white birds hurtled overhead in the twilight, creaking like rusty hinges, some diving into the trees as if to catch insects in the air. The birds passed.

Gallen put his hand to his mouth and shouted, "Everynne? Veriasse?" He stood waiting for an answer. None came.

"I can't smell them," Orick grumbled, standing on his hind legs to sniff at the wind. "Not even the faintest trace of a scent. They didn't come out here."

"What?" Maggie asked. "They had to come out here. They came through not five minutes ago!"

"Maybe," Gallen wondered aloud, "it's not like a gate so much as a hallway. Maybe it branches. Leading to different places. Everynne called it a maze of worlds. Maybe we made a wrong turn."

Maggie looked at the sky full of whirling stars and an odd-shaped moon. The trees smelled strange, and the evening breeze was soft and warm. Nothing like Tihrglas. She couldn't begin to imagine where they might be.

"You mean we got off on the wrong world somehow?" she asked. "Gallen, you reeking bag of fish, I ought to knock you in the head! What did you have to do this for? What were you thinking, going after the key that way? You could have gotten us all killed! I know what you were after—that woman Everynne. You've been hot for her from the moment you first saw her. Why, if someone lopped off your head, it would be no loss. Your gonads would still do all the thinking!"

Gallen shrugged. "The vanquishers had another key. I had to warn Veriasse. Besides, I didn't ask either of you two to come along."

Maggie glared at him. "You left me! Both you and your dumb bear left me. As soon as those ogres began shouting, every wight in the country rushed up the hill toward us. I had to throw in with you! And if I hadn't come to your aid, we'd have all been killed! We could have all stayed home, hidden safe in the woods, but now . . . !"

Gallen said, "I'm sorry. I would never wish any harm on you. I'd never have dragged you into this."

He had such an expression of grief on his face, and he spoke with such sincerity, that Maggie had a hard time staying angry. She pointed her finger at him and then shook her fist. "Just admit one thing. Just be honest about one thing: don't you dare tell me that you came here to talk to Veriasse. It was Everynne you were after. You've been giving her looks all day, and don't you dare deny it, Gallen O'Day, or I'll beat you with a stick."

Gallen shrugged. "I couldn't just let her get killed."

Maggie figured that was as much of a confession as she'd ever get from him. She got up and looked furiously for the crystal key. She had fallen on it when she rolled through the gate. Its lights were gently fading. Maggie picked it up. She could see little worms of silver inside, bits of wire and small circles made of gold, odd things that looked like a priest's communion wafer.

Orick grunted. "I'm hungry. Is anybody else hungry? Where do you think we could get some food?"

"Aye," Gallen said, "I'm hungry. And thirsty, and tired. And I've no idea which way to go, do you?"

Orick gave a little bawl, bear talk for, "No, and it really makes me mad."

"If we head off on a straight path," Gallen said, "maybe we'll meet up with a river or a road."

Maggie looked toward the falling moon on the horizon. It seemed as good a direction as any to take, and if she left it to Gallen and Orick, they'd never make up their minds. She began hiking through the forest and the others were forced to follow.

The uneven ground featured no real hills but few flat spots. They pushed their way through broad-leaved plants that made the sound of tearing paper, and everywhere she could hear mice or rats running through the dry undergrowth. Often, tumbled white stones protruded from the ground.

Every few minutes, Gallen called Everynne's name, but after nearly two hours, Maggie got angry. "Will you quit that bawling. She's nowhere near here, so you might as well put a cork in it."

Gallen fell silent. Though they walked a long time, the moon still lay in the sky like a glowing blue eye, warm and distant. It had hardly moved at all. They found a small pool of water that reflected night shadows and starlight, then knelt to drink. It tasted slightly salty, but quenched Maggie's thirst. Nearby, several white birds flew up in the night, screeching and circling.

Orick snuffled in the grass and shouted, "Hey, you two, over here!"

He'd discovered some nests. Maggie opened the first egg and found a bird embryo in it, so left the rest to Orick. Maggie was exhausted. They hadn't found anything more impressive than what might have been pig trails—no sign of a house or a road.

Not knowing what else to do, she looked for shelter. Aside from the arching trees, she found nothing.

She went to a large white rock, thinking to huddle behind it. It had been sculpted with strange symbols—as if it were part of a building. She looked about. All the white stones had been shaped by hand. They had been hiking through the ruins of a vast city.

Gallen collected two armloads of grass and leaves to use as a blanket, laid them by Maggie in the lee of the rock. The ground was hollowed like a shallow grave or as if some beast often came there to rest, thus packing the soil. Orick lay with Gallen and Maggie, his thick fur warm and welcome.

Gallen called one last time for Everynne. Only the croaking of frogs gave answer. A wind blew cool against Maggie's skin, like the touch of a silver coin in winter.

Maggie wondered if someone should keep watch, but they'd seen no sign of anything larger than a mouse.

Gallen whispered to himself, "So Father Heany is dead. He was such a clean man. Death is such a small and nasty affair, part of me is shocked he would get involved in it." He said nothing more. Soon, Gallen breathed deeply in sleep.

Orick sang some bear lullaby to Maggie as if she were a cub:

"Through winters long and cold we'll sleep.
Don't you weep, don't you weep.
With hides and fat, warm we'll keep,
Though snow grows deep, though snow grows deep.
So let your tired eyes rest, my dear,
And when you wake, I'll be here.
And when you wake, I'll be here."

When the song finished, Orick sprawled a paw over Maggie's shoulders and licked her face. "I have plenty of winter fat stored," Orick said. "Next time we find food, you eat."

Orick closed his eyes.

For some reason, Maggie stared up at the night sky. Hundreds of thousands of stars shone. Directly above was a great pinwheel made of brilliant points of light. Somehow, when she had stepped into this new world, she had not anticipated that all the stars she had known as a child would also be gone. Yet if they were to be replaced by so many stars, in such wondrous arrays, she imagined that she could grow accustomed to them.

Three stars moved fast, in formation, from west to east then dropped toward the treetops in the distance, and Maggie wondered at them. Were these strange stars flying on their own, or were they perhaps distant birds of light, flapping in the darkness?

Maggie gave herself over to fatigue and began to drift. What kind of world have we entered? she wondered. So many trees, nothing to eat. What will become of us?

When Maggie woke, Orick was gone and the moon had set. Gallen slept soundly beside her. Maggie got up, scanned the landscape in a huge circle. It was especially dark under the trees. Orick was nowhere to be seen, but after a few minutes she spotted him in the distance, running toward her between the trees. Orick raised up on his back legs and called, "Hallooo, Maggie. Over here! I've found something! Food!"

Maggie was painfully aware of her empty belly. While working at the inn, providing three meals a day for strangers, she had grown accustomed to eating on schedule. But now she had been fasting for over thirty hours. She prodded Gallen's ribs with her toe. "Get up. It's time to eat."

Gallen sat up, rubbed his eyes. "It's a little more sleep I'm wanting."

"Up with you, you lout! You'll sleep better with some food in your tummy." Maggie realized belatedly that she sounded shrewish—like her own mother before she died. Back in Tihrglas, John Mahoney often warned her about her mouth: "Your mother grew so accustomed to nagging you kids, that she soon started bedeviling everyone in general. I'll tell you right now, Maggie: I'll not have you shrieking like a harpy at my customers, as your mother did!"

Maggie bit her lower lip, resolved to control her tongue.

When Gallen and Maggie reached the bear, he began loping through the woods. "I caught scent of it as I was sleeping," Orick said. They reached a cliff and found themselves looking over a large valley, lush with trees. A broad river cut through the valley. Lights blazed on the water.

It took Maggie several moments to realize what she saw: the river was enormous, and huge ships sailed down it, each bejeweled with hundreds of lights. On the far side of the river was what appeared to be a single building that extended low along the ground for dozens of miles. Fierce bluish lights shone from thousands of windows. In places the land was clear, leaving bits of open meadow and farm. In other places, the building spanned over the water like some colony of mold growing in a neglected mug of ale.

As she watched, bright globes dropped from the sky and fell toward the city, then settled upon rooftops. Perhaps a mile away, a woman in green robes climbed from a shining globe and walked through a door into that vast building.

Maggie drew a breath in exclamation.

"As I said, I picked up the smell when we were sleeping," Orick explained. "There's good farmland down there. I smell ripe corn and pears." Indeed, Maggie saw a few squares of checkered fields and orchards not far off.

"So," Orick said, "shall we go knock on their door, ask for food?"

"It's better than starving in the night," Gallen said.

Maggie felt a deep sense of disquiet. "Are you sure?" she asked. "How do we know what they'll do to us? What if there are vanquishers about?"

"You just saw that woman get out of her sky coach," Gallen said.

"She looked nice enough. Besides, what if there are vanquishers about? They won't know us."

Gallen searched for a way down the embankment and found a narrow footpath. Maggie hesitated, but didn't want to be left in the dark. They climbed down. The starlight was not enough to see by, and Maggie found herself feeling her way forward through the shadows with a degree of apprehension.

At the bottom of the valley was a lush orchard where some sweet-smelling, pungent fruit had fallen. Orick licked one. "This stuff is pretty good." He said, and he began eating.

Maggie gave the bear a minute, thinking that if the fruits were poisonous, the bear might start gagging, but Orick showed no sign of dying or taking sick.

"Didn't you say you smelled corn?" Gallen asked.

"Yeah, over there!" Orick pointed toward the city with his snout. "But why eat feathers when there's a chicken to be had?" he quoted an old proverb often spoken by bears. Obviously, he preferred this strange fruit.

Maggie cautiously followed Gallen toward the river. Halfway there, he stepped into some bushes and disturbed a buck that leapt up and bounded through the brush.

Maggie's heart began thumping.

The deer charged uphill toward Orick, and the bear bawled in startlement and ran downhill to pace nervously at Gallen's side.

They found a paved road by the river and followed it. Often through the trees Maggie glimpsed boats sailing the river or sky coaches rising from the city, yet the night remained quiet.

At last they found a field of ripening corn, the tassels shining silver-gold in the starlight. The corn stalks, at twelve feet, grew taller than any in County Morgan; the huge ears were sweet and full.

Maggie shucked an ear, knelt to eat, and Gallen followed.

Maggie was on her second ear, the sweet kernels dribbling down her chin, when Orick roared, "Spider! Run!"

The bear lunged away.

Maggie looked up. Towering above her, its belly just skimming the corn tassels, stood an enormous creature with six thin legs. The spider's body itself was a yard across, and Maggie could discern green glowing eyes. One enormous leg whipped out with blinding speed and knocked the cob from Maggie's hand, another lashed at her.

Gallen shouted and charged, grabbed one of the spider's legs and twisted, wrenching it free from its body.

The spider shrieked and tried to retreat, but Gallen caught another foreleg and wrenched it free.

The leg brushed against Maggie, striking her with a metallic ring. Maggie screamed and backed away. Suddenly Orick was back at her side, standing on his hind legs and roaring, raking the air with his claws.

The spider's torso became unbalanced, leaned forward precariously. In that split second, Gallen used the torn leg to club the spider between the eyes. It crashed to the ground, emitting a loud squeal.

Gallen jumped forward and began bludgeoning it. Orick pounced at the same time, holding it down. The two green lamps of its eyes kept shining, and Gallen had to pound at them for several moments before they cracked and the lights faded. Only then, when the lights were out, did Gallen stop beating the creature.

He stood over the broken monster's carcass, panting. An odd wailing sounded in the distance, a horn that rose and fell, rose and fell.

Maggie turned a full circle, looking for more giant spiders. She wondered if this city, these fields, belonged to the giant spider, or maybe a family of spiders. She was in the magical realm of the sidhe now. Who knew what wonders lay in store?

The wailing continued. Orick growled, sniffed at the spider. He pricked his ears up and said, "Something's coming."

Maggie heard whispering movement among the cornstalks. Gallen took her hand, and they ran. They crossed the road and hid in the brush, watching as ten more enormous spiders came to patrol the perimeter of the field.

The spiders discovered their dead comrade, and one of them dragged the carcass off while the others raced through the field in a frenzy, hunting.

Gallen frowned. The corn might as well have been a hundred miles away. They wouldn't dare try to harvest any more from that field. "Come on," he whispered, pulling Maggie's arm. "Let's get out of here."

Orick crept ahead, using his night vision and keen sense of smell to scout until the spider-infested fields fell behind. The sky began to brighten, turning to a dull silver as it will before dawn.

A spur of the city sprawled across the river just ahead, and the three had to make a choice—forge on into the city, or return to hide in the wilderness.

Orick glanced back at Gallen and Maggie. The sun was rising quickly. Behind him, the colors of the city walls could be seen, vague swirls of green and purple, like a field of alfalfa in bloom. The walls had rounded contours. Tall trees grew in certain clearings, rising above the city. The forest obscured the road ahead.

"I'm going to sneak up on the highway," Gallen said, "just to take a look."

Maggie nodded. Gallen began climbing. As soon as he left, she knew she had to go up there and join him. She hurried to follow. Behind her Orick grumbled, "Damn you for trying to leave me behind!" He rushed after them.

As Maggie climbed onto the highway, it seemed that magic struck. Suddenly, two brilliant lavender suns climbed above the distant mountains, casting a complex network of shadows over the city. As their light touched the highway, it glowed a deep red as if it were made of rubies. The trees at the roadside hissed in the breeze, their long fronds of leaves swaying. Maggie caught the sound of distant music blowing on the wind.

Ahead a shadowed archway led into the city. Several men and women milled about near the arch, seating themselves at tables. The scents of roasting meat and fresh breads wafted from the arch.

"That's an inn," Maggie said. "I know an inn when I see it."

Maggie stood, not quite sure what she saw. Neither Gallen nor Orick dared move forward. Not all of the creatures stirring in that inn were human. A yellow man with enormous spindly limbs leaned his back against one wall near the entrance to the arch. He was bald and naked but for a burgundy loincloth. Maggie suspected that the man would stand over ten feet tall. Other things moving about in the shadowed inn looked like ivory-skinned children with enormous eyes and ears.

Yet there were plenty of normal people inside. Some wore robes in brilliant greens and blues and darkest black, others wore pants and vests of gold with silver headpieces. Yet others were dressed all in silver body armor.

Then the wind shifted and the music swelled with the clear calling of pipes, rumbling drums, and the mellow tones of instruments that Maggie had neither heard before nor imagined. The combination of music and scents and movement of the glittering people in the city called to her, and Maggie knew that if it were the last thing she did, she had to go.

They rushed to the gaping arch, and the yellow spidery man stood to greet them. "Welcome, welcome travelers!" he called in an odd accent. "Food for all travelers, food near the road. Heap a plate to your liking. Enter to eat!"

"How much do you charge for breakfast?" Gallen asked.

The tall man opened his mouth in surprise. "You must have traveled far indeed! Food is such a small thing. Here among the Fale, all eat for free. Please, come in."

They entered the inn, and the shadows felt cool on Maggie's face. The music was louder. Maggie cast her eyes about, searching for the band, but the music came from the ceiling, as if the living walls of the building had broken into song. Overhead, small gems shone from dark niches of the room, glowing like lamps that did not burn. In one corner of the inn, people were pulling trays from a stack and piling on cups and silverware. Gallen got in line, and they followed it to a narrow aisle where a row of bushes hid the sounds of a kitchen. Each person in front of them went to a small opening and ordered food, then stuck their tray into the opening. When they pulled the tray out, food was on it.

Gallen set his tray in, asked for rolls, fried potatoes, sausage, fresh raspberries, and milk. He pulled out his tray and had all that he'd asked for.

Maggie looked into the hole. In a well-lighted room on the other side, men made of gold and porcelain were cooking. Each man had six arms and moved so quickly that her eyes were baffled.

Maggie found her curiousity piqued. She would have stared for hours if more people hadn't gotten into line behind her. Instead, she set her tray into the slot and ordered breakfast. It felt odd, asking for food when she could not see the faces of the metal men. She realized that they must have had phenomenal hearing.

She got her food, and Orick stuck in his tray, ordered quadruple portions for himself. He pulled the tray out a moment later, carrying it in his teeth. He had muffins heaped on a pile of eggs, a string of sausages dangling over the tray, and the whole affair was smothered in honey.

They found an empty table and began to eat. Maggie could not help but watch the strangers around her. At a nearby table sat several people in silk tunics with swirling patterns of green and red and blues. They were talking vociferously and laughing. Beyond them, two other tables were filled with young men and women who wore pants and vests of gold, and silver crowns adorned their heads. Their skin was well-tanned, and they did not speak as they ate. Instead, they looked at each other knowingly and sometimes laughed as if a joke had been spoken.

Those in bright cloaks and those in gold seemed to be of separate castes. The small ivory-skinned men and women who hugged the shadows made up a third group. They wore no clothing at all, but while they sat at their benches, the women's breasts were so small it was hard to distinguish sexes. And then there were the machines—a fourth caste, Maggie decided. From outside they had looked like warriors in armor, but now she saw that the silver men were only machines like those in the kitchens. They moved smoothly through the room, refilling mugs, cleaning tables.

Neither Gallen nor Orick had spoken since entering the building. Maggie wasn't sure what to say. Should they talk about the strangers? Discuss the wonders they beheld? Something warned her that neither would be prudent. She did not want to call attention to herself.

Maggie felt ignorant. The people here lived among so many marvels—walls that sang, machines that cooked and could fly. Compared to such people, she was a savage. Maggie had always had a quick wit, and for the first time in her life, she felt profoundly undereducated.

Halfway through breakfast, Maggie realized that people were watching them with furtive glances. She whispered to Gallen and Orick, "People are staring at us."

"Maybe we're not dressed to their liking," Gallen whispered.

"Or maybe I'm the only bear they've ever seen," Orick growled. "I can't smell another anywhere." Maggie was used to seeing bears in Tihrglas—they often would try to panhandle in town. She hadn't even noticed the absence of them here.

Gallen glanced around the room and said softly, "Orick, can you pick up Everynne's scent here? Even the slightest whiff?"

"Believe me," Orick answered, "if I could catch the slightest trace of that dear creature's fragrance, I'd pounce on her like a hound on a hare. She's nowhere near."

The folks at the nearest table left, affording Gallen, Maggie, and Orick a moment of privacy.

"What now?" Gallen whispered. "Do we throw ourselves on the mercy of these townsmen? Do we look for work and try to scratch out a living? Or do we hunt for Everynne?"

"We can't announce ourselves," Maggie warned. "We left those vanquishers behind, but for all we know, they could be on our trail at this very moment. If we were to be going around telling everyone that we were strangers, we'd only attract attention. They might even turn us over to the vanquishers."

Orick said, "By the way folks are staring at me, they must know we're strangers. Yet they seem mighty hospitable. Free food for everyone! If these are Everynne's enemies, then maybe we've taken up with scoundrels."

"Hmmm," Gallen said. "You and Maggie are both right. The folks here seem nice enough, but the vanquishers might be hunting us. We should lie low. Still, there's more to this city than this one corner. Everynne and Veriasse may be here. I want to go look for them."

"And leave us alone?" Maggie asked.

"I'd be less conspicuous that way. It would only be for a bit," Gallen said. At that moment, Gallen caught a startled breath. Maggie followed his gaze.

A man stood in the doorway to the dining room, a man in a black robe with black gloves and tall black boots, a man with a face that shone like golden starlight. Gallen got up clumsily.

"What is it?" Maggie asked, taking Gallen's wrist.

"Nothing," Gallen said. "I thought I recognized someone."

Maggie looked at the silver-faced man. "Him? Where would you have met the likes of him before?"

"Not him," Gallen said. "The one I saw was dressed the same, but his skin shone lavender. Besides, the man I met was younger and thinner."

"Where did you meet him?" Orick asked.

"In Coille Sidhe. Last night, a man dressed like that saved my life." Gallen stretched. "I'll be back in a couple of hours—sooner, if I find Everynne." He left the dining room, passed the stranger, and moved into a well-lighted hall.

Maggie watched his back. Right, Gallen O'Day, go chase your mystery woman. I wish you both all the happiness.

The room seemed to close around Maggie. Every few moments,

someone would bump her as they tried to get past. The room filled with diners, becoming cramped. She and Orick moved to a table that let her look out over the broad, muddy river. Green barn swallows were skimming over the river, dipping for drinks.

Maggie nibbled at her food and began to think that this place might be heaven. The weather was beautiful, the food delicious, and life here appeared to be simple.

But when Gallen had been gone for nearly an hour, the truth became more apparent: on the ruby road outside the city, six black dronons appeared. They wore odd shoes that let them glide along the road as swiftly as water striders. One of them skated to the inn. Maggie and Orick moved back against the wall, fearing that the creature was searching for them.

The inn became deathly quiet. The dronon was so wide that it could not easily pass between tables, but the gleaming black creature folded its wings and pulled itself slowly under the arch. Its head swayed from side to side as it moved. It held a long, black incendiary gun in one chitinous hand.

It stopped beside Maggie and Orick, and a single long feeler twisted up from beside its mouth. The feeler wrapped around Maggie's wrist. She stood abruptly, wanting to run, but found she was trapped between two tables with her back against the wall.

The dronon's feeler held her like a thick cord, binding her in case she should try to flee. Beneath the creature's mouth was an organ that looked like dozens of small, blunt fingers poised above the stretched membrane of a drum. The fingers began rhythmically tapping, creating an odd thrumming noise not unlike the sound that some deep-voiced locust might make. Yet the thrumming varied greatly in intensity and pitch. Maggie could distinguish words in that music. The dronon was speaking to her.

"You are not from this world. Where are you from?" the dronon demanded.

Maggie froze, not knowing how to answer. She pressed herself farther against the wall. The dronon's grip tightened, and it raised one arm overhead. She looked up—the arm was heavy, like the claw of a crab, and had a serrated edge. The dronon's tiny segmented hand had retracted, leaving a single large hooklike claw. If the dronon struck her, the arm would chop her in half like an axe. The dronon hissed, threatening to strike her into oblivion if she did not answer.

"You are not of this world. Where are you from?"

At a nearby table, the man dressed in black robes, the man with a golden face that glowed like starlight, stood and answered. "Great Lord, she is a Silent One from Pellarius!" he stepped forward. "She cannot speak. The singers there thought her voice lacked beauty, so they cut out her vocal cords and sterilized her so that she could not breed. Still, I have purchased her as a worker so that she might serve the greater glory of the dronon empire."

"What is her function?" the dronon asked.

"She is an aberlain, highly skilled in installing genetic upgrades in the unborn."

"If she is an aberlain, where is her Guide?" The Dronon's feeler began probing Maggie's scalp.

"She has been a class-two aberlain," the stranger said, "and is ready to be promoted to class one. I am having a new Guide created for her at this very moment."

"Where is her current Guide?" the Dronon demanded.

"Here, in my pocket." The stranger pulled out a wide band of silver, a crown with small lights in it. He held it up for the dronon to see. The dronon warrior abruptly lowered its battle arm.

"May your work prosper the empire," the dronon said, addressing both Maggie and the stranger in the same breath. It regarded Orick for a moment, then hunched and dragged its massive body through the cafeteria. It turned at the hallway and disappeared into the deeper recesses of the building.

Maggie found herself shaking, dizzy. She could not move. Terror held her in place. The dronon's feeler had left a gray powder on her arm that burned slightly.

The people in the cafeteria resumed talking. Maggie sagged into her chair. The stranger with the golden face watched her unabashedly. For the past half hour, Maggie had noticed that he had been studying her and Orick with an intensity that others in the room could not match. She did not know how to thank him.

The stranger came to their table. He took her arm, and poured her mug of drinking water over the skin where the dronon had touched her, then began to sponge it with a cloth napkin. "I don't know where you are from," he whispered, "but you obviously know nothing of the dronon. I envy that." He sponged her face and scalp. "The first lesson you must learn is that the dronon's exoskeleton produces a weak acid. They come from a dry world, and the acid coating is an effective addition to their immune system. But if they touch you, you must wipe off the acid to avoid getting burned."

He set down the napkin and peered into her face, ignoring Orick. The stranger had a strong jaw, penetrating brown eyes. Up under his black hood, he wore a silver headdress, much like the one Everynne had worn. Long silver chains dangled from it with hundreds of small triangles, like some metallic wig. She wondered why he would hide this beautiful headdress under a cloak, but did not ask.

"So," the stranger said, "my name is Karthenor, Lord of the Aberlains."

"I . . . I saw you watching me earlier," Maggie said.

"Forgive my inquisitiveness," Karthenor said. "I did not mean to offend you. But I have never seen anyone dressed like you, nor have I ever seen anyone like your friend." Karthenor glanced at Orick and said with a tone of dismissal as if Orick were a child, "I recognize the species. He is a bear."

"A *black* bear!" Orick grumbled.

"Excuse me," Karthenor said, raising a brow. He looked at Orick with a new degree of respect. "He is a genetically enhanced black bear." He addressed Orick, "I am pleased to make your acquaintance."

Karthenor pulled up a chair. Maggie could sense an eagerness in him, an expectancy she associated with traders who wanted to sell something. "You and your friend have been watching us, too. I suspect that you find us to be as strange as we find you. Am I right?"

Maggie studied his golden face. She could not think of a lie. In fact, she didn't know if she should tell one. She knew only that she wanted an ally, and Karthenor offered help. Gallen's brief mention that another man dressed like this had saved his life inspired her to a degree of confidence that was perhaps dangerous, but on impulse she said, "We came here through the World Gate. Yes, we do find it strange."

Karthenor leaned back in surprise, his voice so neutral that Maggie could not guess what he might be thinking. "You came through a World Gate? What is your name? Where are you from?"

"My name is Maggie Flynn—from the town of Clere."

Karthenor looked at her impassively, then bowed deeply. "I am honored to meet you, Maggie Flynn from the town of Clere. I . . . hope that I am not being too inquisitive, but may I ask what *world* you hail from?"

"Earth," Maggie answered.

The stranger seemed perplexed. He stared at Maggie and Orick with a bemused expression, rested his elbows on the table and touched a gloved finger to his lips. "Which Earth are you referring to? You obviously speak English, so you've been genetically engineered to remember our language. Yet you speak it with an odd accent, one I've never heard."

"Earth," Maggie said. "Where I live."

The stranger turned his head to the side, thinking. "What continent are you from on this Earth of yours?"

"Tihrglas," Maggie said.

"Ah, that Earth!" The stranger smiled. He folded his hands, looked at Maggie and Orick appraisingly. "Surely you did not find a gate key just lying around on Tihrglas? How did you come by it?"

Maggie felt inexplicably frightened. It had nothing to do with Karthenor's mannerisms. He seemed kindly, hospitable. But Maggie froze, not letting the stranger prod her further.

"Ah, forgive me! I've frightened you," Karthenor whispered, and his golden face crinkled in a beneficent smile. "Obviously, because you are a stranger to our land, you do not know our ways. Here on Fale, we are very open with each other. Perhaps you find this . . . disconcerting. Please, ask me any questions first, if this will put you at ease."

"Are you human?" Orick asked.

Karthenor smiled, touched his own cheek. "You mean the mask? Of course I am human, by most standards."

"Why do you wear the mask, then?" Maggie asked.

"To reveal," Karthenor said, taking Maggie's hand companionably. "It is a style here. The masks reveal our innermost selves. Those who do not wear the mask may hide emotions from one another, but when one wears the mask of Fale, he cannot hide behind his flesh and is ever forced to reveal his true emotions. Those of us who wear masks can practice no deceit. That is why, among all worlds, those who wear the mask of Fale are known to be trustworthy." He smiled gently at Maggie, and in that moment, Maggie felt ashamed for having distrusted him.

Karthenor held her hand, as if she were a child, and smiled as he looked out past the veranda to the swallows dipping in the wide river.

Children were out on the water now, riding the backs of giant geese. "If you like, I can give you a tour of our city," Karthenor offered. "If you come from Tihrglas, you will find it quite marvelous. Not at all like your home, I dare say."

"You've been to Tihrglas?" Orick asked.

"Heavens no," Karthenor answered. "I don't travel, but there are records. What do you know of Fale?"

"Nothing."

"Well then, it is time you learned. Our ancestors once lived together on the same world, long ago. A planet called Earth, but not the same Earth that you live on now."

Maggie looked at Karthenor suspiciously but said nothing as he continued. "On that planet, our ancestors had descended from animals, and there they acted the part—always warring, seeking wealth.

"Eventually, they developed space flight and journeyed to distant stars. There was an explosion of knowledge and technology unlike anything ever before. Machines learned to think. Men learned to hold death at bay and extend their lives for millennia. We met new races, new allies who also traversed among the stars.

"Still there were wars, still there was poverty and sadness. So some of our ancestors rejected technology, decided to live on backward planets in rustic settings. They came to be known as Backwards, and eighteen thousand years ago, some of them settled on your world. They took only the most basic tools—a few genetic upgrades that would let them remain relatively healthy and transmit an inborn memory of English. They took seeds for house-trees and plants.

"That is where our ancestors split: my ancestors were Forwards. They embraced technology and traveled to the stars." Karthenor waved his hand in a gesture that encompassed the sky.

"How do you know about our ancestors?" Maggie asked. "I've never heard these tales."

Karthenor touched the silver headdress, the tiny triangles. "My mantle is telling me about it," he said. "The mantle is a teaching machine that knows far more than any human." Maggie studied the ringlets and triangles. "Would you like to learn about such things? I have another teaching device here." His golden face was strangely intense. He reached into his pocket, pulled out the silver crown and gave it to Maggie. She held it, turned it over. The outside of the band showed only a single opening, a small window. But inside were colored lights. Two tiny prongs protruded so that they would push gently into the back of the wearer's neck.

"This is a Guide," Karthenor said. "Here in Fale, it is considered to be a thing of great worth. I want to give it to you, as a gift. You are a beautiful young woman. You will need it if you are to make a living here."

Maggie asked, "What does it do?"

"It is a teaching device, to make you wise," Karthenor said. "It is not only beautiful when worn in your hair, but very valuable. If you wear it, you will learn all of the secrets of how to become an aberlain. You will learn how to create life, shape the human genome into new complexities so that future generations will be wiser, stronger, and better servants of society than they are now. If you choose to wear such a Guide, you would become rich beyond imagination, and in time your wealth and power will rival that of the Lords. Here, let me show you how to put it on."

A hundred questions flooded through Maggie's mind: If it was so valuable, why would Karthenor simply *give* it to her? She realized now that many of the people here in the cafeteria wore similar Guides. They were the ones who ate silently, seemed to have no need to communicate with words. She wondered how long Karthenor would let her wear the thing.

Karthenor lifted the crown. It was bow-shaped and would not fit completely around Maggie's head. Instead, Karthenor began to put it on from behind, so that the ends of the bow touched the top of Maggie's neck. Just as it touched her, another question flooded into Maggie's mind, one that had nothing to do with the Guide: If Karthenor's mask kept him from lying, then how could he have lied to the dronon?

The cool metal Guide wrapped around Maggie's forehead. A faint itching pierced her skin where the prongs touched.

"There now," Karthenor said. "This will be your Guide. It shall teach you all things that you shall do. It will be your comforter and your constant companion. With it, you shall learn many great things."

Maggie looked up. Karthenor's black robes silhouetted his golden face, and Maggie looked into his malicious grin. She clawed at the Guide, trying to pull it free, and a raging fire seemed to sweep through her head. Tears rolled down her face, burning like molten lead. Maggie cried out and fell to the floor, gasping.

"Get that off her!" Orick roared. Karthenor glanced back at the bear, waved his hand. A web of thin gray wires, so small that they could hardly be seen, shot out from a device at Karthenor's wrist. The web struck Orick and the wall, gluing the bear in place. Orick roared in terror and tried to claw his way free, but the tiny net held.

"Help!" Maggie shouted, rolling on the floor, looking to the others in the room.

Karthenor's image swirled, and Maggie watched him through a fog of pain and dismay. He bent low and hissed, "No one can help you. I am a Lord here. Don't try to remove the Guide—it will only punish you for your efforts! Now: tell me how you got through the gate at Tihrglas! Where did you find the key?"

Maggie's muscles went limp, and though she fought to move, she could not control her arms, could not budge a muscle. Yet as Karthenor had promised, the Guide began to teach her.

In an overwhelming instant, knowledge coursed into her like a pure foaming river, filling her with more facts than she'd ever thought she could know. The tide of human learning cascaded over her, drowning her, and she despaired.

In one marvelous moment, Maggie understood the work of an aberlain. With the Guide to help her, she would spend the rest of her life altering the genetic makeup of unborn children, making them into better servants for the dronon empire. In return, each child and their offspring in perpetuity would become indebted to Maggie and her Lord Karthenor. Though they sweated for a thousand generations, a portion of all their earnings would be deducted for payment. The work of aberlains had been illegal until six years ago, had been considered immoral.

But now the dronon ruled, and in dronon society, each creature was born into a caste he could never escape. Images flashed before Maggie's eyes of her dronon leaders: the Golden Queen, Tlitkani, who had so recently seized control of six thousand worlds; the black Lord Vanquishers, her soldiers; the small, sand-colored artisans of dronon society, and the vast oceans of white-skinned workers. Each was born to its place, and the dronons now sought to remake mankind in their own image.

Karthenor, Lord of Aberlains, was one of mankind's greatest enemies on this world. Through genetic manipulation, he hoped to engineer a race of slaves and reap endless profit.

And through the Guide, Maggie would become a slave. The Guide stored information on an atomic level. The silver band housed billions of volumes of data along with transmitters and receivers. Already, the Guide's nanotech components were creating artificial neurons to thread through her cerebrum and brain stem, binding her to the machine. Within hours, she and the machine would be one.

Maggie looked up at Karthenor with undisguised hatred. "I know you!" she growled. The effort caused her great pain.

Karthenor laughed, "Now, see, your eyes are beginning to open already. In your own small way, you are becoming like one of the gods. I want you to think about gods for a moment, and tell me where you got their key."

Karthenor waved his hand. Two silver android servants came to the table, lifted Maggie by each arm, and began dragging her into the recesses of the building. Orick roared and growled in rage, but he could not save her.

When Karthenor said the word "gods," the world went gray as information flooded her senses. Just as Maggie had this small Guide enmeshed in her brain, others across the galaxy were joined to larger intelligences. Karthenor's silver mantle stored far more information than Maggie's Guide, yet some immortals were connected to intelligences the size of an entire planet. They were gods.

In her mind's eye, Maggie saw Semarritte, the great judge who had ruled this sector of the galaxy for ten thousand years. She was a woman of proud bearing and dark hair, very much like Everynne, but older. Semarritte had built the gates at the beginning of her reign as a means of traveling between worlds quickly. Yet to protect herself, she had kept the method for constructing the gate keys a secret.

In one bitter moment, Maggie understood that Everynne was the daughter of Semarritte, and that Everynne had stolen the gate key in a desperate bid to win back her mother's worlds.

Karthenor and his servants dragged Maggie down a long hall. With each jarring step it felt as if the androids would pull her arms from her sockets. They passed shops and hallways and came to a blank wall which turned to mist when Karthenor touched it.

They entered a living room with comfortable sofas and luxurious white rugs. The androids laid Maggie on the floor, and Maggie's lips began to move against her will.

She lay helplessly and listened to herself tell Karthenor of the Lady Everynne, of the dronon that dogged her trail in Tihrglas, and of Gallen's own naive efforts to aid Everynne. With each word, Maggie betrayed Gallen, herself, the Lady Everynne—every human on every world.

Sometimes Karthenor would stop her, ask a question, such as, "And where is your friend Gallen now?" No matter how hard Maggie sought to lie, the whole truth came out. She could not will her mouth to shut.

When Maggie finished, tears rolled down her face. Karthenor said, "Go to your quarters."

Maggie suddenly knew where her sleeping quarters lay in an upstairs loft. She willed herself to run away but could not move her feet. She moved to the rhythm of the machines.

This is your home now, the Guide whispered. You will serve Karthenor. I will teach you what you must do. Stiffly, the Guide moved Maggie's legs and arms, taking her down a sterile white corridor, up a long staircase. Maggie watched, knowing that she was no longer human. She climbed into bed, then lay down, thinking. The Guide was always thinking.

Maggie had one hope: Gallen O'Day.

Seven

Gallen wandered the pale green hallways of the city. The air was warm, moist, like the air inside a house-tree. The very city was alive, growing.

Windows in the roof let in some light, while glowing gems overhead provided the rest. As Gallen moved deeper into this living catacomb, he twice came upon open-air bazaars where merchants in colorful swirling robes sought to sell him fabulous merchandise: a pair of living lungs that could attach to his back and let him breathe underwater; the seeds to a flower that could be planted one day, grow six feet overnight, and break into glorious blooms; a hood that would let him talk to a dead man; a tiny plug that he could place in his ear so that he could always listen to music; a cream that not only removed wrinkles and blemishes from skin but also left the wearer pleasantly scented for a number of years.

Gallen recognized that much of it was junk and gadgetry, trifles for a people who had everything. But still vendors hawked their wares, trying to engage his attention in odd ways. At one shop, a beautiful woman appeared out of thin air. She was tanned and strong and wore only the slightest scrap of clothes. She smiled at Gallen and said, "Why don't you come in here and try me on?" Then she walked into a shop. Gallen followed, and she went to a stack of pants, pulled a pair on and wriggled into them, then disappeared.

Gallen found himself staring at a display of pants, looking about for the woman, but she was nowhere to be seen. Suddenly he realized that she had been created only to lure him into the shop. He left, found that similar devices were at nearly every store. Voices would speak from nowhere, demanding that he buy here and now in order to save. Spirit women would appear, begging him to purchase something from the shop, and always they were so beautiful as to make him dizzy.

A manic glee fell over Gallen, and he wandered the long corridors as if in some intoxicated daze, sampling confections that tasted of ambrosia, yet always declining to buy.

In one square, he found a beast that looked like a huge gray toad sitting in a chair, surrounded by bright containers filled with colorful powders. The toadman wore an immense wig of silver with many ringlets and triangles that cascaded down his shoulders. On his back he wore a number of tubes, and each tube had dozens of tiny appendages rising up from it—some with hairs on them, others with clamps or scalpels. All these appendages rose overhead and by use of various joints managed to converge on a small table in front of the toad. Children had gathered around, and Gallen stopped to look.

The toadman's limbs all pointed to a small object at the center of the table, and Gallen stood breathless, watching. A purple dragonfly sat on a thin reed there, motionless. Dozens of tiny needles, or perhaps hairs, met at the focal point of the device, and Gallen saw that the hairs seemed to be stroking one of the dragonfly's wings. Part of the dragonfly's wing was missing, but the toadman's machines were stroking it, creating a new wing.

Gallen's jaw dropped open, and he walked around so that he could watch over the toadman's shoulders. The old gray fellow was looking at writing that appeared in the air, fiery red letters that blossomed and departed so fast that Gallen couldn't read them. An image of the dragonfly, magnified many times, sat in the air above the toadman's head, and every few moments the toadman would look up at the image whenever a new layer of wing had been placed. He would stare at the image a moment, until new veins and an expanded portion of wing appeared, then glance down. His machines would begin constructing the rest of the dragonfly.

Within five minutes, the toadman finished. "Now, children, which of you would like this dragonfly I have formed?" he asked, and the children clapped and pleaded.

The toadman reached out with one warty gray finger, touched the dragonfly, and it climbed onto his long nail. He held the dragonfly aloft for a moment, then turned to Gallen.

"I think I will give this one to the child who looks like a man." He extended the dragonfly to Gallen.

Gallen touched the toadman's finger, and the dragonfly crawled to Gallen's thumb and sat, wings pulsing. It was vivid purple with touches of red under its belly and in its wings. The children walked away, disappointed.

"Thank you," Gallen said.

"It is nothing. In a few moments, its wings will dry, and it will fly away," the toadman answered.

Gallen studied the toadman. He had yellow eyes, warty gray skin, and a mouth wide enough to swallow a cat whole. His arms and legs were thin, with baggy skin.

"You have never seen a Motak," the toadman said.

"Is that what you are?" Gallen asked.

"Yes," the toadman answered. "And if you knew of us, you would know that you are supposed to avert your eyes and not stare. On Motak, we stare only at those who are ugly."

"I'm sorry," Gallen said. "I didn't mean to imply that you are ugly."

"I know."

"I was simply curious."

"I know that, too," the toadman said. "It has been ages since I have seen an adult so interested in the doings of a creator."

"Is that what you do?" Gallen asked. "You create life?"

"Not true life. Only viviforms, artificial beings. Still, they look true enough, and they don't know that they aren't living creatures."

"Can you create people?" Gallen asked.

"For a price. I can make a viviform that looks and acts any way that you like. Between jobs, I create pets for the children." The dragonfly began flapping its wings.

"Thank you. I'm very grateful," Gallen said, and he cupped the dragonfly into his palms, determined to carry it back to show Maggie.

"I thank you in return," the toadman said. "It is good to see such light in the eyes of an adult again, especially during such hard times. May joy burn brightly in you."

When Gallen returned to the cantina, patrons of the restaurant were freeing Orick from a net, and Maggie was nowhere to be seen.

Orick growled at those who freed him, "Why didn't you stop him, lads? Why didn't you stop him?" No one answered.

"Stop who?" Gallen asked, setting the dragonfly free. He pulled out a knife to cut at the fine webbing. Each tiny thread was tough as a nail and seemed to be glued to the wall.

"A man named Karthenor kidnapped Maggie!" Orick shouted. As Gallen helped cut through the last thread, Orick urged, "This way, Gallen!" and rushed down a corridor toward the heart of the city.

Orick barreled down the hallway, navigating by smell. Sometimes he would come to an intersection and stop, testing the scent in both directions. At other times, he would lunge down a corridor and then come up short, only to test the scent of some side passageway. After a few minutes, they reached a hallway that led to a dead end.

"They came here," Orick said. "They came at least this far." Orick sniffed the creamed-colored wall, stood up on his back legs and smelled the ceiling.

Gallen took Orick by the shoulders. "Now," he said, "tell me everything that happened."

Orick told Gallen of the visit by the vanquisher and how a man named Karthenor, Lord of the Aberlains, put a silver band around Maggie's head and took her captive.

Gallen considered. As in any battle, he took stock of his assets and liabilities. He had his wits, his skills as a fighter, and two knives. Yet he did not know his enemies or their weaknesses. One old sheriff down in County Obhiann had often warned: "When you are confronted by an outlaw, always take stock of the terrain. Look for what cover you can find, watch to make sure he doesn't have a bowman or a couple of lads sitting in the same bush you might want to hide under."

Obviously, when it came to terrain, Gallen was at a phenomenal disadvantage. "Come on," he said. "Let's get you under some cover. If we go hunting for Karthenor together, he'll spot you a mile off. But he's never seen me. I will leg it back here and study the situation."

They made their way back to the highway. The road was filling with people—coaches floated over its ruby surface. Some people had shoes that floated in the same manner, and they skated over the road faster than any horse could run.

Gallen and Orick walked north along the river for a mile until they came to some low wooded hills. Here they slipped into the brush and made camp. Gallen worried about Maggie. Every few moments he would verify some details. "This Karthenor said that Maggie would be working for him? Did he say where?"

"No," Orick answered, yet Gallen felt more easy. If Karthenor needed workers, then Maggie should be all right. Karthenor wouldn't want to harm a servant.

"I'll to have to find Maggie," Gallen said. "To do so, I'll need to sneak through the city. You can't come with me."

"But what should I do?" Orick asked. "I don't want to just sit and wait."

"I still need your help. We know Everynne came through the gate before us, but we don't know where she may have come out. I'd like you to hunt for her trail. Maybe you can find her. I want you to make a thorough search, then come back here in two or three days."

Orick agreed reluctantly, headed south. He looked over his back. "You'll get her out all right, won't you?"

"I'll do my best," was all Gallen could promise.

When Maggie woke in the morning, her head burned with a fever. She wondered at the pain. A voice whispered in her mind, "It is I, your Guide. I have been creating neural pathways into your brain and spinal column all night, and this causes your discomfort. By nightfall the process will be complete, and we will become one."

Maggie tried to get up but could not move. Instead, the Guide let her lie abed for a few moments and began feeding her information at an incredible pace. "If you have questions," the Guide said, "ask."

The Guide began by showing her the structure of DNA in all of its intricacy. In brief visions, it revealed the function of each set of genes in the human genome, and how these genes were affected by variations. It showed her machinery and taught her how to run the tools that aberlains used in their work—chromosome readers, gene splicers, tissue samplers, DNA dyes. She learned how to remove egg cells from women and sperm from men, divide them into lots based on desirable characteristics that the cells would transmit, and then infect each lot with tailored genes to ensure that all progeny were properly upgraded to standards set by the dronon overlords. Once a batch of eggs and sperm were perfected, they could be mixed and incubated for sixty hours, then the resulting zygotes would be implanted into a woman's womb.

The lesson lasted for nearly an hour, then the Guide forced Maggie from her bed, had her shower, and let her go down to the dining hall for breakfast. Maggie sat at a table with other aberlains, men and women who all wore Guides like hers. And though none of them spoke, she could hear their voices in her mind as they discussed the tasks that each would need to complete that day. She ate greedily, but the Guide forced her to stop just before she felt satisfied.

She spent the morning working in a clinic. Couples who had sought a license to bear children were there, and Maggie took egg samples from women, sperm from men. She laboriously tagged and labeled each sample, but since the dronon would allow only people with certain body types to reproduce, she ended up throwing most of the samples away. Instead, the women were implanted with zygotes from approved parents.

Several times during the day, the women asked Maggie, "Will I really be getting my own child? You won't implant me with someone else's child?"

Each time, Maggie's Guide responded by comforting the potential mother and answering, "Of course you will get your own child. We take great care in labeling every sample, and there is no chance that the samples could get mixed. We will simply invest the cells with some standardized upgrades, and you will then have your own embryo returned to you."

Each time she told this lie, Maggie would fight her Guide, try to scream out a warning, and the Guide would respond by doing something that Maggie could only describe as "tickling" her: suddenly her head would itch, and then a sweet feeling of euphoria would wash through her, the greatest contentment she had ever known.

Once, when Maggie was away from the patrons of the clinic in a storage room, she said to her Guide, "How can we lie to them? Why should we lie to them?"

"We do them a favor. Why should we let them harbor ill feelings about a process that they cannot change? Our system maximizes efficiency and insures an even distribution of genetically upgraded offspring."

"But their children will all be brothers and sisters, even though they come from different families," Maggie whispered to her Guide. "They won't be able to marry."

"Within each hive, our dronon masters are brothers and sisters. Each queen bears a hundred thousand eggs, and vanquishers are born brothers to architects, workers are sisters to queens. The new family revels in unity; thus the hive bonds. When our human offspring discover that they are all brothers and sisters, they will revel in that kinship."

The Guide tickled her again. A new and stronger wave of pleasure washed through Maggie. It was a mystical, magical feeling, to be involved in such a great work, a work approved and loved by the Golden Queen and her overlords.

In the late evening, Maggie took a young woman into a back laboratory and had her lie on the operating table. Maggie took out a tissue sampler which she would use to remove egg cells from the patient. The sampler was a long, thin piece of metal with a small scoop at the end to catch a slice of ovary. Maggie was removing its sterile covering when the patient looked up at Maggie and asked, "How free are you?"

Maggie turned to the woman, unsure if she had heard correctly. The woman looked deep into Maggie's eyes. "How free are you? Do you want to escape from your Guide? If so, blink twice."

Maggie tried to blink, struggled until tears formed in her eyes, but she could not blink. The Guide whispered, "Do not be alarmed by this woman, the guards are coming for her."

Maggie stared at the woman. She was small, with mousy blond hair cropped close to her scalp, and a firm chin. She was nervous, sweating, and she whispered. "I'm in danger, aren't I? I think I'll go."

She leapt off the table and opened the door. A green-skinned vanquisher with large orange eyes stood behind it.

The small woman tried to slam the door. The vanquisher shoved it open, grabbed the woman by the throat and one arm. She kicked and screamed, trying to escape, but he held her tight, dragged her away.

Maggie stood, staring out the door, shocked, her heart hammering. The Guide flooded her with pleasant sensations, whispering peace to her soul.

That night, as Maggie prepared for bed, her Guide transmitted a report to Lord Karthenor, detailing her accomplishments for the day. Her Guide reported that Maggie proved to be "culturally retarded," and the Guide had to instruct her in the use of even the simplest machinery.

Karthenor was not concerned by this. Given Maggie's background, it was only to be expected. But the Guide also reported that it had been forced to stimulate her hypothalamus over fifty times during the day, keeping her in a state of vegetative euphoria. Such overstimulation was dangerous. Within a week, it would lead to severe depression, a depression that could not be reversed for months. Under such circumstances, the Guide could still use her, but she would become despondent, an unreliable host. If the Guide temporarily lost control of her under such conditions, she might kill herself.

Karthenor considered the report, called to one of his technicians, a human named Avik whose parents had been integrated into dronon society two generations ago. He was a young man with hair so golden it appeared to be silver, and he had a sleek, well-muscled body. Avik reported quickly.

"My lord?" Avik said when he reached the door.

"The new servant, Maggie Flynn, needs someone to help make her adjustment smoother," Karthenor said. "I would like you to talk to her, befriend her. I'll instruct her Guide to give her free reign during your contact."

Avik nodded. He was a young man, with burning blue eyes. "Would you like me to seduce her?"

Karthenor considered. These dronon-bred technicians mated like animals. Perhaps because they were forced to work under the domination of Guides, they had become emotionally stunted. They tended to confuse sexual gratification with the more permanent rewards of a committed relationship. "Yes," he said after a moment. "I think the physical contact might be appropriate, comforting for her. However, I would like you to take her slowly, at her own pace. Don't rush her."

"Very well, my lord," Avik said, giving a deep bow as he left.

Eight

Gallen began to canvass the city an hour after leaving Orick. That day, he stopped at numerous shops and studied local merchandise while quietly pumping proprietors for information. He methodically stepped off passageways and learned the ins and outs of the city.

The locals called the place Toohkansay, and Gallen learned about the various housing quarters, the manufacturing sectors, and the business districts. Some of these places denied access to the public, and this left gaping holes in his mental map of the city. For example, with only a few questions he learned where Lord Karthenor's two hundred aberlains worked night and day in some mystic enterprise that a businessman said would "improve mankind," but when Gallen went to the place, he found only a small clinic where men and women waited for some mysterious ministrations to be performed on them.

Gallen surveyed the area around the clinic—studied Toohkansay's exits, found each window and skylight, hunted for likely places to hide.

Most of the city's inhabitants fit within certain categories: those who wore silver bands on their heads either could not or would not speak to Gallen. The merchants with their lavish robes soon became easy to spot. In a dark cafe near one manufacturing district, Gallen sat at a table filled with the small white men and women with enormous eyes and ears. His questions elicited raucous laughter from them, yet they answered good-naturedly. They called themselves the Woodari. Their ancestors had been created to work on a distant planet where the sun was dark. Here on Fale, they worked as miners and built ships to carry cargo from one world to another. The Woodari starfarers claimed that their guild was so powerful that they did not fear the dronon.

Gallen asked so many questions of one little Woodari named Fargeth that the little man said, "Your vast ignorance amuses me, but I have work to do. You are so full of questions, why do you not go to the pidc?"

"The pidc?" Gallen asked. "What is that?"

"It is a place where all the questions you can ask in a lifetime will be answered in moments."

"Where is it?" Gallen asked. "What do they charge for their service?"

Fargeth laughed. "Knowledge carries its own price. Gain it to your dismay."

Gallen wandered the halls until he spotted the creator at work in his stall, making a child. In his past two days here in the city, the old alien was the only person Gallen met whom he genuinely liked. Gallen recalled the sadness in the old creature's voice as he talked of "troubles in the city." Gallen suddenly knew that the old man was an enemy to the dronon.

Gallen said, "A friend of mine has been taken by Lord Karthenor of the aberlains. I need to learn how to free her. Can you tell me where the pidc is?"

The old toadman nodded. "I feared such a thing might befall you. I will take you there."

The toadman unhooked the various mechanical devices from his back, led Gallen down a familiar corridor to a business where young parents took children into little cubicles, set them in plush chairs, then attached silver bands to their children's heads for hours at a time. The bands had a calming effect on the children, and Gallen had thought this was the only benefit the devices imparted.

The creator set Gallen in a white chair, showed Gallen how to strap a silver band to his temples, and whispered, "Good luck, my friend. For most people, this is all they ever learn in life, and a session here becomes the end of knowledge. If you were from Motak, you would know that filling your mind with trivia is only the beginning of study. Right action will lead to greater light."

The toadman left, and Gallen held the silver strip a moment. He placed it on his head as if it were a crown. A gray mist seemed to form before Gallen's eyes. The room went dark, and in the distance he could see a bright pinpoint of light. A voice within the light said, "I am the teacher. Open yourself to knowledge. What do you wish to know?"

Gallen couldn't decide where to begin. "I know nothing of your people or customs. I can't figure out what your machines are, or how they work—"

"I can teach you of people and customs—save those things that each community might consider too sacred to share. I can teach you the basics of all technology, though each industry has its own manufacturing secrets that are private property."

"Teach me," Gallen said. And if Maggie's education was rough and painful, Gallen's was sweet and filled with light. It began with a knowledge of mathematics that coursed into him evenly—beginning with the basics of number theory, moving up through advanced spatial geometry. There, mathematics branched into physics and he learned about subatomic particles, relativity, and Gallen memorized the various equations for the unified field theory and its many corollaries.

Then the introduction to physics moved into applied technologies, and Gallen was given to understand the workings of starships and incendiary rifles and gravcars and ten thousand other items.

He learned how thinking machines developed until they reached the point where they began evolving on their own and now could store more information than any human. The Guides were one form of teaching machines, but they included invasive technologies that let the Guide control the wearer. The chainmail headdresses, called mantles, like the one worn by Everynne were a more advanced type of personal intelligence that did not seek to dominate its wearer, and beyond these were a realm of intelligences that had nothing to do with mankind.

Gallen studied nanotechnology and learned how war machines were built. He learned about the development of viviforms and artefs and genetically upgraded humans—and he learned of some creatures that appeared to be biological in their construction but straddled the line between creature and machine.

He learned how the World Gates tapped into the power of a singularity, a black hole, where time and space were warped to the point that they did not exist, so that those who walked through the gate were whisked in a stream of atoms and recreated at a chosen destination.

At the end of an hour, Gallen's head was sweaty. The teacher interrupted the session. "You are learning too much, too quickly," it said. "Your brain can form only a limited number of neurological connections within a given time. Now, you must rest."

"When can I come back?" Gallen asked.

"You will need to eat, nourish yourself, and return tomorrow," the teacher answered.

Gallen rose from his chair, and the world seemed to spin. He fell down, grabbed the chair to support himself, and waited until he felt steady enough to walk to a cafeteria. He ate heavily and felt gloriously elated for an hour, then found himself slightly nauseated and absent-minded.

In three hours, his head began to clear. He walked through the bazaar for a bit and felt a new man. He looked at the vendors with new eyes now, appreciating the craftsmanship of their wares, understanding the utility of items that he could not have fathomed hours before. Indeed, he had become a new man. Before, he had walked through the bazaar shaking his head in wonder, certain that many items worked on principles of magic beyond his ken. Now he saw that there was no magic—only creativity and craft.

He watched the people with open eyes, marking those who wore personal intelligences. Those who wore Guides, he saw now, were often slaves or bond servants. Some submitted to the indignity of wearing a Guide in the hope of earning greater rewards.

Those who wore the chainmail headdresses called "mantles" were vastly wealthy in ways that Gallen had not imagined. Their mantles served them and were far more intelligent than the little Guides.

Merchants were frequently freemen who made themselves useful, but the vast majority of mankind were worthless in this society, and so long as they were free to eat and breed and be entertained, they seemed content.

Here on Fale, there was no need for a man with a strong back or quick wit. There was nothing a human could do that an android could not do better. So those who did not have some type of relationship with a personal intelligence—either as a possessor or as one possessed—were considered only waste, the excess of humanity. And as Gallen studied the peons of Fale, he began to see that behind the well-fed faces, there was a haunted, cramped look.

Gallen went to his camp that night and lay looking up at the stars, smelling the wind. On this world, despite all of his strivings, the people would consider him worthless, and this was something that he had never imagined.

He considered what Karthenor had done. Perhaps in the lord's mind, by giving Maggie a Guide, he had made her a person of worth, bestowed upon her some dignity. Yet such a gift was bound to carry a terrible price.

On the morning of her third day on Fale, Maggie's Guide completed the task of injecting its own artificial neural network into Maggie's nervous system. The Guide now commanded a secondary network of neurons that led through all of her extremities, so that it could control the rate of Maggie's pulse and breathing, feel with her fingers and toes, watch with her eyes and hear with her ears.

When it finished, it reported its progress to Maggie, flashing a three-dimensional image of the new nervous system to her. A sense of panic rose in her when she saw what had happened, but the Guide did not tickle her, did not send her its calm assurances. Instead, it left her with her fears.

Now that the Guide had extended its control over her, it announced that it was free to begin its greater work of teaching Maggie the intricacies of genetic manipulation. The Guide gave her routine tasks for the day. During one marathon twenty-hour work session, Maggie extracted, sorted, and upgraded over a hundred egg cells from one woman. Afterward, she added genetic enhancements to several hundred thousand sperm. She then mixed the cells and put them in the incubator before she left for the night. Her Guide reported her daily accomplishments to Karthenor, and Karthenor set up a credit account to give her advances on the future earnings of the children she was creating. In time, one hundred children would each pay her one percent of their life earnings. In one day, she had sewn a crop that would in time reap a fortune. The Guide made sure that she understood and felt properly grateful to be so employed.

As she worked that day, there was little to distract her. In the late afternoon, she heard an explosion in a storage room. For a few moments sirens blared and dronon vanquishers rushed through the smoke-filled compound, securing the area. Maggie could hear the screams of a wounded woman. Her Guide merely informed her that terrorists had exploded a small bomb, and one of her fellow workers was injured. The Guide instructed Maggie to continue working.

Maggie was too heavily tranquilized to even consider disobeying. All through the morning, the Guide had been dumping information into her, data gleaned from genetic engineering experiments over eighteen thousand years from a hundred thousand worlds. A thousand distinct subspecies of mankind had been formed in that time, and billions of minor alterations had been tried. Maggie learned how to engineer people to live underwater, in reduced or increased gravities, or to cope with chemically altered atmospheres.

Yet the dronon Guide also taught her the glorious plans that it had for Maggie's people, and as the plans unfolded, Maggie was tickled so that she felt as if she were floundering in a pool of ecstasy. The genes that Maggie inserted into that day's batch of children were specifically designed to decrease a female's infant mortality rate and at the same time engineer a subspecies of future women to become breeders. These breeders would bear litters of ten or more children. The women that Maggie engineered would be tall, languid, wide at the hips, and would spend a great deal of time eating. They would require little in the way of cerebral stimulation—would shun mental exercise, physical stimulation. In effect, they would be sacks to bear children.

In a few days, Maggie knew that she would be allowed to work on a second subspecies of females who would be sterile workers, filled with an incredible amount of nervous energy that would be released in the joyful pursuit of labor. Other colleagues were developing males that would consist of one subspecies of dreamy-eyed artisans and creators, while another subspecies would form a caste of giant warriors with superb reflexes, immense strength, and an instinct for killing. These would burn a path across the galaxies, uniting all mankind under a common banner.

In all aspects, human society would come to emulate the more perfect dronon society, and the worlds would embrace a new, superior order.

That night, Maggie ate a quick dinner and then threw herself on her bed, contemplating the riches she had earned. Her Guide tickled her so that her blood raced at the thrill of it.

A few minutes later, her Guide announced a visitor only seconds before he entered the room.

He was a tall man, perhaps twenty-five years of age, with pale blond hair. The sculpted muscles of his chest and shoulders revealed a body type that Maggie recognized from her studies—the human equivalent of a dronon technician.

He entered her small bedroom and sat in her single chair. He watched Maggie with an intensity peculiar to those raised in dronon society. It was as if Maggie were food, and the man was feeding on her with his gleaming blue eyes.

"My name is Avik," he said. "Lord Karthenor asked me to speak with you. He feels that you are not adjusting well to your new assignments. You've been distressed, and your Guide is devoting considerable resources in an effort to make you happy. Is there anything I can do to make you happy?"

Maggie stared at him, and it was as if suddenly her Guide shut off, and she was falling, swirling toward ruin. The false euphoria left her, and she felt helpless, abused, physically exhausted. Her head was spinning with visions of the children she was creating, the mothers with their vast wombs, the legions of sexless workers, the deadly warriors with their quick wits and killer's eyes.

Maggie found herself sputtering, trying in one quick burst to express the rage and horror that the Guide had been suppressing for two days now. "I can't . . ." she cried helplessly. She wanted to launch herself at Avik, claw his eyes out, but the Guide would not let her.

Avik took her hands, held them. "What you need," he said softly, "is another human to help you cope with this change."

Maggie glared at him and thought, *If there were another human in this room, I* would *do that.* She was painfully aware that Avik's enhancements made him unlike other men. He had a dreamy look in his eyes, a soft-spoken nature, a predisposition to move his hands as he spoke. In every way he was a dronon technician, as distinct in his characteristics as a bloodhound would be among mongrels. Yet Maggie could not hate him for something he could not change.

"Set me free," Maggie pleaded. "I can't live the way you want me to."

"Of course you can," Avik said. "It takes time, but you can become dronon. In fact, you have no choice in the matter. Believe me, you will find peace among us."

"I can't," Maggie said. "Don't you see how different they are from us? We weren't meant to live like the dronon."

"The differences between us and the dronon are superficial," Avik said. "They have chitin, we have skin. But we are both a species of conquerors, and both of us found the need to overwhelm nature, expand our domain to the stars. Do you realize how few sentient species have done this?"

"We are nothing like them!" Maggie shouted. "If we were, they wouldn't need to force us into their castes. . . ."

Avik smiled, sat back smugly. "They are not forcing us into castes. Don't you see what they are doing? They are merely enhancing the differences that already exist between us. Even in the natural state, some of your men are born to be warriors. The urge to compete in them is so overwhelming that they can hardly control it." Maggie suddenly thought of Gallen. "And others of your men are like me, dreamers and creators. Some of your people are workers—unable to stop, unable to enjoy any other facet of life but the workplace. And some of you are nurturers, breeders who find comfort in sprawling families and take joy in raising children. And some of you are born to become leaders. In every age of humanity, it has been this way. The hive mind is within us, just as it is within the dronon. Believe me, once your people make the transition to our order, your children will enjoy greater peace and prosperity than they have ever known."

It was disconcerting in a way to watch Avik, so human in form, talk about humans as if they were alien. But she could see the alienness in his eyes, in the hungry way he watched her.

"But you have no freedom. Our children will have no choice in their decisions," Maggie shouted. She found herself shaking with rage, her muscles spasming.

"Perhaps we lose a little," Avik countered, "but we gain much in return. We have no crime on dronon worlds, for the Guides do not allow it.

We have no confusion over making simple choices. We don't spend vast portions of our youth uselessly vacillating as we struggle to learn what we shall become. Among the hives, each child knows what he or she will do as an adult. We are bred to our positions, and we *do* find peace, a peace that is greater and more profound than any you can imagine. It may appear to be a contradiction, but though our laws seem restrictive to you, they free us to find that peace." Avik spoke evenly, a thin sheen of sweat on his forehead. Maggie looked into his wild eyes, wanted to shout him down, yet he so obviously believed in the dronon order, she realized that to argue would be futile.

Still, she could not resist the temptation to say more. "Avik, don't you see—your order doesn't really free you, it merely limits you. You could choose to be more than an architect—you could become anything you want: a father, a leader, a warrior. The dronon haven't freed you. They've merely made you comfortable. You have become content slaves, when you could be gods."

Avik's nostrils flared. Maggie could see that she'd struck a chord. He backed up in his chair, looked at her appraisingly. "You will never speak against the order again."

Maggie tried to argue, but the Guide stopped her tongue and would not let her speak, so that his words seemed to carry the weight of a prophecy.

Avik got up from his chair, put his hands on her shoulders and looked into her eyes. "I will instruct your Guide to continue tutoring you in the ways of the dronon, and in your job. Each time you think of the order, your Guide will give you comfort, and perhaps in this way, over time, you will learn to love the order. Tomorrow you will begin working on the Adoration Project, and as you learn to love our order, you will in turn be teaching others to love it. Maggie, don't fight us. You can't win, and you might get hurt in the struggle."

He cupped her chin in one hand, and her Guide sent her a spasm of lust that knotted her stomach and made her face burn. She tried to fight it, to give vent to her anger, but she realized that Avik was controlling her Guide, forcing this emotion on her. "You're such a pretty thing. I like red hair. Lord Karthenor has asked me to give you physical companionship. You will find that having sex while wearing a Guide is more compelling than anything you have ever dreamed. No beast in heat will ever find greater satisfaction than you will find with me this night."

Maggie locked her legs together and curled up in a ball on the bed. She knew that fighting would be no use. Her Guide could take control of her muscles at any moment, force her to open her legs and give herself to him. But she needed to do this, to commit one small act of defiance.

Avik grinned. “So, is that to be the way of it? Then I'll leave you to this lust, and it shall keep you company tonight. Tomorrow, when I return and make the offer again, you will be grateful.”

Avik left the room. The lights dimmed as he exited, and Maggie was left in pain, screaming inside, aching for Gallen.

Gallen returned to the pidc that morning, put on the instruction hood. “Teach me about mankind,” he said. The teacher began with genetics and showed the path of evolution, including ancient species of mammals and dinosaurs whose DNA had been salvaged and reproduced on many worlds. The teacher taught him the genetic structure of man, showing how genetic engineers had developed mankind into over a thousand distinct subspecies, each bred to a specific purpose, to live in a specific environment.

He learned the schemes humans used to achieve life extension. Thousands of drugs and procedures had been developed to cheat death. Most who died had their consciousness transmitted to virtual heavens that existed within computers. Some had their memories downloaded to machines, like the artefs, which were simply colonies of self-replicating nanotech devices. The most ambitious plans to beat death involved life extensions coupled with downloading memories into clones. Such plans culminated in virtual immortality—a commodity that had once been reserved for the most deserving but now available only to the wealthiest.

Last of all, the teacher showed Gallen the crowning achievement of genetic manipulation, the Tharrin, a race fashioned to embody nobility and virtue, a race designed to integrate fully with personal intelligences without losing their humanity. The Tharrin were to be the leaders and judges of mankind, a subspecies that would control the naval fleets, the police forces, and courts of a million worlds.

The Tharrin's physical features embodied strength and perfection. Certain glands secreted pheromones that attracted other humans so that the Tharrin constantly found themselves at the center of attention. Yet the Tharrin seldom became conceited. They did not see themselves as leaders or judges, but as the servants of mankind.

Gallen was not surprised when an image of a Tharrin formed in his mind, and he recognized Everynne in a thousand details.

Yet the Tharrin represented only half of a human/machine intellect. The machine half, the planet-sized omni-minds, stored information on the societies, moral codes, and political factions of tens of thousands of worlds. All such information was used when debating criminal and civil suits, but the data was all considered to be obsolete when passing a judgment. When a Tharrin passed judgment, it did so based on information stored in its omni-mind, but human empathy and understanding were meant to vitiate judgment. In the end, the wise and compassionate Tharrin ruled from the heart.

In his lessons, Gallen learned the brief history of Fale, how here the Tharrin ruler Semarritte had been overthrown by the alien dronon.

For decades, the dronon had presented a threat to mankind, but Semarritte and her Tharrin advisors refused to go to war. Semarritte had created more guardians to protect her realm—creatures who were as much nanotech machine as flesh, creatures who could be controlled only through her omni-mind. Yet always Semarritte and the Tharrin had hoped that the humans and dronon might someday learn to live together in peace. They could not reconcile themselves to the horrors that would result from an interspecies war.

But in a surprise attack, dronon technicians won control of Semarritte's omni-mind, then manipulated her fleets and guardians, sending them to war against their human creators. Then the dronon killed Semarritte herself and murdered every Tharrin who fell into their hands.

Gallen had to rest and eat again, but he came back late that night and questioned his teacher on matters of law, hoping that he would find some legal means of freeing Maggie. Under the old Tharrin law, slave-taking had been criminal. But under dronon law, Lord Karthenor could capture or buy servants who were not claimed by more powerful lords. Since his work ranked as a top priority among the dronon, he was free to choose servants from ninety percent of the population.

Seeing that he had no legal recourse, Gallen sought information on current war and battle techniques, but the teacher let him study only some very basic self-defense. Obviously, the dronon controlled this teaching machine to some degree, and they would not let it teach tactics that might be used against them.

In his last session that evening, Gallen downloaded a map of Toohkansay. That night, he dragged himself back to the woods late. Orick had returned to the camp.

"I searched all around the spot where we entered," Orick said. "I couldn't smell Everynne anywhere. I couldn't find any other cities."

"I know." Gallen sighed. "Toohkansay is the only city for—" he converted kilometers to miles in his head "—eighty miles."

"I don't understand," Orick said heavily. "We all went in the same gate, but we didn't come out at the same place."

"The making of gate keys is hard," Gallen said, "and our key was stolen from someone who may have fashioned an imperfect key. Obviously, it dropped us off in the wrong spot. Each gate leads to only one planet, so I'm certain we are on the right world, but Fale is a big place. We might be two miles from Everynne, or ten thousand. There is no way to tell."

Orick studied Gallen. "You're certain of this, are you?"

"Aye, very sure," Gallen said.

"What else did you learn in the city?"

Gallen could not begin to answer. He had studied handwritten books in Tihrglas, but in only a few hours here on Fale, the equivalent of a thousand volumes of information had been dumped into his head. How could he explain it?

"I went to a library," Gallen said. "I learned some things from a teaching machine, like a Guide—but this machine doesn't control your actions. I learned so much that I can't begin to tell you everything. But I can take you there tomorrow, if you have a mind to learn something."

"I'll not have one of their devices twisting my brain, thank you!" Orick growled. "I saw what it did to Maggie!"

"It's not the same," Gallen said. "This is a different kind of machine. It won't hurt you."

"Won't hurt me, eh?" Orick said. "What have they done to you? There's a new look in your eyes, Gallen O'Day. You're not the same man who left here two days ago. You can't tell me that you're the same, can you?"

"No," Gallen said. "I'm not the same." He reflected for a moment. Only a few days before, Everynne had told him that she found the naivete of his world to be refreshing. She'd wished that all worlds could be so innocent. And now Gallen lived in a much larger universe, a universe where there was no distinct boundary between man and machine, where immortals wielded vast power over entire worlds, where alien races battled the thousand subspecies of mankind for dominance in three separate galaxies.

Gallen could have described the situation to Orick, but he knew Orick wanted to be a priest. He wanted to sustain the faith of those in Tihrglas, ensure the continuation of the status quo, and Gallen saw that this too was a valuable thing. In one small corner of the galaxy there could be sweet, blissful ignorance. In one small corner of the galaxy, adults could remain children. Knowledge carries its own price.

"I have learned some of the lore of the sidhe," Gallen said at last. "Not a lot, but perhaps enough. I'm going to try to steal Maggie back."

In a darkened room in the city of Toohkansay, nine lords of Fale sat around a table in their black robes and boots. Their masked faces shone in shades of crimson starlight. Veriasse and Everynne sat with them, both masked and cloaked as lords, Everynne in a pale blue mask, Veriasse in aquamarine. Though they had been on the planet for less than an hour, Veriasse had set up this meeting nearly five years earlier, and as Everynne watched her guardian, she could see that he was tense to the snapping point. His back was rigidly straight, and his mask revealed his profound worry.

All their years of plotting came to this. If anyone down the long trail of freedom fighters had betrayed them, now was when they would be arrested. And everyone in the room expected to be arrested: one of their number had not been seen in two days. Surely, the dronon had captured him, wrung his secrets from him. Because of this, they had been forced to change the meeting place at the last moment.

One crimson lord, a woman whose name Everynne did not even know, pulled from the depths of her robe a small glass globe, a yellow sphere that could easily fit in Everynne's palm or in a pocket. "As Lord of the Technicians of Fale, I freely give you this in behalf of my people," the woman said. "Use it wisely, if you must use it at all."

Everynne took the globe, held it in her palm. It was heavy as lead. Inside, was a small dark cloud at the machine's core—a housing where the nanotech components were stored, along with a small explosive charge designed to crack the globe and set its microscopic inhabitants free. In ages past, only a few weapons like this had ever been used. People called it the Terror. It seemed only right to Everynne that something which could destroy a world would be so gravid, so weighty.

"How fast will it work?" Everynne asked.

The crimson lady's mask showed sadness. "The Terrors reproduce at an explosive rate. We designed them to seek out carbon molecules and form graphite. On a living planet, every animal, every plant, the atmosphere itself will be destroyed. Only the Terrors will survive for more than a day. They will appear as a blue shimmering cloud, moving outward through the sky at two thousand kilometers per hour. On the ground and in the sea, they move somewhat faster. The Terrors would destroy most worlds within a matter of twelve to eighteen hours."

Everynne watched the woman's face. The crimson lady was old, centuries old, and in that time she had probably learned to control her emotions exquisitely, yet her voice cracked as she spoke of the machine's capacity for genocide.

"And how fast could this destroy Dronon?" Veriasse asked. "Will the Terrors be slowed significantly by being forced to reproduce on such a dry, desolate world?"

Even as Veriasse asked the question, Everynne cringed. The thought that the weapon might actually be used disturbed her. Time and again, she had begged Veriasse not to fashion such a weapon, to create only a simulated Terror. If the glass case broke, an entire planet would be destroyed. But Veriasse would not hear her arguments. He planned to take the Terror to the planet Dronon itself. He wanted the Golden Queen to fear him, and the only way he could arouse such fear was if the dronon knew that a working Terror lay hidden on their world.

But sometimes at night, Everynne wondered if he had a hidden agenda. If the Golden Queen refused to concede to his demands, she wondered, would Veriasse hesitate to lay the planet Dronon to waste?

"Dronon's atmosphere is heavier in carbon dioxide than most. The Terrors will find it to their taste."

Another of the masked lords smiled cruelly and said, "I designed the package with Dronon in mind. The planet can be terminated in six hours and fourteen minutes. Just make sure that you are near the imperial lair when you set it off."

Everynne was disturbed by the man's maleficent air. It pained her to see her people given over to such hatred. Though she knew that the dronons had killed her own mother, Everynne did not hate them. She understood them too well, understood their need for order at any cost, their instinctive desire to expand their territories and control their environment. "Let us have no more talk of genocide," Everynne said. "Even if we tried to fight the dronon on such terms, they would be forced to retaliate. In such a war, there can be no victors."

"Of course, Our Lady," the crimson lords agreed, and almost as one they breathed a sigh of relief. They had spoken treasonous words and not been arrested. Everynne could feel the clouds of doubt and fear lifting from her. For a long moment, they all sat and simply looked at one another around the table. For five years the crimson lords had worked, and now their part was done. Everynne watched them relax and wanted only to relax with them, take one last rest before her part in the great work began.

"We must go now," Veriasse said. Everynne knew he was right. They had left Tihrglas only an hour ago. The vanquishers could transmit news of their escape over tachyon waves. Within another few hours, word of their escape would reach Fale, and the vanquishers would seek to block all of Everynne's escape routes.

"Wait, please," the crimson lady begged. "I have one last favor to ask before you leave."

"Which is?" Everynne said.

"Your face," the crimson lady asked. "Once, before you leave, I want to see your face."

On Fale, the lords never went unmasked in public. It was a tradition millennia old. The crimson lady would never have asked such a favor of one of her own neighbors. Everynne had little time to spare, but these people had risked so much for her that she could not resist.

She peeled off her pale blue mask, and the lords stared at her in awe for a moment. "You are truly a queen among the Tharrin," the crimson lady said. Everynne felt sick at the words. After all, what was a queen among the Tharrin but a specific set of genetic codes given to those who were born to be leaders? It was nothing she had done, nothing she had earned. Her genetic makeup gave her a certain sculpted beauty, a regal air, a measure of charisma and wit that probably would never have been duplicated in nature. Yet Everynne saw all of this as a sham. It was simply a station she was born to. Her flesh was the clothing she wore.

The crimson lady peeled off her own mask, showed herself to be a handsome, aging woman with penetrating gray eyes. "My name is

Atheremis, and it has been my pleasure to serve you. I will never betray you," she said.

One by one, the other crimson lords around the room also peeled back their masks, spoke their names and their gratitude.

That is when Everynne knew for sure that they would kill themselves. If they had not been planning suicide, Everynne was sure that they would not have revealed themselves. But one of their number was missing, so they were choosing to die now by their own hands rather than risk that they might be captured and forced to reveal damning evidence.

The crimson lady cried; tears rolled down her cheeks. Everynne wanted to stay with them a little longer, hoping to keep them alive. If looking into her face gave them pleasure, then she would stand here for hours. But Veriasse took her elbow, and whispered, "Come, we must hurry."

Together they walked from the darkened chamber and headed down a long green corridor past the shops and apartments of Toohkansay. Only Everynne's mask hid the fact that she was sobbing inside.

They had hardly gone a hundred meters when a blinding flash of light erupted behind them, and the blast from the explosion buffeted their robes like a strong wind. Sirens began to wail, and citizens of the city rushed toward the blast, searching for victims. The living walls of the city did not catch fire, but the distinctive smell of cooked vegetable matter filled the smoking hallways.

They hurried to a cantina on the edge of town where the scent of food beguiled them. Everynne had not eaten for nearly twenty hours, so they went through the dispensary line and grabbed some rolls, then hurried out to a waiting shuttle, a beat up old magcar that would not draw undue attention.

They hopped over the doors, and Veriasse unfolded a thin map and pushed a button until *Fale* appeared on the legend of the world. The map showed them at the edge of Toohkansay, and a three-dimensional image showed the land around them for hundreds of kilometers. There were three gates within that range, but only Veriasse had traveled the Maze of Worlds enough to know which planet each gate would lead to. "This gate here," Veriasse said, pointing to the most distant of the three, "leads to Cyannesse. We will be safe there."

Everynne took the stick and gunned the thrusters. The car raised several inches on a magnetic wave, and she piloted the vehicle slowly at first, fearing that foot travelers might be on the road so close to Toohkansay.

For ten minutes they drove past the yawning farms that sprawled along the calm river. Huge, spiderlike harvesters were at work, cultivating the fields. They turned a wide bend, and Everynne was just ready to raise the windshields so that she could speed up when she saw a bear ahead. It leapt from the road into the woods.

"That's Orick!" she said, reversing thrusters.

"It can't be," Veriasse said. "It's just a bear."

"I'm sure of it." The magcar slowed and idled beside the trees. She gazed into the woods, up a slight rise where white rocks lay in a jumble. There was no sign of Orick—only prints among the fallen leaves that the bear had made as it bowled through the trees. Everynne wondered if it had been a trick of her imagination, yet she let the magcar hover on the road. Uphill, the nose of a bear poked cautiously over some bushes to watch her.

"You're right," she said, distracted. She had last seen Orick only slightly more than an hour ago on a planet nearly six hundred light-years away. Somehow, that recent image must have burned into her subconscious so that she imagined that this bear looked just like Orick.

She gunned the thrusters and the magcar rose and began to move forward slowly. She glanced back, and the bear stood up on its hind legs, sniffing the air.

It yelled, "Everynne? Is that you?"

She slammed on the reverse thrusters.

"Orick?" Veriasse called. The bear dropped to all fours and ran toward them with astonishing speed.

"It's you!" Orick shouted. "Where have you been? I've been searching for you everywhere! It's been days!"

Veriasse and Everynne looked at each other. "What do you mean, 'days'?" Everynne asked. "We left Tihrglas less than two hours ago. How did you get here?"

"Gallen stole a key from the dronon. He was afraid they would use it to catch you. When we got here, we couldn't find any sign of you. Maggie's been kidnapped, and we can't get her back. Gallen and I have been here for nearly four days!"

"The dronon tried to make a key?" Veriasse asked, incredulous. "Only a great fool—or a very desperate person—would try to make his own key to the Maze of Worlds. That explains how you got here before us. Your key is flawed."

"You mean to say we got here four days early because of a busted key?"

"Of course," Everynne said realizing what had happened. "The gates move us from one planet to another faster than the speed of light—but any method of locomotion that can do that can also be used to send things into the past, or the future."

"Still," Veriasse said, "it's a wonder that they broke our access codes at all. We will have to re-tool the gates." Veriasse looked down at the chronometer on the magcar. "We have to go, Everynne."

"Wait a moment," Everynne said. "They need our help."

Anger flashed in Veriasse's eyes. "Many people need your help. You cannot risk staying in enemy territory for *these*."

Everynne looked at Orick. The bear was dirty, had lost a little weight. The whites of his eyes were wide. "I was born to be the Servant of All," she said. "I will take care of these three now, because they need me now."

"Nine people just sacrificed their lives for you back in town!" Veriasse countered. "You can't stay here and risk making that sacrifice invalid. Leave these three. What's the difference? It is an acceptable loss."

"Acceptable to who? To you, perhaps, but not to me. Those nine gave their lives voluntarily for something they understood—" Everynne answered. "These three want to live, and they serve us with innocent hearts. We must give them a little time—fifteen minutes."

Everynne turned to Orick. "Where is Gallen?"

"Hiding in the woods," Orick answered. "I'll get him." He spun and galloped uphill.

"We don't have time for this," Veriasse told Everynne after Orick hurried into the brush. "Every second of delay places you in greater jeopardy. Can't you feel the worlds slipping from your grasp?"

"Right thoughts. Right words. Right actions. Isn't that the credo you taught me?" Everynne said. "Right actions. Always do what is right. That's what I'm trying to do now."

"I know," Veriasse said more softly. "When we win back your inheritance, you will truly be worthy of the title Servant of All. But think:

at this moment, you must choose between two goods. The right action is to choose the greater good."

Everynne closed her eyes. "No, you cannot prove to me that fifteen minutes will make a difference. I'll serve my friends here to the best of my ability, and afterward I'll serve the rest of humanity.

"Veriasse, if not for Gallen stealing that key, we would have jumped out of the gate and found the whole planet mobilized against us. We must help them—you must help them. See, here comes Gallen now."

Gallen and Orick raced through the trees. The young man was dressed in the swirling greens and blues of a merchant of Fale, yet his garments were stained from the camp and his hair was unkempt. He breathed hard as he rushed up to the magcar.

"Orick says that Maggie has been kidnapped," Everynne said. "Do you know who took her?"

"A man named Karthenor, Lord of the Aberlains," Gallen panted. "I've scouted the city. I plan to get her back."

Everynne marveled that such a simple man could have so much faith in himself.

"If Maggie has been taken by Karthenor," Veriasse said, "she is in the hands of a most unscrupulous man. For enough money, he might sell her back to you—or he might become curious and send you to his interrogators to find out why you want her. With the right equipment, you could free her from her Guide and steal her back, but that would be very dangerous to attempt. Both plans carry their risks, and it seems to me that in any event you are likely to fail."

Everynne hesitated to tell them the most logical course of action. She wetted her lips with her tongue. "Gallen, Orick," she said slowly, "would you be willing to leave Maggie behind, come away with me through the Maze of Worlds?"

"What?" Gallen asked, incredulous.

Everynne tried to phrase her argument as succinctly as possible. "I am going to try to overthrow the dronons. If I succeed, then we can rescue Maggie. If, on the other hand, I do not succeed, she will become a valuable member of dronon society, and in the long run she will be better off where she is. So, I ask you again: do you two want to come with me?"

Gallen and Orick looked at each other. "No," Gallen said. "We can't do that. We'll stay and see what we can do to get Maggie free."

Everynne nodded. "I understand," she said heavily. "Then we will both do what we must, even though it takes us on different paths." She turned to Veriasse. "Do you have allies here that might help him?"

"I had few allies here," Veriasse said. "And all of them are dead now. Gallen must forge ahead on his own. The first thing he should do is go learn all that he can about our world."

"I've already been to the pidc," Gallen said. Everynne looked into his eyes, saw that it was true. There was a burden in his eyes, as if he knew too much.

"The pidc can teach you many things, but it is still under dronon control," Veriasse said. "Much of our technology is kept secret. Gallen, if you want to free Maggie, you will have to do it without her knowledge. The Guide sees through her eyes, hears with her ears, and it can transmit messages to other Guides. It will be your greatest enemy, and since it controls Maggie, she will fight you herself if you try to rescue her while she's still connected to the Guide. You will need the help of a Guide-maker to learn how to dismantle the thing.

"At the same time, security around the aberlains will be very tight. Microscopic cameras will be hidden in the main corridors, and motion detectors will be at every window. I doubt that you can make it into the compound undetected. Dronon vanquishers themselves will probably patrol the compound, and they are very dangerous. You will need weapons and an escape plan.

"Gallen, don't be in a hurry to rescue her. This will require careful planning and research."

Veriasse looked down at the chronometer on the magcar. "Everynne, my child, we really must go now, before the vanquishers block our exit."

Everynne gritted her teeth. Veriasse had just outlined an impossible task for Gallen—a task that only Veriasse himself could pull off. She glanced at Gallen, ashamed to be leaving, and said, "Good luck."

"What world will you be going to next?" Gallen asked. "Maybe we will follow you there?"

Everynne considered lying. She had to protect herself from possible danger, yet she knew that Gallen must be feeling lost and alone. As a Tharrin, her presence gave him a sense of comfort that he could not find elsewhere. And the world she was going to was beyond enemy lines.

"Cyannesse is its name," she said. "The gate lies nearly three hundred miles north of here, about a quarter of a mile off the right-hand side of the road. When you put your key up to the gate, it will glow golden. That's how you know you have the right destination."

Gallen looked at her longingly, and Everynne could not bear to watch him any longer. "Take care of yourselves," she said. She gunned the thrusters and headed out.

Nine

Gallen watched Everynne and Veriasse glide off through the forest in their magcar. Orick grumbled and pawed the ground, raking leaves as if he were frustrated. "What now?" he asked. "Do you have a plan to save Maggie?"

Gallen considered. He had few resources: a couple of knives, a key to unlock the Maze of Worlds. A few days before, he'd told Everynne that imagination was the measure of a man, but now he wondered if that were true.

"You heard Veriasse," Gallen said. "If we try to rescue her, the Guide will warn Karthenor. Our only hope is to take her without her or her Guide knowing of it."

"Can we trick the Guide?"

"I doubt it," Gallen said. "It's probably smarter than we are. But I may be able to figure out some way to lure Maggie out of the city at Karthenor's request, so that the other Guides can't hear her talk."

"Och, this sounds like a *grand* plan!" Orick said. "Why, it's no plan at all, that's what it is."

Orick was right, at least for the moment. "We'll have to find a way to disable the Guide," Gallen said. "I'll have to find a Guide-maker."

"So, what are you going to do," Orick asked, "walk right into a shop and ask the fellow, 'By the way, how can I break one of those things?' and then hope he answers you square?"

"No," Gallen said. He knew the means had to be close by. He thought, If you were the most creative bodyguard in the world, Gallen O'Day, what would you do? He waited for a moment, and a familiar thrill coursed through him. He knew the answer. "I'm going to go speak to a past employee of the company that makes the Guides. A dead employee, to be precise."

"What?" Orick shouted.

"When we first went into town, and I was wandering around on my own, I met a merchant who sells a machine that lets you talk to the dead, so long as they're properly embalmed and haven't rotted too much."

"And what if you can't find a dead employee handy?" Orick said. "What then?"

"Well, then I'd stick a knife in an employee and make him dead!" Gallen shouted, furious at Orick's exasperating mood.

"Fine!" Orick growled. "That's fine. I was just asking."

It was early morning. Kiss-me-quick birds sang in the trees, hopping from bush to bush, their green wings flashing.

"I think I'll go ask about this now, in fact," Gallen answered.

"What about me?" Orick asked. "You can't leave me here again."

"And I can't take you with me. Orick, there are some things we'll need—food, shelter, clothing, weapons. You're in charge of finding them and setting up a proper camp. We might be stuck here awhile."

"Right," Orick said.

Gallen hunched his shoulders. His muscles were tight from the tension, and suddenly he longed to be back home in Tihrglas, guarding some merchant's wagon. Hell, on any day of the week, he'd rather take on ten highwaymen single-handed. Ah, for the good old days.

He ambled back to Toohkansay and made his way to the merchant quarters. There, he sold the shillings from his purse along with a bead necklace to a dealer in exotic alien artifacts.

Then he went to the merchant who sold "Bereavement Hoods," and began to haggle. Gallen didn't have enough money to buy the thing. The hoods were designed for those who wanted to "Share those last precious thoughts with the recently departed." Gallen cried and put on a show, talking about his dear sister who had died, until he finally convinced the merchant to rent him a hood.

"Now you understand," the merchant warned, "that your sister is dead. She'll know who you are, and she'll be able to talk through the speaker in the hood, but she won't gain any new memories. If you visit her once, she'll forget all about it, even if you return five minutes later."

Gallen nodded, but the merchant drove the point home until Gallen finally asked, "What are you really telling me?"

"Well," the merchant finally admitted, "it's just that the dead are always surprised and happy to be visited, and they'll tell you about the same fond memories time and again. They tend to get . . . repetitive."

"So they get boring," Gallen accused.

"Most of them, yes," the merchant admitted reluctantly.

When Gallen finished, he went to the pidc, accessed the public records to find out who in Toohkansay made Guides, and found that they were made under the auspices of a Lord Pallatine. Gallen accessed Pallatine's files, got a list of his workers for the past ten years. By checking vital statistics for each worker, he found that sure enough, a fellow named Brevin Mackalrey had been a corpse for less than three months, and poor Brevin was down deep in the crypts under the city, kept in cold storage so that his widow could speak to him on occasion.

Gallen hurried down a long series of subterranean corridors to pay a visit to poor old Brevin. The crypt was a dark, desolate place, with only a few visitors. Corpses were stacked in long rows, sleeping in glass coffins that could be pulled out for display. The temperature in the crypt was near freezing, and perhaps that tended to keep the mourners' visits short. The bodies were stored for a year before final interment. Still, Gallen was surprised to see hundreds of bodies and only five people visiting them. Gallen searched alphabetically until he found Brevin Mackalrey, pulled the man out.

The glass coffin was fogged; icy crystals shaped like fern leaves had built up under the glass lid. Gallen opened the lid. Mr. Mackalrey did not look so good. His face was purple and swollen. He wore only a pair of white shorts. He had dark hair, a scraggly beard, and legs that were knobby and bowed. Gallen decided that this particular fellow probably hadn't looked so good even when he was alive.

Gallen pulled up the fellow's near-frozen head and placed the hood on. The hood was made of some metallic cloth, and electromagnetic waves from the hood stimulated the brain cells of the dead. As the dead man tried to speak, the cloth registered the attempted stimulation of the cerebral cortex and translated the dead man's thoughts into words. The words were then spoken in a dull monotone from a small speaker.

Gallen activated the hood, waited for a few moments, then said, "Brevin, Brevin, can you hear me, man?"

"I hear you," the speaker said. "But I can't see you. Who are you?"

"My name's Gallen O'Day, and I came to ask your help on a small matter. My sister has a Guide on, and she can't get it off. I was wondering if you could tell me how to get one of them buggers off."

"She's wearing a Guide?" Brevin asked. A mourner passed Gallen, heading down the aisle of coffins.

"Aye, that's what I said," Gallen whispered, hunching low. "Is there any way to get it off?"

"Is it a slave Guide?" Brevin asked.

"Of course it's a slave Guide," Gallen hissed. "Otherwise, we'd be able to get it off."

"If she's a slave, it would be wrong for me to help you. I could get into trouble."

"Well," Gallen drawled, "how much trouble can you get into? You're already dead!"

"Dead? How did I die?"

"You fell off a horse, I think," Gallen said. "Either that, or you choked on a chicken bone."

"Oh," Brevin said. "I can't help you. I would be penalized."

"Who would know that you'd told me?" Gallen said.

"Go away, or I'll call the authorities," Brevin's microphone yelped.

"How are you going to call the authorities?" Gallen asked. "You're dead, I tell you."

Brevin went silent for several moments, and Gallen said, "Come on, answer me you damned corpse! How do I get the Guide off?"

Brevin didn't answer, and Gallen began looking about, wondering what kind of barter chip he might use. He whispered, "You're dead, do you understand me, Brevin? You're dead. You got no more worries, no more fears. If there was one thing in the world I could give you, what would you want?"

"I'm cold. Go away," Brevin retorted.

"I'll give you that," Gallen said. "I'm going away. But first I want you to tell me how to take a Guide off of someone without setting off any alarms."

Brevin didn't answer, and Gallen decided to bully him into it. "Look," he said. "I hate to have to do this to you, but you've got to answer me."

Gallen took the dead man's pinky finger and bent it back at an excruciating angle until he feared it might snap. "There now," Gallen said. "How does that feel?"

"How does what feel?" Brevin asked.

Gallen saw that torture was no use. The dead man couldn't feel a thing.

Gallen scratched his head, decided on another tact. "All right, you've pushed me too far. I didn't want to have to tell you this, but the reason you're so damned cold is because you're lying in this coffin naked. Did you know that?"

"Naked?" Brevin asked, dismayed.

"Yes," Gallen assured him. "You're bare-assed naked. At this very moment, I'm looking at your penis, and I've got to tell you that it's not a pretty sight. You were never well-endowed in the first place, but now you're all shriveled down to the size of a pinhead. Did you know that?"

Brevin emitted a low moan, and Gallen continued. "Now, not only are you bare-assed naked," Gallen said, "but I'll tell you what I'm going to do. I'm going to drag your naked carcass upstairs and leave you in a hallway tonight, and every person who walks by is going to see what a shamefully inadequate organ you have. It will be an embarrassment to your whole family, I'm telling you. Everyone in Toohkansay will see your shrunken pud, and when they do, they'll look at your wife and smile in a knowing way, and wonder, 'How could she have stayed with that fellow all those years, what with him being so sorrowfully lacking?' So tell me, my friend, what do you think of that?"

"No," Brevin said. "Please!"

"You know what you have to do," Gallen said. "Just a few small words is all I'm asking. Give me those words, and I'll put your pants on and leave you with your dignity intact. What do you say? You do me a favor, and I'll do you a favor."

Brevin seemed to think for a moment. "A universal Guide extractor can take off the Guide. Simply point the rod at the slave in question and press the blue button. Lord Pallatine has three of them locked in the security vault."

"Tell me about this vault," Gallen said. "How would I get into it."

"You can't. Lord Pallatine has an electronic key, but the vault is equipped with a personal intelligence that will only open when it recognizes that Pallatine alone has come to open it."

"So I don't have access to all that fancy equipment," Gallen said. "I just want to free my sister, quick and easy, and I don't want to get caught. Surely you know how to do it."

Brevin's stomach muscles twitched, and for a moment Gallen feared that he would sit up, even though he was stiff as a twig. But the dead man said quickly, "First, you will need to catch her unawares. You should take her when she's asleep. If you can't take her in her sleep, you need to immobilize her so the Guide can't fight you. It will take control of her body at the first sign of danger. If you can, perform the abduction in a room that has metal walls to block any transmissions the Guide might send. Then insert a knife at the back of the Guide near the base of the skull. You will have to cut through two small wires. This will sever the Guide's neural connection to the victim. When you're done, destroy the Guide."

"What do you mean destroy it?"

"Put it in acid, or crush it, or burn it. It must be thoroughly pulverized on the atomic level."

"What if the Guide isn't thoroughly destroyed?" Gallen asked, half certain of the answer.

"If the Guide is retrieved, its memory will identify you."

"Thank you, Brevin. May you rest in eternal peace. I've already got your pants back on you, and all your secrets are safe with me," Gallen said. He sat back and thought. He knew where Karthenor's aberlains slept, in apartments near the cantina with windows over the river. He would have to work quickly—get in through the window and remove the Guide before the vanquishers responded to the alarm from the motion detectors at the window. Afterward, a simple toss could send the Guide off into the muddy deep. It would take the vanquishers some time to retrieve the Guide from the water. By then, Gallen imagined he could be well away from Toohkansay, on the trail to another gate and a new world.

He removed the bereavement hood, closed Brevin's coffin and shoved it back into its chamber. He knew that he couldn't leave poor little

Maggie any longer than necessary. He stared at the black bereavement hood. Its metallic cloth was of a heavy weave. Perhaps not as thick as the walls of a room, but it might block radio transmissions from a Guide.

Gallen could only hope.

The road from Toohkansay to the Cyannesse gate was clear most of the way, yet Everynne drove with a heavy heart, a sinking feeling of guilt. She had left nine ardent supporters dead behind her and had left Gallen, Orick, and Maggie to fend for themselves in matters beyond their understanding.

Yet she drove on. Everynne skirted two smaller towns in an hour, barely slowing the magcar. When she was four hundred and eighty-one kilometers north of Toohkansay, the land began turning to desert, a sandy plain where only a few volcanic flows marred the surface.

This gate, unlike most, was in open view of the highway. Perhaps ten thousand years earlier, when the gate was built, the landscape had been different. The gate may have been hidden in a forest or swamp, but now it was in open view of the road. Even though the road was nearly empty of traffic, Everynne did not relish the idea of entering from a place where she would be in view of prospective witnesses.

She began to slow the magcar, but Veriasse waved his hand and whispered, "Keep going! Keep going! Don't stop. Don't even slow!"

She engaged the thruster to speed up, and on her rearview display saw six giant humanoid figures rise up from some camouflaged pit out near the gate. Vanquishers had been hiding, and now were watching them pass, perhaps wondering if they should give chase. If six of them were secluded there, many more would also be hiding.

"How did you spot them?" Everynne asked when they were far down the road.

"I didn't," Veriasse said. "I just felt uncomfortable. If Maggie was captured three days ago, then the authorities may have been expecting us. They've had plenty of time to seal off the gates and prevent our escape. In another hour, they will simply receive confirmation of our escape from Tihrglas, and matters will be worse."

"What will we do?" Everynne asked. She looked over to Veriasse. He had been her mother's protector for six thousand years. He was used to intrigue and danger in a way that she hoped she never would have to be.

"We will need to form some new allies here. We won't get through that gate without an armed conflict." He sighed. "I'd say that the city of Guianne is our best hope. It's about five hundred kilometers south and ninety kilometers east of here."

"Where Mother was killed?" Everynne asked.

Veriasse nodded slightly. "There is a shrine to her memory. We shall go and see if anyone tends it. Perhaps our allies will make themselves known to us."

Everynne swallowed hard, trying not to cry. She had never seen her mother's resting place. Of all the worlds they had visited, Everynne had harbored only one secret wish: to see her mother's tomb. And if Everynne died on this journey, as long as she saw her mother's tomb first, then she would feel that she had accomplished at least one significant act.

"I know where three allies are," Everynne said. "They're right on our way, and at this moment, they need our help."

Veriasse sighed deeply. "You are right, of course. We'll stop and get them. But I won't let you put yourself in jeopardy. If they are in trouble, I will try to rescue them. And if I fail, you must promise to go on without me."

"I promise." Everynne's heart leapt. She had not felt right about leaving Maggie in captivity. She turned the magcar around, and as she soared over the highway toward Toohkansay, she felt light and free.

Two hours later, Veriasse crept over the hill to Gallen's camp. The early afternoon sunlight slanting through the trees dappled the leaves in purple and scarlet. Veriasse had pulled the magcar off the highway, hidden it in the brush. He was skilled at moving quietly. In his cloak of concealment, wearing a specially designed scent from the planet Jowlaith that neutralized his body odors, Veriasse could pass through the woods unnoticed by all but the most wary forest animals.

Thus he came upon Orick unawares. The bear had retired to a glade, and there he had been busy making a small shelter by leaning broken pine branches up against a tree. The shelter was finished, and now the bear sat beside it, engaged in fervent prayer. "Holy Father," Orick grumbled, shaking like a cub, "spare Maggie and Gallen. Bring them alive and safe from the realm of these damned sidhe. They are innocent of everything, innocent of any desires to do evil. I brought them here by accident, because there was no other way to save their lives, and I did not mean to break your commandments in doing so. If we have sinned ignorantly, I pray that the sins will be upon my head, and that Maggie and Gallen will be found guiltless—"

"I am sure that your friends will be found guiltless," Veriasse said, startling Orick. The bear tried to stand, and twisted around so fiercely in his panic that he fell over.

"You!" he roared accusingly. "What are you doing here?"

"The gate we sought was guarded by vanquishers," Veriasse said. "We have been forced to make new plans. I came to see if I could be of any help to you and your friends."

The bear gazed from left to right, scanning the woods behind Veriasse. "We don't need your help. Gallen will handle things."

"So, you don't need the help of any 'damned sidhe'?" Veriasse smiled. "Your friend Gallen may be a fine man, but he is a stranger to our world. I doubt that he will be able to bring your friend out."

"Ah, keep your misgivings to yourself," Orick grunted. "Gallen got himself a bit of book learning. He knows plenty."

"At the very least, I can expedite his plans," Veriasse offered. "What were his plans?"

"I'm not sure he has any," Orick said. "Gallen doesn't work that way."

Veriasse considered. "I'll leave Everynne to your care. Right now, she is down by the road. I want you to take her deeper into the woods, then come back here shortly after dawn. I don't want you here to meet Gallen if he comes back."

"Why?"

"Because if he is captured by the vanquishers, then he will lead them here."

"Gallen would never do that!"

"If they put a Guide on him, then he will have no choice," Veriasse countered. "Please, take her with you, and I will see what I can do for Gallen and Maggie."

Veriasse watched Orick head down the valley toward the road. He rummaged through his pack, put on a mantle as a disguise, then walked to Toohkansay. Since he was already dressed and masked as a lord of Fale, no one challenged him. Even if they had, they would find that Veriasse, Lord of Information Managers, was registered as a citizen of the world. His forged records included computerized documentation that detailed much of a fictional life, down to his bathing schedule and the content of meals purchased during the past seventy years.

Veriasse went to the northwest quadrant of the city where the aberlains worked. He found the place to be heavily guarded. Green-skinned vanquishers on roving patrols were a sure sign that dronon guards resided within. In some places, he found that the living walls of the city were blackened by fire. Obviously, resistance bombers had been at work here within the past few weeks, and Veriasse suddenly became very concerned about Maggie.

He had worried before about her treatment by the dronon and her lord, but he had not considered the very real possibility that her greatest threat came not from her captors but from the local freedom fighters. Before, when he'd heard that Maggie was captured, he'd wondered why Karthenor had made such a poor choice of worker, but now he saw that indeed Maggie might have been exactly what the lord needed—someone who was alone in the city, someone who would not be missed. By taking slaves who were well tied to the community, Karthenor would only have earned further resentment.

Veriasse cursed himself, wondering if he might be able to get in touch with some of these freedom fighters. But he had to find Gallen first.

As he had imagined, the exterior of the compound was well secured. In sensitive areas, the dronon had installed heavy doors that would resist bombing.

Veriasse finished his scouting expedition and went down to the pidc. There he requested to view all documents that Gallen had studied. The teacher gave him the information, and Veriasse was impressed. Gallen had tried to retrieve data on Maggie's rooming situation, but the computer had not given him such sensitive information, nor would it supply a map of the interior of the compound. So Gallen had requested information on all areas where the aberlain compound did not extend, and had thus retrieved a negative image of the compound. By requesting maps of the laundry chutes which went through the floors below, he had been able to decipher the location of the living quarters for the aberlain workers. Veriasse studied the map, saw that most of the rooms had exterior exits. But Gallen went one step farther. He had requested computerized readouts on the electrical output for each room. One of the apartments had been left idle for three days, then suddenly recorded a tenant who turned on the lights each evening for a moment before retiring.

Gallen had taken his questioning one final step. The room had a southern exposure, and Gallen had asked the city computer to study the temperature records for the room and then determine whether the occupant left the windows open at night. The computer responded by showing that for the past two nights, the windows were left open, but the computer shut them when the temperature dropped below a certain threshold.

Veriasse smiled, impressed that some rustic could negotiate through the city's information system so smoothly. At the same time, Gallen showed some gaping holes in his education. For one thing, the boy didn't know that he'd left a data trail that would indict him. Veriasse asked the computer to run a credit check on Gallen, found that the boy was attempting to purchase clothing, ropes, and air exchangers—items he would need for his rescue attempt. Yet Gallen was broke. Veriasse used his credentials as a lord of Information Managers to have the computer transfer credits from his personal account into Gallen's account, then he ran a security-delete on most files that mentioned Gallen's name.

He sat for a moment, thinking. Before Gallen tried to climb in that open window, he would need to neutralize the motion detectors. One could build a simple jammer that would disable any warning the motion detectors might send.

Veriasse would have to work fast, if he were to complete the jammer before Gallen tried to rescue Maggie.

Maggie tried to sleep, but after Avik left her, her lust kept her awake. Near dawn, her Guide quit stimulating her sexual appetites, and Maggie was free to dream: she dreamed of Tlitkani, the Golden Queen of the dronon, and in her dream Maggie's heart stirred with passion. The queen walked across a plaza of white stone, and her chitin flashed gold in the sunlight. She was perfect in every respect—without a flaw or blemish, not so much as a nick in her exoskeleton, and all around her was a great celebration. Dronon warriors with their heavy front battle arms knelt at her feet, battle arms crossed and extended in a sign of reverence. Tan dronon technicians with thin little segmented hands stood by to adore her, too, along with the small white workers. But among the insect hordes were many humans in all manner of clothing and attire, worlds of them, dancing and capering about, gazing at the Golden Queen with adoration shining from their eyes. Little human children had made garlands of flowers and strewn them at her feet, and a song rose up from humans and dronons alike, their voices raspy with fervor, praising the Golden Queen.

In her dream, Maggie felt such a profound respect for the golden one, that tears streamed from her eyes. To simply gaze upon her caused a height of religious feeling unparalleled in all Maggie's life.

Maggie woke, eyes still streaming with tears, and her Guide whispered to her, "This is a vision I have given you of the future you shall help bring to pass. When a dronon looks upon its Golden Queen, it feels the ineffable sense of awe and wonder I have shared with you. We shall insert the genes that cause this condition into the fetuses of your children, so that they will no longer view the dronon as aliens, but will see them as brothers. Today you begin laboring within the inner sanctum of our compound, and you will help in the great work of bringing to pass the Adoration."

Having said this, the Guide had Maggie rise from bed, shower, and go down to eat. She was dead on her feet with fatigue, and after breakfast, the Guide had her walk into a part of the aberlains' working compound that she had not visited before. On her previous days, Maggie had worked only at the reproduction labs, but far more of the aberlains' labors were spent here in the research department, the inner sanctum of the aberlains' lair.

Here, she joined Avik's research team, which was supervised directly by Lord Karthenor. Here, Karthenor engaged in decoding dronon DNA so that the genes that carried Adoration might be discovered. To work here was a great honor, and the Guide stimulated Maggie's emotions so that she approached her task with a proper sense of reverence.

The research department was dark and warm, with dim red lights to simulate conditions on the planet Dronon itself. Black-carapaced dronon vanquishers patrolled the corridors while dronon technicians worked side by side with humans in their sterile white coats.

Maggie was put to work on a gene scanner, dyeing and scrutinizing dronon DNA. Thousands of healthy dronon specimens had given tissue samples over the past six years, and all of these were well catalogued. Now, Maggie and the aberlaines studied samples from unhealthy dronon.

So it was that Maggie spent her day encoding the DNA of dronons who were born with lung defects. Genetic aberrations that led to weaknesses were never tolerated in dronon society. The congenitally insane, retarded, and deformed were always killed when their abnormalities were discovered. So Maggie found herself working with tissue from dronon infants. The workers who had shipped the specimens from Dronon had not taken great care to clean and prepare the tissues. Instead, they had shipped crates filled with pieces of the dead. The whiplike sensors had been ripped off the young dronon mouths. The feelers were then placed in refrigerated boxes and labeled according to deformity.

Maggie's job was to carefully unwrap the feelers, remove small samples from each and label them according to specimen, then place each in a gene decoder. Computers would then store information on the mutant DNA, match identical genetic structures from different samples of mutants, and thus by defining the areas of aberration, learn which genes controlled which functions.

Maggie worked at her grisly task all morning. For days she had been fighting her Guide as it attempted to stimulate her emotions. When she was angry or frightened, the Guide continually sought to calm her, send feelings of bliss. Maggie had found herself nursing her anger, trying to overwhelm the Guide. But now she was so weary that she could not fight it any longer. If not for the Guide, she would have collapsed from exhaustion. But the Guide kept her awake.

The Guide carried her about the room, fed her comfort and information. She knew that her work was important, and Maggie found herself wishing that she could do more, hoping she would discover the actual genes that led to Adoration.

But the most important work was left to others, to aberlains with greater skill. They worked with tissues from the criminally insane, decoding genes from those few dronons who did not adore the Golden Queens.

Few such specimens had ever been born in dronon history, and they had been completely eradicated. Since the dronon used their own dead to fertilize their fields, the tissue samples of these insane individuals were rarely available. Still, a great search of the dronon worlds would eventually turn up a few new individuals. Maggie could only hope that when such samples became available, they would be sent here to the laboratories on Fale, so that she might have the honor of decoding them.

The tissue samples that Maggie used came from dronons who were born with a disorder that caused the chitin around their breathing orifices to form scarred nodules that could block the air passages. The breathing orifices on a dronon consisted of a row of nine holes located on the back upper hips of the dronon's hind legs. The orifices led to small lung sacks between the inner wall of the exoskeleton on the hip, and the hip muscles themselves. The dronon could not properly be said to have hearts. Instead, a rhythmic movement of the back legs caused the hip muscles to pump oxygen through the lungs and oxygenated blood through the rest of the body. For this reason, a dronon actually pumped blood more efficiently when it walked or ran. When it stopped walking, it would be forced to crouch and rhythmically bob up and down to keep its circulation going.

By evening, Maggie's work allowed her to isolate a defective gene and thus learn the gene's purpose in the great act of controlling the development of dronons.

The dronon technicians congratulated her and rewarded her by letting her work late. Her Guide fed her a sense of rapture, and she felt thrilled to be engaged in such a great and noble cause. Thus it was that she finally stumbled to her cubicle.

She opened the window, smelled the fresh night air, listened to the sound of the river lapping against the living walls of the city. A hundred thousand stars filled the night sky like white sand, and she looked up at a great swirling galaxy, wondering at its beauty.

She set the temperature of her bed higher, took a quick shower, then put on a thin robe and lay down to sleep. Out in the hall, she could hear the comforting sound of a dronon vanquisher's feet clicking as it patrolled the hallways of her sleeping quarters.

In the middle of the night, Maggie woke to a consuming lust that rolled over her in waves. She knew Avik was coming, and she did not think she could fight the Guide's commands anymore.

She was lying on her stomach, and the air stirred behind her. She realized that Avik must already have entered the room; the light did not go on, but she felt the weight of his body as he climbed on the bed. He moved quickly. She could hear his heavy breathing, and feel his weight as he straddled her back.

She whimpered softly. He pulled at the Guide on her head, thrust what felt like a chisel against the base of her neck. There was a searing pain, and hot blood spurted down her neck, and suddenly she was free from the Guide.

Maggie's only thought was that Avik had decided to kill her. She screamed, twisted to her side so that she could wrestle the knife away.

Gallen sat atop her, knife in hand, lit only by the starlight shining from the window. He thrust the Guide in a sack, then hit the sack sharply against the wall so that it made a sickly crunching sound, like breaking bones.

Maggie's head was reeling from fatigue, from a sudden overwhelming sadness. She couldn't think what was happening. "Get out," she whispered. "Avik is coming."

"Who is Avik?" Gallen whispered.

"A rapist," Maggie said, and behind Gallen the door whispered open. Light from the corridor shone in. Gallen surged from the bed so quickly that Maggie hardly saw him move. He seemed almost to fly across the room, a black shadow in his robes, a gleaming silver knife in his hand.

Gallen's knife fell just as Avik began to cry out. Gallen tossed the body to the floor with a thud.

In the corridor outside her door, the dronon guard shouted and scrabbled to come to Maggie's rescue.

Gallen slammed the door and locked it, saying, "Quick! Out the window! Jump in the water!"

Maggie staggered off the bed; horror overwhelmed her—not just horror at the thought of the dronon guard racing to the door, but a horror at all that had happened here.

In one instant, she realized what kind of work she had been engaged in, and an image flashed in her mind—a vision of the bloated sacklike mothers she had helped engineer, the remembered smell of dronon body parts stacked like cord wood in bins.

Her hands felt filthy; her entire skin felt filthy, and Maggie dropped to her knees and simultaneously cried from the core of her soul and tried to keep from retching up her dinner.

With a squeal of rending metal, the dronon guard hit the door, peeled it back with one chitinous claw, tearing it from its hinges. It held its black incendiary rod forward, pushed it through the door, and Maggie could see the wicked serrated edges on its forward battle arms. Gallen and the beast were dancing shadows in the light thrown from the corridor.

As Gallen rushed to the torn door, the dronon's wings buzzed in anticipation.

Gallen grabbed the dronon's incendiary rod, twisted it away and spun, firing through the rent door. He was far too close to shoot the weapon, and Maggie hoped that the thin metal door would shield them from the heat.

The chitinous black flesh of the guard squealed as its body temperature rose above boiling, and smoke roiled from its carapace and crawled along the ceiling. It became a blazing pillar of white fire. Intense heat filled the room, and the broken door caught flame. Gallen threw up his arms and staggered back to her.

Somewhere in the building, an alarm sounded. Gallen threw his robe over Maggie's face. She struggled up, thinking that they would die any moment, but Gallen scooped her into his arms and staggered to the window.

"I can't . . ." Maggie cried, weeping bitterly.

Gallen pushed her out. The building was sloped, and for a moment she slid out in the darkness through air that felt pleasantly icy, then hit the black water. It was far colder than she would have guessed. She thrashed vigorously and floundered for a moment, found herself underwater. She bobbed to the surface again and called for help. She looked up. Gallen was clinging precariously to the windowsill like a spider, and she wondered if he had somehow gotten stuck, then he splashed into the water ten feet away. Maggie thrashed her legs, went under again. A moment later, Gallen grasped her neck.

He pulled her to the surface, holding her head up from behind. She kept struggling and tried to spin, grab him. "Help! I can't swim!"

"Can't swim?" Gallen asked. "Your father and brothers all drowned. I'd think you'd learn to swim."

Maggie gasped, part from the cold, part from the fear that she would slip under again. Gallen reached around, put something in her mouth. It felt like the mouthpiece to a flute, but it was attached to two small bottles.

"Breath in and out through this," Gallen panted. "It's an oxygen exchanger. It recycles air. As long as you breathe through this, it doesn't matter if your head goes underwater. In a minute, I'll start pulling you to shore. We will have to dive underwater. Don't fight me." Maggie tried breathing through the machine. She had to exert extra force to inhale, as if she were breathing through heavy cloth.

Gallen fumbled to put on his own oxygen exchanger, then dove and began pulling her toward shore. He did not try to hurry, just made a leisurely swim of it, so that by the time they came up, they were far downstream from Toohkansay and had rounded a bend in the river. The lights from the city gleamed over the water, and a lighted barge sailed past them, heading downriver. Gallen swam to the mouth of a small creek, and they waded upstream till they reached a bridge that arched above them darkly, shutting out the powdered light of the stars.

Under the bridge, Gallen stepped from the water, pulling Maggie after him. He bent and opened a cloth sack that was lying in some tall grass, pulled out a single blanket. Maggie was shivering vigorously, shaking from more than the chill night air. Everything that had happened to her over the past few days slammed into her like a giant fist.

"I'm sorry," she cried, feeling ill to the core of her soul. "I'm so sorry." She wanted to explain why she was so sorry but did not know where to begin. She was so cold, she could not feel her fingers. Gallen wrapped the blanket around her; he was shivering violently. She wrapped her arms around him so they could share the blanket.

"You—you had this planned?" she asked between chattering teeth. His golden hair gleamed in the starlight, and she could make out little of his features. The brackish odor of the river was heavy on them both.

"Aye," Gallen said. "I've got some food in the pack, dry clothes. I found a trail along this creek. We can follow it up into the hills, then circle back north of town to where Orick and I set camp. I think we should stay off the road."

The blackness still hung over Maggie, and every few moments the images of her work over the past few days would flash in her mind. The demented gleam in Avik's eye. Sorting the tagged feelers of the dead dronons, the images of the twisted people she had built.

There were no signs of pursuit, but she was sure that the dronons would come after them soon.

The cold, the fear, the darkness of it all was too much for Maggie, and she sank to her knees. Wild vetch grew in a tangled mass here in the shadow of the bridge.

Gallen knelt, hugging her to keep her warm.

"Everynne?" Maggie stammered, and it seemed to her that her thoughts were now unnaturally clear, bright and well-defined, like the chemical fire from an incendiary rifle.

"We found her this morning," Gallen said. "She was heading north for another gate. The dronons were on her trail. She plans to fight them. She asked us to come with her, but . . ."

Maggie looked up, studied his face. It caught only the slightest touch of starlight, and she could not see his eyes. But one thing was clear: he could have gone with Everynne, but Gallen had chosen to stay and rescue Maggie.

She leaned her shivering body against Gallen, felt the firm muscles beneath his wet shirt. His breath warmed her neck. She realized he'd planned the escape in every detail: two sets of dry clothes, two oxygen exchangers. But only one blanket. He'd planned to share this moment with her.

The residual emotions stimulated by the Guide were still affecting her somewhat. The night before, she'd staved off Avik's advances by fantasizing about Gallen, and now she found that an edge of lust still lingered.

Maggie was painfully aware of her thin nightgown, her nipples tight, protruding against the hairs of Gallen's chest. He shivered. She wrapped both hands around his neck, kissed him firmly on the mouth. Gallen pulled away slightly, gasped as if surprised by her action.

"What's wrong?" she asked, aware that he was shaking harder. She recognized it for what it was. He was shaking with desire. "Don't you want this?"

"You're still too young," Gallen said, his voice husky.

She grew so angry, she wanted to hit him. "We don't all age at the same rate, and some things make you old before your time," she said. "Watching your family die, that ages you! Working—working day and night just to stay alive, that ages you. Wearing a Guide—hell, Gallen, I, I can't even begin to tell you what that thing did to me. It's like a vice, crushing you. It teaches you and it rapes you all at the same time, because the things it teaches you shatter all of your deepest hopes—and if it didn't play games with you and make you feel like you were in heaven, you would gladly cut your own head off to be rid of it!"

Maggie began sobbing and trembling. She imagined that she could feel the dronons' black sensor whips on her arms, cold and rough like cornstalks, fouling her. "Gallen, you don't even begin to understand what kind of place we live in—"

"I know—" Gallen said. "I put on a teaching machine in the city. It taught me."

"Did it teach you about the dronon, about their plans?"

"No," Gallen admitted. "The teacher only showed me how the dronon conquered this world."

"In other words, this teacher taught you only what the dronon want you to know!"

Maggie was shivering and angry. Gallen put his arm around her, and she desperately wanted to be loved, to be comforted, for at that moment, it seemed that love was the only token that could be put on the scale that might balance out all the pain and despair that threatened to overwhelm her. Even then, she wasn't certain that love would be quite enough.

At that moment, something touched her back, and Maggie realized that Gallen held something long and hard in his hand. She reached around with her palm and touched the incendiary rod. Amazingly, he had managed to carry both it and her through the water.

And in that moment, she knew what else she needed to balance out her pain. Revenge.

"You said Everynne plans to overthrow the dronon," Maggie whispered. "Do you have any idea what her plans are?"

"No," Gallen admitted, "but I know where her gate is."

Maggie nodded softly and whispered, "Let's go."

But at that moment, a great circle of light shone on the bridge above them. The bridge rumbled and shook, so that bits of dirt rained down.

In horror, Galled clapped a hand over Maggie's mouth. She could think only one thing: They found us!

Overhead, a voice sounded from the sky. "You there: put up your hands!"

Ten

The light shined all around the bridge, bathing every grass blade in a brilliant glow. Gravity waves shook the bridge, making it thunder and vibrate so that bits of dirt and paint rained down. Maggie hugged Gallen. Overhead, Gallen heard someone shout, "I'm not armed! I'm not armed!"

Someone's up there, Gallen realized.

"I was only out for some exercise," a man called. "There is no harm in that." Gallen recognized the voice. Veriasse.

The flier hovered nearer. "Citizen, have you seen anyone pass you on the road?"

"Indeed," Veriasse said. "A magcar flashed past me not five minutes ago."

"Can you describe its occupants?"

"It carried only two—one was a woman. I cannot be sure of the sex of the driver."

Without another word, the flier darted south. Gallen peeked out and saw a second white, saucer-shaped flier that had been zigzagging over the far side of the river do likewise.

Veriasse whispered, "Gallen? Maggie?"

"Down here." Gallen started to climb up. "What are you doing back? I thought you were gone?"

"Shhh . . . talk softer. The gate we sought was guarded, so Everynne and I were forced to retreat. Don't climb up here. The night scopes on the vanquisher's flier can spot a man at forty miles. It is likely that I am being watched. Stay hidden and speak softly. The fliers can discern loud sounds, but softer sounds are masked by the fluctuation of air molecules that are disturbed by the fliers' gravity waves. I'll meet you at your camp at dawn. For now, follow the creek, keeping under heavy cover, then circle back through the woods. As an information manager for Fale, I've taken the liberty of issuing you false identifications. If you are captured, feign innocence. You will not be harmed."

"I wondered how I got credits on that empty chip," Gallen whispered. "I knew I had a hidden ally."

"Good luck," Veriasse whispered, and he hurried away.

Gallen led Maggie through the ravine into the hills. They crept under the starlight, more anxious to keep under cover than make good time. They reached camp before dawn, so they took shelter in a deep grotto to sleep.

At dawn, Veriasse woke them with a whistle. He stood at the top of a small rise, holding three bundles tied with string. He was gazing north. It took Gallen a second to realize that Veriasse was calling to Everynne and Orick. Gallen got up and stretched. In the distance, he could discern Everynne and Orick making their way through the woods. He wondered at the old man's uncanny ability to walk softly in such heavy growth, to find them no matter where they hid.

Gallen shook Maggie awake, then walked up the rise. "Thank you again for your help last night, Veriasse. How did you know we were under the bridge?"

"I watched you from a distance," Veriasse said. "I saw you enter Maggie's room and effect her escape. I was impressed at the last, when you closed her window as you leapt out. I'm sure that it confused the guards, forcing them to search for you within the compound. In fact, they are probably still concentrating their main search inside. Anyway, I saw you leap into the river, and by gauging the flow of the current was able to guess where you would exit. I would say that you planned your escape fairly well, although your lack of education was almost your undoing."

"In what way?" Gallen asked, perplexed.

"You didn't know about the capabilities of modern pursuit vehicles. That was my fault, for not warning you. But you also tried to beat the motion detectors. I suspected you would, so I went to Maggie's window and put jammers down before you arrived."

"You mean you were there?"

"Just for a moment."

"Why didn't you rescue Maggie yourself?"

"And expose myself to unnecessary hazards? As long as you were willing to take the major risk, it seemed reasonable to let you. Besides, if you had failed, you would have needed me to rescue you both."

Gallen stared at the ground, annoyed. Veriasse's argument made sense, but an hour ago Gallen had felt like a hero. Now he felt like a child who had been caught doing something stupid. The older man must have guessed what he was thinking. "You are a talented and courageous young man. I'd like to imagine that I was as good when I was your age, but I was not. I have trained many guardians in my time. Would you like to be one of them?"

Gallen nodded.

Veriasse began unwrapping his bundles. He had brought a black cloak for Gallen, with black boots and gloves and a lavender mask. The outfit bore two scabbards, one for a sword, one for an incendiary rifle. Gallen stared at them in awe, for it was the attire he had seen worn not five nights ago by a man he had thought to be a sidhe.

"Those are the clothes of a Lord of Fale, but who wears these colors?" Gallen asked.

"I wore these colors when I was young," Veriasse said. "They were my colors as Lord Protector. Lord Oboforron purchased them from me a few years back, but he was executed by the dronon recently, so I bought the title back last night. I told you I had issued you a new identity. You will need clothes to match the part. Put on the robe."

Gallen put on the outfit. The boots shrunk around his feet as soon as he pulled them on, and the robe seemed massive, thick enough to foil a dagger blow, but was actually very light and comfortable. There was some type of metal padding in the gloves on the knuckles and at the palm and edge of the hand. Gallen imagined that if he landed a blow while wearing the gloves, it would be devastating. He strapped on the weapons.

With the outfit was a personal intelligence, a fine net with many triangles of silver. Gallen hesitated to put it on, for he had never worn a mantle. He was becoming familiar enough with personal intelligences that he did not know if he wanted to trust this one, but Veriasse urged, "Go ahead. It will whisper the intricacies of the protector's art for you, and it can teach you much that will be of value."

Gallen put on the silver mantle, felt the now familiar thrumming in his head as the intelligence established communication. Yet his mind did not flood with images like it had at the pidc. Instead, his muscles seemed to tighten involuntarily, as if he were preparing to leap into action, yet there was no tension. He felt almost relaxed, and his senses became heightened. Gallen almost felt as if . . . he listened, and in the distance to the south, perhaps twenty miles away, he heard a flier approaching. The vanquisher pilot was giving a report over the radio, telling his supervisors that he had found nothing in his search of the area.

"What?" Gallen said. "What is this thing doing to me?"

"This mantle has many sensors built into it," Veriasse said. "It hears, sees, smells. It detects motions and weaponry better than any mere human ever could. If you want to see something in the distance, close your eyes and think of the thing you want to see. As long as the object is within your line of sight, its image will appear in your mind, in expanded form. Over time you will learn to access the mantle's higher awareness without conscious thought."

"How does this thing teach?" Gallen asked.

"When you are safe, away from harm, in quiet moments it will begin training you in earnest. But for now, you are in danger. The mantle will simply be prepared for whatever comes our way. In the early decades of your training, should anything put you in danger, just let yourself go, follow your instincts. Wisdom will flow to you in your time of need."

Gallen picked up the mask. It looked like a thin layer of gel, but when he put it on his face, it stuck with an adhesive quality. He hadn't fitted the mask perfectly, but like the boots, it flowed to fit the contours of his face.

For Maggie, Veriasse had a yellow-ocher robe with a pale green mask. Her mantle was large indeed, with dozens of round silver icons that flowed down her back to her waist. "I have decided to dress you as a Lady of Technicians," he said. "You will find that this intelligence knows far more than your little Guide did, but it is a gentle servant, not a cruel master. You can remove it any time you wish."

"I don't understand," Maggie said, pulling the yellow robe over her thin nightgown. "These mantles must be expensive."

"Indeed," Veriasse said, "but I have been very wealthy for a very long time. And, so, I am free to give you these."

"You were Semarritte's husband before the dronon overcame her?" Gallen asked.

"Husband?" Veriasse said. "An odd word, and a very old one, and I was not her husband in the way that you think, though I husbanded her. I nurtured her and protected her as much as any man could, and I made a career of it. Indeed, Gallen, I once thought of myself as being very much like you—a bodyguard, a protector. But I think the dronon have a clearer view of what I am.

"I played the part of Semarritte's Lord Escort, the Waymaker. Among the dronon, the escorts battle for the right to become the Golden Queen's personal honor guard. The winner takes the title of Lord Escort. The Lord Escorts from different hives then engage in ritual combat, and the winner's Golden Queen takes the high throne, making her Lord of the Swarm. Thus her Lord Escort is also called the 'Waymaker,' he who secures the path to the throne.

"It was my job to fight Semarritte's battles when needed, to protect her from other powerful lords. But I could never have been Semarritte's husband in the sense that you mean. Only her caretaker. Now, I am the Waymaker to her daughter, Everynne."

"You mean Everynne isn't your daughter?" Maggie asked.

"Not my biological daughter," Veriasse answered. "She is a Tharrin, from a race born to rule. I am from less elegant stock. She sometimes calls me father from affection, and I call her daughter perhaps because I raised her as my own. She is, in fact, a duplicate of Semarritte, cloned from her cells."

As Orick accompanied Maggie to the top of the rise, Veriasse said, "Our magcar can carry all five of us, but I'm afraid that you, Orick, will be easily noticed. We will simply have to take our chances, keep you out of sight. I purchased a cloak to disguise you on our drive to the city of Guianne."

Orick hugged Gallen and Maggie, and his heart swelled with joy. "My prayers have been answered. You are safe."

"You should also thank Veriasse," Gallen said. "The rescue went smoothly because of him."

Orick wondered at this. It seemed to him that they were in trouble precisely for trying to help Everynne and Veriasse. It was only fit that Veriasse should help them in return.

Yet as he watched Maggie and Gallen, Orick realized that this adventure was not over. It had only begun, yet by Maggie's pale features, the lines in her haunted face, he could tell that they had already suffered casualties. Gallen, in his mask of lavender starlight, looked as if he were fast becoming a sidhe. Maggie and Gallen would never recover from this trip. And Orick felt cast off, alone. Of them all, only he had had the strength to refuse to accept this world, preferring to suffer the consequences of that decision.

From his last bundle, Veriasse brought out a cloak in colors of forest brown, then began fastening it around Orick's neck. But the fastener would not let Veriasse stretch the cloak around Orick's neck completely. Orick was forced to stand for several minutes, and he grumbled at being compelled into an uncomfortable position for so long. Veriasse did not hurry.

Orick looked into Veriasse's deep blue eyes as the old man worked at the fastener, and saw in them an intensity, a deliberateness that few men carried. Here was a man, Orick decided, who had become a fanatic, a man who could be driven beyond mortal efforts.

Veriasse managed to fasten the cloak, then led them to the magcar and drove south for an hour through a winding mountain pass. In that time, they had to stop at two inspection stations where green-skinned ogres questioned them. Yet after checking the false identification for Maggie and Everynne, the ogres let them pass.

As the magcar climbed over a last mountain, Orick could taste the scent of sea air even before they saw the water beyond. The city of Guianne gleamed white below them, a collection of exotic domes that rested on a sandy beach like broken eggshells from some giant bird. Above the city, people flew lazily in the air currents, clear wings strapped to their backs flashing like giant dragonflies.

It was only as Veriasse descended toward the city that Orick began to realize how large it must be. He drove for five minutes, and though the buildings loomed larger, they were still very far away.

Just as Orick began to get used to the idea of those enormous buildings, the winged people scattered away from one quadrant of the city, then one round building lifted into the air, defying gravity, and continued climbing straight up into the morning until it vanished behind a layer of clouds.

"By Saint Jermaine's wagging beard, you'll not get me in one of those buildings!" Orick shouted.

"That isn't a building," Maggie said. "It's a starship. All of the domes are starships." Orick looked over at Maggie. She wore a strange expression, one of both profound awe and conquest. He had never seen her so happy, so transformed by wonder. "And I know how they work."

Orick crossed himself to ward off bad luck. He muttered under his breath. "I don't know why I came here. Nothing good can come of it, as I've said all along. You stay right where you belong, Orick. Bears need the woods like birds need sky."

The car skimmed over the highway, then turned onto one of many branching boulevards. When they neared the city, the egg-shaped ships loomed above them. Beneath the ships was a sprawling conglomeration of tunnels and passages that seemed to wind about in meandering patterns like veins in a leaf.

Veriasse pulled up to one huge tunnel-like opening and passed under an arch. The presence of the dronon vanquishers was heavier here than it had been in Toohkansay. A dozen vanquishers manned an outpost at the gate, brandishing oversized incendiary rifles. Veriasse stopped to give his identification.

The vanquishers let the car pass. Veriasse drove down a broad boulevard beneath the covered city, a vast arching tunnel whose ceiling could not have been less than three hundred feet high. Everywhere along the sides of the street were shops with exotic displays. The scent of foods unfamiliar to Orick wafted through the tunnel. Smaller side passages led off to living areas and uncovered parkways. Veriasse drove slowly, for many pedestrians and other vehicles also negotiated the great boulevard. A dozen times, Orick was tempted to ask Veriasse to stop so that he could try out some pastry or other dish sold by vendors, but the old man kept driving for nearly an hour, heading down at a slight angle.

It was getting darker. Orick glanced up at the huge skylights, saw that they had descended below the ocean. Schools of fish swam in the green waters above them.

Far from the gates of the city, Veriasse halted the car in front of a building whose strange facade attracted Orick. The building displayed no markings to explain its purpose to passersby. Lampposts in front had glow globes attached, but the muted lights gave the place a somber appearance. To heighten the solemn atmosphere, Orick saw that there were no businesses nearby for hundreds of yards. The building was silent. A few people hurried in, some away, but all of them kept their heads low, as if to hide their identities. The building's facade showed in bas relief an image of a woman standing with arms outstretched. Behind her glittered a field of gold stars. The handiwork was astonishing, beautiful, but something more attracted Orick: the woman herself.

"Hey, that's a picture of Everynne," Orick said.

"Shhh," Veriasse muttered. "It's not Everynne. That is an image of Semarritte, Everynne's mother, who was once our great judge. This is her tomb."

Now Orick understood why the place was so quiet, so solemn.

"Why are the lights so low?" Everynne asked. "It looks as if the building is closed." Indeed, beside the doors were two burly vanquishers, watching the entrance like ogres.

"The dronon would close the tomb, if they dared," Veriasse said. "They want the memory of Semarritte to die with her. But too many remember her still. Too many revere her, and this confuses the dronon. Reverence for the vanquished is a concept that is alien to them."

Orick didn't say anything, but he doubted that anyone would revere a mere woman as much as the old man said. Semarritte was, after all, only human, but Veriasse spoke of her with an awe that Orick reserved only for God and his servants.

They got out of the car. Both Everynne and Veriasse refused to slouch and scurry to the entrance as others had. Instead, they walked tall and proud up the broad steps, toward a large ornate door. The green-skinned ogres stood silently, but when they saw Gallen, one of them reached out a hand to Gallen's shoulder, stopping him. The guardian said, "There was a time when I served one who wore those colors."

Gallen turned, looked up from beneath his black hood, and his lavender mask of starlight twisted in rage at being stopped, as if the ogre were some gnat that Gallen would squash. "Many things are changing," Gallen said. "I hope you served him as well as you do your new lord."

The ogre removed his hand from Gallen's shoulder, and the group passed through the doors into what Orick recognized as a cathedral. The room was silent, heavily carpeted with red fabric, and the sound of a muttered word or cough did not echo back from the ceiling. They walked up an aisle between rows of pews, where a few mourners sat quietly. Most of the mourners were lords, with their glowing masks and somber robes, and Orick wondered at this. Apparently, the inside of this building was off limits to common folk. Or perhaps commoners feared to worship here.

Ahead was a great stone pulpit with what looked to be an image of the stricken Christ carved upon it. Upon the stone pulpit stood a ghostly apparition of Semarritte, speaking softly to the crowd. Her clear voice seemed to issue from her lips, saying, "The rightful duty of one who would be your leader is to become the Servant of All. We Tharrin believe that those who serve must do so in both thought and deed, subjugating all selfish desires. Any leader who does less is not worthy of either position or honor. . . ."

Orick listened enrapt, for the Lady Semarritte's teachings were not like those he had ever heard from any puffed-up mayor or clan chieftain back in County Morgan. These words recalled to Orick's mind the teachings of Christ to his disciples when they argued about who would become the greatest in the kingdom of heaven: "Let him who would be greatest among you, become the servant of all." The hair began rising on the back of Orick's neck, for here among the sidhe, this was indeed their church, and the Lady Semarritte had been their god.

As Orick got closer, he saw that it was not Christ at all carved upon the pulpit but a blackened skeleton fused against the stone. Here were the remains of Everynne's mother. The flesh had burned from her bones and turned into a black, oily substance, but the whole skeleton was intact, hands clawed out protectively as if the dead woman had raised them to ward off a blow, legs tilted askew. Bits of dark hair and the chainmail netting of her mantle were fused into the stone, along with a necklace and other metal items.

This is what someone looks like after getting shot with an incendiary rifle, Orick realized. He'd seen Father Heany go down in flames back in Clere, but he had not realized the full magnitude of what the weapon could do.

The five of them lingered before the blasted remains. Veriasse knelt on one knee, and Everynne got down on both knees and wept softly over her mother's body. Above them on the pulpit, the image of the dead queen continued her sermon for several minutes, detailing the rightful duties of a judge, pledging to fulfill those duties for as long as her people wanted her. When she finished, the image faded, and a voice floated through the hall, saying that the dead woman's oration would be repeated in five minutes.

Veriasse touched Everynne's shoulder and whispered, "It's time, my daughter, my lord." Several people got up to leave, but Veriasse walked to the back of the room, closed the inner doors to the chapel while Everynne went to the podium. When she reached the top, she pulled back her robe to expose her face, peeled away the pale blue mask.

She began speaking, reciting what Orick was sure must have been the beginning of Semarritte's oration. "Through all the heavens, at all times, among all peoples, the greatest treasure of a nation has always been the quality and number of its good leaders. No abundance of wealth can quell the rapaciousness of a tyrant. No nation can count itself fortunate while groaning under the iron foot of war. No people can afford to tolerate corruption at the hands of a governor, whether that governor was chosen in free election or has maneuvered himself into position through influence."

Orick's hair bristled, and he wondered that Everynne would dare to speak so with the vanquishers out at the gates of the cathedral, but Everynne did not shrink from her duty. Instead, as she spoke she seemed to grow in size and power and majesty. She pulled off her outer robe, and beneath it she wore a pale blue gown. The light that had been shining upon the skeletal remains of Everynne's dead mother now shone fully on her, and Everynne stood in the darkness, shining like a bolt of lightning.

Orick looked back at the pews, and these handful of mourners who had come to pay homage to the dead Semarritte now all stood, mouths agape, to see their great judge standing before them, as one raised from the dead. Some of them wept openly, and Orick watched one woman put her hand to her mouth and repeatedly cry out in astonishment.

Everynne continued. "And so you have fashioned us Tharrin to keep the peace among you, to establish order and ensure that every person is granted the right to life, liberty, and the freedom to prosper according to their best abilities.

"The rightful duty of one who would be your leader is to become the Servant of All. We Tharrin believe that those who serve must do so in both thought and deed, subjugating all selfish desires. Any leader who does less is not worthy of either position or honor." At this point she cut the oration short, and said. "I stand before you, offering to become the leader you have sought. I am Everynne, the daughter to Semarritte, and I was born Tharrin. I seek to cast the dronon from the midst of our realm, but I cannot do it alone. Who among you will come to my aid?"

From every corner of the room, the people erupted with shouts of "I! I! I will help you!" and the proud lords in their gleaming masks rushed forward, weeping in glee like children to fall at Everynne's knees. They knelt at her feet, reaching up their hands in adoration so that she could touch them, not daring to touch her on their own, and Everynne grasped each person's hand firmly and thanked each lord.

And somehow, Orick the bear, who had always believed that he would become a servant of God, found himself rushing forward into the small crowd. He sat down and raised his paw, and Everynne smiled at him in surprise, tears filling her pale blue eyes. "Orick!" She laughed. "Even you?"

"I will aid you, lady, though I be the humblest of your servants," he said firmly.

"No doubt you shall be among the most valiant," Everynne said as she knelt to kiss his paw. And even though she had not asked it, Orick felt as if he ought to take his priestly vows of poverty and chastity.

Eleven

That night, Gallen could not sleep. All night long he lay in a fever, waking in a sweat. For a time he worried about his health, but then he lay back calmly, realizing that the mantle had begun its instruction. He had been dreaming, and the dreams were memories of things that had happened to Veriasse.

He dreamed first of Fale. He had been escorting Semarritte on this world when the dronon warships fell from the sky in dark clouds. The dronon came in vast numbers, sealing off Guianne so that its residents were trapped in tunnels beneath the ocean. Guardians tried to fend them off, but the dronon were too numerous; like dark grains of sand they swept over the land.

Veriasse and Semarritte had become trapped here in Semarritte's judgment hall. Dronon by the hundreds of thousands had surrounded the building, a black wave of warriors clambering over one another's bodies, until at last they cleared a path so that the Golden Queen and her Lord Escort could enter.

In his dream, Gallen struggled fiercely with the Lord Escort—landing blows on the beast's chitinous body, ripping off one of its feelers, smashing eyes with a leaping kick. But in time he wearied, and the Lord

Escort lashed forward a wing—an unprecedented move that would have availed the creature nothing in a battle with one of its own kind. But the dronon's wing slashed through Veriasse's belly like a saber, and suddenly he was reeling away from the battle, his entrails spilling across the floor.

The Lord Escort then rattled its wings in a thunderous roar, leapt into the air, and in one swift kick disemboweled Semarritte while Veriasse watched. The dronon vanquishers who encircled the room raised a rattling howl of congratulations. Then the Lord Escort gently removed Semarritte's Mantle of Command, placing it on his own Golden Queen, crying to his people that Tlitkani of the dronon had become the new Lord of the Swarm, queen over all peoples both human and dronon.

Afterward, a dronon vanquisher rushed forward with an incendiary rifle, firing into Semarritte's body. Smoke and the scent of chemical fire rose through the building. Veriasse pulled his intestines in as the world faded to gray, pinching the skin closed, unsure whether the nanodocs in his body could heal such a massive wound.

In the dream, Gallen could not feel Veriasse's pain. He could discern the man's thoughts, observe his actions. But the dream carried no emotional weight.

Gallen woke and thought long about the dream, wondered if there were any way that Veriasse could have defeated the dronon, and suddenly images of the planet Dronon filled his mind. He saw a brown world filled with odd plants, where insects had developed interior lungs that allowed them to grow in size far beyond anything on Earth. Dronon was a vast world, and it orbited its sun once each four Earth years. Its axis tilted at a forty-two degree angle, with the result that each year, each polar icecap would melt. During a summer, one hemisphere would bathe in perpetual daylight while the other suffered perpetual night.

As a result, the dronon were forced to migrate over vast continents with each changing season, foraging for shrublike fungi. Each hive continually competed with others for food and space, for the finest nesting sites, for water that became scarce during the dry seasons. The order of their universe was clear: expand your territory or die.

In each hive, as the first few females hatched, they would battle among themselves, fighting in order to remove the exterior ovaries from one another. The female who managed to keep her ovaries established her dominance as a future queen, and soon the others recognized her authority as a princess. She would bide her time until a Lord Escort flew in from another hive, one who would kill the reigning Lord Escort and queen, making the princess the new queen of the hive.

Those poor females who were neutered could never form the secondary sexual characteristics of a queen. They grew only to a small size, and their color remained as white as that of any grublike larvae. Their boundless energy was channeled into work, rather than procreation, and they became the most menial servants of the hive.

Among the males, a similar battle would take place, but only after the larvae had exited their cocoons as adults. Adult male vanquishers, with their flashing wings and huge battle arms, engaged in ritual combat, seeking to remove one another's testicles, until only six males remained. These six princes would then fly to new hives, hoping to win their own kingdoms, while the neutered vanquishers remained with their hive.

A third sex often hatched without functioning sexual organs—neither male nor female. These had deformed wings and less energy than workers, but often had facile minds, suitable for solving problems. These become the technicians of the hive, the architects, counselors, and artists.

Over the eons, the queens had evolved to become more and more virile—laying more eggs, living longer lives. Only the strongest survived, and it was in the interest of the queens to root out the weak, destroy competing hives.

But among the queens, one great lady ruled each swarm. She could not begin her rule until she reached the age of one hundred and fifty Dronon years. At that point, her exoskeleton would change color, bleaching from its pale wheat to a beautiful gold. If the queen survived to this age without injuries—broken appendages or a cracked exoskeleton—her offspring would gather near, carried into ecstasy at the sight of a new Golden Queen.

The Lord Escort of the hive, stricken with adoration, would pilgrimage with his Golden across the continents, seeking out the reigning Golden Queen.

The Lord Escorts for each Golden would then battle for the right to rule a swarm of one thousand hives. When one of the escorts was killed, his foe would attack the opposing queen and maim her, damaging her so that she would lose the adoration of hives. Such a queen was often allowed to cower back to her own hive and continue laying eggs until she died.

But the Lord Escort and the vanquishing Golden Queen became Lords of the Swarm. They would choreograph the great works of the hives—the migration across the vast plains of Dronon and through the reaches of space; they would choreograph battles with legions of the vanquishers as they sought to enlarge the swarm's territory.

Gallen lay in a half sleep, and the mantle displayed battles that had been filmed between Lord Escorts. Veriasse had made a great study of the battles—had noted the various fighting stances, attack forms, the use of feelers, mandibles, serrated battle arms, and the clawed legs as weapons. He had performed autopsies on dead dronon vanquishers—had determined how much force was necessary to crush their faceted eyes, to pull off the hooked claw of a forearm, to rip out a feeler, to pry off a head. He had measured the thickness of their chitinous exoskeletons, searching for thin spots.

The dronon had few weaknesses. Their exoskeletons offered superb protection for the head, belly, and back. They were most vulnerable on the hind legs, where their respiratory orifices weakened the hip, but reaching those legs was a task—the dronon could protect themselves well from a frontal assault, and with the dronon's flight and leaping capabilities, it was nearly impossible for a human to attack from behind.

Gallen lay for a long time, thinking about how one could engage a dronon in hand-to-hand combat with the hopes of winning. Sometimes, he would doze and wake to find himself sleepwalking, performing arcane exercises, stretching muscles he did not know that he had, leaping and kicking at imaginary foes in the quiet halls of the temple.

In one such session, Maggie came to him, half asleep herself. "What are you doing up so late?"

"I can't sleep," Gallen said. "Veriasse said this damned mantle would teach me when things were quiet, but it's kept me up all night."

Maggie simply said, "Have you tried talking to it? Just tell it to let you rest for the night."

Gallen gave the command, and immediately the mantle relinquished its lessons. He went back to bed, found himself compelled to lie next to Maggie, recognized that the mantle was whispering for him to lie beside her. "Why?" he wondered, and the answer flooded into his mind. "You are a Lord Protector now. You must have someone to protect."

Over the next few days, Orick became inseparable from Everynne. He would disappear into his room for a few moments, and then while Everynne was speaking in a secret meeting with the masked Lords of

Fale, she would suddenly turn and find him lying on the floor near her foot like some great hairy dog.

She did not mind his attentions. Few men could best a vanquisher in single battle, and she did not forget that the bear had already saved her life once. More than that, she found his presence somehow morally calming. Everynne was acutely conscious of the fact that she had been born to lead, that every facet of her appearance, even the chemical combination of her pheromones, had been designed to make her appealing to other humans.

From childhood she had been keenly aware of how easily she could manipulate people through a thousand seemingly insignificant things—by sitting when making a request of a man, she could appear more helpless and in greater need. By standing with head erect and back straight, she could more easily seem in control of any situation. By holding eye contact and softly making requests when someone hesitated to give allegiance, she could force the person to make a choice. By taking great care of her clothing and her appearance, she could make herself more desirable to men. By emphasizing the things she held in common with other women, she could convince a woman that they were sisters rather than competitors. The list was endless, and Everynne knew that her very ability to learn the art of manipulation was bred into her. Billions of people had none of her talent and as a result were born destined to become socially inept.

Orick, by not being human, should have been immune to her charms. Yet he stayed at her side, seemingly for his own purposes. Everynne wondered at his motives. Perhaps it was only the crowd. In the past two days, each of the Lords of Fale had come to her, detailing some startling atrocity committed by the dronon. A merchant told of vast assets the dronon had seized for war efforts, so that now he was poor. A mother told of a son who had disappeared. A builder told of a mass grave he'd discovered, filled with the corpses of handicapped children, or "defectives," as the dronon called them. The tales of horror were far-reaching and personal, and Orick listened in startled silence, then would listen even more keenly as the lords told of their fondness for Everynne's mother, told how they dreamed of her return. And though Everynne knew that her mother had never been a perfect governor, she had truly sought to be a Servant of All. There had been peace in the land, honest strivings for justice. But the dronon did not value peace or justice.

Their biological imperative told them to vanquish all, then reap the spoils. To them, human lives were simply merchandise for the taking.

And if the tales that Orick heard were his motive for staying by her side, then she worried what he would think when he discovered her inadequacies.

On their first day in Guianne, Everynne collected her confidantes, and together they had devised a plan to escape from Fale. The dronon had been systematically sealing off the planet. Guards were at every gate to the Maze of Worlds, and warships were being diverted to block the skies above.

Right now, the beleaguered vanquishers were spread too thin. They could hinder Everynne from escaping, but they lacked the manpower to effectively search for her. But once their warships arrived, they would form a picket, reinforce the troops, and begin searching Fale in earnest. Everynne had to leave now.

In order to escape, Veriasse had designed a system of thrusts and parries that included three attacks: first, they would feint at another gate, forcing the dronon to send for reinforcements. Everynne's forces would then attempt to hijack a starship. If the starship made it to hyperspace, the dronon would think she had escaped the planet. If it was destroyed, the dronon would believe she had died in the attack. In either case, they would be off their guard.

While the dronon had their support drawn off and were reeling from the belief that Everynne was on a spaceship, her forces would begin an aerial assault against the gate that led to Cyannesse. If that attack succeeded as it should, Everynne could leave.

Now, the morning of the assault, Veriasse drove up the highway in an ancient hoverbus. It was an old model—a long aluminum cab suitable for ten people, with flaring wings where the exhaust vented.

Beneath them, the highway rolled flat and smooth. For the moment, they simply looked like tourists, floating along the highway. Everynne glanced at her chronometer. It was nine in the morning, and three hundred kilometers to the south, the Lords of Fale had mobilized their workers in a ground assault at the gate to Bilung. The gate served well as a diversion, being close both to the city of Guianne and to the gate to Cyannesse.

Everynne closed her eyes and let her mantle connect to Lord

Shunn's personal intelligence via telelink. She watched his attack progress—silver fliers swept through the sky in a wedge, shooting low over the forest toward the gate, dropping a barrage of explosives along with canisters of chlorine gas, which was particularly toxic to dronon. As soon as the fireballs began erupting over the treetops, Lord Shunn's attack force moved in.

Under cover of the trees, long-range laser weapons were nearly useless, so Shunn's forces all wielded only incendiary rifles. No human could bear the weight of the armor needed to ward off an incendiary blast, so Shunn's men were protected only by gas masks and lightweight heat-resistant combat fatigues. The men ran forward in loose formation, moving cautiously. Since the battle was meant only as a diversion, they were not in a hurry to engage the vanquishers.

Lord Shunn himself flew in behind on his hovercar, with its hood down, observing the battle. He glided through the trees, and only the distant smell of smoke signified that a battle had been launched. For fifteen minutes, Everynne watched the battle progress, until Lord Shunn's troops met several dozen vanquishers. Suddenly the woods filled with fire as incendiary rifles began discharging. Flaming balls of sulfurous white whipped through the air with incredible speed.

She watched a civilian try to dodge behind a tree in hopes of eluding a ball that flamed toward him, growing in size. The chemical charge from the rifle splattered across the tree and across the man's arm, erupted into flames hotter than the sun. He screamed and held his arm out, spinning once, kicking up detritus from the forest floor. In less than a second, he succumbed to the heat and lay burning.

The sight horrified Everynne to the core of her being. As a Tharrin, she was bred to be empathic. She detested violence. Somehow, knowing that Lord Shunn and his workers had volunteered to die in the woods this day made Everynne feel ashamed, weak. She only wanted the killing to stop, everywhere, but she was forced into a deadly contest and could not escape.

Suddenly on the highway ahead of Everynne, sirens began blaring as army hovertrucks approached. Veriasse pulled his own old bus off the highway to let them pass. Everynne disengaged the telepresence link and looked up. Three truckloads of vanquishers were heading south at full speed, perhaps sixty green-skinned giants. Ahead of her, Veriasse relaxed in his seat for a moment, breathed easier. The soldiers could only have come from the Cyannesse gate. Their ruse was working.

Veriasse let the soldiers pass, gunned the throttle. Everynne engaged her telepresence again, saw how the battle was progressing.

For four more minutes, the battle continued. Suddenly, far to the south, a spaceship lifted over the horizon, a distant white sphere that floated higher and higher into the morning sky. Lady Frebane began broadcasting urgent messages to Shunn and his troops, "My lord," she called, "the lady's ship is away! Repeat, the mission has succeeded. The lady's ship is away. Break off your attack!"

Lady Frebane continued broadcasting for two minutes. The dronon vanquishers sent low-altitude fliers to intercept the ship, but they did not make it in time. Lady Frebane jumped into hyperspace before the fliers got into range, and Everynne was filled with a deep sense of regret. If she'd been on that ship, she would have made her escape already. But Veriasse had insisted that the ship was too dangerous, too large a target. He had opted for the double feint. The real battle lay ahead.

"We're about sixty seconds from our gate," Veriasse warned. "Gallen—" he began to say, but the young man was already playing his part. He lowered the hood to the hovercraft and got out his incendiary rifle, flipped it on so that its indicator glowed red.

For a moment, as Gallen's black robes flapped, Everynne caught glimpses of the silver bangles of his personal intelligence, the lavender of his mask, and Gallen reminded her of Veriasse. But he turned and she caught the profile of his face, and the illusion dissipated. Everynne gazed across the desert. Three kilometers north of the gate was a line of low yellow hills. At any moment, three phalanxes of fliers would stream over the hills at four thousand kilometers per hour. The vanquishers would have less than three seconds to take cover.

Veriasse focused on the gate. The hoverbus hummed, bouncing as it hit small thermals. In the distance, Everynne spotted a flash of sunlight reflecting from the flier's windshields, and she began counting: three, two . . . one. The saucer-shaped fliers were in a tight *V*, fifteen of them; suddenly the formation split and the fliers veered east and west. Antiaircraft fire erupted from the vanquishers' outpost at the gate; Everynne watched gray pellets rain from the fliers, beacons designed to fool intelligent missiles.

Then the incendiary bombs landed. They were so small that Everynne did not see them drop. Instead, the ground around the gate erupted into a wall of flame that leapt thirty meters into the air. Everynne found it hard to believe that anyone or anything could survive that inferno, but Veriasse had insisted that the fliers make a second pass, and then a third.

By now, their hoverbus had reached the turn where the highway veered west, but Veriasse simply kept his northern course, slowing dramatically; the hoverbus leapt from the shoulder of the highway.

The engines roared, straining as they raced down a small ravine, throwing up clouds of dust. The second wave of fliers was sweeping over the hills now, sooner than Everynne had anticipated, and they dropped a barrage of conventional explosives. Dust and burning bodies pitched into the air, twisting in a great whirlwind. Smoke and fire obscured the nearly indestructible gate, but Everynne pulled out her key and pressed the open sequence. The light under the arch shimmered.

Already the flames from the incendiary bombs were beginning to die. The third and final phalanx of fliers closed over the hills, spraying out their ordnance, an oily black substance that civilians referred to as "Black Fog." It had no toxic properties, but absorbed light so completely that in seconds the sky turned black.

A black cloud boiled toward them, and Veriasse stared in concentration as they hit the wall of darkness. Everynne felt as if her eyes had been painted over. At first she could see no light at all, yet they were hurtling toward the gate; she feared that Veriasse would crash into a post.

Some vanquishers must have heard their hoverbus, for two balls of white fire whizzed over Everynne's head. She screamed and ducked. Gallen returned fire at the unseen targets. Veriasse shouted, "I can't see the gate!"

Gallen fired his incendiary rifle; a fireball of actinic light spattered one gate post, only twenty yards ahead. Veriasse hit the reverse thrusters, shouting, "Run for it."

Everynne leapt from the hovercar. It was so dark, she could see only the fiery light above the gate. Orick tried to leap out of the hovercar but slipped. He yelled, "Damn!"

Everynne turned but could not see the bear. Maggie, Gallen, and Veriasse could be detected only by the faint shimmering of their masks;

they floated above the ground like wraiths. Maggie grabbed Everynne's hand, urging her to hurry forward, but they tripped over the body of an ogre. Everynne was just struggling up when the creature grabbed her ankle. She screamed and simultaneously the thing shouted weakly, "Vanquishers to me!"

"Gallen, help!" Maggie cried.

Everynne tried to kick free, but the ogre held her tight. Orick, hidden by the inky blackness, roared and pounced on the creature. The vanquisher let go, and Everynne heard more than saw the ensuing scuffle.

Suddenly the vanquishers surrounded them, too close to use incendiary rifles, faintly visible in the light from the arch. Gallen and Veriasse pulled out their swords and began swinging, but the vanquishers were armored. By the time Veriasse and Gallen brought one down, three more had taken its place.

Everynne had no choice. She reached into her pocket, pulled out a ball of glowing light. "Stop!" She stood defiant, holding the ball high, though her heart was faint.

"You vanquishers, do you see this?" she asked. "You know what it is?"

"A Terror," one vanquisher said, a sergeant in heavy armor.

"If you don't surrender now," Everynne said, "I'll destroy this world. My mantle is linked to eighty-four other Terrors spread across the galaxy, including one on Dronon itself. I've already initiated the arming sequence. They will begin detonating in three minutes, unless you surrender now! You will not have time to issue a warning. You will all die!"

Everynne gasped for breath. She did not know if the vanquishers would fall for her ruse. She was a Tharrin, dedicated to peace. All her training, all the engineering her ancestors had built into her, screamed that even to risk destroying a world was wrong. Yet she held a Terror aloft, hoping the dronon would treat her threat seriously.

From the darkness, a dronon limped forward. The fire had burned its wings, and it dragged one hind leg. A familiar clicking began as mouthfingers tapped its voice drum. "I am broadcasting your demands to Lord Annitkit, our supervisor on this world. He will contact the Golden Queen, Tlitkani, and learn her will in this matter. It will take several hours to learn her reply."

"You don't have that long," Everynne said. "We're leaving." She turned to the others. "Get through the gate, now!"

She began inching backward through the crowd of vanquishers, moving carefully. It might be that Lord Annitkit would order them to kill her, risk losing eighty worlds in order to keep the thousands they had gained. But Everynne had to hope that he would take her threat seriously. The dronon were often as paranoid as they were violent, but they loved their queen. She did not know of a dronon who would risk the chance that his queen would be killed.

The dronon vanquisher rushed forward, and a segmented hand erupted from the hidden compartment in its battle arm, grasping her arm, pinning Everynne to the spot.

"I do not believe you will detonate the Terror," the dronon said. "A Tharrin would not destroy a world."

"Can you be so certain?" Veriasse shouted from behind the dronon. "Others of our people have detonated Terrors on your worlds. My mantle, too, has the access codes for these weapons, and I am not a Tharrin. Believe me, if you do not let us go, we will kill your precious Golden Queen."

The dronon hesitated. He seemed to be stalling as he waited for further orders. "If you have a Terror on Dronon, why have you not used it? I do not believe you have another Terror."

Veriasse strode forward, put his face close to the vanquisher's, and looked into its eye cluster. "Perhaps we only take our orders from a higher source," he whispered threateningly. "Perhaps we do not completely comprehend their plans for your queen. I only know that I am not free to contravene those orders. Friend, take your hand off the woman's arm. If she drops the Terror, it could break open. We wouldn't want any accidents. . . ."

The dronon held Everynne's hand. It had a tiny metal device clipped to one of its feelers, and the device buzzed. The dronon addressed Veriasse and Everynne simultaneously.

"Lord Annitkit demands your word of honor that if we release you, you will relinquish your attack on Dronon!"

"Once I pass through the gate, I will initiate the disarming sequence. I will spare your queen, for now," Veriasse said.

The dronon began walking, wrenched Everynne toward the gate.

Maggie and Orick leapt through ahead of her, but Gallen and Veriasse stood on each side of the gate. The chemical fire of the incendiary rifle burned white across the arch. With their dark robes, weapons drawn and faces masked, Gallen and Veriasse looked like doormen to some hell.

They each took one of her hands. Together they leapt into the light.

Twelve

Gallen stood up to his knees in the warm water of a new world, panting, holding onto Everynne's hand. He spared the world a quick glance: twin white-hot suns spun on the horizon. In every direction, a shallow sea reflected the yellow sky, and fingers of vapor climbed from the water. The sea was calm, with only tiny lapping waves, and when Gallen looked toward the distant suns, a strange prismatic effect caused the waves to sparkle in a rainbow. Maggie and Orick were searching about, unable to spot land. But to the southeast, Gallen's mantle showed him distant bluffs of coral, rising from the water.

"Where the hell are we?" Gallen asked angrily. He was shaking—they'd come close to getting butchered on Fale, and Gallen didn't like that. Even worse, he didn't appreciate Everynne hiding things from him—like the fact that she carried a weapon that could destroy a world. She put the Terror into a fold of her robe. Veriasse opened his map.

"We're on Cyannesse, of course," he said. The map showed them as a fiery dot of red, but showed no gates. Veriasse pushed a corner of the map, and its scale expanded to display a continent—if continent you could call it. Cyannesse was mostly ocean, and the land here looked to be only a rough archipelago. "Ah, here is the gate," he said, pointing to a blue arch. "Only about a thousand kilometers. We're not far from a city." He pointed southeast, toward the cliffs. "Let's go."

"I don't get it," Orick bawled. "Why don't we see the gate from this side? Why did we get dumped in the water?"

"You don't see a gate from this side," Veriasse explained, "because the gate doesn't have two sides. Each gate on a planet is like a bow, shooting you toward a single destination, and you are the arrow. You simply land where you are pointed, within reason. An intelligence is built into each gate, and that intelligence continually tracks the destination planet. There is a beacon buried beneath us that tells the gate how deep the soil is, so you don't land in a bed of rock. When this gate was built, this spot was on land, but now the oceans have risen. Still, I've been through this gate before—this spot is only underwater during high tides. We can make it to shore easily enough." Veriasse made as if to depart.

"Wait!" Gallen said, looking first to Veriasse, then to Everynne. Gallen still had not sheathed his sword; it dripped blood into the clear, warm water. "Neither of you are going anywhere until I get some answers."

"What?" Veriasse said. "You wear the mantle of a Lord Protector for two days and think you can beat me in combat?"

Gallen stuck his sword into the sand under the water, swiftly pulled his incendiary rifle, aimed it at Veriasse. "I've known you less than a week, but I have heard two very different stories about your plans. First, you said you planned to start a war to win back your realm. But a minute ago, you said you plan to destroy nearly a hundred worlds. I may be a Backward, but I've learned a few things in the past week. If that Terror breaks, it will destroy this planet. You are jeopardizing every world you set foot on. No one has that right! You've been traveling between the Maze of Worlds, and by your own admission you have sabotaged world upon world. Though you may be a Tharrin, Everynne, I have yet to see evidence of the compassion that you claim as your birthright."

Maggie and Orick kept still, not daring to interrupt. Veriasse held back. Everynne watched Gallen and licked her lips.

"You are right, of course," she said. "I'm not what I seem. On Fale, they so wanted a new incarnation of their great judge that they were willing to believe I was her without any evidence. But I am not so certain that I am my mother's daughter."

"Don't say that!" Veriasse interrupted. He said to Gallen, "How dare you! How dare you set yourself up to judge her, you miserable little piece of filth!"

"And how dare you create a god to judge me without my consent!" Gallen shouted. "I'll not aid you further. In fact, I'll kill you both dead right now, unless I get some answers!"

"Don't, Gallen—" Orick growled.

"If he must know the truth," Everynne said to Veriasse, "I prefer to answer his questions." She held her head high, gazed evenly into Gallen's eyes. He could detect no fear in her, no deceit.

"You're right about me. I don't deserve to be the Lord Judge of your world or any other. I haven't earned that right, and I doubt I'm worthy of it. Certainly, my people would never approve of me. The Tharrin do not just insert a Lord Judge as a ruler. They breed and train and test tens of thousands of candidates for every position that is filled—and they would be horrified by me. Yes, I carry a device in my pocket that could destroy this world! Yes, I've let hundreds of people throw their lives away so that I can win back my mother's place. I—I don't even want the position! Maggie—" She looked at the girl. "You told me the other day about how you hated working in your little inn, scrubbing dirt from the floors, washing, feeling like a slave. Yet can you imagine being asked to clean the filth from ten thousand worlds? Can you imagine being the sole arbiter in a hundred thousand disputes per day, sentencing thousands to die every hour? I—I cannot imagine any post that would make me feel more corrupt!"

Tears filled her eyes, and Everynne began coughing, heaving in great sobs. She fell to her knees in the water, folding her arms over her stomach. "Did you see how many died for me today? When I look at the things I've done . . ."

"Shhh . . ." Veriasse said, sloshing through the water to comfort her. "No matter, no matter. You must only take the post for awhile—long enough for the Tharrin to send a replacement."

Gallen studied them. It was said that the Tharrin were bred for compassion. He could now see how Everynne suffered. She carried weapons to destroy a world, yet those weapons tore at the very fabric of her sanity, and as he watched her sobbing, saw her self-loathing, part of him realized that if he were to be judged by a god, she was the one he wanted.

Veriasse held Everynne, but he stared up at Gallen with angry, brooding eyes. "What are your plans?" Gallen asked, "I want every detail."

"We are going to make war with the dronon," Veriasse answered. "The Terrors are set on their most heavily occupied worlds. We will only detonate them if we are forced to."

"Father, don't!" Everynne said. "No more lies! They've earned the right to learn the truth."

"You can't—" Veriasse urged, but Everynne said, "Veriasse and I are going to Dronon, to battle the Lords of the Swarm in single, unarmed combat. If Veriasse can defeat them, then by dronon law we will become their lords, and I can order the dronon to retreat from human territory. It's the only way to save our worlds. It is what my mother wanted. Everything we've done—the Terrors, the talk of war, all have been a ruse."

Gallen considered—his mantle carried a great deal of battle information, and he recalled the dreams it had been sending. Veriasse had made detailed studies of how to fight the dronon in unarmed combat, and Gallen pondered upon the possibility. Nature had gifted the dronon vanquishers with armor. They were larger, stronger, and more mobile than a human, and had an array of weapons that was frightening. A human could hardly hope to win against one in unarmed combat.

"Why not a full-scale war?" Gallen asked. "You could win a war like the one you described on Fale. Destroy Dronon and the occupied worlds. A few fleets could then clean up the mess."

"We could win a war temporarily," Veriasse said, "but we would weaken this entire arm of the galaxy. The dronon despise weakness. They try to root it out, destroy it. We would open ourselves to certain attack by other swarms. In time, we would lose. The only way to defeat them with any hope of retaining our territories for an extended period is to beat them decisively while retaining a strong navy. This means that we cannot risk destroying our old guardians, the ones you call "ogres." Each guardian takes orders through the omni-mind. We have to win Everynne's omni-mind back and regain control of our navies. We must make the dronon fear our species more than they already do."

"What do you mean, fear us more than they do? I have seen no evidence that they fear us."

"The dronon rule by a rigid hierarchy," Veriasse said. "When a Golden Queen takes over as Lord of the Swarm, then the lords of her defeated enemy do obeisance, accepting her as their rightful leader. But it has been six years now since the dronon conquered us, and few of our lords have subjugated themselves to dronon authority. Instead, our resistance fights the dronon continually, while our lords publicly apologize to the dronon for the 'madmen' in our midst who have not yet accepted their queen. But the dronon are not stupid—they see the pattern. Although it goes against their very nature to destroy all members of a defeated hive, they have resorted to xenocide on dozens of our defeated worlds. They fear that, as a species, we are insane."

"Why do you keep your plan a secret, then?" Gallen said. "If you plan to challenge the Lords of the Swarm in combat, why not be more forthright?"

"Some factions would try to stop me," Everynne said. "The aberlains, for instance, hope to reap great profits under the Dronon Empire, and they would sabotage our efforts. But there is a more compelling reason to keep this a secret: by dronon law, those who do battle against the Lords of the Swarm must earn 'Charn'—the right to pass through hive territories—by battling each lesser queen and her escorts."

"We've had to pass through fourteen occupied worlds so far," Veriasse said. "If we had kept dronon law, I would have had to fight the ruling Lord Escort on each planet. You are wearing my mantle, Gallen. You know how difficult it will be for a mere human to win against dronon vanquishers in unarmed combat. I can't risk fighting many Lord Escorts. In any given battle, if I lost, then the Lord Escort would try to mar Everynne by wounding her. If Everynne is wounded, she would forfeit her eligibility to succeed the Golden Queen."

"What do you mean?" Maggie asked.

"Among the dronon, the Golden Queens must be unblemished," Veriasse answered. "And though some humans have been integrated in dronon society for sixty years, we are not even sure that the dronons will accept a human as Lord of the Swarms. But if they will even consider her as a contender, Everynne can have no visible defects, no scars. I hope the dronon will accept Everynne as an example of one of our own Golden Queens—one who is flawless. One born to rule. For her entire life, we have managed to keep Everynne from ever taking an injury that would leave a scar. That is why I work so hard to keep her from jeopardizing herself."

"I have one question more," Gallen said. "You carry a Terror. If you plan only single combat, why do you need such a device?"

"In case we lose totally," Veriasse said. "Everynne and I are going to the planet Dronon itself. If they reject our suit for the right to engage in ritual combat, they may try to kill us outright. Under such conditions, we have no choice but to begin the fruitless war that we have tried so hard to avoid. We hope that the very presence of the Terror will force the queen's hand, so that she will have to let us challenge. But, if necessary, Everynne's mantle will detonate the Terror. When the Golden Queen dies, the dronon will lose contact with the omni-mind. Their automated defenses will close down, and our freedom fighters will attack."

Gallen did not need to ask what would happen next. His mantle whispered the answers. If Dronon was destroyed, forty percent of the hives would die with it. Lesser queens might take over their own realms on distant worlds, but a long and bitter civil war would begin as hives battled to determine who would become the new Lords of the Swarm. Other dronon swarms around the galaxy would be tempted to invade during that time. Even if new lords were found, the inexperienced leaders would be weak. Leadership might turn over several times within the first few months. During such turmoil, the humans would be given time to win back lost territories, gain a stronger foothold. But as Veriasse had said before, it would pose a terrible risk in the long term.

"There is one scenario that you have not described," Gallen said, "and I am afraid it is the most likely. What if the dronon let you battle for succession and you lose?"

"Then we will at least have established a precedent that would give humans *the right* to battle for succession," Veriasse answered. "I have provided key people on several worlds with tissue samples from Everynne. Thousands of clones could be made. In time, one of her escorts could win the battle."

"Would you then detonate the Terror on Dronon?"

Everynne shook her head. "We couldn't. Our best hope for success in this contest is to fight the dronon within the bounds of their laws. My mother and the Tharrin considered this course of action for many years. This is the best way to win back our worlds. Otherwise, billions of innocent people will die on both sides of the battle. Surely you see that this is how it must be?"

"But if you don't win," Maggie said, "you will be subjecting your people to years of domination by the dronon. You can't let that happen. The aberlains are making such far-reaching changes, that in another generation, our children will no longer be human. You can't let that happen!" Maggie's eyes went wide. Though she had appeared calm over the past two days, Gallen could see how her experience on Fale had devastated her.

Veriasse sighed, and Everynne tried to comfort her. "It will be a sad day, even if we win," Everynne admitted. "Under Tharrin law, we also permitted upgrades on humans—but only within the limits agreed upon by their parents. We wanted all people to be decent and free, and earn the right to immortality. Sometimes we allowed upgrades of whole civilizations so that a people might become better adapted to their own world. But these sad creatures the dronon are forming—my heart bleeds for them. I fear that there will be little place for them in our society. We will give them the opportunity to go to Dronon, if they so desire, carve a niche among the hives. Those who choose to remain with us may have their children reverse-engineered. And I promise you, the aberlains will be punished."

Gallen could see that Everynne was not gambling with the future of her people. She would either win and live, or she would die and give her people new hope in the process. In either case, Gallen suddenly yearned to go to Dronon to see what would happen—even if it meant dying in the nanotech fire of a world-burning Terror.

Gallen thrust his incendiary rifle into its sheath, pulled his sword from the sand, and began to dry the dripping blade by whipping it over his head in complex patterns.

"Veriasse," Maggie said, "I have been wondering. Even in my short time working for the aberlains, I concluded that your guardians could have been engineered better. They could be more heavily armored, could be virtually invincible. Since they were Lady Semarritte's only police force, I find it odd that they are this weak. Orick killed one with his teeth."

"Lady Semarritte did not rule with an iron hand," Veriasse said. "The Tharrin rule by the will of the people. Yes, the guardians are imperfect. Part of their weakness stems from the fact that they are based upon models that are very old. But we have always known that someday, someone like the dronon could gain control of an omni-mind. Since guardian officers wear Guides and receive orders directly from the omni-mind, any usurper who controls the omni-mind also controls fleets and armies with billions of warriors spread out across ten thousand worlds. Isn't it a comfort to know that a human has some hope of beating them?"

Gallen thrust the blade into his sheath. "Let's go," he said as he turned and began walking toward the distant shore.

They chugged through the warm water for the next three hours with only one brief rest. The sea had little salt in it and remained marvelously clear. By picking a trail through shallows, they spent most of their time in water that didn't reach their hips, though they could often look out into deeper pools. In places, rock formations thrust up to create submerged islands. Here, fish swarmed in great silver schools that darted out to the depths and then raced back to the shelter of the rocks. Twice they saw great beasts swimming in the depths, chasing fish. Veriasse warned Gallen to watch for the creatures. "Puas, they are called," he said. "They feed on fish and anything else they can swallow."

At last they reached dry land—a beach that extended for miles. The beach was home to sand flies and some soft creature that reminded Gallen of a pine cone with eight legs. Small reddish black spiders fearlessly scuttled about carrying small rocks. If anyone got too close to the spider, it would toss a stone, flipping it over its back with its hind legs. They were fearless spiders, lords of the sand. Gallen saw no birds.

A stiff gale blew from the sea; soon it began driving water over the beach. At last they reached a stony ridge—a metallic green expanse of sculpted limestone like a chimney, flat on top. The ground here was rocky, thick with tide pools.

Gallen and Orick climbed one steeple of pale limestone, looked southeast. In the distance they saw a city built on stilts, but just below them a group of four children were hunting in the tide pools. The children had red skin and were so long of leg that they looked like cranes as they waded through the pools. They had tied colorful rags into their hair, and they wore bright tunics.

With them was a beast, striped with gold and brown scales. It had large carnivorous teeth and used its tail to balance on its strong back legs. Its front legs were small and heavily clawed. Gallen recognized the creature as a dinosaur, some type of raptor. On its back was an ornate leather saddle. Gallen watched the children and their dinosaur hunt. The beast would run through tidal pools, splashing, using a bony crest near its nose to push over heavy rocks. The children would then leap in with capture sticks and scoop up large, yellow lobsters. Some of these they put in a sack, others they fed to their pet.

At last a small child noticed Gallen's shadow on the ground and looked up. She smiled and waved, pointed at Gallen. The other children glanced at him, then returned to hunting lobsters.

Gallen and Orick climbed back down, and the group made their way around the ridge. The children were just fishing their bag of lobsters from the water. An older boy, perhaps ten, greeted them and asked their destination. Veriasse said that they were heading to the city, and the children seemed happy to see visitors.

The two smallest children were eager to announce the strangers. The children mounted the dinosaur and headed toward the city in the distance, letting the dinosaur run in a long, loping gait. Soon they had nearly raced out of sight. The city, six miles distant, rose from the ground like some vast collection of mushrooms.

Gallen and the others walked through a maze of stony tide pools as an afternoon thunderstorm brewed, until they reached the city. They climbed a wide, winding stairway, like the stem of a mushroom.

When they reached the top, the terrain was uneven, like rolling hills. Small clusters of cement domes made up the homes. No glass was in the windows, no doors in the doorways. Apparently the temperatures here remained warm all year, and no annoying insects flew about. Each doorway led out to a wide parapet where people sat and cooked at communal fires and listened to music. Atop the dome houses were lush gardens.

Everynne removed her mask and pulled back the hood that veiled her face, walking into the city undisguised. The people came out on their verandas to cheer her entrance to the city with loud whistles. Gallen looked at Veriasse, wondering why Everynne was so bold here, and Veriasse explained. "Here on Cyannesse, the dronon are but a distant threat. We are over forty thousand light-years from the world of Fale, well behind our battle lines with the Dronon Empire. Their warships will not reach here for many years. Still, the people here have heard of our long war, and they know Everynne for what she is."

So it was that by early afternoon, Gallen found himself in the ancient city of Dinchee by the Sea of Unperturbed Meditation on Cyannesse, and there tasted the peace that had once been the rule among Everynne's people.

That evening there was music and feasting in the city of Dinchee, on the city's uppermost tier. The suns went down in a blaze of gold, and a cool wind blew thunderheads across the wide ocean. Children roasted whole lobsters over cooking stones and brought them to the guests on great heaping trays, along with melons and roasted nuts and tubers. Gallen could not identify all that he ate, but he ate to his fill, then lay back on the grass with his mouth open, letting the wind play over his face.

Out over the gardens, three youths played mandolins and guitars while a young woman sang. Everynne sat beside them listening, while Veriasse sat beside an old Tharrin woman who insisted on being called only Grandmother, a silver-haired matriarch with small bones and a beauty undiminished by age. She sat on the stones, her long legs folded out to the sides. She wore an ancient mantle that was made of brass-colored plates with ornate symbols of knowledge. The young people of her city served her with great deference.

As Gallen sat under the oncoming night, he saw that these people were not rich. They did not have great stores of food, but instead harvested from the sea and from their gardens. Their entertainment was simple. Shops did not crowd the plazas, as they had on Fale. Everyone wore tunics in bright colors. But if they were not rich in worldly goods, they had enough, and they seemed rich in peace. Their children were strong and smart and happy.

Veriasse talked softly with Grandmother, asking for a couple of airbikes and provisions. The old woman smiled and nodded, saying that they had few airbikes. Yet she granted all of his requests.

Veriasse stopped talking for a moment, looked at Gallen, Maggie, and Orick. "Our three friends," he told Grandmother, "would like to rest here, taking refuge with your people until they can return home."

"They will be welcome," Grandmother said. "As friends of the Grand Lady, we will be glad to attend to them."

"Pay no attention to that old rooster," Gallen said quickly. He nodded at Veriasse. "I'll be going with Everynne when she leaves."

Veriasse shook his head. "I have given it some thought, and I've decided that you shall not come. The dronon control the next two planets we shall visit, and frankly, Everynne and I will be less conspicuous without you."

"Have you asked Everynne about this?" Gallen asked.

"No," Veriasse said softly. "I don't think I need to."

"Then I will," Gallen said. He glanced over at the singers. Everynne had been listening to them, but now she had gone. He spotted a flash of blue in the twilight, saw her walking over a small hill among the trees. He got up, made his way through the crowd until he found the trail she had taken. It led down a small gully and off into a miniature woodland where crickets sang in the evening. Of all the things on this planet so far, only the crickets reminded him of home. The path was broad and well-maintained.

He couldn't see Everynne, so he let his mantle tweak his hearing and vision. He moved silently as a mist down the trail, passed a pair of naked lovers rolling in a deep bed of ferns.

After a hundred yards, he reached a railed balcony at the edge of the city. There he found Everynne on a parapet at the forest's edge, watching the suns set. The tide was rushing in over beaches they had negotiated a few hours earlier. The sea had turned coppery orange, and huge white breakers smashed against the limestone rock formations. Beneath the wild, tormented waves, he could see a vast line of green lights.

Everynne stood very quietly. Though she held herself erect, proud, she was so petite that he could have lifted her with one hand. Though her back was to him, he saw tears on her cheek. She shook softly, as if she tried to hold back a wracking sob. "Have you come to watch the torchbearers?" she said, jutting her chin toward the waves and the green lights beneath. "They're beautiful fish. Each bears its own light to hunt by."

Gallen walked up behind her, put his hands on her shoulders. She started a bit, as if she had not expected his touch. Beneath his hands, her muscles were tense, strung tight, so he began kneading them softly.

He wanted to ask permission to follow her, but she seemed so troubled, he could not bear to do so. "I don't want to talk about fish. They aren't important. What are you crying about?" Gallen waited a long moment for an answer.

Everynne shook her head. "Nothing. I just—" She fell silent.

"You are sad," Gallen whispered. "Why?"

Everynne looked off, staring at the sea. "Do you know how old my mother was?" Her voice was so soft, Gallen could hardly hear it over the crashing of breakers.

"A few thousand years," Gallen guessed. She had, after all, been immortal, and Veriasse claimed to have served her for six thousand years.

"And do you know how old I am?"

"Eighteen, twenty?" Gallen asked.

"Three, almost," Everynne answered. Gallen did a double take. "Veriasse cloned me after my mother died. He raised me in a force vat on Shintol, to speed my growth. He couldn't risk that I might have a normal childhood—couldn't take a chance that I might cut myself or break a bone. While I grew in the force vat, he used mantles to teach me—history, ethics, psychology. I feel as if I have learned everything about life, but experienced none of it."

"And in a few days, you fear that your life may end?"

"No—I *know* it will end," Everynne said. "My mother was far older and wiser than I. The dronon had been lurking on her borders for thousands of years. She had millennia to prepare for her battle with them, and still she died. I think my chances of winning are nil. But even if I win, I will be changed. You know what it is to fuse with a personal intelligence, the wonder and pain that all burst in on you in a moment. But an omni-mind is the size of a planet and stores more information than a trillion personal intelligences combined. I am . . . less than an insect compared to it. My mother and it grew to become one, and when her body died, it would download her personality into her clones. It stores everything that was my mother—all her thoughts, her dreams, her memories. And if I fuse with it, I will no longer be me in any way that matters. Her experiences will overwhelm me, and it will be as if I never existed."

"You would still be you," Gallen said, hoping to comfort her. "You wouldn't lose that." But he knew he was wrong. As far as the omni-mind was concerned, Everynne was just a shell, a template of the Great Judge Semarritte, waiting to be filled. In the space of a moment, Everynne would grow, learn more than he or billions of other people could ever hope to know. Yet her personality, her essence, would be swept away as something of no importance.

She turned and looked into his eyes, smiled sadly. "You're right, of course," she said, as if to ease his mind. The wind blew her dark hair; Gallen looked into her dark blue eyes.

"Maybe," Gallen offered, "someone else could take your place. There are other Tharrin. Perhaps Grandmother would reign in your behalf."

Everynne shook her head. "She is a grand lady, but she would not take my place. A Lord Judge must earn that position, but Grandmother could not earn that title. All of the Tharrin knew of Semarritte's plan to return as a clone. I sometimes wonder if I am worthy to become a Servant of All, but the Tharrin treat me as if I am but an extension of Semarritte. They say that once I join with the omni-mind, my own short life will have meant nothing. I will be Semarritte." She paused, took a deep breath. "I want to thank you for what you did today."

"What do you mean?"

"When you pulled the incendiary rifle on us. I'm glad that you're not the kind of person who would follow me blindly. Too few people question my motives."

"Do you feel that your motives need questioning?"

"Of course!" Everynne fell silent for a moment; Gallen heard someone laugh in the distance. It was growing dark, and Gallen felt he should go, but Everynne was standing close to him, only a hand's breadth away. She gazed into his face, leaned forward and kissed him, wrapped her arms around him.

"Question my motives," she whispered fiercely. Her lips were warm, inviting.

Gallen took her request literally. "You're afraid that you will die soon," Gallen whispered, and he kissed her back. She leaned into him, her firm breasts crushing into his chest.

"I think I'm falling in love with you," she whispered. "I want to know what it's like for *me* to be in love."

Gallen considered the way that she had said it, pulled back. "Veriasse was your mother's escort. Was he also her lover?"

Everynne nodded, and suddenly Gallen understood. Once the omni-mind downloaded its memories, Everynne would become Semarritte in every way. Veriasse was not just trying to restore the Great Lord Judge to his people. He was rebuilding his wife. "He has never touched me, never made love to me," Everynne said. "But I can see how I torment him. I'm but a child to him, a shadow of the woman he loves. Sometimes he watches me, and I can see how his desire tears at him."

Everynne leaned close for a long moment. Gallen could feel her heart hammering against his chest. "Give me this night," she said. "Whatever comes later, let me stay with you tonight."

Gallen looked into her wide eyes, felt the heat of her body next to his. "I know you want me," she said. "I've felt the intensity of your gaze from the moment we first met. I want you, too."

Gallen found himself shaking, stricken. She was indeed the most beautiful, most perfect woman he had ever seen, and it hurt to know that they could never be together. He could not deny what he felt. If she asked him to become her Lord Escort, fight the dronon in her behalf, he would gladly do so, lay his life on the line day after day, hour after hour.

Yet she could only promise him one night of love. Everynne pulled off her own robe and undergarments, stood in the dusk and let him hold her. Her breasts were small but pert. Her hips were shapely, strong. She began breathing deeply, pulled off Gallen's robe, then pulled him down to the deep sweet grass there on the parapet, and together they made love long and slow.

Afterward, they lay together naked. Down in the sea below, the waves covered the limestone and the torchbearer fish lit the ocean in pale green. Above them, the clouds passed and stars sprinkled the sky, until everything was light. The warm winds blew through the trees, and Gallen felt peace inside.

Everynne cuddled closer, and they slept awhile. When he woke, the winds were beginning to cool. The great school of torchbearer fish had departed, and the night draped over them like a tent. Gallen kept his arms wrapped around her protectively. He could not help but think that this was the beginning and the end of their love. They had sealed it with one, small, nearly insignificant act. Now, the future lay before them, and no matter what happened, tomorrow the winds of change would blast them apart like two leaves scattered in a storm. The sky above them was so vast, so nearly infinite in size, and it seemed to Gallen that they were lying naked while the infinite, appalling darkness prepared to descend.

Thus it was that at last Gallen looked up to see Veriasse standing in the shadows at the head of the trail. Gallen startled, tried to sit up and throw his clothes on in one move, but Veriasse raised a finger to his lips.

"Careful, don't wake her," he said, his voice ragged. "Throw her robe over her, keep her warm."

Gallen did so, slid into his undergarments, then his own robes. He watched Veriasse from the corner of his eye, half afraid that the older man would attack him, but Veriasse seemed more hurt than angry. He kept his arms protectively folded over his stomach and turned away, began walking slowly up the path.

Gallen finished dressing and followed Veriasse. The old man walked with his back straight, tense. Gallen needed to break the silence, so he said softly, "I'm sorry, I—"

Veriasse whirled, stared hard at Gallen. "No apologies are necessary," he said at last, with hurt in his voice. "Everynne obviously has chosen you over me. I suppose it is only natural. She is a young woman, and you're an attractive man. I, ah, ah . . ." He raised his hands, let them drop in consternation.

"I'm sorry," Gallen said, unable to think of anything more.

Veriasse advanced on him, pointed his finger. "You shut your mouth! You know nothing of sorrow! I've loved her for six thousand years. I love her as you could only hope to love her!"

"No!" Gallen shouted, and suddenly a rage burned in him. "You loved her mother, you miserable bastard! Everynne is *not* Semarritte! Everynne may be willing to do your will, she may be willing to wear the omni-mind for the good of her people, but if she puts it on, you will have destroyed her. You will have murdered your own daughter in order to regain the woman you love!"

Veriasse's eyes blazed and his nostrils flared. Gallen realized that his mantle was heightening his vision. Gallen's own muscles tightened and when Veriasse swung, Gallen ducked under the attack, sought to remain calm, emotionally detached. He punched at Veriasse's belly, but the old man dodged, kicked at Gallen's chest.

Suddenly they were both moving, spinning in a blur of fists and feet in the darkness. Veriasse was like a ghost, impossible to touch. Guided by his mantle, Gallen swung and kicked in a steady barrage of attacks that would have overwhelmed any dozen ruffians back on Tihrglas, yet never did a blow land with any force. Sometimes Veriasse would turn a blow, and in one brief portion of a second, Gallen's hopes soared. But after three minutes, he had not landed a blow, and he was beginning to tire. He knew that Veriasse would soon attack.

Gallen stepped back from the fight, took a defensive stance. Veriasse was not winded. "I wore that mantle for six thousand years, and would be wearing it now if I didn't fear that it would jeopardize my right to fight in ritual combat," he said. "I taught it most of what it knows."

Then he leapt for the attack. Gallen dodged the first few swings and kicks, but Veriasse threw a head punch that Gallen tried to deflect with his wrist. The old man was far stronger than Gallen had ever imagined, and the blow felt as if it would snap Gallen's arm. The punch grazed his chin, sent him sprawling.

Gallen leapt back to his feet, let the mantle guide his actions. Veriasse began a deadly dance, throwing kicks and punches in combinations that were designed to leave a victim defenseless. Gallen's mantle began whispering to him—this is a fourteen-kick combination—flashing images of what would happen in his mind quickly so that Gallen could escape the final consequences.

After forty seconds, Veriasse leapt back, apparently winded, studied Gallen appreciatively for a second, then leapt into combat once more. He swung and kicked in varying combinations so fast that Gallen's mantle was overwhelmed; Gallen had to fend blindly, retreating through the woods. Veriasse was swinging and leaping, his fists and hands in Gallen's face so much that Gallen was sure he would go for a low kick. But suddenly Veriasse vaulted into the air and kicked for his chest. Gallen reached up to turn the kick with his arm, but the old man shifted in midair, aiming the kick at the blocking arm.

The blow landed with a snapping sound on the ganglia in Gallen's elbow, numbing the entire arm. A second kick landed as Veriasse dropped, hitting Gallen's ribs hard enough to knock the wind from him. Veriasse twisted as he fell through the air, and a third kick grazed Gallen's head, knocking off his mantle.

Gallen hit the ground, gasping for breath, and glared up at Veriasse. He would be no match for the old man without a mantle. Even with a mantle, he'd been no match for the old man.

Veriasse stood over him, gasping. Sweat poured down Gallen's face; without the mantle, he could see little in the darkness, but he could make out Veriasse's blazing eyes. Gallen held his aching arm, found that he could only move his numb fingers with difficulty.

"I don't need you," Veriasse said. "You are not coming with us."

"I'm sure Everynne will have something to say about that," Gallen said.

"And I'm equally sure that I will not listen to her."

"Just as you've never listened to her?" Gallen asked. "You send her to her death and think you can ignore her cries?"

"You find that appalling?" Veriasse said roughly, his voice suddenly choked.

"Yes," Gallen said. "I find *you* appalling."

The old man nodded his head weakly, stood by a tree and suddenly grabbed it for support, looking about absently as if he had lost something. "Well, well, so be it. I find myself appalling. There is an apt saying among my people, 'Of all men, old politicians are the most damned, for they must live out their days in a world of their own creation.'"

Gallen was surprised that Veriasse did not argue, did not defend his actions. "Is it so easy for you to be appalling?"

"What I'm doing," Veriasse said, straightening his shoulder, "appalls even me. . . . But, I can think of nothing else to do. Gallen, an omni-mind takes thousands of years to construct. Once it is built, it is meant to be used by only one person throughout the ages. If another person tries to wield it, the intelligence cannot function to full capacity. We *must* win back that omni-mind! And though I wish it were not so, whoever deigns to use it will be consumed in the process. I knew this when I first cloned Everynne. I knew she would be destroyed. Somehow, the sacrifice seemed more . . . bearable at the time." Veriasse turned away, his breath coming deep and ragged. "Gallen, Gallen—how did I get into this mess?"

Veriasse needed a way out of his predicament. He stood for a moment, his back turned to Gallen. "What if you get killed in your match with the dronon?" Gallen asked. "What will happen to Everynne?"

"She may be killed also."

"But, if I remember your words correctly, that is not what the dronon do to their own Golden Queens who lose the combat. Instead, the losing queen is only marred and may never compete in the contest again."

"True," Veriasse agreed, "sometimes. But the decision whether to mar or destroy the queen comes at the whim of the victor. I fear that the dronon would not spare Everynne. They murdered all of the Tharrin they could catch in this sector after the invasion, then obliterated their genetic matter."

"I am coming with you to Dronon," Gallen said. "If you lose, perhaps I can convince the dronon to only mar Everynne. Of all possible outcomes, this one alone gives her some hope. She would be free to live her own life."

Veriasse looked down at Gallen, raised an eyebrow. "You would risk everything on this one chance to save her? It sounds like a noble gamble," he admitted. Veriasse paused, drew a breath, and he suddenly straightened, as if a load had been lifted from his shoulders. "I will welcome your company, then. And if I die in the contest, I can only hope that you will succeed in bringing Everynne away safely. She is a great treasure, the last of her kind in this part of the galaxy."

Veriasse helped Gallen to his feet. Gallen's arm and ribs ached. Veriasse said heavily, "I would like to ask you an important favor. When I gave you my mantle, I did so with ulterior motives. Gallen, I have seen tapes of the Lord Escort's battles. His name is Xim, and among the Lord Escorts, he is the most capable warrior in many generations. I do not think I have a great chance to survive this fight. If I die, I want you to be my successor. Would you become the next Lord Escort?"

"Me?" Gallen asked, suddenly aware that Veriasse had made a complete turnabout. "But I'm no one. Certainly you have better warriors than me."

"We created the guardians to fight for us," Veriasse said, "and so we have not needed human warriors. You wear my mantle, and in time, given a few years, it will teach you. You could become as great a warrior as any I might hope to find."

Gallen considered the request. He was tempted to say yes. If Everynne died, another like her would be created, and her need would be just as great. Yet if he promised to do as Veriasse asked, he would be bound to labor for many years with perhaps nothing but an ignominious death as a reward. He recalled his oath, that when his heart was hot to aid another, he would always do so.

"As you wish," Gallen said.

Thirteen

As night fell, Maggie and Orick sat talking to Grandmother. The old woman let the children build a bonfire with branches from the nearby woods, and Grandmother asked Maggie many questions about her home in Clere.

Maggie told Grandmother of her work in the inn, how she cleaned and scrubbed and cooked all day. She told how her mother died of sickness after giving birth, and of her father and brothers, who had all drowned when their small fishing boat capsized. It seemed to Maggie that Tihrglas was a cold and bitter place, where she had felt cramped, forced into a corner, and as she talked, Maggie realized that she did not want to go back. To live here on Cyannesse, even to live on Fale as a free woman, would be better.

Yet when she finished telling Grandmother about Tihrglas, the old woman smiled and nodded sagely. "We are like you, in that we keep no android servants. This lets us serve one another and take pride in our work. A simple life is best," she said, as if she were agreeing that, yes, life on Tihrglas must be peaceful.

Maggie wanted to growl and scream in the old woman's face, but

Orick chimed in with, "Och, well said! I'll drink to that!" and he lifted a goblet of wine in his great paws and poured it down his throat.

The wind was blowing through the trees, and it sounded like the wind that blew through Tihrglas on a summer's night, warm and comforting with the taste of the sea in it. It was the same kind of wind that had lulled Maggie to sleep as a child, and she felt a pang of longing, not for that damned Tihrglas, but for her childhood, for the blissful ignorance she felt before she'd heard of the dronon, and Maggie realized that if she had never heard of the dronon, even if she'd never left home, she would probably have grown old and been content. "Yes," Maggie agreed at last, "a simple life is best."

Veriasse had gone out to look for Gallen and Everynne quite awhile ago, and Maggie was growing worried. Veriasse had said that there were factions who would fight Everynne. Maggie wondered if such factions existed here on Cyannesse, among these seemingly peaceful people.

"I think I'll go look for Gallen," Maggie said, and she went uphill, past the singers who sat around a small fire.

By now the stars were out. A red moon was rising and the ocean had slid in under the city. With the wind, Maggie felt pleasantly cool, and she strained her senses as she entered the woods. She found dozens of trails and had no idea which to take, but soon she found one that led to the railing looking out over the ocean. There were benches by the railing, and a path that followed the rail around the city. Maggie imagined that if she just followed the path, she would find Gallen and the others sitting on some bench, talking quietly.

She grabbed the iron rail and used it as a guide, walking through the forest. At the third intersection to another path, she still had not found Gallen and Veriasse, but just as she was ready to pass, she looked down in the cinnabar moonlight, saw Everynne lying in the grass, dead. Her robe was draped over the body, as if to hide it.

Maggie gave a startled cry, rushed to Everynne's side and pulled off the robe. Everynne was naked. She opened her eyes, looked up.

"What?" Everynne said, sitting up. She looked around in a sleepy daze. "Where's Gallen?"

Maggie could think of nothing to say. Her heart was hammering and her head spun. "You slept with him, didn't you?"

Everynne crawled through the grass, picked up her underclothing and put it on, watched Maggie without saying anything. She began to put on her robe.

"You took him, just because you could!" Maggie said.

"On many worlds," Everynne said, "men and women sleep together whenever they want. It means nothing."

"Yeah," Maggie said. "Well, where I come from, it means something, and you knew that!"

"I didn't *want* to hurt you," Everynne said.

Hurt me? Maggie wondered. You've crushed me. Maggie found her heart pounding. She didn't know who to be maddest at, Gallen or Everynne, but she knew they were both to blame. "Maybe you didn't want to hurt me," Maggie said. "But you knew that this *would* hurt me, and you did it anyway. You bought your pleasure by giving me pain. Think about that when you're the Servant of All."

Maggie turned and stormed away. Everynne called for her to come back. Maggie refused to listen.

Maggie did not sleep well that night. She returned to the fire, stayed up late listening to the music of this world while waiting for Gallen, but he didn't return. Veriasse ambled from the woods later. Maggie asked if he had found Gallen. He nodded soberly, saying only, "Gallen and Everynne are talking. They wish to be alone."

When the music ended and the crowds dispersed, Grandmother conducted Maggie to a large but modestly furnished room, where Maggie bathed in warm water and lay on a soft bed to sleep, with Orick sprawled at her feet.

The longer Gallen and Everynne stayed away together, the more despair tugged at Maggie. She knew she had no claim on Gallen, they weren't promised to one another, yet she could not help but feel stricken to the core. Two years earlier, when Maggie's father and brothers had all drowned, a horrible sense of loss had overwhelmed her. But somehow it was less than what she suffered now. To watch family die caused more grief than Maggie had ever believed she would suffer again.

But when Gallen slept with Everynne, Maggie didn't just grieve from the loss but agonized with the numbing realization that no matter what she did, she could never match up to Everynne. Maggie could love Gallen, serve him, offer everything she was and ever hoped to become, but she wasn't good enough.

Part of her wanted to be angry at Everynne, to hate the woman for stealing Gallen. But the more she thought about it, the less Maggie found that possible. She had been jealous of Everynne from the first. Everynne was beautiful and kind, and in her own way she bore an air of profound loss and loneliness. It was hard for Maggie to resent someone who was in such pain.

A part of Maggie wanted to be angry with Gallen, but she kept reminding herself that he had never promised her anything. In the end, his loving Everynne seemed inevitable.

In the morning, Maggie stayed in bed late, hoping to get some sleep. Orick left for breakfast quietly, then returned.

"Grandmother and Everynne want to see you," Orick said. "They have gifts. Everynne and Veriasse are planning to leave. They want to say good-bye."

Maggie lay on the bed, her eyes gritty from lack of sleep. She could not think straight. "No. I'm not coming."

"Are you sure?" Orick asked. "They have some nice gifts." Maggie's curiosity was piqued, but she didn't want to let it show. "And there's something else. I guess I'd better break the news to you myself. Gallen is going with Everynne and Veriasse."

"He is?" Maggie asked, pulling the covers down so that she could look at Orick. The bear stood on all fours at the head of the bed, his nose only inches from her face so that he could sniff her as he spoke, the way that bears will. She could smell fruit and dirt on his moist breath.

"No, I can't go," Maggie said.

"That's a shame." Orick turned away. "Gallen will be hurt that you didn't say good-bye."

"He doesn't know what it means to hurt," Maggie said.

"Hmmm . . ." Orick grumbled. "I suppose you're referring to what happened last night? There's a lot of folks out there giving guilty looks and shuffling their feet. Even a bear can figure out what's going on." Maggie didn't answer. "Och, what are you thinking, girl? Gallen loves you! How can you believe otherwise?"

"He loves Everynne," Maggie said.

"You humans are so narrow!" Orick replied. "He loves you both. Now, if you were a bear, you wouldn't get so all bound up in trivial affairs. You would come into heat, go find some handsome young man if one was available—or an ugly old geezer if nothing better could be had—and you would invite him to perform his favorite duty in life. Then you would be done with it. None of this moaning and moping and wondering if someone loves you."

"And what if someone else wanted your lover?" Maggie asked.

"Why, that's easy!" Orick said. "You wait until he's done, then invite him over. Just because a bear is interested in one female today, doesn't mean he won't want another tomorrow."

Maggie found herself thinking of evolution, such a new concept, yet one her Guide had taught her much about. Human mothers and bear mothers had different needs. A female bear didn't have to spend twenty years raising her cubs the way a human did, and bears ate so much that having a male bear around to compete for food just didn't make sense.

"Of course," Orick offered, "if you're in a hurry to get a lover, you could just go bite the competition on the ass, chase her away."

"I can't do that, either. They're leaving together. Besides, it's not that easy with people."

"Sure it is," Orick said. "If you love Gallen, you'll fight for what you want. Get mad! Oh, hell, what am I talking to you for? Don't you realize that Gallen made his choice long ago when he rescued you from Lord Karthenor?"

Maggie watched the bear trudge away, his belly swaying from side to side. "Stupid people," he grumbled. "Sometimes I don't know why I bother. Maybe I've had things backward. Did my mother tell me to eat sheep and talk to people, or was it eat people and talk to sheep?" He wandered off.

Maggie tossed on the bed, angry at herself. Everynne, Veriasse, and Gallen would be leaving, and there was a strong possibility that they would be killed. Yet Maggie was lying here pouting. She steeled her nerves, threw off her covers.

Outside, the bright morning suns rose in an amber haze. The water had dropped during the night, revealing a vast beach, wet and gleaming. Already, the children were running out over the sand toward the rocky tidal pools to hunt.

Maggie found Gallen and the others just outside her door, sitting on stone benches in the plaza. Grandmother had three airbikes sitting in the open—machines that were all motor and chrome with a set of stabilizing wings both fore and aft. At Grandmother's feet sat several packages wrapped in silver foil.

"Ah, Maggie, I am so glad you made it," Grandmother said, clapping her wrinkled hands. "You are just in time for gifts." The old woman smiled so graciously that Maggie could not help but believe Grandmother took great pleasure in her company. Indeed, they had spoken together for a long time the previous evening, but Maggie had become so distracted afterward that the pleasantness had been driven from her mind.

Grandmother looked through her packages. "First," she said softly, "I have a gift for Lady Everynne, who is already rich beyond anything I can offer. Still, I was thinking last night that you will be going to fight the dronon, who esteem their Golden Queen higher than any other." Maggie looked at the old woman in surprise. She had forgotten that, as a Tharrin, Grandmother had been apprised of Semarritte's plans. "Since you will be our Golden Queen, you must look the part. I have for you some golden clothes and a mantle of gold." She brought out two packages. Everynne unwrapped them.

The outfit included long gloves and boots, stockings and a tunic, all in brilliant gold. The small mantle was made of golden ringlets and fit over her hair. "You will find that the gloves and clothing are very tough," the old woman said. "Almost as tough as symbiotic armor. Often, a dronon queen will defend herself if a Lord Escort chooses to do more than mar her. If you are forced to defend yourself, these clothes will help protect you. In addition, we have bonded a selenium matrix into the fists of the gloves and toes of the boots. A solid blow to a dronon body will let you crack its exoskeleton."

Everynne thanked Grandmother, and the old woman turned to Veriasse. "For our Lord Protector, I doubt that we have anything on our world that could match the weapons you already bear. And so, I give you a special hope. It is a small thing, but perhaps it will carry you through a dark time." She handed him a small package, and he opened it. The package contained a crystal vial. Veriasse took out the glass stopper.

Immediately a heavenly scent wafted through the air of the open courtyard, and Maggie was filled with such enthusiasm and a boundless sense of strength that she wanted to leap from her seat with a battle cry. Veriasse suddenly seemed to become a younger man—all the cares and worries that so creased his brow melted away. He threw back his head and laughed deep and easy. In that moment, Maggie had no doubt that

Veriasse would slay the Lords of the Swarm. He was a powerful man; he could not fail.

Veriasse stoppered the vial, yet Maggie's sense of boundless fervor was slow to diminish. From Maggie's work with the aberlains, she knew that the vial must contain an extract of simple proteins—the chemical components of enthusiasm to act upon the hypothalamus, along with some type of airborne delivery system so that "hope" could be absorbed through the sinus membranes as a person breathed.

And yet, even having some idea how the hope was borne, she couldn't help but admire the craftsmanship inherent in the gift. The artist had combined the hope with some exotic perfume and had probably taken great pains to mix the right proteins so that he could elicit the perfect response.

Grandmother looked over the little group. "For Gallen, the Lady Everynne has asked a special thing. He once asked for eternal life in return for his service. And even though he rescinded his request, he has more than earned his reward. She would like to begin payment." She lifted a small packet from the ground, handed it to Gallen. "Inside, you will find six tablets containing a full set of nanodoctors. They will help heal your wounds, slow your aging, cure all ills. You have only to swallow the tablets. You will not be immortal, of course. You can be killed. But before you leave here today, we will take a template of your intellect and gather gene specimens. Then, if you should die, we can build you again."

Maggie knew something of how valuable a gift this would be. Even in Everynne's world, such things were reserved only for the most deserving. Yet Gallen took the small package, hefted it, then glanced into Maggie's eyes. He tossed the package to her. "I want you to have this. I wanted it for you all along."

Maggie sat with the package in her lap, too surprised to reply.

"Ah, a gift of true love," Grandmother said, and Maggie realized that it was true. Gallen would only give such a treasure to someone he cherished.

"I don't know what to say," she offered. "Thank you."

Grandmother patted Maggie's knee. "I have something for you, but it will not be ready until tomorrow."

Maggie thanked her, and Grandmother turned to Orick. "And now, for the bear. I have considered many things, but as I talked to you last night, of all the people I have ever met, you seem to be the most self-sufficient. You yourself admit that there is nothing you want or need, although you grumble more than anyone else I know. So, I put the question to you: what one thing would you ask of me?"

Orick stepped forward and licked his lips. "Well, you have a lot of nice things here. The food is good, the music and the company is even better—but I'm just a simple bear from the woods, and the land provides for my needs. I think if there were one thing I'd ask for, it wouldn't be yours to give." He looked at Veriasse and Everynne. "I didn't start this journey because I wanted to, but I'd sort of like to tag along with Everynne and see it through to the end."

Gallen and Veriasse looked at Everynne, letting her make the decision. Maggie suspected that even Everynne had no idea how much this would mean to the bear. For days now, Orick had been showing her a special kind of devotion, and Maggie suspected that as unseemly as it might appear, the poor bear was as lovesick for the woman as he could get.

"You've been a good friend, Orick," Everynne said. "But if I were to be a true friend in return, I would deny your request. I've tried to put a calm face on when speaking of it, but this last portion of our trip will be extremely dangerous."

"Gallen and I have been in a few tight spots before," Orick said. "And I've always been right there at his side."

"Please, don't ask this of me." Everynne's eyes misted over. "Orick, I love you. I couldn't endure the thought that you might get hurt on my account."

Orick watched her with longing in his brown eyes, turned away. "All right, then," he said. "If you don't want me. I'd probably just get in the way." He turned and began loping back toward Maggie's room.

"Wait!" Everynne said, and she rushed to him. She got down on her knees and scratched the thick fur under Orick's ears, then looked into his eyes and said lustily, "If you were a human, or I were a bear, wouldn't we have a *fine* time?"

She kissed him on the snout, and Orick's red tongue flicked out, licked her forehead. Orick gave a sharp little roar of grief and lunged away to Maggie's room.

Everynne stood watching after him a moment. Veriasse said, "He'll be okay. Male bears get used to being sent away by females." He did not say it to be unkind, merely stated the fact. Young cubs never left their mother voluntarily. Instead, she chased them off. And later, when a male mated, he would usually run with the female until she chased him away.

Everynne nodded wistfully while still watching after Orick.

Grandmother glanced at Everynne. "Do not feel bad. You've given him the thing he most wants: your love. It is something I could not give him, and he will treasure it always."

"Can you give him something more?" Everynne asked. "Will you make him a locket with my image inside? Something to remember me by."

"Of course," Grandmother answered.

Everynne and the others prepared to leave. Veriasse began teaching Gallen the basics of riding an airbike. Maggie found it odd that Gallen didn't know how to ride the thing. She realized that the mantle she wore must have been teaching her in her sleep, for Maggie understood the most intimate workings of the bike, and as she listened to Gallen rev the thrusters, she heard them whine just a bit, suggesting that a turbine wasn't properly lubricated. She considered pulling out the toolkit stored under the airbike's seat, just to tinker.

Everynne went to get her pack, and Maggie went to get Gallen's. Orick was lying at the foot of the bed. Maggie rummaged through Gallen's pack until she found Gallen's defective key to the Maze of Worlds. He'd placed it in his old black leather money purse, drawing the string tight. Maggie removed the key, glanced around the room, looking for something of similar size to put in the key's place. In one corner was a potted plant with purpling flowers. She removed a flat stone from the plant's container, placed it in the purse, and returned the purse to the pack.

Orick watched the whole affair, then said, "What are you doing?"

"You want to go with Everynne, and I want to go with Gallen. All we need to follow them is a key."

"Do you know where they are going?"

"Veriasse was looking over his travel plans last night at the campfire. I watched over his shoulder. My mantle has stored the coordinates of all the gates but the last. We should be able to find them easily."

"But Veriasse said that using a defective key is risky," Orick warned, shaking his head.

"Everything we've done has been risky," Maggie shot back. "I'm not going to let that stop me now." Her mantle could not tell her specifically how the key worked, but obviously an electronic signal unlocked the gate and gave it the coded information on how to make a jump. True, the key was defective, but they hadn't been hurt in that first jump. Maggie decided that the key time/location send coordinates were probably out of synch with the gate destination decoder. The gate key would simply perform as it had before—sending them back in time as they traveled.

She looked at Orick sharply. "We both know that Gallen and Veriasse think we've been as helpful as a pair of mallards on this trip, but even they might need our talents. Are you coming with me, or are you just going to let the woman you love walk out of your life forever?"

"I'm with you," Orick answered.

"Good," Maggie said. "Now do me a favor and get out of here. Gallen is going to be coming in for his pack in a minute, and I want some time alone with him."

"Always being nagged by women," Orick grumbled as he left the room. "Doesn't matter if they are human or bears, they're all the same."

Maggie stood by the foot of the bed, waited for Gallen to come in. She found her heart pounding, tried to compose something to say, but nothing came to mind. All too soon, he stood in the doorway, a circle of morning light silhouetting him. In his black robes, weapons at hand, the mantle of a Lord Protector on his head, he looked somehow different, strange. No one on Tihrglas had ever worn such clothing, and Gallen seemed to stand taller in his costume, walk in more of a rolling gait. This trip was changing him, leaving an indelible mark, just as it was changing her.

"I'm surprised that you, too, didn't ask to come with us," Gallen said after a long moment.

"You wouldn't have let me," Maggie said.

"How do you know?"

"You protect people for a living. You're always watching out for others. You must know that the best way to protect me is to leave me out of harm's way."

Gallen smiled weakly. "I'm glad you understand." He walked over to her, took her by the shoulders and kissed her firmly, passionately. "Everynne told me that you know what happened last night. Can you ever forgive me?"

Maggie was confused, unsure how to answer. She thought—or at least she wanted to believe—that he really did love her. Some things pointed to it—his protectiveness, his tenderness to her now. Yet she couldn't accept that he would sleep with Everynne one night, then come to her in the morning and try to pretend that nothing had changed. She slapped his face, hard, and it barely moved him, so she punched him in the stomach. "Don't you ever do that to me again!" she hissed. "Do you understand me? Don't you ever put me in second place again!"

Gallen nodded, the lines of his face set in hard angles. She couldn't read what he was thinking. "I know that an explanation will just sound like an excuse, but in all likelihood, by tomorrow night Everynne will either be dead or else so . . . changed that she will be at least as good as dead to me. She wanted something last night that only I could give. I cannot be sorry for what we did, though it pains me terribly to know how it must hurt you. What Everynne and I did last night—that was just saying good-bye." He considered for a moment, then said, "I will never put you in second place again."

Maggie studied his face. When Gallen O'Day took an oath, he'd keep it or die trying. She knew that much about him.

"Just promise to come back to me," she said. Gallen reached out to her, stroked her jaw with one gloved hand. He made no further promises. She fell against his chest and began weeping. Gallen wrapped his arms around her and hugged her until it was time to go.

Orick spent much of the day sleeping, worrying about Everynne. He wanted to leave immediately, but Maggie insisted that they wait until dark to sneak away. Maggie and Orick were both exhausted, so he tried to rest.

In spite of his nervousness, he enjoyed the hospitality of the Cyannesse that day. Once again, the day ended clear and beautiful. He and Maggie ate a sumptuous dinner, and Grandmother announced afterward that an actor wanted them to watch a play he had written in their honor.

So when the campfires had burned low, they watched the actor perform the story of an old man who became lost in a magical wood filled with wise beasts.

The old man worked for a long time, searching for a path home, but by the time the beasts helped him discover that path, he desired only to stay in the forest forever. The old man was tremendously funny, and Orick enjoyed his performance, but the thing that impressed him most was the scenery. The play was set in an open amphitheater, and when a scene changed, an entire forest would grow up as needed, or a moon would rise and shine down on a glen, or a pool of water would begin lapping where only a moment before there was solid ground. The animals, too—the gossiping deer, the overbearing badger—would appear or disappear as needed.

When the play finished, Orick thought longingly of the woods at home, the sweet mountain grasses, the trout-filled streams. Yet when they got back to their room, Maggie asked Orick, "Did you enjoy the play?"

"Och, it was a grand play," Orick said honestly. "My favorite character was the fox, most amusing."

"But what of the message of the play? What did you think of it?"

"There was a message?" Orick asked, perplexed.

"Of course there was a message. The actor was asking us to stay. We are the people lost in their magic woods."

"Oh," Orick said. "Are you sure? It only made me homesick, thinking of the woods."

But Maggie seemed sure. She sat on her bed, looking at the box of nanodocs that Gallen had given her, as if wondering whether or not to pack them. Orick asked, "Are you going to eat those?"

"Not yet," she said firmly.

"Why not?"

"Gallen might need them still."

Orick studied her. She seemed deeply occupied. "If he died, would you take them?"

"No. I don't think so." She shoved them into her pack. "You had better get some rest. When the others are asleep, we can go borrow an airbike. There's got to be one somewhere in town."

"That would be stealing," Orick said.

"We'll bring it back, if there's any way we can."

Orick grunted, sniffed the floor and lay down. He envied Gallen. Not every woman would choose to die if her lover died. No bear would ever do such a thing. The sense of romance behind it overwhelmed him until he almost wanted to laugh with glee. Instead, he lay down and rested.

Half an hour later, Maggie grabbed her pack and whispered, "It's time to go." She led him out into the night, under the red moon.

Grandmother sat outside the door, in the moonlight, wearing a deep robe to keep out the night air. "So, you are leaving us so soon?"

"I—" Maggie started. "Please don't try to stop us."

Grandmother smiled, her face wrinkling in the dim light. "I was once young and deeply in love," she said. "And I could never have left the man under these circumstances. Gallen gave me this before he departed." She handed Maggie the black coin purse. "He said there was a gate key in it, so that you could go home, but I found only a rock. It was not hard to guess who had taken the real key."

"What are you going to do about it?" Orick asked.

"Veriasse made a map, telling you how to get home, but I am a Tharrin. I cannot stop you from going where you will, so I shall give you your gifts now," Grandmother answered. She waved toward the shadows of a nearby home. An airbike sat beside the wall, and Grandmother escorted them both across the plaza.

Grandmother hugged Maggie, gave her a piece of bent metal. "I don't have much in the way of weapons," she said. "You are going into dangerous territory, and though I abhor violence, this gun might come in handy. Keep it hidden. Also, I have packed some meals for you to eat on the road. They're in the container under the seat of the airbike."

Maggie stifled her tears, thanked Grandmother graciously.

The old woman reached into the pocket of her robe and pulled out a large golden disk, perhaps a foot long. "And this is for you, Orick," she said. She pushed on a latch. The disk opened, and Orick felt as if he were gazing into another world. Everynne stared out at him, and she smiled and said, "Remember, I'll always love you." Behind her, the oceans of Cyannesse lapped in early morning amber light. Orick could see Everynne perfectly, smell her. He reached up his paw, touching the image, but some soft gel would not let his paw through.

"Everynne had us record this just before she left," Grandmother said. "This memento has captured her voice, her image, her scent. It will stay good for many centuries, and I hope that when you look at it, you will not only be reminded of Everynne, but of all of us here on Cyannesse."

Grandmother closed the disk, and handed it to him. It was slippery in Orick's paws, but he wanted to hold it for awhile. Grandmother hugged him and Maggie goodbye.

Maggie got on the airbike, asked Orick to straddle it. The airbike was obviously not designed for a bear. His legs were too short to reach the foot pads and his tail was crushed at a very uncomfortable angle. Still, he managed to get on, rest his front paws against Maggie's shoulders. But he had to have Maggie put the huge locket in her pack.

Maggie pushed some buttons, and the thrusters roared to life behind his feet. He could feel the heat of the engines, and he feared that his fur would catch fire, but Maggie pressed a throttle and the airbike bucked under their combined weight, then lifted with a kick.

Orick looked back one last time at Grandmother, who stood straight in the darkness and waved good-bye. Maggie applied full acceleration. The airbike whizzed into the night, along the streets of Cyannesse until they reached the winding stair that led down to the beach, then she slowed. Still, the bike seemed to slide down, going faster and faster until they hit the sandy beach, bounced once, and then were off.

They drove straight through the night mists, out over a wide sea. The wind whipped in Orick's face, and lantern fish with their luminous backs lit the water. In some places, it seemed that Maggie and Orick whisked over a road of green light. Tiny silver fish sometimes jumped toward the headlamps of the bike.

After a while, Maggie relaxed, and the machine carried them on until they reached land near dawn. There, Maggie stopped and they ate a short meal, stretched their legs, then rode the airbike up onto a large island, through some rough terrain.

Soon they spotted a gate gleaming gold in the morning. Maggie pulled out the key, thumbed some buttons. Orick was amazed that she could learn how to work such a thing, but ahead of them the gate began glowing white between the arches.

"Where are we going?" Orick asked.

"The planet Bregnel," Maggie shouted. She slowed the airbike until they hit the light wall and were swallowed in the mists.

The airbike skated into profound darkness, into a world where the very air burned Orick's lungs, then lay in them like a clot. The ground was thick with ash, and dead trees raised tortured black branches to claw the sky. Buildings towered above them on every side, like squatting giants, and the buildings too were blackened over every wall.

Maggie coughed, hit the throttle, and the airbike whipped through the night, raising a cloud of ashes as it roared down the empty streets. Here and there on the ground, Orick could see blackened skeletons of small gnomelike humans among the ash, many still wearing their mantles, some holding weapons. It looked as if they had been caught and burned in the midst of a battle. There was no clothing left on the skeletons, no flesh on the ebony bones.

There were no lights in any window, no footprints among the ashes. The world was dead, uninhabited, and by the smell of the air, perhaps uninhabitable.

As bad as the air was, a certain heaviness fell upon Orick as well, as if he weighed more here than he had elsewhere. Upon reflection, he realized that he had felt somehow lighter and stronger upon Cyannesse, but had not noticed it then.

As they hurried forward, Orick saw a corpse on the ground, half covered with ash. Its arms were curled close to its ribs, as if the person had died protecting some great treasure. Orick almost called for Maggie to stop, but as the airbike rushed over the corpse, scattering ashes, Orick looked back. In its hands, the corpse held the bones of an infant.

"What happened here?" Orick bawled, the air burning his lungs.

Maggie shouted back, horror in her voice. "Someone released a Terror on this world."

"Did you know about this?"

"Veriasse told me that the people here were fighting the dronon."

"You mean the dronon killed them?"

Maggie shrugged.

The headlights on the airbike cut a grim alley through the darkness, and Maggie soared over winding roads through a maze of stone buildings. Up ahead, the lights shone over a pair of footprints in the ash.

Someone had lived through this catastrophe. Maggie veered to follow the trail a short way. After two blocks, they came to a dead end in an alley. There, lying in a heap on the ground was the corpse of a small man, his mouth open and gasping. Above him on the wall, he had scratched a message in the ash: "We have won freedom, not for ourselves, but for those who shall follow after."

Maggie stared at the message a moment, then hit the bike's thrusters and rode away. The airbike raced through the city, left the sprawling wastes. The countryside was no better. Fields and crops had been transformed to blackened ash. On the outskirts of town, they saw a red light up the road ahead, and Orick's heart lifted a little, hoping that someone perhaps had survived this devastation.

Instead they came upon a vast machine, a walking crablike city with eight legs and hundreds of gun emplacements sprouting from its back and head. In one lonely turret on the head, a red light gleamed like a malevolent eye. The machine reminded Orick of some giant tick, bristling with strange devices, and Orick knew instinctively that the dronon had created the thing—for no human would have built such a monstrosity.

"What is that?" Orick shouted to be heard above the roar of the airbike, hoping that Maggie's mantle would give them some clue.

"A dronon walking fortress. They built them on their home world to carry their young during their migrations."

"How long must we endure this?" Orick asked. "I can hardly breathe."

"We'll get out fast," Maggie wheezed.

"Maggie, can the Terror still hurt us?"

"If it were going to burn us up," Maggie said, "we'd already be dead by now."

After that, they did not speak. Maggie revved the thrusters, giving the bike its full throttle, and they plowed ahead. It took a great effort to breathe. Orick began gasping; his lungs starved for fresh air. He felt insufferably hot, and the world began to spin. He feared that he might fall from the bike, so he clung to Maggie. She reached up and patted his paw, comforting him. Orick closed his eyes, concentrated only on breathing. He tried holding his breath to save his lungs from the burning air, but then he would become dizzy and have to gasp all over again.

It became a slow torture, and he kept wishing that he would faint, fall from the bike and just die in the ashes.

They crossed a long bridge over a lake, and muddy ash floated on the water, creating a thick black crust. The water bubbled. Dark billowing clouds obscured a pale silver moon, and ahead was a black wall of rain. Orick imagined how the air would be cooler and fresher there in the rain, imagined tasting the water on his tongue. But they hit the wall and found that the sky rained only ash.

An hour later, they reached another gate, and Maggie got out the key, pressed some buttons until the gate glowed a soft orange, the color of sunset, then she gunned the thrusters and the airbike plunged through the white fog found between worlds.

At first Orick wondered if it would stay white forever, for the cool fog gave way only to more white mist, but then they were roaring down a snowy mountain trail through the mist, passing between large pillars of black rock.

As soon as Maggie saw that it was safe, she turned off the thrusters. The bike skidded to a halt. Maggie crawled off, fell to the ground gasping and coughing, trying to clear the foul air of Bregnel from her lungs. Orick climbed off, fell to the ground. Bears rarely get sick to the stomach, but Orick found that the brief trip through Bregnel had left him both wrung out and positively ill.

He lay in the snow and vomited, and though it was freezing, he could not muster the strength to move. After twenty minutes, Maggie got up, rubbed herself.

"Are you all right?" Orick asked.

She shook her head. "That air was too foul. Another few minutes, and I would have fallen off the bike. I'm not sure I could have gotten back up."

Orick understood. He felt grateful to be alive and offered up a silent prayer of thanks. When he finished, he asked, "Where are we?"

"A planet called Wechaus," Maggie answered. "I didn't get time to ask Veriasse about it. He said there was some danger here, but the only gate to Dronon is here, somewhere on Wechaus."

"Are any towns nearby? Someplace we can get a bite to eat, a beer maybe?" Orick looked about in the fog. If a bear could eat rocks, he'd never fear starvation on this world, that much was certain. But other than the rocks, Orick could not make out any sign of trees here, just a few small bushes.

Maggie shook her head. "I'm not sure. We still have some food in the pack. If my guess is right, we should be four or five days ahead of Gallen and the others. I thought we could find a place to stay, then follow them to the Dronon gate."

Orick looked around. It was getting darker out, and he could not see far. He wondered about things: right now, back in Tihrglas, he and Gallen were most likely lazing about at John Mahoney's Inn in Clere, drinking a beer and dreaming about tomorrow, totally ignorant of Everynne or the Maze of Worlds. At the same time, he and Gallen were on the planet Fale, trying to rescue Maggie from Lord Karthenor. In a couple of days, he would reach Cyannesse, and he didn't know when he'd be on Bregnel. Somehow, the idea that he was simultaneously mucking about on at least three different worlds at once left him shaken, and if they kept walking through the Maze of Worlds, things would get even more confusing.

It all seemed sacrilegious, as if they were playing with powers not meant to be comprehended by either men or bears. It reminded Orick of an incident when he was a cub. He and his mother had gone hunting for nuts and had climbed to the top of Barley Mountain. There, under an evergreen, they sat munching at pine nuts and looking out over mountain peaks that seemed to go on forever, fading to blue in the distance. To a small cub, it seemed as if they were viewing infinity, and Orick had asked his mother, "Do you think I'll ever get to see what's on the other side of all of those mountains?"

"No," his mother had answered.

"How come?" Orick asked, thinking that perhaps this would be his life's work, to travel far roads and learn about the world.

"Because God won't allow it. No matter how many mountains you cross, he has always made more."

"How come?"

His mother rolled her eyes at him and sighed. "Because that is how he stays God. He knows what is on the other side of every mountain, but he doesn't tell all of his secrets to others."

"How come?" Orick asked.

"Because if everyone knew the answers, everyone would be gods, even people who are evil. So in order to keep evil people from gaining his power, he hides the answers to the most important questions."

Orick had gazed out over the purpled hills and felt a rushing sensation of awe and thankfulness. God had willed him to be ignorant, and for that Orick felt profoundly grateful.

Yet now he was trying to help Everynne steal the powers of the gods. It seemed only just that he should be punished.

Maggie got a blanket from the pack and wrapped it around herself. A cold wind was stirring.

Orick sniffed the air. "Maggie, child," he said, "I think we'd best get back on that flying scrap pile and see if we can't find some shelter. Something tells me this place gets colder than a lawyer's heart at night, and you shouldn't be out in such weather."

She nodded wearily, got back on the bike, and Orick climbed on behind her. They slowly drove down the mountainside through the rocks and mist. After a few hundred yards, the fog cleared and they got their first view of Wechaus: a rocky, barren world for as far as the eye could see. Off in the distance several miles, Orick could make out one of those sidhe highways.

Maggie made her way down a steep canyon, then wound through it until they reached the highway. Once they hit the highway, the airbike seemed to know the path, and Maggie quit steering. By then, the cold and the wind were having their way with Maggie. She wrapped the blanket tighter around her and kept her head low so that the bike's windscreen protected her somewhat, but within minutes she was shaking fiercely from the chill, sobbing in pain. Orick did not know what to do: should he tell her to stop and try to get warm? It was already so cold that if he stopped, he might never get her going again. On the other hand, the poor little thing could hardly travel farther in her current condition.

So it was that they topped a mountain and looked across the line of the highway to a distant valley and saw a small village. It was an outpost of some kind—a collection of stone huts shaped like domes, well lighted with pale green lights. Orick could discern several emerald pools. Smoke was pouring from them, filling the night air.

Maggie redoubled her speed, and in five minutes they closed in, and Orick saw that it was not smoke filling the night at all, but steam. The buildings sat alongside a natural hot spring, and he could see the dark shapes of people splashing in the waters, swimming in the deep green pools. As they neared, Orick let out a whoop of delight, for among the many swimmers, he saw dozens of bears.

Fourteen

Everynne led the others through the gates on the way to Dronon. After making love to Gallen last night, it seemed that everything was ruined. Both Veriasse and Maggie knew of the tryst, and somehow it had all turned into a fiasco. Now, as she drove, she thought that perhaps it would all end. Perhaps today she would die, and thus put to death her guilt.

The vibration of the airbike mirrored her shaking. Her nerves were frayed, jangled, and she found that her teeth chattered even though it was warm.

She drove the thousand kilometers through Cyannesse at top speed, hit the gate and roared through Bregnel into the early afternoon. Veriasse cried out in shock when he saw the devastation, and all of them drove through the place in horror.

In the daylight, everything was gray and foul. Blackened human bones rotted in the streets, and dronon war cities squatted all across the countryside like dead beetles. Everynne counted twenty of them in the distance.

The air was so foul, that Gallen stopped beside a bubbling lake, got a pair of oxygen exchangers from his pack. He gave one to Everynne.

Veriasse gazed out over the countryside. His eyes were glazed with tears. "Look at all the hive cities. The dronon were building a vast military presence here."

"It looks as if the people of Bregnel decided to wipe them out at any cost," Everynne said.

Veriasse shook his head sadly. "I feared this was coming. The battle to free Bregnel was not going well. They could not have loosed the Terror more than two or three days ago. If they had only waited, perhaps this could have been avoided."

"Let's go," Everynne said. "Let's get to Dronon today." She gunned her thrusters, sped away.

Everynne let her mantle switch through open radio frequencies, trying to catch a clue as to what had happened. She locked onto only one dim channel, far away, probably a transmission beamed from satellite. It broadcast the warning, "Resistance fighters have loosed a Terror. Please take appropriate measures."

The only appropriate measures were to take flight and leave the planet.

Everynne looked out over the wastes in horror, thinking, If we go to war against the dronon, this is what it will be like. Terrors loosed upon hundreds of worlds. Fleets of starships bombarding planets with viral weapons.

Veriasse and Gallen drove side by side, sharing an oxygen exchanger from breath to breath. An afternoon wind kicked up, raising black clouds of ash that swept over the plains. Everynne hurried down the road, passed three skeletons that were half standing, half kneeling, fused together as if they had held each other for comfort in that last moment just as the burning wall of fire swept over them and the invasive nanoware burrowed through to their bones.

Everynne knew that as long as she lived, the images she saw on Bregnel would haunt her.

They broke through the next gate to Wechaus, headed down a snowy trail in the mountains. It was early morning here. They had not gone a hundred meters when they rounded a corner, spotted bloody paw prints in the snow, and Gallen shouted, "Halt!" raising a hand.

He idled his airbike, sat looking at the prints: a bear had rolled on the ground, leaving behind marks of blood and mud, compacting the snow except in one small circle. Within that circle was one firm red print with two scratch marks beneath it.

"Bear tracks," Gallen said. "Orick's here! He left a message."

"Orick?" Veriasse asked. "But I didn't show them how to get to Wechaus."

"Maggie's a smart girl," Gallen said. "And you spent enough time looking at routes on your map that she could figure it out." He pointed at the paw print. "The marks are a code. Back home, when I guard clients, Orick walks up ahead. No one ever bothers a bear, and he can smell an ambush better than any human. He leaves a print by the roadside if the path ahead is clear, but he leaves scratch marks under it if I'm to take warning. One scratch means something has him spooked. Two scratch marks means he is certain that an ambush waits ahead."

Everynne studied the bloody marks, worrying. The poor bear had to be terribly wounded. "But who would be lying in wait?" she asked. "The dronon?"

"Perhaps," Veriasse said. "When last I was here, their numbers were not great on this world, but after our escapades on Fale, they will be more wary. We should move forward cautiously." He pulled out his incendiary rifle, and Gallen did the same.

They followed Orick's footprints down to a small valley; among the snow-covered rocks they found evidence of a great battle—scorch marks from incendiary rifles, bloody tracks.

The torn body of a vanquisher lay in the snow, his naked green flesh ripped by teeth, clawed by strong paws. His incendiary rifle lay nearby, yet Everynne searched the ground with growing discomfort. The signs seemed to indicate that more than one vanquisher had fought here. Everynne could make out tracks of at least three of the giants. But if there had been only one casualty, then it seemed that Orick had fought in vain.

Veriasse looked up at Everynne. His face was rigid, fearful, and Gallen seemed equally disturbed.

Veriasse powered down his airbike, leapt off and surveyed the site. "The dead vanquisher was taken off guard," he said after a moment. "Orick ripped out his throat, and the vanquisher pulled his incendiary gun and tried to club the bear off, perhaps fired in hopes of attracting attention. Then the vanquisher pulled a knife and drew blood, but by then it was too late." Everynne looked at the frozen corpse. There was a certain look of surprise in the creature's dead face, a blankness in his orange eyes. Veriasse took up the vanquisher's bloody knife, cut open the creature's belly, then stuck in his hand. "The corpse is still warm in the bowels. He can't have been killed more than a few hours ago."

"These tracks are crisp around the edges," Gallen said, pointing to the tracks in the snow. "They had to be made last night." He got off his bike, studied the site.

"It looks as if the vanquishers set an ambush here. They waited several hours, then Orick came up behind, killed this one. The other two ran that way!" He pointed north, shook his head. "But I can't imagine them running from an unarmed bear."

"They didn't," Veriasse said. "Those tracks are too evenly spaced, too confident. They're not the tracks of someone sprawling headlong in fear. I think those two left before the battle took place. Perhaps they were drawn off, or were redeployed. In any case, they left their companion alone, and Orick attacked the vanquisher from behind."

Everynne searched the hills above, scanning for more signs of the enemy; thick snow covered the rocks. The vanquishers could not travel through this terrain without leaving a clear trail, but Everynne could see no other footprints—only the one trail coming up from the road, and the vanquisher prints heading north parallel to the highway.

Gallen said, "After the battle, Orick didn't bother to follow these other two. Instead he left us his message, then headed back down the trail."

"Of course," Veriasse said. "Orick knew he couldn't win a battle against two vanquishers, but felt he had to leave us a warning."

"What are these vanquishers doing here? How did they anticipate us?" Gallen shook his head in disgust.

Everynne was not surprised to find the vanquishers so alert. She and Veriasse had used their key to travel to over twenty worlds in the past six months, and many of those worlds had been under dronon control. It had seemed only a matter of time until the dronon caught them.

"You know," Veriasse said as if to himself. "Maggie stole Gallen's key and experienced a temporal loss on her travels once again. Given this loss, the vanquishers who met us on Tihrglas can only have come from our own future. Which explains why they are obviously searching for me and Everynne. Somehow, the dronon learned our identities. We will have to be doubly cautious."

Veriasse wiped his bloody hand on the snow, put his gloves back on. "We'll have to disguise you," Veriasse said to Everynne. "On Wechaus, the lords do not wear masks, and this will make it difficult. Unpack your blue cloak, and tie the hood up to cover your face."

Everynne dutifully pulled the clothes out of her pack, did as Veriasse said, even though with the bright sun the morning was not terribly frigid. When she finished, they started the airbikes, followed Orick's bloody trail down to the highway and headed north.

They had not gone more than a few hundred meters when they saw bear tracks leave the road again to the east; other tracks showed where vanquishers had pursued Orick across the road from the west.

Gallen shouted when he saw the prints and took off following the trail with Everynne close behind. Not fifty meters from the road, they found the site of the last battle, and Everynne cried out in horror.

A heap of blackened bones was all that the incendiary blasts had left of the bear.

Fifteen

Maggie and Orick got off their airbike. Maggie's legs were so cold she found it difficult to walk, and for a moment she just stood shaking in the snow outside the hot springs, wrapped in her blanket. The place was obviously an inn of some kind. Bears and humans were playing in the water, leaping and splashing, while androids manned dinner tables in a large common room. But it seemed to Maggie to be an odd inn, a relic.

The inn was not a living thing like the trees on her home world or like the city of Toohkansay on Fale. Instead it was made from some poured material, perhaps, Maggie considered, so that it could retain the organic lines of a living hostel even in such a cold environment. It was designed much like the buildings found on other worlds, and if Maggie had not been wearing her mantle, she wouldn't have recognized that Wechaus was Backward. The androids waiting on tables were ancient models, a few thousand years behind the times. Few human patrons wore personal intelligences, and even those who did wore unsophisticated models. Perhaps it was the atmosphere of the inn itself, but Maggie imagined that if people here were any more relaxed, they'd have to be dead.

There was no sign of dronon or vanquishers on the premises, and Maggie took that as a good omen.

Maggie opened the front door for Orick. A golden android hurried up with a jaunty gait and said in a prissy voice, "Welcome to Flaming Springs! We're so glad you could join us!" He eyed Maggie's mantle and said, "May I set up an account for our honored guest in the name of . . . ?"

"Maggie Flynn," Maggie answered, somehow surprised that these people would require money for their services. This was new. She immediately began to wonder how much they would require, but knew that when Veriasse came, he would be able to settle the debt. At the very least, she could sell a knowledge token from her mantle. Each of the metal disks stored thousands of volumes of data, and would be valuable to anyone who wore a mantle.

"Of course, Maggie Flynn," the android said, feigning that he recognized the name. "Let me show you to a room. You may order food at any time, and the pools are always open."

He led them through a complex of small huts scattered like hills over the ground. Maggie guessed that steam piping kept the area free of snow. Around the grounds, alien treelike plants with purple fruit lived in containers.

The android opened a door, and Maggie suddenly saw why the rooms appeared so small from the outside. The upper room served as entryway to a luxurious submerged apartment below.

"Will this be adequate?" the android asked.

"Yes, thank you," Maggie answered. "Do you have the time? And the date? Galactic standard."

The android told her the time. They were one day and sixteen hours ahead of when they had left Cyannesse. Maggie made some quick calculations, realized that the temporal distortion was inversely proportional to the distance they jumped between gates. The shorter the jump, the more time they lost.

The android left, and Orick went out to the hot pools to swim. Maggie had had enough of the cold and darkness outside. A side room contained its own small pool where mineral waters cascaded down some falls. The room was decorated to look like a forest, with deep mosses and beds of ferns. Maggie retired there and lay in the water for a long time, letting the warmth seep into her bones. A startling thought struck her: she had left her pack out on the airbike, where it might get stolen.

She climbed from the pool, toweled dry, then dressed and ran out for her pack. It was still sitting in the dark, nearly frozen to the seat. She pulled it free, walked back into the common room of the inn. She had eaten a bite an hour before, but the smells were so enticing that she took a seat, asked an android for a steak dinner with mushrooms and wine.

While she waited, she took out a brush from her pack and brushed her hair. She could not resist the urge to check her pack, make sure that nothing of value had been taken. She opened it a little, dug through. Her gate key was there, and she rummaged for a moment, pulling out clothing, looking for the gifts that Grandmother had given Gallen and Orick.

Dinner came soon, and Maggie tried to enjoy the food but kept glancing up furtively.

Someone was watching her. Most of the guests at the inn were couples—young men and women out to celebrate, frequent pairs of bears. But not all of the couples looked so innocent. A thin man with a hawkish nose, long dark hair, and a thin goatee sat at a nearby table, hands folded under his chin. He did not hide the fact that he was watching her.

Yet he kept glancing toward the doors—both the front doors and those that led to the pools and the rooms at the side. Maggie lost her appetite.

She got up to leave, but the dark stranger came and discreetly took her arm, forced her to sit again, then sat next to her. "By any chance," he asked, "have you been to Fale recently?"

"Yes," Maggie said, then realized that because of the way her gate key sent her back in time, she was currently on Fale, held captive among the aberlains. "I mean, no."

"I thought so." He smiled. "Eat with me."

"No, I have to be going," Maggie said.

But the man gripped her arm, holding her, pulling her back to her seat. "Come now, you've hardly touched a bite," he said, a gleam of excitement in his eyes. "Besides, you've only had the main course. You must try the desserts."

"No," Maggie said, trying to pull her arm from his grasp. "I must be going." She yanked free.

"You won't get far," the stranger warned in a whisper, "not to the next gate."

"What?" Maggie asked, her heart hammering.

"Come follow me to your room. We must talk in private, before it's too late," the stranger said. He rose from his seat, walked out the back door. Maggie didn't know why, but the man terrified her. There was a certain calculated power in his gestures, a toughness about him, and she imagined that if he got her alone, she would not be able to protect herself. She tried to still her heavy breathing, looked around the room for some sign of help. He expected her to come, but she couldn't follow him out into the dark.

She stayed at the table, pretended to eat for an hour. She wanted to go to the pools, find Orick, but the pools were too close to her apartments. So she sat, hoping the stranger would leave. A patina of sweat broke out on her forehead, and she kept worrying that people were watching her, until Orick came in.

"Hey, Maggie!" Orick called loudly from across the room. "You should try these pools—they're great!" He swaggered over to her table, his fur still wet. "Maggie," he said with uncontrollable excitement, "half of these she-bears are in heat! I tell you, I can hardly believe my luck. Why, I met this she-bear named Panta, and she's panting for me, the dear girl, I assure you. She's invited me to her room tonight—"

"Good, good," Maggie said without enthusiasm. She didn't know how to tell him that something was dreadfully wrong. She especially did not want to talk here where every word could be overheard. Right now, she only wanted Orick to get away from her safely, keep him out of danger. "Why don't you go with her?"

"Well, I don't know," Orick said. "Do you think I should? Are you all right? You look sick?"

"I'm afraid," she whispered, hoping none of the other diners could hear. "This world may be more dangerous than we thought."

"Oh, nonsense," Orick growled too loudly. "This place is grand!"

"Yes, of course it is," she said, hoping to quiet him. "Please, just go. I'll be all right."

A female bear came to the side door, stood up on her hind legs, sniffing the air. She saw Orick, walked over on all fours, and stood at the side of the table, demurely watching Orick with big brown eyes that fairly shouted her desires.

"It's nice to meet you, Panta," Maggie said. "I'm afraid I'm feeling tired. Why don't you two take this table. I'll see you in the morning, Orick." She got up, realizing that she needed to go out the side door to reach her room, see this thing through on her own. If the stranger was waiting in the darkness to accost her, she would have to face him sooner or later. She did not want to place Orick in jeopardy.

She stalked back through the night. The hot pools had raised a cloud of steam that lingered in the air between buildings, shrouding everything in heavy fog. The faint green footlights set by the sides of the trail and under the trees gave the only illumination, and they seemed inadequate as she walked back through the maze of apartments.

But the stranger was not waiting for her in the shadows. She reached her own room, glanced skyward before entering. A line of fire ringed the sky, arching from horizon to horizon, and Maggie could just see it through the fog. Her mantle whispered that this planet had a ring around it.

Maggie spoke to the door. It registered her voice and opened. She walked into the room, looked down the broad staircase to the apartments below. There was no sign of the stranger. She closed the door behind her, crept downstairs. The apartment was empty.

She was just feeling safe when the door chimes rang, startling her. She opened the door. A short, bald, fat man stood at the door, his broad arms sticking deep in the pockets of his cloak. Both his leather cloak and his deep frown looked as if they had been worn constantly for years.

"Excuse me," he said. "Maggie Flynn, is it? My name is Bavin. I own this establishment. May I speak with you for a moment?" He looked up at her with sad, baggy eyes.

She nodded. He glanced back nervously, closed the door. "The, uh, the thing is—" Bavin explained, "is that I want you to settle your bill and clear out before morning. I won't have you bringing any trouble down on my inn."

"I don't understand," Maggie said. "What are you talking about?"

"I'm talking about that *thing* you're carrying in your bag," Bavin said, wringing his hands. "I'm not the kind of man who would turn you in for the reward, but there's others who will. I won't have you bringing any trouble down on us poor folks."

"What are you talking about, 'reward'?"

Bavin looked about cautiously, as if someone in the room might be listening. "The dronon—" he confided, "they're looking for a beautiful woman who is traveling the Maze of Worlds. She's rumored to be accompanied by several protectors. When you first came in, I wasn't sure you were the one, because you rode in with only that bear. That cast some doubt in my mind. But you rode an airbike that no one would ever bring down this far south in the cold, and that seemed strange. Then you pulled that key from your bag at the table, and you had the planetary police asking about you. . . ."

"I don't understand," Maggie stuttered. "Are you sure they are looking for me?"

"The dronon sent more vanquishers just a few days ago, using the gates, same as you," Bavin said. "Oh, they've got people scared—scared evil. Good people that would never have thought of doing business with their kind are scrambling now, and there's some that would turn you over in a second, thinking it might give them some leverage in the future. But not me—not me!" Bavin was shaking his head, and Maggie realized that he denied any possible turpitude simply because he was tempted to turn her in himself. "So like I said, I want you to settle up your account and get out of here."

"But where will I go?" Maggie said. "What will I do?"

"Don't go to the gates, whatever you do. They're watched. Beyond that, I don't care what you do. Just settle your account."

"But, I don't have any money," Maggie said.

The little man looked at her, a dangerous gleam in his eyes. "What do you mean, you don't have any money? How did you plan to pay for this?" He spread his arms wide, indicating the luxurious apartment.

"I planned to work, make some money," Maggie said. Maggie reached up to her mantle, pulled off a small silver disk with the emblem of an android on it. Regretfully, she handed it to the man. She would be giving up all her knowledge about androids.

"I—I can't take this," Bavin argued, apparently having an attack of conscience. "It's too much!" The little man grumbled under his breath, looked about the room. "Get out of here. Just get your things and sneak away."

Maggie still had the pack she'd carried in. She went to her bedroom, got her blanket and robes. The soil of the day's travel was still on them, and she was loath to wear the dirty robes, but she slipped into them quickly, wrapped her blanket around her shoulders. When she was ready to leave, she returned to the living room. Bavin was gone. He'd left the front door open for her.

She followed the little footpath through the fog toward the common room, thinking to warn Orick. But as she reached the corner by the pools, she could see the front of the inn.

Three green-skinned vanquishers hunched over her airbike. Two were ogres—typical military grunts—the third was a tracker.

The tracker leaned down, sniffing the airbike, his flat orange eyes tilting about like those on a fish. "This bike was driven by a woman and a bear. They traveled through two worlds in a matter of hours."

"Then we've found her?" one of the soldiers asked.

"Yes," the tracker said. Maggie began fading back into the shadows, looking for a way to escape. She wanted to circle the inn, approach the bike from the other side. Orick was eating in the common room and he needed to be warned, but she dared not go back into the inn. She thought that, instead, perhaps the vanquishers would go into the common room searching for her. If she reached the far side of the inn without being seen, she could hop on the airbike and speed away, creating enough of a diversion so that Orick could also escape.

She ran down the trail and circled to the back of the inn where there were no lighted trails. One moment she was rushing around a building, and the next someone leapt from the shadows, knocking her to the snowy ground.

Maggie screamed, tried to leap up and get some footing. But her captor held her arm, hissed, "Quiet!" then pulled her to her feet with great haste. She stood in the darkness, looking at the thin man she'd seen earlier in the dining room.

"Hurry—they're after us!" he said, pulling her arm. She heard shouts at the front of the inn, and Maggie didn't need coaxing. They ran over frost-crusted snow to a small field at the back of the inn, where dozens of aircars hunkered in the cold night.

Maggie looked back, saw vanquishers rushing toward them past a green footlight. One pulled out an incendiary rifle and fired.

The actinic chemical light shot out in an expanding ball, and the thin man pulled her down to the right. The fireball whooshed overhead, singeing Maggie's face as it passed, then splattered against an aircar.

She and her benefactor weaved between several cars. Maggie spotted one with an open hatch. A guard dressed in black stood at the door, carrying an incendiary rifle.

Maggie glanced at the man, caught her breath. He was a twin to the thin man. She froze at the sight of him, but her companion urged her forward. As she lunged into the back seat of the aircar, the guard leapt away into the shadows.

The thin man started the ignition, began firing the thrusters, and Maggie looked out the window. His twin took cover behind another aircar and fired his incendiary rifle at the vanquishers. The tracker burst into flame, burned like a pillar in the night, his huge spiderlike body twisting in pain. From around the far end of the buildings, three more thin men rushed from the shadows, and two loped around from the front of the inn.

The vanquishers dove for cover behind some planters and began laying down suppressive fire while shouting for help.

The aircar rose, began sliding away into the darkness, and Maggie cried, "Wait! I've left a friend down there!"

"I know!" the thin man said, though he did not slow the aircar. "I was trying to warn him when the vanquishers arrived. They sent for reinforcements, so we had to move fast. We hope that by killing the tracker, it will give your friend a chance to escape."

"We?" Maggie said.

"My doppelgangers," the thin man said.

Maggie had never heard the word *doppelganger*, so her mantle filled her with understanding. Some people chose to become immortal by cloning themselves and downloading memories into the clones. Among those immortals were people who often kept multiple copies of themselves running at the same time so that they could work toward a common goal. Their leader was called the primary, while the copies were doppelgangers.

The aircar slid smoothly up into the sky, and Maggie looked down. White volleys of gunfire were whipping through the air. The hot springs looked like cloudy green gems from up here, and she watched another vanquisher turn into a living torch, then saw a doppelganger take a hit to the left leg and stagger. He managed one last shot before he toppled; the shot went wide and torched one of Bavin's apartments.

She looked down at the dying man and felt peculiarly detached.

Though he was human, he was, after all, only a copy of a man, and therefore not real. But she knew that the man had felt pain and desires like any other person; he had hopes and dreams, and he'd just chosen to give his life for her.

Maggie looked up at the thin man who piloted the aircar. Somehow it was comforting to know that he was the kind of man who would be willing to die for her.

Sixteen

Maggie leaned back in the padded seat as the aircar roared out over snowfields. The cabin was pressurizing, and her ears popped. She took her eyes off the green gems of flaming springs, hoping Orick would escape.

If I get through this alive, she thought, I'll never go near another inn again. She twisted some hair around her finger, chewed the ends nervously.

The thin man glanced at her. "Your bear friend will be all right. My men just took out the last vanquisher. As one would suspect, the guests of the inn are checking out in record time."

The thin man appeared to be thirty-five years old, though appearances would mean nothing on this world. He did not wear a mantle or guide. He wore a work suit of nondescript brown. He was not particularly handsome. "How do you know that your men killed the last vanquisher?"

"Implants." He pointed to his ear. He sighed and leaned back. The aircar was piloting itself now. He glanced at Maggie. "I must say, I'm disappointed. I had been informed that a Tharrin was traveling between worlds, Semarritte reborn. And the man accompanying her fit the description of Semarritte's Lord Protector. Yet I risked my life and the lives of my doppelgangers for what, a bear and . . . ?"

Maggie shrugged. There was something more in the question than mere curiosity—a demand. His face remained impassive as he waited for her answer. "My name is Maggie Flynn."

"My name is Primary Jagget," he offered, stroking his goatee. "So why are you on Wechaus, and where is Semarritte's clone?"

Maggie did not know if she trusted Jagget. Her first impulse was to lie. Yet she suspected that some of his men were searching for Orick, and in time Jagget might question the bear. She had to make the lie plausible, so she forged ahead.

"Everynne was her name," Maggie said. "She came to my home world of Tihrglas two weeks ago with her escort, an old man who didn't mention his name. They hired me and my bear to lead them through the woods to an ancient gate, but there were some vanquishers and dronon after them. The old man fell behind to slow the vanquishers, sent us up ahead to the gate. We were at the gate when we heard his death scream. Everynne gave me the key, showed me how to use it, then rushed back through a clearing to help the old man. Just then, the vanquishers came out the far side of the clearing and shot her. The bear and I saw that our only chance for escape was to jump through the gate. We've been traveling ever since, trying to find our way back home through the gates."

"What of your mantle?" Primary Jagget asked. "Surely you did not get that on Tihrglas."

"The woman—Everynne—had it in her pack. She handed me her pack before she got killed."

Primary Jagget studied her with dark eyes, his face lit only by the running lights of the aircar. He sighed deeply, closed his eyes. "So, Semarritte's clone is dead," he said. "What a loss. What a tremendous loss!"

"Was she a friend of yours?" Maggie asked.

Primary Jagget shook his head. "I've never actually seen her, but yes, she was a friend of mine."

He fell silent for a long moment. "What shall we do with you? The dronon have offered a reward for the woman who is traveling the Maze of Worlds."

"I've done nothing," Maggie said, realizing that she had a hole in her story. If Everynne was already dead, the dronon wouldn't still be searching for her. "Why should they want me?"

"Isn't it obvious? They want your key."

Maggie breathed a sigh of relief. "Of course." She looked out the window. There were no moons above this planet, only a ring of light, and that was partly in shadow. The aircar sped over a frozen ocean.

"So, you and your friend want to get home," Primary Jagget said. "I can help you—in return for the key." Maggie did not know what to answer. She didn't really want this stranger trying to escort her back to Tihrglas. "Of course, if you think the price is too high, I could sweeten the bargain."

Maggie listened to the tone of his voice, realized that she might have just stumbled upon a universal trait for the inhabitants of Wechaus—they all seemed greedy.

"I will think about it," Maggie said. "When your men find my friend Orick, I'll discuss your offer with him."

"Fine," Primary Jagget said. "I'll take you to my compound. You'll be safe there. I personally can vouch for the character of every person on the premises. It's secluded, well defended. The dronon won't find you there."

"Thank you," Maggie said. She leaned back in the comfortable cushions of her seat, watched the land go by. They were flying very fast. They were in a Chughat XI, an expensive car used by diplomats, and her mantle whispered that its top speed was Mach 12. She guessed that they were nearing Mach 10 when the car suddenly began slowing and dropped toward a city of stone. Bright lights ringed one large building, and Maggie could see dozens of people driving along streets, standing on corners. They all moved with a common gait, stood with a familiar stance. They were all clones of Primary Jagget.

"How many copies of you are there?" Maggie asked.

"All told, right now I would estimate about nine hundred thousand," Primary Jagget answered.

"Why so many?"

"I am a man of great ambition, but I have too little time. So my doppelgangers and I work together."

"And what is your great ambition?" Maggie asked as the aircar slid to the ground.

Primary Jagget didn't hesitate to answer. "To keep my homeland free. That is my sole desire."

The car skidded to a halt, and Primary Jagget climbed out his door. Two doppelgangers hurried up to Maggie's door, opened it for her. One reached out to give her a hand from the car. She took it, stepped onto the pavement.

Primary Jagget said, "I'm sorry that I can't see you to your room, but I have urgent business elsewhere." Maggie turned to glance at him, and there was a soft whispering sound of wings.

Primary Jagget turned into a swarm of cream-colored butterflies that flew away in a cloud.

The butterflies vanished into darkness just beyond the streetlights. Maggie stared at the butterflies, astonished, for Jagget's body had not been flesh and blood but an artifice created through nanotechnology.

Maggie felt something poke her back. Her muscles spasmed and her legs went numb. She saw lights and whirled, staggering. She grabbed a doppelganger's shirt to keep from falling. For a moment the world spun, and she hung on precariously. She twisted and looked down at the doppelganger's hands, saw a blue arc of light issuing from a small grip. She smelled burned cloth and ozone.

Maggie blinked, looked at the arc, and her mind suddenly registered that it was an electric stun gun. The doppelganger shoved the gun into her belly, and the world went white.

Orick had been sitting with Panta in the dining room at Flaming Springs, enjoying a salmon dinner that was more feast than dinner when he looked out the window and saw three vanquishers outside the front door, their breath steaming in the cold as they examined Maggie's airbike.

"I think we'd better haul our tails out of here," Orick told Panta. The young she-bear glanced out the window.

"I think you're right," she said, wiping her greasy paw on the tablecloth.

Orick wanted to leave quietly, but it appeared that Panta had a greater distaste for the vanquishers than he did. She hurried to the side door, making for the apartments, and broke into a run. The front door to the inn opened behind them, and a vanquisher shouted, "Stop!"

Orick halted, but Panta hit the door full tilt, knocking it down. Out by the pools, Orick saw Maggie beside a lighted tree, her back turned as she raced around a building. Two vanquishers rushed through the dining room, ducking their heads to keep from scraping the ceiling, dashing over tables.

When they tried to pass Orick, he veered left as if to avoid them, then swerved right to trip them. He roared an apology as they tumbled to the ground, then backed against the wall as if he'd only been trying to get out of the way. The vanquishers leapt to their feet, dashed into the night.

Panta had disappeared into the fog beyond the buildings, and the vanquishers turned the corner, rushing toward Maggie, apparently determined to capture anyone who tried to run from them. Orick looked out the row of windows behind him. One of the vanquishers—a tracker—was racing around the building in the other direction, as if to cut Maggie off.

Orick didn't know how best to help, so he roared a challenge and rushed out the door, following the two largest vanquishers, hoping that if need arose, he could jump them from behind, gain an element of surprise.

He reached the corner apartment by the pools, and three identical men carrying incendiary rifles rushed past him. He stopped to give them the road, wondered who they were.

Behind the cluster of apartments, the white fire of incendiary rifles broke out with a distinctive whooshing sound followed by a pop as each round ignited. Orick passed the last buildings, saw a battle in progress. Several men were shooting it out with a vanquisher. Tracers of white flame filled the sky. Two other vanquishers were already in flames.

A bunch of cars were parked in a field, and an aircar shot up into the sky. Panta sat cowering behind another aircar. When she saw Orick, she ducked low to the ground, roared for him to stay down.

Orick watched one human defender then another take hits with incendiary fire, but the vanquisher was surrounded. Within seconds, the ogre burst into flames.

The human defenders raced through the parking lot for a moment, shouting to one another, then leapt away north through the darkness and fog. The parking lot was well-lighted by vanquishers and vehicles blazing in raging flames.

Panta rushed through the smoke to Orick. "Let's get out of here!" she shouted. She ran toward an oversized magcar.

"I can't!" Orick said. "I've got to find Maggie!"

"She left in an aircar!" Panta said. "Let's go."

Orick stopped a moment, astonished. It had never occurred to him that Maggie would leave without him, but it only made sense. If it hadn't been for his lust, he would have listened more seriously to her warning. He simply felt grateful that she'd escaped.

"Did you see those men?" Orick shouted at Panta's back, running to catch up with her. "Are they brothers or something?"

"No!" Panta said. "They're Jaggets. If there's anyone I distrust more than the dronon, it's a Jagget. And your friend is with them."

Panta leapt up onto the oversized magcar, and Orick climbed in beside her. "Car," Panta said, "put up the hood, and take me home. Hurry!" A glass hood slid over the top of Orick's head, and the magcar's thrusters revved.

"What's wrong with a Jagget?" Orick asked as the car surged forward, weaving among the flaming wreckage.

"It's hard to put it into words exactly," Panta said. "They used to be the protectors of this planet, but now that the dronon have taken over, the Jaggets have all gone crazy. They've been cloned for too many generations. Their DNA is breaking down, and each new generation is more unstable than the last."

Orick didn't understand what she'd said. Right now, he felt just a bit giddy. He sat in a closed vehicle with a handsome young she-bear who was in estrus, and the scent made him dizzy. Add the excitement of the past few days, the element of fatigue, and the poor bear could hardly think straight.

Panta's vehicle whizzed south over the highway Orick had traversed only a couple of hours before. Orick felt nervous, vulnerable, and wanted to get under cover. After what seemed like a long drive, the car turned abruptly and headed into the hills on a winding road until it reached a small stone house on a knoll. Lights shone warmly from the window, and Orick could see a nice stone fireplace inside, a dining room with a large table, bright flowers growing from pots that hung above the windows. He stared in awe. In all of Tihrglas, no bear had ever owned such a fine home.

He felt nervous. The car stopped and the glass hood rolled back.

Cold air hit him, and he sat for a moment, breathing deeply, steam coming from his breath. Panta looked at him, made a soft whining noise. "Will you come in with me?"

For no reason he could discern, Orick's mouth began to water. He knew that if he went into the house with Panta, he would lose his virginity. Only days before he had been tempted to take his vow of chastity, but now temptation was sitting here beside him, batting her brown eyes and filling the car with the scent of desire.

In the past few days, Orick had seen a lot. He'd let the peace of Cyannesse seep into his bones, and he'd thought it heaven. He'd seen the bones of dead children and tasted the poison air of Bregnel. He'd seen Everynne's powers nearly unleased on Fale, and he wondered at it all. Was God letting him see beyond hills that no other bear had ever seen? Was this his reward for seeking to serve God, or was God showing all of this to him for his own purposes? Could it be that he was meant to make a difference? And how did Panta fit into God's scheme?

Some priests in Tihrglas held that God's commandment to Adam and Eve to "go forth and multiply" was given to all. But Orick had always believed that only by taking a vow of chastity could he give his full devotion to God.

Oh God, Orick whispered in prayer, you're the one that led me here. I would have resisted her advances, but you brought me here. I swear that after this one night, I'll come crawling back to you on my knees, and I'll take my vow of chastity then.

Panta waited for Orick's answer and asked huskily, "Orick, were those vanquishers hunting for you?"

"I think so," he admitted.

Her eyes grew wide. She licked her lips and said, "I find that soooo exciting!"

Orick trembled with anticipation as she led him into the house.

Maggie woke to a yellow haze. She heard a voice speaking, realized it was her own. But someone else's questions were running through her brain: Where is Semarritte's clone? Why did you lie to Primary Jagget? Where did you expect to meet Semarritte's clone? How many Terrors is Semarritte's clone carrying? You testified that Veriasse and the clone have told you several conflicting stories about their plans; how do you know that they have not planted bombs on each world they have visited?

The questions were all ringing through her mind, and Maggie willed herself not to answer. Her voice quit speaking.

Maggie's head felt as if it would split. Some viselike instrument was crushing her temples. She tried to move her arms and kick, but could not move.

Nearby, Jagget or one of his clones said, "Sedate her again, quickly."

"No!" she shouted, and was swallowed by the cold.

She woke, perhaps hours later, with a headache. She was in a small, cold room made of stone. It had one light, no windows, no furnishings. The white walls were cracked, like rough skin. Maggie felt her head. Her mantle was gone. From the cold seeping to her bone, she realized so were her underwear and her shoes. She had only the pale green robe she'd worn for the past few days. The place was empty, except for some dirt on the floor and her own ripening scent.

There was one door in the room. Maggie got up off the floor, approached the door. It slid open. Two Jaggets stood against the far wall of a corridor, and they smiled at her. They wore crisp, identical tan military fatigues.

"Are either one of you Primary Jagget?"

As one, the Jaggets shook their heads. One answered, "He's asked you to join him for lunch."

"Lunch? Was I out all night?" Maggie asked.

"Yes," the Jagget answered. "We found it desirable to sedate you. We don't like strangers walking around our compound." Maggie looked deeply into the Jagget's dark eyes, saw them glittering with something that might have been madness. She'd reacted to it instinctively the night before.

"I see," she said softly.

"Shall we go to lunch?" the other Jagget offered.

"Please." Maggie nodded so that one of them would lead the way.

"We don't like to walk in front," one of the Jaggets said. "Please, you lead."

"But I don't know where we're going."

"Just walk," the Jagget offered. "We'll tell you when to turn."

Maggie shrugged, headed down a hall dirty with disuse till it reached a side passage. "To the right," a Jagget said. He guided her through an underground construction facility, and everywhere Jaggets in dull brown coveralls hauled containers, worked at monitoring stations, or stood supervising others. She could not guess from the odd components what they were making. It looked to be some type of personal flier in a new design.

They climbed some stairs that led to the surface. It was a cool day with blue skies and fresh snow on the ground. Once she saw the compound in the daylight, Maggie saw that this was a military installation. Several towers held gun emplacements, and on the perimeter of the city she spotted heavy generators that powered energy shields. Only then did she notice the faint shimmering in the sky above as sunlight refracted on the shields.

They climbed a stair that zigzagged uphill to a large house, a stately affair with marble columns. Primary Jagget sat under the portico at a table covered with a white cloth. Sunlight splashed down upon him. The day seemed cool to Maggie, with snow on the ground in most places, but Jagget luxuriated in the thin sunlight, as if it were a warm and pleasant day. Lunch waited on the table. Wine goblets were filled, and an assortment of silver platters held steaming foods. Two Jaggets busily served vegetables onto plates.

Primary Jagget stood as Maggie climbed the last few steps, smiled warmly. "Greetings, Maggie! Well met! Well met! Are you thirsty after your little climb?" She wondered why he didn't ask if she was thirsty after her interrogation.

She was both thirsty and had to urinate, but she didn't want to admit it to Jagget. She was mad, but in control of her anger. Still, he grabbed a wine goblet, handed it to her.

A cool wind blew out over the fields of Wechaus, and Maggie drew her robe tight. Primary Jagget raised his glass in a toast and said, "To my kingdom." He waved in an expansive gesture, indicating the countryside around them.

She didn't want to toast with him and wondered how offended he would be if she declined. Primary Jagget noticed her hesitancy and said, "You don't have to pretend that you like me. I assure you, it is quite uncommon for a woman to take any kind of romantic interest in a Jagget. When I was a lone man, women seemed willing to give their hearts. But now that I am an organism, with hundreds of thousands of individuals acting as cells, people are more . . . reluctant to accept me. Indeed, as a young man they hailed me as an idealist, but now that I am old, they ridicule me as a fanatic—even though my notions have never changed. Believe me, I have grown accustomed to scorn."

"I . . . don't scorn you," Maggie said.

"Ah, you feel pity," Jagget said. "A far more noble emotion. Or is it fear? A far more reasonable emotion."

Yes, both, Maggie thought, but she would not speak it. She wanted to change the subject. She looked out over the valley. A mine shaft sat off to her left, and four Jaggets drove a car up to the edge of the mine. The car had a trailer, and the trailer carried a large white ball. When they got to the mouth of the mine, the car stopped. The Jaggets exited the car, and one of them climbed up on the trailer and opened some fastenings to the white ball. The ball flipped open, revealing a hollow interior like an egg. One Jagget stood talking to the others for a moment, laughing and slapping their backs, obviously saying good-bye, then he climbed into the egg, flipped down the lid. The others got up, made sure the egg was fastened securely, then drove the car on into the mine shaft.

"What are those men up to?" Maggie asked.

"Ah, we are storing some of our personnel for future use," Primary Jagget said.

"What do you mean, storing?" Maggie asked, wishing that she had her mantle back.

"In stasis chambers. We are a defeated planet, you understand. We could choose to flee in starships before the Dronon Empire, but the costs would be prohibitive even for me. So, I am storing some of my clones so that I can wake them when the political climate is more favorable."

Maggie shook her head, wondering at this man. She downed her wine, thinking it might be advisable to be drunk for this encounter.

"I'm sorry for having to take you captive and drug you," Jagget said. "I needed to check you for weapons, and I couldn't have you conscious for the procedure. Aren't you going to ask how I knew you were on Fale in my future?" The smirk on his face assured her that she would have to find out sooner or later.

"How?" Maggie said.

"I learned it from the dronon," Jagget answered. "A huge number of reinforcements landed on the planet through a gate last week. They bore holotapes showing how you and your friends blackmailed them during your escape from Fale. I found it intriguing to watch a newscast from our own future. But the dronon must also have some earlier news, for they suspected that Everynne and Veriasse might have traveled here alone. Anyway, the images of you and your bear friend were not clear in the videos, but I managed to enhance them. The dronon had a gate key that would take them into the past, so they were moving back in time, searching frantically for Terrors on all of their worlds. Since Wechaus is a conquered planet, and since it is rumored to have a gate that leads to Dronon, we received a great deal of attention from the Lords of the Swarm." Primary Jagget stood posed with his wineglass in hand, obviously pleased with himself.

"So, what will you do with me?" Maggie asked.

Primary Jagget shrugged. "In a few moments, we should be receiving a live broadcast of your exploits on Fale. The dronon have been searching for you all night, and they're trying to mobilize the public against you. If the people here believe that Everynne will leave a Terror on this world, I fear that she will receive a typical Wechaus welcome—a cold welcome."

"But you know that's not true!" Maggie said. "Everynne wouldn't destroy a planet."

"I know nothing of the sort!" Jagget snapped. "Everynne has told different stories on at least three different worlds. All I know about her is that she is a talented liar who seems to practice her art at every opportunity!"

"What will you do to her?" Maggie asked.

Primary Jagget smiled, stroked his goatee. "I will decide once I have her in my hands."

Seventeen

Orick woke in Panta's home. The fire in the fireplace had burned down to ashes, and he and Panta sprawled exhausted on the floor like a pair of rugs.

The night had turned into a heavenly ordeal. Like most species of animal that mated only every few years, bears tended to try to make up for lost time. Panta had exhausted Orick after three hours, but demanded his services for two more. Orick was beginning to see that the ritual battles between male bears back on Tihrglas might have served a real purpose. The winners of such battles tended to be the males who had the most stamina, and servicing Panta had certainly tested Orick's stamina to the limits.

He lay staring at the female. She was beautiful—a soft, thick pelt; sensual snout; claws polished to a bright shine. Orick roused himself, went into the kitchen. A bowl of fresh fruit sat on the table, and as he helped himself, he began wondering about Maggie. He felt guilty for not following her, trying to help her. He'd let his gonads do all the thinking last night.

Panta stirred in the other room, and he called out. "These brazen fellows that Maggie went off with—"

"The Jaggets?"

"Aye," Orick said. "Where would they have her?"

"Just about anywhere," Panta said, padding into the kitchen. She stood in the doorway on all fours, put her front paws out and stretched seductively, her rump in the air. "There are Jaggets all over the country. Perhaps before saying where they might take her, I should ask you why they might take her."

Orick had already explained to Panta that he was from Tihrglas, so now he told her all about their exploits on Fale and other worlds. He had no reservations in telling her things that he might never mention to a human. Though many a bear will grow grumpy and irritable, there never was a bear with an ounce of avarice, and avarice is what led humans into so many errors.

"If the Jaggets have taken her to keep her away from the dronon," Panta said, "they'll have her at one of their fortresses. It's beyond the power of a bear to get into one of those places, and I wouldn't try, if I were you."

"The poor child," Orick said, "she's had such a rough life, I wouldn't want to add to her burdens. I'm worried sick over her."

"Perhaps your friends can help when they get here," Panta said. Orick grunted in appreciation, and Panta licked his face.

The door chimed. Panta went to the corner, looked out the window. "Vanquishers!" she whispered. "Stay out of sight."

She hurried to the door and opened it. A deep voice said, "Citizen, records indicate that you were at Flaming Springs last night."

"Yes," Panta said. "I had dinner and swam with a friend."

"Were you there at the time of the shootings?"

"There was a shooting?" Panta asked in mock horror. "I had no idea. I left early."

"It is strange how many people left early," the vanquisher said.

"I was only there for a short time," Panta said. "I went only to choose a mate. It's that time of year."

"Did you find someone?"

"Yes, an old friend named Footh. He left just an hour ago. He can verify my story."

"We shall speak to him, citizen," the vanquisher grumbled.

Panta closed the door, walked swiftly back to Orick and spoke to a grill on the wall. She talked to it for several moments before Orick realized that she was talking to Footh, using little code phrases to make sure that he would verify her story.

"Stay home," Footh told her. "The vanquishers are all over the highways. The holovid networks say that someone carrying a Terror escaped from Fale. The vanquishers tried to arrest her here last night."

She thanked him, and said "Off." The box quit speaking. Orick had seen so many wonders over the past few days it only made sense that folks who could walk between worlds could talk to each other while miles apart.

"Well, you heard him," Panta said. "We need to stay inside today. We could try calling the Jaggets, ask to speak to your friend, but the dronon will be monitoring all the phones. I don't think we can do anything until your friends get here."

Orick looked around the house forlornly, wondering what a simple bear could do. "The fool rushes blindly down the rocky trail, while the superior bear makes sure of his path," Orick said, recalling the only bit of wisdom he could dredge up. "I should never have come here. I'd quit the place if I could. I'm afraid I've made a mess of this."

"You've made a mess of nothing," Panta said. "Why, your friends are all over the news. They're just as likely to get caught with you as they would have been without."

"That's not true. Maggie and I stirred up a hornets' nest, and now Gallen is going to walk through the gate and get stung. I have to fix this if I can, Panta. Once it gets dark, I have to go warn Gallen."

Panta watched him for a long time. "Do you really believe that this Everynne is a good person?"

"Och, the woman's nothing but cream, as we'd say back in Tihrglas," Orick assured her. "I'd bet my life on it."

"You're betting all of our lives on it," Panta said.

"I'd do that, too."

"Then I'll come with you," Panta offered. "You'll need a cover story, and two bears out for a ride isn't uncommon."

Orick smiled, and they spent the day in the house, eating what they would, frolicking when the mood took them. Panta worked for a textile company, designing prints for cloth. She showed Orick her samples, and Orick found that her art spoke to him like nothing he'd ever seen. She wove cloth in the colors of the forest, greens and grays and the shades of the sky. She wove pebbles under rushing water, sunlight streaming through leaves. Many of her patterns featured bears, cubs running through fields of tan, an old bear staring at the moon. Orick could look at the cloth, and sometimes he would hear sounds, bear voices talking, the grunting of a sow as she dug for tubers. The pictures awoke his racial memories, and when he looked at the pictures, he looked through them into the dimly recalled dreamtime of bears.

Though Panta's people had left the wilds, the wilds had not left her, and Orick saw that he would miss Wechaus, would miss Panta when he left.

That night, after dark, Orick could not sleep. Gallen and the others would not drive through the gate until near dawn, but he was eager to get to the hills, prepare a message to warn Gallen.

He paced through the house on all fours, his claws raking the hardwood floors. Finally, near midnight, Panta said, "Let's go," and they went to her car.

She drove along the highway in the darkness. Once they passed a convoy of magtrucks filled with vanquishers. They appeared to be moving large numbers of soldiers. Another time they passed a roving patrol, and Orick felt nervous. He watched the snow-laden hills until he spotted the beaten path where he and Maggie had driven down from the gate. He told Panta to slow the car and lower the hood. As soon as she did, he smelled vanquishers.

"Drop me here, then off with you," Orick growled. He could not take a chance that she would linger near this spot—not with the vanquishers patrolling the area.

"I'll come back for you," she said.

Orick studied her profile in the darkness, and he longed to stay with her forever. "Do that," he said. He leapt from the moving car, and Panta sped away.

Orick sniffed the ground. The vanquishers had walked up the path. A cool wind drifted down from the hills, carrying their scent. Orick began stalking, his head low to the ground.

He took nearly an hour to reach a small hilltop. The light was faint—the stars were thin here, but a fiery ring ran up the sky at the horizon, giving almost as much light as a moon. Orick looked down into the glade, smelled vanquishers for a long time before he finally spotted them.

Three of them sat as still as stones in the snow, hidden beneath a white sheet, watching up a small draw. Orick was surprised to find so few of them and wondered why they kept so far from the gate. Apparently they had followed the trail a ways, saw that the airbikes had materialized from thin air, but perhaps they just couldn't believe their luck, or maybe they did not realize that the beaten snow led to a gate opening.

Orick watched them for awhile, studied the hills. He could see the forbidding snow-covered top of the mountain, the slopes along two arms. The problem was that he could not circle up to the gate opening without being spotted. The vanquishers had set their surveillance post here precisely because it did allow them to view the area on all sides.

So Orick waited. Given the circumstances, he had no option but to stay through the night. When Gallen and Everynne came downhill, he could roar, warn them of the ambush, and then wade into battle. But until then, he could do nothing.

After nearly an hour, two of the giant vanquishers stood, then headed uphill, running along a ridge. Apparently they had been redeployed. Orick decided to strike.

He crept downhill, his feet padding through the snow. When Orick closed to within a dozen yards, the lone vanquisher turned and glanced at him for a moment, but Orick had bear-sized boulders behind him. He merely stood still in the shadows until the vanquisher turned away again.

Orick raced over the snow, leapt at the vanquisher's back, climbing over its shoulder to rip at its throat. The vanquisher tried to stand, raised the butt of his incendiary rifle and smashed it against Orick's face, but Orick merely wrapped his arms around the ogre, ripping at the green skin.

The vanquisher fired his rifle, then threw himself on the ground, and for a moment Orick rolled free. He twisted and leapt at the vanquisher, grabbing the creature's Adam's apple. The vanquisher unsheathed a knife and plunged it into Orick's shoulder, slicing through tendons.

Orick slapped the vanquisher's head with a paw, knocking it down, then tore out its throat.

When the vanquisher lay dead in the snow, Orick turned and rushed uphill till he found the end of the trail where he and Maggie had first materialized. Orick and Gallen had long ago worked out a system to warn one another of dangers on the road. Orick left his paw print and scratched twice beneath it. Since Orick was not sure if Gallen would enter this world before or after dawn, Orick rolled in the snow, beating it down so that his message would be more likely to attract attention. Then he rushed downhill, heading back for the road.

Halfway there, he discovered that his right shoulder hurt, and he began to limp. Blood was pouring from the wound, but he had not noticed it in the heat of the battle.

He licked at the blood, made his way down to the highway. Panta was nowhere to be seen. Orick grumbled under his breath and began limping down the road, watching for signs of movement in the hills, hoping he did not meet a patrol.

The cold night air sapped his warmth. His blood was leaking away, and he felt small, helpless out here in the wilds, so far from home. Once, he heard voices and raised his head in fear. He did not think he could outrun trouble, but after a moment, he realized that he had been dreaming voices. Another time, he found himself feeling weak, and he just sat on the roadside for a moment. A passing vehicle roused him from his sleep, and he looked about, headed north again, wondering what had become of Panta.

He felt like a cub, lost in the deep woods. For a time he walked again, thinking he could hear the mesmerizing sound of wind rushing through trees.

He had not gone far when he heard the deep voices of vanquishers shouting up ahead to his right. His head spun. He was so weak he didn't know if he could leap from the road.

Gallen looked down at the ruined body of the bear. Many of the bones were burned all the way through, and it looked as if the bear had died while trying to paw fire from its face. Gallen could not cry. The pain went too deep for that, tasted too bitter. He felt only a hardness, a cold anger that demanded vengeance.

Veriasse shook his head. "We must go. Our friend gave his life trying to warn us. Let us heed that warning."

Veriasse powered up his airbike, turned and headed back down the trail to the highway. Everynne pulled her bike up beside Gallen, touched his shoulder. "I don't know what you are thinking, what you might be planning. But there is nothing we can do for Orick now."

"I know," Gallen said. He squinted at the morning sun, pulled his robe tightly about him to keep out the cold. They rode their bikes downhill, hit the highway and turned north.

They drove for twenty minutes in silence. A creepy sensation stole over Gallen, as if he were being watched. Once, the feeling was so powerful that when they entered a valley, he was forced to stop and gaze out over the white, empty hills. There were no trees, just small bushes and rocks to give shade. No birds sang from the bushes; nothing moved. Even the wind was still. Yet Gallen felt watched.

Veriasse stopped beside him. "Do you feel it, too?" he said. "My bones are trembling in anticipation."

"I haven't seen anything. Nothing has moved," Gallen answered.

Veriasse glanced slowly from side to side, only his fierce blue eyes moving. "That is what bothers me. Gallen, listen with your mantle. See if you can hear any radio conversations. Let it scan for military channels." Veriasse pulled off his gloves, raised his hands in the air as if he were surrendering.

Gallen closed his eyes, freed his senses. The thrusters on their airbikes sounded suddenly loud, but Gallen listened beyond that, began picking up radio frequencies. Images flashed through his mind from commercial holo broadcasts, music played from radio stations. Beyond that, he could pick up some chatter—pilots to the north seeking landing clearance in a city.

"Nothing," Gallen said at last.

Veriasse put his hands down, shook his head. "The same here. I smell nothing. Last time I was here, the dronon had a fairly strong presence on Wechaus. Don't you think it odd that you would hear no military calls at all?"

Gallen agreed. Yet there was nothing they could do but go forward. He hit the thrusters. The bike lifted and hummed down the highway, until at last in the distance he saw smoke rising from a small compound of buildings.

Veriasse pulled beside Gallen. "There's a good inn ahead. Let's stop and see if we can get some news."

As Gallen neared the inn, he could discern white limestone buildings around green pools of steaming water. There were many swimmers near the pools, shivering in the cool air, eager for the water.

Gallen had not bathed in several days. He felt grimy, tired. It looked like a good place to stay.

They pulled up to the front, stopped their airbikes, looked through the windows. The dining room was nearly full, dozens of young couples eating breakfast, smiling, some of them laughing.

Gallen felt disconnected from them, found it somehow abhorrent that these people were laughing when he felt such profound pain. Orick was dead, and Gallen wanted the world to mourn with him.

Everynne and Veriasse got off their bikes, but Gallen just sat for a moment. There was an odd smell of smoke in the air, as if something had burned nearby.

Veriasse went to the door, and it slid open at his approach. A golden serving droid rushed to greet them, and Veriasse looked back at Gallen questioningly. "Are you coming?"

Gallen shook his head. "You eat. I'm not hungry. I'll keep watch out here." Gallen arched his back to loosen muscles tightened by too much driving.

Everynne said, "Are you sure? You'll feel better if you come inside where it's warm. Please, come in with me."

"I want to be alone," Gallen said.

Everynne squeezed his hand, went inside. He watched Everynne and Veriasse through the windows, saw them take a seat. A soft breeze stirred, and Gallen used his mantle, listened to the swimmers laughing at the pools. Yet there was something odd, a sound of whispering in the back parking lot. Gallen could not be certain. It might only have been reeds rattling in the wind, but he needed to stretch, get off the bike, so he climbed off and walked nonchalantly around the left side of the building.

The back parking lot held several dozen aircars and magcars. He stared at them a moment, wondering. It seemed that the lot held more cars than the inn could warrant.

His mantle picked up whispering ahead and to his right, at the back of the building. Gallen crept around a small potted tree, looked at the back of the building. Fifty feet away, three men hunched over a box that was linked to an absurdly large transmitter antennae. They wore white cloth combat armor. One of them looked up at Gallen guiltily.

Gallen did not have time to think. His mantle did it for him. He pulled out his incendiary rifle and fired. At this range, to hit one was to hit all. The chemical discharge slapped over two men. They blazed white as the sun. Gallen flinched, looked away, and found himself running to the front of the building.

Just as he rounded the corner, he met four men in cloth combat armor. He holstered his rifle and pulled out his sword in one move, whipped it overhead and decapitated the first in line. He leapt in the air, kicked one man in the face and sliced through two others, then bellowed as he reached the front door of the inn.

He could see Veriasse inside, sword in hand, swinging like a madman. A dozen "patrons" of the inn had him surrounded, and they held small stunners. They were trying to knock him down, but their weapons had no effect. Everynne was down, half sprawled across a table, blood pouring from her nose, apparently unconscious. A dozen warriors with heavier arms were rushing from the back apartments beside the pools.

Gallen leapt through a large glass window, landed on a table. He pulled his incendiary rifle, fired at the side doors, hitting a droid that had scrambled for cover. The resulting fire effectively sealed the door, and Gallen jumped, giving a flying roundhouse kick to the back of the head of one of Veriasse's opponents.

Within seconds, Veriasse's sword put down the nearest attackers, and he scrambled for Everynne's pack, pulled out the Terror and tossed it to Gallen.

"This is what they want!" he shouted. "Gallen, send the arming code."

Gallen held up the Terror as if it were an icon, and every eye in the room fastened on him. People froze at their tables. No one moved.

"All of you get back!" Gallen shouted. "I've instructed my mantle to detonate this if you don't give us the road!" Gallen could only hope that his ruse would work.

"We've got jammers! We've got jammers!" one soldier yelled.

"You mean the jammers that were out back?" Gallen shouted. "I fried them."

"We have a backup!" the soldier shouted, trying to rally his people.

"Are you willing to bet the lives of everyone on this world that your jammers will work?" Veriasse asked.

That seemed to cow them. The soldiers hesitated. None dared step forward.

Veriasse pulled at Everynne's arm, turned her on her stomach and lifted her, cradling her like a child. He began walking toward the door, and Gallen stalked behind them, holding the Terror high.

Outside, Gallen got on his bike. Dozens of infantrymen in white cloth body armor were rushing from the back apartments. Gallen began counting. There had to be over two hundred of them. He looked at the patrons in the dining hall. None had shock on their faces, no expressions of horror. Only anger, disappointment. He suddenly realized that all of them were military personnel.

Veriasse got Everynne on her bike, and one man walked forward. Gallen could not mistake his stride. He carried himself with dignity and a calm assurance. He had been in charge of this operation.

He was an older man, with long dark hair and eyes as black as obsidian. He wore a small goatee. "Well done, Veriasse," the stranger said. "We meet again."

Veriasse nodded at the man. "Jagget."

"Yes, Commander Jagget, of the planetary defense forces. To tell you the truth, Veriasse, I was not sure I would be able to take your Terror away, but I had to try. No offense, I hope."

"Of course not. But I am curious—why do you call yourself planetary defense forces when this is a dronon world?"

"I work under their direction now," Jagget said, "The dronon appreciate competence, even if it does come from the hand of an old enemy. I was able to convince them that we could handle this situation better than their green-skinned oafs. The element of surprise, you know."

"I find your wavering loyalty unsettling," Veriasse said. "In fact, I cannot believe it. Primary Jagget would never give his loyalty to an alien usurper. I would expect more from even one of his mad clones."

Jagget shrugged. "Believe as you will. I caught your act on Fale, Veriasse. The incident is being broadcast all over the galaxy." He looked at the Terror, licked his lips, glanced at his men, as if trying to make a decision.

Then he gazed deep into Gallen's eyes. "Young man, if you really are linked via ansible to Terrors on eighty-four dronon worlds, detonate them now, this very second. And if you feel you must, destroy this world, too!"

Jagget stepped forward threateningly, walked several paces toward

Gallen. Jagget's eyes went wide, and Gallen could tell that he planned to die. He was trying to force Gallen's hand. He wanted to start the war.

"Stay back!" Veriasse shouted, pulling out his incendiary rifle.

Jagget raised his hand in a commanding gesture. Three men among the crowd shouldered their own weapons. Jagget clones.

"Young man," Jagget said, walking up to Gallen, looking deeply into his eyes, "ignite it, now! Other worlds have burned themselves down in order to keep from falling to the Dronon Empire. It is a worthy trade. Release the Terrors, and someday this sector of the galaxy will remember your name in honor!"

Gallen held the Terror aloft, looked out over the warriors. These were humans whose genes had not been twisted by the dronon. They could not have been subjugated long enough even to feel any loyalty to their conquerors, yet for the most part, they had sided with the dronon. They would have captured Everynne if they could, would have turned her in. As it was, she was unconscious, and Gallen could not tell how badly hurt she might be. And they had killed Orick.

Even now, only their fear of Gallen held the locals at bay. Except for Jagget. Jagget alone seemed to be a true patriot, and he was begging for Gallen to end it all. Set this world afire rather than leave it in the hands of the Dronon Empire. Perhaps he knew the hearts of his people too well.

In that one moment, Gallen would have freed the nanotech warriors within the Terror, if he had had the ability. Jagget walked up to him, grabbed Gallen's wrist, shook it so that the Terror fell to the ground. He stared into Gallen's eyes.

"You can't do it, can you?" Jagget whispered fiercely, as if Gallen had just betrayed all of his hopes. "You've got only one Terror, and you're trying to get it to Dronon—just as Maggie said."

Jagget spun, spoke to his soldiers. "I'll be escorting these people to their destination."

"Sir," one young woman objected, "shouldn't we report their capture to Lord Kintal?"

"You may report it to the dronon bastards if you wish," Jagget said calmly with just the slightest hint of a threat. "But of course, our orders to stop these people were based upon the false assumption that they had many Terrors in their possession. Since that report is obviously spurious, we have no reason to detain them."

The woman looked at him warily, took a step back. "I'll report that everything was quiet on my shift," she said. "May I take a car thereafter, along with my personal leave?"

"Yes," Jagget said. "I think that would be wise."

"You mentioned Maggie," Veriasse said to Jagget. "Where is she?" Veriasse had Everynne on the bike, his arms cradled around her. Everynne's eyelids fluttered. She tried to raise her head, struggled to regain consciousness, then fell back.

"She will join us shortly." Jagget unclipped a small commlink from his belt, spoke swiftly in some personal battle code.

"We'll need a room for a few minutes," Veriasse said. "And some hot food."

"Very well," Jagget said.

Veriasse lifted Everynne, carried her to the back of the compound, down to a small apartment. There he laid her on a bed, lightly tapping her cheek as she struggled to awaken. A dozen soldiers followed them into the apartment. Veriasse turned on them, shouted for them to leave.

Only Gallen, Veriasse, and Jagget stayed to nurse Everynne. Veriasse removed her robe, turned her on her back. She had two burn marks from the stunners, a light one on her lower back, a severe wound on her neck.

Veriasse caught his breath, pointed to the neck wound. "This one may leave a scar." Jagget went to a sink, returned with some water and began spooning it over Everynne's back. Meanwhile Veriasse took out his sword, nicked his wrist and let the blood flow over her wounds.

"What are you doing?" Gallen asked.

"The nanodocs in my blood will help heal the skin," Veriasse said. "Unfortunately, the burn has seared the blood vessels at the subdermal level. The nanodocs in her own system will not be able to combat the wound very effectively. I am hoping to prevent a scar."

Gallen sat, and together they watched the wound. Over the next fifteen minutes, much of the burned and blackened skin dissolved; the swollen red welts reduced in size. Everynne finally woke during that time and whimpered at the pain. Veriasse bid her to be still.

At the end of the fifteen minutes, fresh new skin began to grow over the wounds, but there was a distinct red mark on the back of Everynne's neck, shaped like an *I*.

Veriasse put his head in his hands, sat still for a long time. "I fear," he said heavily, "that all my years of preparation have been jeopardized. Now that the nanodocs have finished knitting the tissues together, we can do nothing to speed the healing process. The blemish should clear in a few days but . . . We must delay our trip. Everynne's blemish makes her ineligible to challenge the Lords of the Swarm."

"How long of a delay do you need?" Jagget said.

Veriasse shook his head. "A few days."

"Veriasse," Jagget said, "the dronon have been sending in troops all week. They know you're here. I could try to hide you, but I don't think I could hold them off that long. At this very moment, the vanquishers have this entire area surrounded. The sooner you leave here, the better your chances of making a clean escape."

"It's only a small mark," Gallen said. "Her clothing might hide it."

"The dronon wear no clothes," Veriasse said. "They will have the right to inspect her without clothing."

"Cosmetics," Jagget said. "Body paint?"

Veriasse looked up, skeptical. "If the dronon discover our deception, they will kill her outright."

"It's worth a try," Jagget said. "You can't wait for her to heal. The dronon have already built one gate key. They can build another. In a week's time perhaps, none of the worlds will be closed to them."

Gallen studied the two men, feeling trapped. Their inability to make a choice galled him. He wished the scar was permanent. Everynne had never wanted to come on this trip. She had been chosen as a sacrifice, and only her generosity let her continue the journey. The only way she could hope to win this battle was to walk away. At least, then, she could live her own life. A scar on her neck would have been a ticket to freedom.

"It will have to be some form of makeup that will not leave a detectable scent," Veriasse said. "At least nothing the dronon can smell. And it must match her skin color precisely."

"I don't know," Jagget said. "That will be a hard order to fill on such short notice."

Everynne turned over, looked at Gallen for a moment, considering her options. "Please, do what you can," she said to Jagget. "I must challenge the Lords of the Swarm quickly."

"Are you sure?" Jagget asked.

"Yes," Everynne said.

Jagget nodded, "I'll be back in fifteen minutes."

Gallen lay down on the floor, weary to the bone, thankful for a few minutes' rest.

A moment later, the door opened again. Gallen did not bother looking up, thinking that one of the Jaggets had entered the room. Suddenly Orick was beside him, licking Gallen's face. "Top of the morning," Orick grinned. "I see you ignored my warning and blundered right into the trap anyway."

"Orick!" Everynne shouted, rousing up in her bed. Gallen threw his arms around the bear. There was a white bandage on Orick's shoulder, a look of pain in his eyes.

"We thought you were dead," Gallen said. "We found bones by the roadside."

"A friend," Orick said soberly. "I left my message and was on my way home, dodging vanquisher patrols. My friend, Panta, stopped to pick me up on the highway, and the vanquishers caught us. She lost her wits and ran for cover. I was too weak to follow. Afterward, they brought me here for questioning, then left me with the Jaggets."

Gallen could tell that there was more than casual friendship involved with this she-bear. He could hear the hurt in Orick's voice. "I'm sorry, my old friend," Gallen offered. Orick limped over to Everynne, gave her a hug. They sat and talked quietly.

Two soldiers brought in some plates of food. Gallen and Everynne sat on the bed and had a bite to eat. Veriasse paced, looking at the wall clock as he waited for Jagget.

Minutes later, two Jaggets came into the room, escorting Maggie. She looked tired, worn, but she smiled in relief to see Gallen. She hugged him and whispered, "I am glad you're well."

One of the Jaggets, an older man, was better dressed than the others Gallen had seen. Captain Jagget introduced him with great flourish as Primary Jagget.

Veriasse stood in deference and said, "Primary Jagget, I thought you were dead." Gallen could not miss the tone of respect in Veriasse's voice. Veriasse glanced at Gallen and explained. "Primary Jagget is one of the great Lord Protectors of our time. He was a Lord Protector three thousand years before I was born."

Primary Jagget said softly, "I *was* a Lord Protector, Veriasse. Now, the dronon have conquered my world, taken my title and position. I have worn out my flesh and been forced to download myself into an artifice. The dronon would not even have allowed that, but for my clones. They have retained enough power to force an uneasy truce."

Primary Jagget clapped a hand on Veriasse's shoulder. "I regret having detained you and your friends, and I regret the harm I've caused here. What I have done, I have done in order to protect my world and my people. I had to be sure of your intent."

Veriasse hesitated a moment. "I suspect that I would have done the same in your position."

Gallen sensed that much was being left unsaid between the two men, and he wondered what kind of relationship they had. They were both Lord Protectors, and though their interests ran afoul of each other, they shared a mutal respect.

Primary Jagget begged them to be at ease, then knelt over Everynne, applied a flesh-colored salve to her neck, and rubbed it in until Gallen could hardly see the scar. When he finished, he stepped back and looked at Everynne admiringly, then bowed. "You are the exact image of your mother Semarritte. I had to come see you for myself. May you grow in power and grace and beauty. I wish you could stay and enjoy my hospitality, but I am afraid that I have just started a war in your behalf, and it will not be safe for you to remain."

"A war?" Veriasse asked.

"The vanquishers must have learned you are here. They began moving in just moments ago. I've ordered my men to wipe out every vanquisher within three hundred kilometers," Primary Jagget answered. "It has long been rumored that you built a gate to Dronon. I know the location of every gate on the planet. Tell me where you must travel, and I will clear a path for you."

"North, sixty kilometers," Veriasse said.

Primary Jagget raised a brow. "There isn't a gate in that region."

"I disguised it so that it does not look like a regular gate," Veriasse said. He glanced at Everynne. "We must go now."

"Wait a moment more," Primary Jagget said. He reached into a fold of his brown jacket, pulled out a mantle. "This is the mantle I wore as a Lord Protector," Jagget said. "I do not want it to fall into enemy hands. I would like you to take it. You have long been a Lord Protector yourself, and I doubt that there is much it could teach you. Still, when you battle the Lords of the Swarm, I would ask that you wear it. Perhaps it could be of help."

Veriasse took the gift. It was an ancient thing of black metal, not nearly so elegant as the mantle Veriasse had given to Gallen. Still, Veriasse took it for what it was, a symbol of hope.

Eighteen

Primary Jagget took a quick survey of the room at the inn, as if he were checking to be sure he didn't leave something when he departed. "We must hurry," he said. "Are you ready to go?"

"Five minutes," Veriasse answered. "When we jump out of the gate, we will be on Dronon. Everynne should be dressed appropriately."

"A couple more minutes, then," Primary Jagget said. "But hurry. Time is of the essence."

Everyone left the room but Veriasse and Everynne. Veriasse opened his pack, unfolded Everynne's golden attire. The metallic robe was made of a flowing material that felt cool, almost watery under his touch. It had an odd sheen to it and was peculiarly heavy, as if it were actually made of microscopic ringlets of pure gold.

Veriasse let his fingers play over the robe. It seemed somehow appropriate that Everynne should wear it this day. She truly was golden, the human equivalent of the dronon's great queen. He had seen it in people's eyes a thousand times: they would look at Everynne and respond with adoration. And though there were physiological reasons for their devotion, something in his bones whispered to Veriasse that mere science could not explain Everynne's power over him. Everynne was sublime.

Some said that she was perfect in figure, that the proportions of each bone in her body were designed to conform to some racial dream, an image of perfection shared by all. Others claimed that it was only a combination of scents that she exuded, a carefully selected range of pheromones that turned men into mindless creatures, willing to sacrifice themselves at her feet.

But Everynne's beauty seemed to him to be more than perfect. When she touched him, he shivered in ecstasy. When she spoke, something in her voice demanded attention, so that the softest words whispered in a noisy room would hold him riveted. Everynne transcended the hopes of the scientists who created her, and in his weaker moments, Veriasse would have admitted that he believed she was supernatural. There was something mystical in the way she moved him, something holy in the way she could transform a man.

And so, today she would wear gold, an appropriate color for the last Tharrin alive on the conquered worlds, the sole child of a race dead in this sector of the galaxy.

When all was ready, he left the room. Everynne dressed quickly in her golden robes, boots, and gloves, then put on her mantle of golden ringlets. Though she was a woman, and fully as beautiful as any of her previous incarnations, Veriasse looked at her and thought that there was something special about this incarnation of Semarritte. Perhaps it was only her youthfulness. By having been force grown in the vats, she had attained the appearance of being twenty years old by the time she was two. Perhaps that was part of it: there was an innocence, a freshness to this incarnation that had been missing in the previous generations.

When she finished dressing, she sat on her bed and smiled up at Veriasse, weakly, her face pale with fear. But for her expression, she looked the part of a queen. He said, "You look wonderful. You look radiant. Are you afraid?"

Everynne nodded. Veriasse himself had great doubts about this plan. "You will do well today, my love," Veriasse assured her. "Never has there been a woman more worthy to represent the human species in such a contest. I can only hope that I shall be as worthy."

Everynne took his hand, looked into his eyes. "I trust you," she said. "If your devotion for me can grant you power, then I know you cannot be beaten today."

Veriasse kissed her hand, then they went outside to meet the others.

Gallen, Orick, Maggie, and Jagget sat in front of the inn, straddling their airbikes. Far to the south, Veriasse heard a dim concussion, the sound of heavy artillery.

"Hurry," Primary Jagget whispered. "Every minute is costing the lives of my men."

Veriasse hopped on his bike, and Everynne climbed aboard hers. She was shaking, unsettled, and Veriasse would have reassured her, but she twisted the handlebars, revving her thrusters, and the rest of the group was forced to hurry to catch her.

They roared over the highway, which was ominously devoid of traffic. Ten kilometers up the road, they came upon a magtruck that had exploded, throwing out the corpses of dead vanquishers, and two kilometers farther along, they whipped past a score of Jaggets lying dead by the roadside.

Primary Jagget held his commlink to his mouth, shouting orders in his personal battle language, a code that was thick with nasal tones and grunts.

Forty kilometers from the city, a wall of scintillating lights blossomed ahead to his right—portable shielding. Just beyond the shields, a curtain of flames and black smoke erupted.

Dronon fliers—swift, saucer-shaped craft—whipped through the air at Mach 15, dropping ordnance on some unseen front. The very ground shook and buckled under the force of the assault, and Veriasse hoped that the saucers wouldn't target them. Jagget screamed into his commlink, and a squadron of slower V-shaped fighters piloted by humans swerved from the north, perhaps forty strong. They would be no match for the dronon. They could only serve as a diversion.

Veriasse and the others continued north for five kilometers, heading toward the front until a vast pall of smoke hung over the little party. It was nearly dark as night, yet Veriasse did not turn on his airbike's headlights.

They had not gone far into the cloud when Primary Jagget shouted to them, "Our front is collapsing ahead. My men can't maintain it. Can we veer off the road?"

"Yes," Veriasse shouted. "There is a river to the right. We can follow it north."

Veriasse alone knew where the gate to Dronon lay. He wondered if he should tell the others its location. Two hundred years ago, he had ordered his men to build the gate. In trying to plant the destination markers at Dronon, he had lost three complete technical crews. Afterward, Semarritte had forbade him from trying to put more gates on Dronon, just as she had always forbade him from building a gate that would lead to her omni-mind. She said some risks were not worth taking. But unlike the gates of old, constructed in simpler times, this one was hidden. He had built it into the arch of a small bridge that spanned the river.

He pictured the location, sent the thought to his mantle, ordered it to transmit the knowledge to Gallen. Gallen suddenly turned, caught Veriasse's eye, then nodded.

Two kilometers farther, the black clouds of soot began to thin. Suddenly light flashed across the sky far behind them, brighter than the sun, followed by a second blinding flash nearby. The light continued to glow redly through the sooty sky.

"They're using atomics!" Jagget shouted, and Veriasse glanced back. Mushroom clouds were forming where the inn had been, and again at a point perhaps nine kilometers behind. "Open your speed up."

Veriasse's heart raced. They were still ten kilometers from the gate. The atomic bombs would raise a wall of dirty, swiftly moving air as the air super-heated. The dust storm would rush away from the bomb site at over a hundred kilometers per hour—a speed impossible to match in such rough terrain. Yet if they did not beat that surging storm of radioactive dust, it would kill them all.

"Vanquishers ahead!" Jagget shouted. On the highway ahead, two kilometers away, a convoy topped a steep hill. Veriasse swerved from the road into a snow-filled ravine, and the others followed. The airbikes kicked up rooster tails of snow, millions of tiny motes that glittered like slivers of ruby, reflecting the atomic fires behind.

Veriasse began counting the seconds, listening for the blast, trying to discern exactly how far they were from the detonation site. Fifty seconds later, the air filled with a high-pitched shriek, indicating that the Jagget's shields had collapsed, followed by a deep booming.

The ground rumbled and rolled in waves. To the northeast, a volcano began to spit a sluggish flow of lava down its sides.

The airbikes raced over a rise, down a rock-strewn gully, then swept onto a river, skating over flattened stones and lead-gray water that reflected the winter sky and the towering mushroom clouds that filled the heavens behind them like elementals of flame.

Veriasse glanced at his speedometer. They were traveling at only seventy kilometers an hour—fast over such uneven terrain, but not fast enough. He opened his throttle. "Faster," he shouted.

The river was an old one, and canyon walls soon rose around them as they surged through a narrow gorge. Veriasse's speed hit a hundred and twenty. Everynne pulled ahead of him. She had her head low to combat wind resistance. She threw a trail of icy water in his face, and he only hoped that she could make it as she raced ahead.

Time and again she flirted with death, weaving through the rocky gorge, taking corners so fast that she was only a hair's breadth from destruction. For eight more minutes they raced, and whenever they reached a straight portion of the river, Veriasse would glance back, each time hoping anew that the others had negotiated the last turn. Maggie's bike was both slow and dangerously unstable with the bear on it. Jagget stayed at the far end of the train, bringing up the rear.

The gate to Dronon waited for them somewhere ahead at the end of a wide bend. Through his mantle, Jagget transmitted a message: "We have pursuers behind me." Veriasse glanced back, thinking the saucers would be shooting overhead. He saw no saucers—only a great black wall of dust rushing toward them, the frontal tide of the nuclear storm.

Veriasse rounded a corner. Ahead, the river stretched straight for a kilometer, its troubled waters winking in the sunlight. At the far end spanned a bridge, a simple monstrosity of gray plasteel arching over the river. Veriasse looked at it, and his heart fell. The gate was built into a bridge, but he could not remember ever having seen this one before. Was this the bridge?

"Everynne," he shouted, "initiate your key."

Everynne reached into the pack behind her, fumbled for a moment, and slowed her bike as she grabbed the key.

Veriasse slowed, pulled beside her, glanced back. Gallen whizzed past them, followed by the bike with Maggie and Orick on it. Orick's eyes were wide in terror, and the bear's tongue lolled from his mouth.

Jagget held up the rear, and as he rounded the corner, he looked at Veriasse and Everynne in surprise, slowed his throttle at the mouth of the narrow bend. He whipped out his incendiary rifle with one hand, raised it in salute to Veriasse.

Everynne took the key firmly in hand, opened up her throttle, and Veriasse followed directly behind, drenched by plumes of freezing water.

Everynne thumbed the unlocking sequence. Ahead a silver light began to glow beneath the bridge. Behind them, Veriasse heard vanquishers whoop in delight as they rounded the corner. He glanced back.

Three vanquishers in aircars whipped down the river channel, negotiating the tight turn.

Primary Jagget fired his rifle, and pure white light shot down the river. A vanquisher burst into flame, and his burning car screamed toward Jagget. Another vanquisher swerved to avoid the explosion, and his car erupted into a fireball as it smashed against the canyon walls. The last in line killed his throttle, and his car slowed and bogged down in the water.

Jagget did not have time to avoid the burning car that hurtled toward him. In less than a heartbeat, his body transformed into a swarm of butterflies that lifted above the collision.

Overhead, the nuclear winds roared toward them all, a black tumult. Veriasse turned to face ahead. Maggie, Orick, and Gallen plunged through the gate while Everynne slowed to match Veriasse's speed. As he hurtled toward the gate, Veriasse spared one last glance back. The last hapless vanquisher had stalled his aircar. He frantically struggled to restart it as the black storm swept over him.

Then came the white and the void, and Veriasse felt the kiss of the cold breeze that blew in this crack between time and space. He could feel the fabric of his robes whipped by the gale, but there was no sound, no seeing here. Instead, there was only a rushing sensation. The hand of a god lifted him to a distant place.

When his vision cleared, a drab plain sprawled before them, filled with pockmarks and covered with rocks. Thin clouds made the sky a dim reddish gray. The air was hot and sticky. He could see no buildings, no roads or any other signs of habitation—only desolation.

A soft wind sighed over the ground, and Veriasse began to recognize that there was some plant life around, a deep gray-brown fungus that grew in tight knots like rosebuds. Things that he'd first taken to be pale rocks also proved to be fat, fanlike plants of palest blue, and the pockmarks in the ground were so numerous that they could not have been formed by any natural means that he knew of. They could only have been formed by the walking hive fortresses of the dronon.

"Where do we go now?" Maggie said.

Veriasse turned to Gallen. "Which way is magnetic north?"

Gallen consulted the sensors in his mantle, nodded to his right. The sun lay to their northeast. Obviously, winter was coming to this section of the world. The walking hives would be migrating.

"North," Veriasse said. "Look for fresh pockmarks in the ground. Maybe we can track a hive."

They hit the thrusters, let the airbikes carry them over the gloomy terrain. They saw only a few animals—often things that looked like a conglomeration of sticks could be seen sunning themselves or dragging pieces of vegetable matter to their burrows.

Once they came to a cloud of round, slightly opaque gray leaves that fluttered slowly over the landscape; it wasn't until the leaves splattered against the windscreen of his bike that Veriasse saw that they were some kind of winged insect, with tiny red heads attached to a single wing. He could not imagine how the creature sustained flight.

After two hours, Dronon's sun set, rolling quickly, a dull shield dropping before the onslaught of darkness. In the distance ahead, they spotted a huge black saucer. Massive legs rose in the air around the saucer like hinged towers.

They drove to it, found a deserted hive city with gaping rust holes in it. The armor was pitted from incendiary fire. The city provided the best shelter they had seen all day, so they stopped to camp. They laid out a few blankets beneath the crook of one towering leg, built a cooking fire, and began heating some food bags.

Then they sat, listening to the night sounds of an alien world: something on the horizon kept making a noise like a popping bag. Elsewhere, a creature called out, "wheeeee," in a high, buzzing voice.

Veriasse felt disappointed at not having found a hive, and after he checked the back of Everynne's neck to see how the wound was healing, Everynne lay down on her blanket just staring up, as if deep in thought. Orick grumbled about the inconvenience of always finding dronon where you didn't want them, but not being able to find them on their own home world, then lay down protectively beside Everynne. The poor bear had been listless all day, and his stab wound, although slight, had cost him much. He fell asleep within minutes.

"Don't worry," Veriasse said to the others. "The chances are good that our fire will attract some attention in the night. Perhaps by morning we will meet the dronon, and then we'll find out how they feel about our intrusion on their world." He lay back and thought. Everynne's scar was mending well, but he somewhat hoped that they could wait a few more days.

Gallen and Maggie were restive. Maggie wore her mantle, and she fairly buzzed with excitement as she studied the legs to the hive city, talked about the engineering feats of the dronon who had made such a thing. At last Maggie took a torch, led Gallen up into the body cavity of the dead city. There they stood on the black metal of a turret mount and gazed into the deep shadows.

To Veriasse they looked as if they were peering into the shell of a huge turtle. Maggie shouted and whistled to hear her voice echo.

The two climbed inside to explore.

Veriasse watched the light from their torch dim as they entered the recesses of the city, and soon he was alone with Everynne and Orick. Veriasse felt weary, tense, and he laid down beside Everynne. Orick snored; it was getting very dark.

He had thought Everynne slept, but she said softly, "Well, here we are."

"At last," Veriasse said, trying to sound hopeful.

Everynne laughed, not the musical sound of joy, but a derisive chuckle. "At last."

"Do you regret having come?" Veriasse asked.

It was an unfair question, he knew, but Everynne answered, "This is the planet where I will die, one way or another. I guess I'm disappointed that it is taking so long. I had myself braced for a battle today."

"I know that you think you will lose something if I win this battle," Veriasse said, "but I promise you—when your consciousness is subsumed into that of Semarritte's, it will not be a death for you. Instead, it will be a wonderful awakening. I have seen it happen with clones before. It will be such a powerful experience that it will overwhelm you, and you will fall asleep for a few moments. But you will awaken a much wiser and more powerful being. Trust me, my daughter, trust me."

Veriasse looked at Everynne's face, lit only by the campfire. She was more frightened than he'd ever seen her. She trembled violently. Her lips pulled back in terror, and a heavy perspiration lay on her forehead.

Veriasse took her hand, caressed it, but Everynne did not turn to him. Instead, she laughed coldly and said, "Father, if I turned around and walked away from here, would you hate me?"

This was a subject that Veriasse had hoped to avoid—a discussion about other options, other plans for defeating the dronon. He had already considered all of his options, discussed them in depth with Everynne and Semarritte before her, rejected them one by one. She couldn't walk away from this, and Veriasse could not afford to let her be weak. He wanted to warn her against trying to take the easy path, remind her of billions of others who would suffer and die under dronon rule if she quit now. Instead, he only spoke the truth. "I would love you, even if you turned away. You are as much a daughter as I have ever had, and I've watched you learn and grow these past three years with great joy and a great deal of pride."

"But you will love me more when Semarritte fills me, won't you?" she said bitterly. "I'll bet you can't wait until she succeeds me. How long do you think it will take before you bed her?"

Veriasse had rarely seen Everynne angry. Never had he heard her say an unkind word, yet he had to remind himself that emotionally she was still a child, and he had to make allowances for that. "Everynne, don't torture yourself this way. No good will come of it."

"I'm not torturing myself," she said. "You're torturing me. You're killing *me!*" She rolled away from him and began weeping.

Veriasse wanted to say something to comfort her, but there was so little he could say. At last he whispered, "If you want to walk away from this, then tell me, and I swear I will do everything in my power to get you home safely. If this is what you want, we can raise armies, take our keys and open the gates. People everywhere love you. They would fight if you asked them to, and in a matter of days I swear I could raise an army of billions to fight in your behalf. They would scream across the worlds in a rampage of blood and fire. Terrors could be unleashed on a thousand worlds. If this is what you want."

He did not have to tell her that the losses from such a war would be immeasurable. The dronon would begin destroying those worlds they had already captured. The images of mushroom clouds were still fresh in his mind from this afternoon, and images from the terror-burned world of Bregnel lay in his mind like a black clot, but this war would be far worse than anything that had occurred before. The dead would pile up quickly, mountains of corpses so vast that no one could ever begin to count them.

But Everynne already knew that. She could not turn away from so many in need. She lay crying, and said at last, "Hold me, Father. Please?"

Veriasse put his arm over her shoulder and snuggled against her back. She gripped his hand, hard. He held her until she stopped shaking, nearly an hour, and at last he whispered, "Are you all right? Do you feel better?"

"I'm all right," she said firmly. "I just wish it were over. I was frightened for a minute."

"There's my brave girl," Veriasse said, and he lay with his body cupped around hers, smelling the sweet scent of her hair. After awhile she began to breathe deeply, as if she would soon fall asleep, and he wondered about Maggie and Gallen. Though they had been in the dead hive city for a long time, he reminded himself that it was a huge place. He imagined that they might keep exploring for hours. He gave himself permission to sleep, and soon fell into a fitful dream.

Maggie rushed through the dead dronon hive city, feeling wild and free. Her nerves jangled in anticipation, and Gallen ran behind her. They would meet the dronon soon, and she fully expected to die, but for the moment, the mantle she wore wanted images of this city. It drove her forward in a mad rush through the beast, gleaning images of an engine room where monstrously large hydraulics assemblies had once driven the massive legs. She studied the power system and the exhaust nacelles.

Though the city was dead and much of the equipment had been scavenged, the dronon took great care of their equipment; they had even protected the abandoned machinery by coating it with oil.

The heavy odor of rusting iron and dust filled the city. The corridors were dark. Wind whistled through the hallways high overhead.

For an hour Maggie and Gallen studied the engine rooms, then found what could only have been egg warmers in a huge nursery. But Maggie's mantle drove her on, ever curious. It fed its discoveries to her in a constant barrage, so that she felt as if she would burst at the wonder of it all.

She ran laughing into the bowels of the city, and Gallen ran beside her, bearing the torch, sometimes touching her shyly.

At last they reached a storage chamber and walked down a long corridor. Various implements of unknown intent had been piled along the walls, the machinery of a forgotten age. Enormous capacitor coils rose up for ten meters, sitting like huge thimbles. Spare legs for the hive city were strung from the ceiling. Bits of round, antique flying message pods lay heaped in a pile, and Maggie's mantle warned her to fill her pockets with them so she could disassemble them later. Things that looked like dronon heads made of glass—with three sets of compound eyes—lay in a heap, as if in some distant past the dronon had tried creating androids. Or perhaps, Maggie wondered, there were even now dronon-shaped androids running about in the hive cities. But her mantle whispered that if such things existed, they had never been seen on any world.

Much of what she saw her mantle could understand—bits of cabling, servomotors, a shelf heaped with mechanical brains, outdated egg-warming chambers. These things she would explain to Gallen. Yet much of it was equally mysterious to her. Most of the dronon equipment was bulky, five times as heavy as anything a human would use. The dronon seemed to prefer their machinery to be durable rather than lightweight or convenient.

In one vast chamber, they found what could have only been a spaceship. It was a small vessel, eighty feet long, forty wide, shaped like a Y. Maggie didn't know if she could fly it.

She opened the hatch, went inside, and her mantle whispered to her as she studied the engines. She told Gallen, "This has a gravity-wave drive. We couldn't take it out of the solar system. Still, I'll bet it's fast." She went to the control board. The chairs before the panel were saddle-shaped affairs meant to hold a dronon body, and various foot pedals on the floor looked too intricate for any being with less than four legs to operate. The hand controls were set on a dashboard nearly five feet away and could only be manipulated by something with long arms. Maggie grinned, realizing that this must be an ancient dronon warship, for only the vanquishers with their long battle arms could have worked those controls.

She was giddy with excitement, grinning in wonder. She laughed, then laid back on one of the saddle-shaped chairs and stretched.

Gallen set the torch in a groove on the ship's control panel, then turned and looked at her, perplexed. "I've never seen you in this kind of mood before."

"What kind of mood?"

"So ecstatic. So free."

Maggie laughed. "That's because I've never been happy or free before," and she realized that there was more truth in it than she would have dared admit to herself.

"Your smile looks good on you," Gallen said. He swung his leg over the saddle, sat facing her, his legs wrapped around hers. He lay back with his arms folded behind his head. His half-closed eyes looked tired, and the flames from the torch flickered, showing only half of his face. She felt electric, wanted to kiss him now, make love, but Gallen only studied her a moment.

Maggie's mantle whispered for her to get up, look deeper into the storage chambers. She took it off and held it in one hand, not wanting to be distracted by its insistent promptings.

Gallen leaned forward, stroked her jawbone tenderly with his fingers, and kissed her. It was an odd kiss, she thought. It wasn't insistent with desire, nor was it one of the guilty little pecks that Gallen had given her back home. It was slower than dripping honey and tasted just as sweet. It spoke to her, saying, "I love you just as you are, and right now I am content with that."

They held each other and kissed for a few minutes, then Gallen leaned back again, pillowing his head with his hands.

"Damn you, Gallen O'Day," Maggie said. "It took you long enough."

"I suppose it did," Gallen smiled, self-satisfied. "When we get back to Tihrglas, will you marry me?"

Oh course I'll marry you, she thought. But then her heart fell. "I'm not going back to Tihrglas."

"Not going back?" Gallen asked.

"Why would I want to go back? What's for me there? You said it yourself not a moment ago. In all my life, you've never seen me so happy. Gallen, how can I begin to explain this—right now, I want to tear this city apart," she said, waving toward the ship and the dronon city around her, "and discover exactly how it works. Like those little dronon message pods. Until two hundred years ago, that was the only form of communication the dronon used. They hadn't discovered radio waves at all, until we showed them. The pods have miniature antigravity drives in them, and no technician that I've ever heard of has disassembled one of the buggers and figured out how it worked. Gallen, I've got a pocket full of dronon technology, and right now I feel as rich as can be. It's amazement and discovery. Here I'm free to learn and grow. I can't get that on Tihrglas. Pick any other world we've been to. I don't care which. I could go back and be happy, but you'll never see me smile again on Tihrglas."

Gallen stumbled over his words. "Maggie, I—we don't belong here. I can't protect you here."

"I don't want your protection," Maggie said. "You asked to be my husband, not my bodyguard."

Her flippant words didn't answer his real concerns, she realized. He was a bodyguard. It came naturally to him. Part of him cried out that at all costs he had to protect those around him, maintain a semblance of order. But in these past few days, they had staggered through so many worlds that he was left confused, overwhelmed. He had not been able to discern the underlying order in the worlds around him, simply because the human societies they had visited were all experimenting and growing, twisting away from any predefined shapes.

"You have your mantle," Maggie said. "It has to be teaching you something. In time, you'll become a Lord Protector, like Veriasse." Or perhaps a frustrated fanatic, like Primary Jagget, she wondered. When Jagget's world had twisted out of shape on him, he had not been able to adapt. He kept calling Wechaus "my world," but it was peopled by folks who over the millennia had become strangers to him.

And suddenly Maggie understood. In his way, Gallen already *was* a Lord Protector. Back in Tihrglas, he'd planned to run for sheriff of County Morgan, and in a few years he'd have become the Lord Sheriff of all the counties. He'd been born to become the Lord Protector of Tihrglas.

Gallen's eyes misted. After a moment he said softly, "Maybe, maybe I can find a world we could both live with."

Maggie took his hand in hers. "Maybe we can find that world together."

In his dream, Veriasse rode his airbike, speeding over the dull plains of Dronon with Everynne beside him. Ahead were dark clouds, gray as slate. He could hear the distant rumble of thunder. They drove hard toward the sun as it prepared to dip below the clouds, and he passed under the sprawling leg of a dronon hive city. There was so little daylight left that Veriasse despaired of ever making it to the horizon.

The sun dipped below the distant hills, and Veriasse gasped. Grief passed through him as the night descended. Yet suddenly the white sun flared out on the horizon as if it had reversed in its course, blazing across the blasted land, filling him with hope.

The dream was so real that Veriasse stirred, heard a distant rumble and realized that thunder was brewing on the horizon. He would have gone back to sleep, but Gallen shouted, "Over here! Come over here!"

Everynne stirred from his arms.

Veriasse sat up. Gallen had fired his incendiary rifle into the air. White chemical fire streamed in the sky like a brilliant flare, then arced toward the ground. Gallen and Maggie had come out of the dead hive city and were now standing on a gun mount. They shouted and waved, and Veriasse looked out over the horizon. In the distance, something massive and black moved in the darkness, crawling over the plains, heaving its bloated body along like a gigantic tick. Veriasse could only see it by the lights at its battle stations, lights that glowed in the night like immense red eyes.

The ground shook and rumbled in pain. Veriasse had not heard thunder in his dreams but the sound of a dronon hive city groaning as it pulled itself over the broken earth.

Gallen hooted and shot another round from his rifle, shouting in an exaggerated brogue, "Come on, you lousy bastards! Drag your ass on over here! We're tired of chasing after you!"

The dronon city changed course and began moving toward them, its turrets swiveling as the dronon searched for sign of enemies. Veriasse's heart pounded in his chest. His breath came ragged. They had found the enemy.

Nineteen

Veriasse could almost not believe his luck. Of all the scenarios that he had imagined, this perhaps was most ideal—to spot a dronon hive city in the distance at night. He went to his pack, pulled out his various paraphernalia. Some of it had taken him years to acquire. A translator he clipped to his mantle was equipped with a microphone that he could speak into, loudspeakers that would throw his voice, and a tiny speaker that plugged into his ear. With it, he could speak his native English softly and have his words translated into dronon in a commanding roar. Meanwhile, the device would translate the dronon's own clicks into English and feed them into the earpiece.

Veriasse plugged in the earpiece, then flipped on the translator, noticed that Everynne was doing the same with her own translator.

He also pulled out some protective goggles that would keep acid from his eyes, in case a dronon spit at him.

Under dronon law, those who engaged in ceremonial combat were not allowed any weapons to fight with, but for his own defense, Veriasse had brought a small holo projector. He got it out, set it on the ground before Everynne, turned it on: the air above her shivered for a moment, then blazed with an image of a Golden Queen, a hive mother whose abdomen was a great saucer-shaped, bloated sac. Her small useless wings were neatly folded over her back, and she stood regally, her clublike forearms raised as if to do battle, her head held high so that the uppermost of her three eye clusters allowed her to look behind her back while the other two arrays scanned the horizon at one hundred and twenty degree angles. The whiplike sensors under her mandibles swung about wildly, as if she were trying to catch an elusive scent.

Out on the horizon, the great city would drop, then rise on its legs and shudder forward, like a hive mother dragging her egg sac behind her. The earth protested under its weight, and a cloud of dust and heated exhaust poured from behind. Light glowed from the archways above the forward turrets.

Veriasse looked at Everynne. She was tense, standing with arms folded, her face pale. Orick stood beside her on all fours, the hair on his neck raised, his fangs showing as he gazed on.

Gallen and Maggie shouted as they climbed down rungs built into the dead city's huge legs. In less than four minutes, they made it down. Gallen shouted, "Veriasse, watch out! There's a sea of dronon warriors swarming out of that thing!"

"I know," Veriasse said calmly. "They will come inspect us to make sure that their hive queen is not in jeopardy. Then I will battle them for Right of Charn. If we win Right of Charn, then they will lead us to the Lords of the Swarm, so that I can battle one last time. I can only hope their queen grants us the opportunity to battle."

"And if she doesn't?" Maggie asked, coming up behind him.

"Then likely we'll all be killed," Veriasse answered calmly. He glanced back, in the golden light thrown by the holo he saw the stricken look on Maggie's face. "I kept trying to warn you," Veriasse said. "The dronon are highly territorial. If we lose any step of the way, by their own law, the dronon may kill us all." He didn't want to have to tell them this, but knew that he had to tell them how to save themselves. "If I'm killed, fall on your knees and lay your arms out in front of you, with your wrists crossed and your head facing the ground. This is the dronon pose of ritual oblation. A dronon who assumes that posture is both defenseless and unable to see the leaders before him. The dronon vanquishers may spare your life if you maintain that pose, although they might strike you lightly with their battle arms. Given our thin skins, even a light blow might kill us. Still, it is your best chance."

"Are you sure it will work?" Maggie asked.

"It is a part of the order," Veriasse answered. "The dronon crave order. Yes, I believe it will work."

The hive city had approached to within two kilometers now, and by its lights, Veriasse could see the black shining carapaces of countless dronon vanquishers scurrying like cockroaches before the great city. At any one time, dozens of them would rise up on their back legs, sensor whips lashing as they gazed forward and tasted the air. Beneath the rumbling and squeaking sounds of the moving city, a dull roar arose, the clacking of arms and legs slapping against the carapaces of the dronon, the clicking of mouthfingers against the dronon vocal drums as they spoke amongst themselves. The city and its racing warriors moved far faster than Veriasse had imagined.

Veriasse took out his incendiary rifle, fired two shots in the ground in order to give them more light. The chemical fire burned in white-hot pillars, and Veriasse threw off his cloak, stepped forward between the pillars of light, raised his arms over his head and crossed them at the wrists, signaling that he wished to engage in ritual combat. He was dressed all in black—shining black boots, supple black gloves, a vest of black battle armor. Even his mantle was a glossy black, and he hoped that in this light he would look enough like a Lord Escort that the Dronon would recognize him as such.

The dronon hive lurched its last few steps, then squatted. The saucer section of this hive was perhaps twelve stories tall and seven hundred meters wide. Each of its eight legs towered a hundred meters in the air before reaching the first of its three hinged joints. The lights from the city showed dronon vanquishers at the gun emplacements, and smaller white workers rushed around them, bringing food and drink. Veriasse wondered if the dronon frequently fed during battle, or if perhaps the dronon were assuming some brave pose.

A dark wave of vanquishers swarmed forward to within a hundred meters of Veriasse's small band, then climbed one atop another, forming a wall of bodies that bristled with incendiary rifles. The thrumming of their voices rose, sounding like a vast sea of reeds rustling in the wind. The translator speaker plugged into Veriasse's ear was so overwhelmed by their derisive shouts that it seldom attempted to translate, and Veriasse silently cursed his luck, fearing that he would not be able to hear anything a single dronon might say to him.

Veriasse shouted the formal words of challenge, praying that his translator would phrase them correctly. "This land is ours! All land is ours! A Great Queen comes among you. Prostrate yourselves in adoration, or prepare to do battle!" He waited a moment, and his translator began clicking loudly.

Every dronon suddenly fell silent, and from the top of the wall of living bodies, a single dronon vanquisher raised on its back legs, crossed its battle arms overhead and shouted: "You dishonor us! This is no true Golden Queen before us, merely a projection! Are your minds so simple that you think to trick us?" In the darkness, Veriasse could not see if this dronon wore the facial tattoos of a Lord Escort, but the creature spit acid, as if to say, "You are food." Veriasse guessed that only a Lord Escort would dare offer such an insult.

Obviously, this would not go as smoothly as Veriasse had hoped. His stomach knotted. "This holograph is only a banner that we carry," Veriasse shouted. "Our Golden Queen stands behind me! She is not a dronon like you, but all among us humans worship her form. She is flawless and worthy of adoration. A Great Queen comes among you! Prostrate yourselves in adoration, or prepare to do battle!" Veriasse threw his arms out forward in a battle pose and spit on the ground.

The dronon cringed at his insult.

Silently, Veriasse looked backward at Everynne. She held her hands knotted in a fist, and he saw a faint light shining golden between her fingers, showing that she held the Terror in her hand. If these dronon attacked, she would have only a portion of a second to activate the weapon and begin destroying this world. Almost, he hoped that she would activate it now.

The Lord Escort shouted, "I will perform a rite of inspection on this Golden!" Suddenly its wings unfolded and it leapt from the wall, landing within an arm's length of Everynne. Veriasse could see tattoos on its face—golden waves like rods of lightning striking from each eye. The Lord Escort's sensor whips waved over Everynne's head, flashed around her hips. It hesitated a long moment. Veriasse prayed that it would not make her strip, search for flaws.

The Lord Escort pulled at her clothes, but did not remove them. Apparently, it seemed more pleased by the color and texture of the golden material than by Everynne's pale skin. At last the dronon clicked, "I do not find this one worthy of adoration."

"She is worthy," Veriasse said. "She is Golden among mankind, perfect in form, without blemish."

"She is soft, like a larvae. She is disgusting, unworthy of adoration."

"All humans are soft," Veriasse said. "And we find your bodies to be disgusting, unworthy of adoration. Yet we honor your Great Queen despite the differences in our forms. We ask you to do the same. I assure you that you will never see a more perfect human than this Golden Queen, and I challenge you to battle for Right of Charn."

By battling only for the Right of Charn, Veriasse felt that he was making the decision easier for the creature. If Veriasse should win, there would be a second inspection by the Golden Queen and her Lord Escort. In effect, Veriasse was asking for a small thing. The dronon said, "I reject your right to challenge. This is not a Golden."

"If you reject our right to challenge," Veriasse said, "then you will dishonor the Golden Queen of our kind. If you will not honor our Goldens, then all mankind on all worlds will reject your queen's right to rule over us. You will start a war unlike any that you have ever known."

"You threaten us?" the Lord Escort asked. He looked at Everynne, at the Terror glowing in her hands.

"I do not want to be forced into threatening you," Veriasse said. "But you know what we carry. You've chased us across the worlds. If you do not let humans battle for the right of succession, you leave us no alternatives."

The dronon hesitated. "I speak the truth," Veriasse said. "Let us battle for the Right of Charn."

The dronon studied Everynne a moment longer, backed off two steps. "I will go and consult with our queen." It turned, flew up to the hive city and entered. By now the chemical fires from the incendiary rifles were beginning to die, and in the light thrown from the twisting flames, it almost seemed that the wall of dronon bodies wavered.

Neither Gallen, Orick, nor Maggie moved or spoke, and Veriasse was silently thankful for their good sense. The negotiations were at a critical point. If the queen ruled against them, the dronon would attack in a great wave. If she decided to grant the Right of Charn, Veriasse assumed she would come out with her Lord Escort to do battle.

Ten minutes passed, twelve, and then the Lord Escort flew from the battlements of his hive city, landed on the bodies of his own men.

The Lord Escort raised high on his hind legs, crossed his battle arms over his head. "We have consulted with our Golden. She instructs us to honor you by letting you battle for Right of Charn. I am Dinnid of the Endless Rocks Hive. For ten thousand years we have ruled this plain. Our larvae shall eat your corpses. Our vanquishers shall claim your domain. Your hive shall submit to us!"

As one, a hundred thousand dronon vanquishers raised their battle arms and slammed them together with great clashing sounds.

Veriasse shrugged, tried not to show his concern. Until now, he'd had no idea where on dronon he might be, but the name of the Endless Rocks Hive was known throughout the worlds of mankind. Dinnid was relatively young and powerful, a son of the Golden Queen and her Lord Escort. Rumor named him "The Cunning" for his prowess in battle. It was said that he was the finest strategist among the Lord Escorts, and many claimed that he and his queen would become successors to the current Golden. It was said that Dinnid was only biding his time until his nemesis grew older and more feeble.

Dinnid's wings flashed, and he darted high into the air, entered the maw of the hive. Ahead of Veriasse, the dronon vanquishers began clacking and mumbling, readjusting their bodies so that an opening appeared in the wall. Veriasse looked back at Everynne, telling her with his eyes to follow. Gallen, Maggie, and Orick followed, too, and they walked through a tunnel formed by the black bodies of dronon warriors.

When they reached the saucer-shaped belly of the hive, the dronon lowered a ladder much like any that a human might use, except that the rungs were spaced inconveniently far apart. Veriasse climbed, noted the thin gray powder of dried dronon stomach acids on the rungs but decided that his gloves would be ample protection. Only poor Orick among the group did not have gloves, and Veriasse hoped that the padding on the bear's paws would prove adequate insulation.

When they reached the lowest level of the hive city, they came to a security station where strange, gleaming, three-eyed cameras photographed them. Message pods, like tiny balls, whizzed through the air, flying between various levels with a hiss. Small white female dronon workers scurried through the hallways like lice, infecting him with their tremendous energy. They seemed incapable of moving at anything less than breakneck speed.

The group climbed more ladders, and everywhere were tan dronon technicians with green tattoos and long segmented fingers growing from small battle arms. Vanquishers lined the halls. When they reached the mid-level of the hive, Veriasse glanced down one corridor, saw a vast incubation chamber. Thousands of white workers scurried among eggs, adjusting heating devices, catching the grublike newborns as they hatched, regurgitating acidified food into the gullets of grubs.

At last Veriasse climbed to the highest level of the great city, stopped to catch his breath. Dronon vanquishers lined the passage. He stared down the dimly lit hall for a moment, waited for the others to catch up with him. The air here was thick with the acrid scent of dronon, warmed uncomfortably by the heat of hundreds of thousands of bodies. Everynne breathed heavily but tried to stand tall and regal. Orick was panting from the effort of climbing, and Maggie was drenched with sweat when she reached the landing platform. Veriasse let them catch their breaths, then led the way down a long corridor lighted dimly by golden globes.

Some dronon vanquishers raised their battle arms over their heads, crossing them as a sign of respect for Everynne and her retinue, but most of the vanquishers refused that honor.

The air grew hot and fetid as they neared the belly of the city, until at last they came to a wide, circular room two hundred meters across.

Around the room, thousands of dronon lined the walls. Black Lord Vanquishers with their enlarged forelegs and flashing wings seemed to make up the majority of the audience, but as his eyes adjusted to the dim light, Veriasse saw that they were really outnumbered by small whitish workers, plump as lice, who ran about under the feet of the warriors. Dozens of the large tan technicians with their green facial tattoos had also come.

At the far end of the arena, the Lord Escort Dinnid sat beneath the lights beside an enormous young queen. She was a light cream in color, but gold highlights on her upper thighs and battle legs indicated that she would soon develop into a Golden. The queen was perhaps six meters long and three meters tall. Her saucer-shaped egg sac looked as if it were ready to burst, and indeed as he watched, a translucent egg about two decimeters across fell from her sac. A white worker rushed forward and carried it away.

Dinnid raised his battle arms over his head, crossing them as a sign of a temporary truce. Veriasse stopped at his side of the arena and raised his arms in the same token, crossing his wrists.

"You stay here," he whispered to Everynne and the others, indicating a red box drawn on the floor.

As one, he and Dinnid advanced to the center of the arena.

Veriasse studied the battleground—the light in the room was diffuse and came from yellow globes set in the walls all around the arena. The metal floors seemed to be of heavy steel and were uneven, curving slightly like a bowl until they reached a low point in the center of the room. The ceiling was perhaps fifteen meters high—enough so that if Veriasse were the Lord Escort from another hive, he and Dinnid would be able to fly about the room, engaging in aerial combat. Indeed, it was the preferred method among dronon. The males flew at tremendous speeds, batting one another with their heavy forearms, lashing out with their hind legs, grabbing with their sensor whips. The battles tended to be fast-paced and ended quickly.

As Dinnid marched forward, Veriasse studied him. The big male was perhaps two meters tall as he walked, and he bore scars from a recent fight. His right sensor whip had been ripped off near the mandible and had not yet grown back. The right front array of eyes had been damaged. Of the seven faceted eyes of various sizes, two of the larger ones were broken. An ugly white ooze dripped from one mandible.

Yet the dronon lord had impressive forearms. The serrated edges at the bottom of these arms were exceptionally well developed, so that it looked almost as if he had triangular axe heads emerging from those arms. One blow from those battle arms would crush the exoskeleton of nearly any dronon. Veriasse held no delusions. To be hit with those arms would mean his death.

Around him, the dronon began to sing a slow dirge, their mouthfingers tapping rhythmically upon their voice drums. Veriasse looked to the far side of the room, saw that beneath the queen, several white things that he had thought to be workers were in actuality larvae—royal grubs with six small legs and poorly developed eyes.

When the two were forty paces apart, Dinnid uncrossed his battle arms, began to wave them threateningly. Veriasse knew that as soon as he uncrossed his own wrists, the battle would begin. The dronon always considered it a good strategy to strike first, and Veriasse suspected that the Lord Escort would leap into the air, try to strike while flying past. Indeed, the dronon's superior aerial troops had always devastated humans, who relied too heavily on ground-based operations.

Veriasse took a deep breath, uncrossed his arms. Almost before he could see it happen, Dinnid leapt into the air, wings buzzing.

Veriasse dodged right. The Lord Escort twisted his abdomen, tried to kick with a rear leg. Veriasse considered grabbing it, but elected instead to simply avoid this first blow.

Dinnid flew past, circled like a great black fly. It took him several seconds to cross the arena, then return.

Dinnid flew up near the top of the ceiling, then swooped low at the last possible second. Veriasse dodged right again, but the dronon anticipated his move, turned his head and spat the contents of his stomach into Veriasse's face. The acid splashed out in a wave, and Veriasse saw that he would not be able to dodge it. He leapt up in frustration, kicked the forward edge of Dinnid's lower right wing and heard a satisfying crack.

The lord spun, crashing into the metal floor, then rolled upright. He raised his wings and flapped them madly, apparently terrified on some instinctual level at the thought of being grounded. He lifted himself in the air, but moved slower and was forced to flap his wings much harder to fly at all.

Veriasse pulled up his tunic, wiped the acid from his face. The goggles he wore were dirty with the fruits of the vanquisher's stomach, and Veriasse only managed to smear the glasses. He threw them off in frustration, gambling that Dinnid had emptied his stomach and would not be able to spit any more acid in the course of this battle.

Dinnid circled the vast arena, building up speed, and Veriasse clenched his fists. The metal studs sewn into the fingers of his gloves felt heavy, comforting.

He watched the vanquisher circle, saw that Dinnid was breathing hard. His rear thighs flexed and unflexed rapidly, the air holes expanding as he sought to draw air into his lungs.

Suddenly Dinnid swerved and came straight at Veriasse, battle arms thrust dangerously forward, his head tilted back so that his mandibles were extended down and out. It was the perfect posture for a ramming attack.

Veriasse dodged right early, and the dronon veered to intercept, then Veriasse dodged left at the last moment, grabbed for Dinnid's sensor whip. Dinnid responded by smashing with his left battle arm, but Veriasse was already on the floor, rolling beneath the attack. He felt the cordlike sensor whip in his grasp, tugged it with all his might, hoping to pull it out.

Instead, the dronon flipped onto his back. At that angle of descent, Veriasse's added weight was too much for the creature.

In that moment, Veriasse leapt and kicked Dinnid's right front eye cluster with a cracking sound. Veriasse danced backward while the dronon scrambled to his feet.

Veriasse expected Dinnid to retreat, regroup for a moment, but apparently the creature went berserk. It leapt forward, thrashing blindly with its battle arms, trying to chop Veriasse in half. Veriasse staggered back to avoid its blows. Yet the vanquisher kept advancing.

Veriasse dodged right beneath the creature's blind spot and struck the dronon full force in the right thigh of his rear leg, crushing the lord's exoskeleton so that bits of carapace fell into its air holes.

Dinnid spun to attack, but Veriasse leapt under his blind spot and smashed the dronon's left front eye cluster, then staggered back a step.

Orick shouted, "Get him! Kill him!" and Veriasse suddenly became aware of the noise around him. The dronons too were shouting, but he had been so focused during the fight, that he had blocked out all such mundane sounds.

Lord Dinnid was blinded in both front eye clusters. He responded by rushing forward, lashing out with roundhouse swipes of battle-arms. He twisted his head to the left and right, trying to spot Veriasse with his back eyes. After several seconds, he buzzed his wings, flew overhead.

Veriasse's face burned painfully from the acid. He was sweating heavily, pouring salt into the wounds. He could feel the acid eating into his cheeks and neck like fiery ants.

Veriasse gasped for breath. The room was so damned hot, and his head began to spin. Lord Dinnid landed on the far side of the room, turned his back to Veriasse so that he could watch him, then Dinnid began the dronon equivalent of coughing. His right thigh convulsed rapidly, and bits of exoskeleton came flying from his air holes.

Veriasse considered rushing to attack, but he realized that Lord Dinnid would probably like him to try. The dronon would only fly away, forcing Veriasse to tire himself.

Veriasse began walking toward Dinnid, "Surrender now," Veriasse offered. "I do not wish to destroy you!"

"I will not surrender to a soft creature like you," the dronon answered. "You have been fortunate in this contest, and I have been incautious."

The dronon vanquishers who circled the arena were still singing, their mouthfingers clicking softly. Dinnid shouted for silence, and they obeyed.

Dinnid turned, waved his sensor whip high, then stood tall on his hind legs. In such a position, he could not launch into flight, but he raised his battle arms overhead like vicious clubs. He stood silently, waiting for Veriasse to advance.

Veriasse watched the creature warily. The sensor whips collected information in three ways: they were chemoreceptors that the dronon used to smell with; they felt vibrations; and they acted as enormous ears. Time and again, the dronon proved to be more sensitive to sound than humans. Veriasse vowed not to be taken in by Dinnid's apparent vulnerability.

Veriasse's face felt as if it were on fire. He closed on Dinnid. Gallen and Maggie must have recognized the danger, and they began shouting loudly, "Get him! Kill him!" making as much noise as possible so that they could cover Veriasse's approach. Dinnid twisted his head in frustration, slowed, then seemed to center on Veriasse and began stalking.

Veriasse waited. The air in the room was suffocating, and he had to focus, try to forget the pain in his face, the strangling air.

Lord Dinnid began coughing again, stopped to clear his air passages. Veriasse looked for a weakness. There were so few places to attack. The dronon's exoskeleton was so thick that even a heavy kick to the head would do no good. Veriasse considered the mouthfingers down beneath the mandibles. He might be able to crush its voice drum—which would have much the same effect as putting a hole in its lungs—but the mouthfingers were too close to those heavy mandibles.

There were only a few places he could strike with much effect. The air holes on the thighs were one target. The wings were another. The sensor whips were a third. Yet he looked at the huge lord, a consummate warrior, and he despaired of winning this battle. Dinnid was too powerful.

Veriasse backed away a step, gasping for air, and caught a sweet scent of flowers. He laughed as he realized that Everynne had opened the bottle of Hope he had received on Cyannesse. An adrenaline surge poured through him, filling him with light. And then Veriasse considered ways to use the dronon's own power against it.

Dinnid stalked closer, and Veriasse jumped forward and shouted, causing the monster to swing both battle arms down, slamming into the metal floor. Veriasse leapt, kicked Dinnid's voice drum. His foot connected with a sharp thud. Dinnid raised his battle arms protectively, hitting Veriasse in midair, knocking him away.

Even that minor touch was too much.

Veriasse hit the floor on his back. Some ribs cracked on impact. For a moment, he lay gasping in pain, unable to move. Dinnid swung his head from side to side, biting down with his mandibles in case Veriasse tried to kick his voice drum again.

Veriasse didn't move, didn't stir a muscle, forced himself to still his breathing. Lord Dinnid was so fond of pointing out the weaknesses of the human's soft body that Veriasse decided to let the creature think he'd done some damage.

Dinnid shouted, "Human? Human?" his voice garbled. Of the dozens of voice fingers under Dinnid's mandibles, half were crushed.

Veriasse didn't answer, and the dronon decided that now was his opportunity to strike. He leapt forward, waving his sensor whip and chopping down with his right battle leg. In that moment, Veriasse leapt up, grabbed the sensor whip and pulled it in front of the swinging leg.

The serrated chitin of the foreleg sliced through the whip. Dinnid groaned in pain, spun away so that his back eye was on Veriasse, then buzzed his wings, lifted off in flight.

Veriasse picked up the sensor whip. It was over two meters long and very heavy. Veriasse snapped it overhead as if it were a bullwhip, cracking the air.

Everywhere, the dronon in the audience hummed in disapproval.

Veriasse imagined how he would feel if a dronon were to pull the leg off a human and use it as a weapon. He imagined how it would anger him and hoped that Dinnid too would be appalled. Perhaps it would break his concentration.

Dinnid buzzed forward, hit the far wall and fell. He turned, leapt into the air again and rushed toward Veriasse. Veriasse cracked the sensor whip, and Dinnid veered toward him.

Veriasse crouched low, and Dinnid swooped over. Veriasse dodged and swung the whip with deadly ferocity, hoping to get the creature's back leg. Instead, the whip cracked against the stub of Dinnid's damaged sensor. The dronon flapped his wings so rapidly that they buzzed, creating a keening that was the equivalent of a dronon scream of pain. He doubled his speed and crashed into the far wall with a tremendous smack.

Dinnid fell to the ground, tried to get up, but his legs wobbled. He turned in a semicircle as if dazed, and Veriasse watched in horror. Dinnid's skull had cracked. White ooze seeped from the wound.

Somehow, even though Veriasse had struggled from the outset for a clean kill, now that the moment was upon him, he was repulsed at the task.

He ran to Dinnid, and the dronon vanquisher wobbled about feebly, trying to prop his massive battle arms so that he could support his own weight. Dinnid was not thinking of fighting now, only of crawling to safety.

Veriasse leapt into the air, aimed a flying kick at the crack in the dronon's skull. He hit with a thud, managed to open the crack a bit wider. Dinnid wobbled feebly on his front legs, and Veriasse leapt again, was forced to kick a third time. His foot entered the skull, and he pulled it away in disgust.

Lord Dinnid shuddered and fell. For a moment there was silence. Veriasse crawled back a pace and sat, gasping, horrified by what he had done.

All around him, the dronon began thrumming their mouthfingers against their voice drums loudly, creating a deafening roar.

Veriasse turned, looked across the room to the young queen of the hive. She was little more than a bloated sac for laying eggs. Her battle arms were small, unformed, and with her great egg-filled abdomen she could not fly, could hardly walk. Yet by dronon law she could defend herself against his attack.

Veriasse walked to the queen, panting. He was exhausted, ready to faint, and could not take any more of the hot air. "I do not want your death, Great Queen," Veriasse said. "We came here seeking only the Right of Charn. We wish to pass through your land, so that we might do battle with your Golden."

"You have earned Charn," the queen said. "If you promise not to kill me, you may mark me. I will not resist."

Veriasse could not escape this symbolic act, the maiming of the queen. He went to her side, made a fist and swung into her egg sac with all his might. The queen's abdomen did not burst, nor did it break, but the metal studs in Veriasse's gloves left a long gouge in her carapace.

A great hissing noise of displeasure rose from the dronon. All around the arena, dronon put their battle arms over their heads, crossing them in token of surrender. Yet they were not looking at Veriasse. Instead, they turned to face Everynne to do obeisance, their drumming voices crying out over the translator, "Behold the Golden! Behold our queen!"

Veriasse held his lungs, sucking air with great pain. The room seemed to spin, until he was forced to his knees.

Twenty

Maggie rushed to Veriasse. The skin of his face was red, burning away. She looked around desperately, then dabbed at his face with the hem of her robe and called to Everynne, "Help me, please!"

Everynne stood alone watching. The dronon were clattering their battle legs in token of surrender. She walked over to Veriasse, with Gallen and Orick in her wake, but Everynne said, "You have to clean him. They call me a Golden now. I cannot be seen doing work." She looked into Maggie's eyes, pleading. She could not jeopardize what she had gained thus far.

Gallen pulled a canteen from his backpack, bathed Veriasse's face. Veriasse knelt on one knee, panting.

"How badly are you hurt?" Everynne asked. She had been surprised at the ferocity of the battle. With his upgraded nervous system, Veriasse was phenomenally quick. In two minutes she had seen him take apart a dronon Lord Escort, his fists and feet blurring. Yet he had done it at great cost. His face was terribly burned, and she'd heard something crack when he'd fallen.

Veriasse pulled the microphone away from his mouth. "My ribs," he groaned. "I think some are broken."

"What can we do for you?" Gallen asked.

Panic took Everynne. She could not think. She only knew that if Veriasse failed the next battle, she would die.

"Rest. I need to lie still for awhile. My nanodocs should be able to heal the wounds in a couple of hours."

Everynne's mantle told her that he was wrong. It would take days for his nanodocs to heal the breaks. She needed to get him away from here, take him somewhere so they could speak in private.

Everyone turned to the hive queen and said, "We have won the Right of Charn. We now demand that you alter the course of your hive city. Speed us on our way to Queen Tlitkani."

The hive queen clicked her mouthfingers against her voice drum, and Everynne's earpiece translated. "She is not on this world. She has moved her hive to another world, to facilitate her use of the human's mechanical mind."

"You mean she has taken up residence on the omni-mind?" Everynne asked.

"Yes," the queen said.

"Where has she taken the omni-mind?"

"It is orbiting our sun."

Everynne said, "Then take us to the nearest spaceship."

The queen spoke to one of her Lord Technicians, then turned back to Everynne. "Our technicians will prepare a ship for you immediately. We will send a squadron of our Lord Vanquishers as an honor guard."

The dronon queen watched Everynne for a moment. "We have received orders from our ruling dronon. She asks that we relieve you of the Terror you have been carrying."

Everynne reluctantly pulled the ball from her pocket. It had been her insurance, and part of her was loath to give it up. But it had accomplished its purpose.

She held it out for the queen, but a trio of Lord Technicians rushed forward and carried the thing away, presumably to be destroyed. The dronon queen turned her back, began dragging her bloated egg sac away.

When they were alone again, Maggie touched Everynne's arm. "We can't leave yet. Veriasse needs time to heal."

"Neither can we delay," Veriasse said, pulling on Gallen's arm as he staggered to his feet. "We have won Right of Charn, but according to dronon order, we must leave in all haste."

Everynne doubted that Veriasse could fight another battle in his condition.

Gallen stood tall, his hands on his hips. "Veriasse, you're in no shape to fight. It would be wrong to even try. You can't take a chance with Everynne's life this way. Let me fight the next battle."

Veriasse looked up, his jaw firm. "I wore the mantle of a Lord Protector for six thousand years. You have worn it for less than three days. You are a good man, Gallen, but you're not a Lord Protector yet. Even though I am injured, you couldn't beat me. How could you then take my place?"

"I watched you fight," Gallen said. "I know I could win! Veriasse, you're all done in."

"You can't just take my place, Gallen," Veriasse said. "I am Everynne's Lord Escort. By dronon rules of conduct, she can only take another Lord Escort if I die."

"I could switch clothes with you when we're alone," Gallen said. "The dronon would never know."

Gallen turned to Everynne, pleading. "You decide between us. It's your life."

"And yours," Everynne said. She looked at the two men. Gallen was probably correct. The dronon might never know if the two men switched places. Veriasse was gravely wounded, and Gallen still fresh. Yet Veriasse had proven himself in combat against a dronon.

"Will you, too, hold with my choice?" Everynne asked Veriasse.

He glared at her. His next words seemed to cost him more than the pain of drawing breath. "Gallen is right. You should have a say in this." By those words alone, Everynne knew he was severely wounded. Veriasse would never relinquish his title if he thought he could still fight.

Everynne turned her back on them, looked out over the arena. Orick ran to the center of the arena, retrieved Veriasse's goggles. A few meters away, the dronon had circled the corpse of Dinnid and were dismembering it, feeding it to the royal grubs. Everynne could not help but think that within a matter of hours, other dronon might be doing that to her.

She considered her options. Veriasse was sorely wounded, but his nanodocs would ease his discomfort. Within an hour, he should be feeling somewhat better. And Veriasse outweighed Gallen by thirty kilos. When he'd managed to break the carapace around Dinnid's air holes, she'd found it hard to imagine a human with such strength. Everynne doubted that Gallen could equal the task.

Yet, even with all of Veriasse's great accomplishments of the past, somehow at this moment, she trusted Gallen more. He was still healthy. And even though he didn't have an upgraded nervous system, Gallen was fast. Veriasse had been astonished by his strength when they first met. She considered choosing Gallen and wondered at the wisdom of such a move.

Maggie put her arm around Everynne's shoulder. "You can't let Veriasse fight anymore!" she whispered. "It would be murder."

Everynne looked into Maggie's eyes. They were no longer the eyes of that innocent child she'd met on Tihrglas a few days before. Instead, her eyes were filled with wisdom, the kind of knowledge that comes only through pain.

"You love Gallen, don't you?" Everynne said.

"Of course," Maggie answered. And in her mind, Everynne heard Maggie's accusation of a few days before: *You took him, just because you could.*

Everynne nodded. She had stolen something from Maggie once before. She determined not to do it again. Even if I die, Everynne thought, I will not steal from her again. She turned to face the two men. "I choose Veriasse as my champion."

Gallen gasped in astonishment, obviously hurt, and Veriasse breathed deeply, tears of gratitude glistening in his eyes. "I will not disappoint you, my lady. Give me a few moments' rest. I promise I will not disappoint you."

The journey to the omni-mind seemed shorter than it was. The dronon technicians took only an hour to remove a spaceship from the bowels of their city, and another hour to alter accommodations so that humans could travel in it. The alterations were limited simply to removing some seats and installing a pallet for Veriasse to lie on.

The old warrior lay on the pallet, put himself in a meditative trance to slow his breathing as they traveled. The ship was light and fast. With its antigrav drives, it moved fluidly between worlds, its rapid acceleration apparent only as one looked out the windows and watched Dronon shrink to a tiny glowing ball, lost between the stars. Forty dronon fighter ships escorted them.

After two hours, they swooped low over the omni-mind, and Everynne got her first glimpse of the great machine. It glowed with a soft silver light. Trillions of computer crystals lay upon its surface, reflecting sunlight like a sea of molten glass. Here and there across the planet, vast tachyon communication towers rose above the plains, pointing like metallic daggers to the heavens. Beyond that, there was no hint of the monolithic processors built into the planet's interior, no sign of its power supplies.

It was beautiful.

The dronon ships flew in a *V* to a great city, perhaps thirty kilometers across, ringed with light. Everynne watched from the portals. The city was built under large domes, and parts of it were green with grass, blue with pools of water. She could see hills and forests under the glass, and clear streams.

The dronon ships hissed low over the city, taking nearly half an hour to make their slow procession. Everynne gazed down on small estates that had once belonged to her mother's Tharrin advisors. Hundreds of thousands of people could easily live there.

The dronon went to the interior of the city, circled the largest central dome. There was a small palace beneath it situated in some woods. Nothing exotic or costly, simply a functional building where her mother had sometimes performed her duties.

The dronon fighters circled this building twice, then dove toward a gray docking portal at the dome's edge and landed so softly in the docking bay that Everynne never felt them touch down. She went to Veriasse, stroked his cheek and whispered, "Come, Father. We're here."

Unaccountably, Veriasse had fallen asleep. They had not really rested much in nearly twenty hours, and Everynne herself was exhausted. She felt a bit dizzy, unconnected from her body, but she could never have fallen asleep with the end of the journey so near. She jostled him again, and Veriasse woke, blinking. "Yes, yes. I'm coming."

She got him up, and he stretched, walked straight and tall through the ship's exit. Gallen, Maggie, and Orick followed them down a long glass corridor into one of the domed cities.

The dronon waited at the entrance to the dome. A wall of dronon vanquishers had formed under the clear canopy, and it seemed strange to Everynne to see their black carapaces shining in the pristine daylight.

Everynne breathed deep in amazement at their sheer numbers. She estimated that at least forty thousand vanquishers had gathered to meet them. Their acidic stench filled the dome, overwhelming the scent of the green grass that they trampled. In the distance, beyond the woods, she could see the palace, a building of purple-gray stone with ivy trailing up its sides.

Atop the wall of living dronon stood their leader, a Lord Escort with facial tattoos that looked like white worms strung beneath his eyes. Veriasse had talked of him often. Xim.

Xim shouted insults in dronon, and Veriasse gave his ritual hand signals, shouted insults in return and challenged the vanquisher to ritual combat, so that he and Everynne could take their rightful place as Lords of the Swarm.

Whereas earlier she had been terrified, now Everynne felt some sense of calm. She controlled her breathing. Xim called for the Rite of Examination, flew down and stalked around her. Unlike Dinnid, he was thorough. He used his whiplike sensors, grasped her dress and pulled it up to examine her skin. Xim tasted her scent thoroughly and stopped at the back of her neck, his sensor brushing against her small scar.

"What is this strange substance?" the vanquisher asked, rubbing at the body paint.

"It is a perfumed soap that our Golden uses to clean her skin," Veriasse said evenly. "Do you not like the scent? We find it quite pleasing."

Xim rubbed at the paint. "What is this mark?" Behind Everynne, she heard Maggie gasp.

"It is the mark of a Tharrin," Veriasse said reasonably. "A coloration variance similar to that found on our nipples. It is common to some of our Goldens." Everynne was not surprised that Veriasse had chosen to lie. The burn would heal in a few days, but it would be difficult to explain its presence now.

Xim hesitated, and Everynne imagined that he would kill them now for the attempt at deception.

He raised on his hind legs, crossed his battle arms and shouted, "I am Xim, Lord of the Swarm. Our larvae shall eat your corpses. Our vanquishers shall claim your domain. Your hive shall submit!"

His wings flashed, and he flew high into the air, buzzed around the ceiling. All around them, the dronon vanquishers beat their battle arms together, and their carapaces rustled as they shifted, creating a tunnel of living bodies for Everynne and the others to walk through.

They stepped into the dark cave. The dronon vanquishers had stacked themselves so that they could watch the procession, and myriads of heads swiveled to follow their progress. Sensors writhed overhead like black snakes, and many a battle arm hung overhead threateningly.

They did not have far to go. A field of grass lay a hundred yards beyond, ringed with countless dronon. The Golden Queen stood on the far side, proud and tall, whip sensors waving above the crowd. She wore the mantle of Semarritte on her head, a silver headdress with long flowing rows of medallions. Everynne looked at the mantle, the icon she had sought across light-years. To win it would mean her death. To lose it would mean her death.

Royal larvae huddled under Tlitkani's legs. Xim circled her in the air, then landed in front of her protectively, raised his battle arms high and crossed them. He shouted, "Veriasse, Lord Escort of the Golden Everynne. I have watched your battle with Dinnid. I come now to kill a worthy opponent!"

Veriasse raised his own wrists and crossed them. The two proceeded over the field. All around, dronon began their chant. A familiar thrumming filled the air, and the sound of it raised the hair on the back of Everynne's neck.

When they were ten meters apart, Xim's wings flashed and he soared into the air. The ceiling was far higher here than it had been on Dronon, and the vanquisher took full advantage of the larger area, sweeping in faster than Dinnid ever had. He flew toward the setting sun, then turned and screamed toward Veriasse, battle arms outstretched.

Veriasse stood tall and proud in his black robes of office, the dark chains of his mantle flowing down his shoulders. He raised his fists as if to strike, but Xim flashed his battle arms in a rolling blur and flew straight at Veriasse.

Veriasse was forced to dodge, roll away.

Xim repeated the tactic four times, each time veering nearer to Veriasse, and each time Veriasse had to retreat. On the fourth pass, Veriasse got up, holding his ribs painfully. He gasped for breath, and Everynne suddenly saw Xim's plan. The dronon knew of Veriasse's injury. Xim sought to aggravate it.

Xim circled the room, continued his charges. On the seventh swipe, he swerved near, slashed with a sensor, whipping Veriasse across the forehead, knocking Veriasse's goggles aside. Veriasse tried to dodge the attack, rolled to his feet and staggered. Jagget's black mantle fell from his head.

Blood flowed down his face, covering his eyes. Veriasse tried to wipe the blood away, and Xim swerved short of the roof to the glass dome, pressed the attack. He shot low over Veriasse's head, spat the contents of his stomach. The acid hit the wound, and Veriasse rolled to the ground, writhing. He tried to wipe his face with his robe.

Faster and faster Xim circled the great room with seeming effortlessness, his legs pumping rapidly as he flew.

Veriasse staggered to his feet, got up and spun in a circle, blinking frantically, his eyes a swollen mess. He tried to wipe the acid from his face. "Everynne!" he shouted.

Everynne cried, "I'm here!" She reached into her pocket, pulled out the bottle of Hope that Grandmother had given her on Cyannesse, opened it and sprinkled a drop on the ground.

Veriasse was still blinking, and though he fixed on the sound of her voice, he didn't seem to see her. Yet he suddenly breathed easier, stood tall. He closed his ravaged eyes, listened for the sound of Xim's wings.

Xim came screaming in from above, and Veriasse blurred as he leapt high into the air and blindly kicked.

Yet the dronon had anticipated his attack. Xim had come in high, and now he lashed down with the claw of his hind foot. It cut through Veriasse like a knife, and blood spattered darkly across the grass.

Around the arena, the dronon vanquishers' humming raised to a roar, and thousands of them began beating their battle arms together. The sound was deafening. Some of them rushed into the arena a couple of paces, as if they would tear Veriasse apart and begin feeding now.

Veriasse climbed to his feet, blood streaming from his leg, and he shouted. His voice came to her faintly, "Everynne? Everynne?"

"I'm here," Everynne called. Xim had swerved back into battle, letting the roar of dronon applause block out the warning sound of his clattering wings.

Everynne shouted, "Watch out!"

But it was too late. The dronon vanquisher dropped to the ground, simultaneously chopping with his battle arms. One huge serrated arm crashed down on Veriasse's head, slicing him nearly in half. The other fell at an angle, chopping him across the belly.

Xim picked up the mangled corpse, held it overhead and paraded with it a few steps, then tossed it to the ground. All across the great arena, the vanquishers fell silent as Xim turned his attention to Everynne.

Twenty-one

Everynne backed away, feeling faint. Xim leapt into the air, landed before her at ten yards, and advanced with battle arms fully extended.

Everynne recalled dully that her gloves were weapons with metal inserts in the knuckles. She raised her hands and shouted.

Suddenly Gallen jumped in front of her, arms crossed at the wrists. He fell down on his knees and shouted, "Lord Xim, I beg you to show mercy to our Golden, as Lord Veriasse showed mercy to your queen. Do not kill her, but mar her only."

Everynne did not know if the dronon understood Gallen. He did not have a translator. Everynne repeated his words, shouting so that the microphone roared her plea.

Lord Xim leapt over Gallen, advanced on her. His mouthfingers tapped over his voice drum, "I will not spare a Tharrin. You have lost your right to live."

For one second, Everynne stared up into Xim's faceted clusters of eyes. Each eye reflected a small image of her, fists raised, defiant.

Xim lifted his battle arms for the killing blow, and she suddenly realized that he thought she would make it easy, he thought she would submit to his punishment as if she were a dronon queen.

She screamed and leapt, smashed his right eye cluster with a fist. Xim twisted, caught her with his sensor whips, and smashed her to the ground. There was a great rushing in her ears, and the world twisted violently. In the distance, she could hear Orick shouting her name.

Gallen leapt up from his kneeling position, spun. He had not understood Xim's reply to his plea for mercy, so he had remained kneeling.

Now Xim had Everynne on the ground. He raised a battle arm and clubbed her. The blow struck home with a sickening thud, and Orick roared in grief, jumped on the dronon and grabbed Xim's rear leg, biting into it and pulling back.

The dronon vanquisher leapt, trying to flee the unexpected attack, and part of his carapace came away in Orick's mouth. Gallen could suddenly see Everynne's body, crimson blood washing over her golden clothing. Her hand trembled violently.

Orick roared and charged in for a second attack, but Xim backed away, raised his battle arms and chopped a slicing blow that ripped through Orick's right shoulder.

Orick yelped in pain, spun away from the battle, and Xim buzzed his wings and jumped into the air. He flew a lazy pattern while Orick madly danced in circles, blood and hair spattering across the grass. The dronon's intent was clear. Orick was already mortally wounded. He did not need to engage in battle until the bear weakened further.

Maggie shouted at Gallen, "Do something! Save them!"

Gallen watched it all, and knew that by dronon law he could do nothing. If he tried to protect Everynne, he would only be destroyed, and he had promised Veriasse that he would clone Everynne, come at some time in the future and challenge the Lords of the Swarm again.

He shook his head at Maggie, shouted, "We can't," and saw the horror in her eyes. He recalled Primary Jagget's predictions. Now that the dronon had formed gate keys, they would march through the Maze of Worlds. The Lords of the Swarm would conquer every realm. There would be no future. He had to act.

Everynne twisted on the floor, struggled for something in her pocket. Gallen stood, amazed that with such a wound she could still be alive.

He watched her pull out the small vial of Hope. It rolled from her hand.

If I were the greatest warrior in the world, what would I do? Gallen wondered. And he stood, closed his eyes and tried to clear his mind. He waited, but nothing came.

Maggie shouted at him, raised her hands over her head, crossing her wrists. "Gallen, I am Golden!"

He studied her face, wondering at the possibility. Could she challenge the dronon? And even if she won, what could she do. Maggie had suffered tremendously by wearing a Guide. The knowledge that it so ruthlessly imparted had ripped at the very fabric of her sanity, yet it was nothing compared to the wisdom of the omni-mind. To wear the mantle of Semarritte would destroy her. Even if it did not crush her as the Guide would have, it would tear away her identity.

All of Maggie's hopes, all her thoughts and dreams would be like words written on a sandy beach, waiting to be erased by the onrushing tide.

"Are you sure?" Gallen shouted. No matter what happened, he was consigning her to destruction. Yet she alone had worked under the dominion of the Lords of the Swarm. She knew the price that whole worlds would pay if she failed.

"Please!" Maggie cried.

Gallen turned. Lord Xim was flying low over the arena, circling back to finish Orick.

Gallen raised his hands, crossed his wrists. "This world is ours! All worlds are ours! A Great Queen comes among you. Prostrate yourselves in adoration, or prepare to do battle!"

The room fell silent, and ten thousand vanquishers looked to Gallen. Lord Xim flew low over Orick, dropped in front of Gallen. The dronon began clicking his mouthfingers, and Gallen went to Veriasse's corpse, pulled out the translator from his ear, plugged it into his own.

"You claim this woman is also Golden?" Lord Xim asked.

"Yes," Gallen said. "She is a Golden from the world Tihrglas. All who know her adore her. I am Gallen O'Day, Lord Protector of that world, and her Lord Escort."

He looked at Maggie, standing there with her long red hair streaming out, her clear blue eyes. He'd seen the longing in men's faces as they watched her work in the inn back home. Nothing he said was a lie.

Yet Gallen feared that his plan would not work. The dronon lived by their rigid order, their code of honor. He only hoped that his actions and words fit within that order.

Xim seemed agitated by Gallen's claim. His head swiveled from side to side, and he walked in a circle, dragging his injured leg. "You bring two Goldens and two Lord Escorts?" he asked confused.

"Yes," Gallen said. "We humans are soft. We did not think that one pair would be enough."

Xim stopped in his tracks, raised his head questioningly, whip sensors waving. He tilted, so that his rear eye cluster faced his Golden Queen. "You must rule on this," he begged.

The Golden Queen raised her head, studied Maggie and Gallen. "She is not a Tharrin," the queen said, "and therefore cannot be a Golden among the humans."

"Do you accept challenges only from the greatest hives in your realm?" Gallen asked. "Do only the Goldens who come from your greatest families deserve the privilege of battling for the Right of Succession? Maggie and I come from a small world, a Backward world. We don't have any fancy lineage. We had never even heard of the Tharrin until a week ago, but on my world, Maggie is as Golden as they come."

The Golden Queen's whip sensors stopped waving as she considered his argument. "The omni-mind contains no useful information about your world or your culture," she said after a long moment. "I cannot corroborate your claims. Still, if you seek to battle Xim, you will find only your own death. You may battle."

Xim stalked over to Maggie, his whip-sensors waving. He pulled at her clothing, searched her scalp. Gallen didn't know if Maggie had any scars. He'd never seen her undressed. Gallen held his breath. Xim's prodding revealed a few moles on her back, nothing more. Throughout the search, Maggie simply glared at the lord, as if she wished only to bash in some more of his eyes.

When he finished, Xim raised his wings and shook them angrily. "Our offspring shall eat your carcasses! We shall rule your land! Your hive shall submit!"

Gallen could not remember what challenge Veriasse had called out next, so he was forced to innovate.

"Bullshit!" Gallen raised his fists. "I'm going to knock out your brains and use your hollow skull for a planter!"

Xim stood silently, apparently perplexed by this nonstandard verbal affront. All around the arena, dronon vanquishers began making thrumming noises.

Xim launched into the air, circled high above the arena. Gallen watched him, considered how best to handle the creature. Veriasse had opted for low dodges, a kicking attack. Gallen's mantle flashed images before his eyes, showing the dronon's weak spots.

Gallen wondered what Xim would do if Gallen opted to go over the top.

Xim swerved, dove toward Gallen, a frontal assault with his battle arms extended. Xim swept low to the ground, as if afraid Gallen would dive from his reach. Gallen rushed forward, vaulted into the air and twisted, kicking at the vanquisher's face with all his might, hoping that he could avoid its serrated arms.

Xim was traveling at tremendous speed, and Gallen's assault took him by surprise. His face smashed into the steel-toed boot with more force than Gallen could ever have mustered.

Gallen felt a sensor whip snap off at the impact, and Xim's head slammed into the ground. Gallen tumbled through the air, fell on his back. His mantle got knocked off his head, was tangled in the claws on Xim's rear leg.

Somehow in the impact, one of Xim's battle arms had grazed Gallen's leg, slicing it open. It bled profusely, but Gallen didn't have time to bandage it. Gallen scrambled to his feet as Lord Xim rushed toward him, but Xim suddenly buzzed his wings, flew high in the air, and tossed Gallen's mantle over the crowd.

Only seconds before, Gallen had felt confident, controlled. Killing a dronon in unarmed combat had seemed not only possible but easy. From moment to moment, the mantle had sent him images of the weak points on a dronon's carapace, but suddenly he felt emptiness, a yawning void.

Gallen got up, struggling to recall where he should strike on a dronon, remember the films of Lord Xim's previous fights.

His leg felt numb from the blow it had taken, and he shook it, tried to keep limber.

He recalled that Xim was supposed to be a consummate tactician. In his first fight with Veriasse, the dronon had sliced the old man open with a wing, using an appendage that could not serve as a weapon against other dronon.

Now, Xim was fighting a battle of attrition. He had removed both Gallen's and Veriasse's mantles, played against their weaknesses.

Gallen stood, sweat streaming down his face. He had plenty of weaknesses. If I were the greatest warrior in the world, he wondered, what would I do now?

He cleared his mind, let the old peace settle over him. He was breathing hard, and his tongue felt dry. The dronon vanquishers were humming loud, and Xim's wings buzzed above the crowd. God, I love a fight, he thought. All his senses were alive, and he reveled in the energy that flowed into him.

He watched Xim buzz around the room, and he realized that Xim fought a battle of attrition because with a fully armored dronon opponent that was the only kind of battle there was. Strike at an eye cluster in this pass, rip off a wing on the next.

Xim circled the great dome, gaining speed. Gallen realized that it was a ruse. The dronon knew of Gallen's bleeding leg, and he was waiting for the loss of blood to weaken the human.

Gallen couldn't afford to fight this kind of battle. He was already losing.

Gallen closed his eyes, focused, and all of the sounds went away. He tried to ignore the numbness in his leg. Faintly, he tasted the sweet scent of flowers, and energy coursed through him. Maggie had retrieved the bottle of Hope, removed the stopper.

Gallen opened his eyes and looked up. Xim was diving toward him from the top of the dome—sweeping in with the sun behind him.

And suddenly Gallen understood why Veriasse had lost. He'd performed countless tests, trying to discover how much pressure it took to shatter a dronon's exoskeleton. But he'd performed the tests by striking the skeleton of a stationary body. He'd never calculated how much force a dronon added to a blow when its body slammed into a fist at a hundred and twenty kilometers per hour.

Gallen couldn't afford to fight a battle of attrition. He stood his ground. At the last moment, he feinted a left dodge.

Xim swerved to intercept, swung a battle arm, and Gallen veered back right, simultaneously dodging a blow and striking at the dronon's head, putting all his force into the blow. His fist connected with a loud smack, and instantly pain flared up his arm, into his shoulder. Xim's momentum threw Gallen back, and human and dronon rolled together in a tumult. Gallen's arm was loose in its socket.

He rolled to his belly, climbed up, blinded by pain. He reeled in a circle, dazed, looking for Xim. Gallen suddenly spotted the dronon lord a dozen meters off, crawling away.

He raced toward the dronon. Xim swung around to meet his attack, and Gallen leapt into the air before the dronon could raise his battle arms. Gallen's kick landed in Xim's face, and Gallen fell backward.

He looked up. Xim wobbled feebly, raised on his hind legs, extending his battle arms in the air. There was dirt and grass all over Xim's face, rubbed into his broken eye clusters. A thin grayish ooze dripped from a crack in Xim's skull.

Gallen panted, scrabbled backward to get out of Xim's reach. The dronon dropped his battle arms, rested a second.

Gallen stood up. His shoulder was dislocated, and the bones made a sickly rasping noise as they grated together. His leg was spurting blood.

Xim raised back up on his hind legs, prepared to meet Gallen's attack. Gallen staggered forward and stopped just out of Xim's striking range. He stood for a long moment, looking into the dronon's eyes. Xim waved his single remaining feeler in the air. His head leaked a gray-white fluid; an eye cluster was gone; one of his rear legs was ripped. Gallen had seen a hundred men back down from a fight, and though he didn't know what might be going on in the monster's mind, he decided to give it one last chance.

"Beg for mercy," Gallen said, "and I'll spare your life."

"Fight me!" the dronon clicked.

"If you insist." Gallen leapt in, feinting a strike. Xim swung his battle arms, and Gallen danced back. The creature's reaction time was slow, terribly slow.

Xim raised his battle arms again. They were wobbling, and Gallen fell back, panting.

Xim stood on his hind legs for a moment, and his battle arms waved feebly. He tired and dropped his arms. The white ooze was running thickly from his skull, and Gallen knew then that the creature was dying.

All around him, dronon vanquishers began thrumming, and the translator in Gallen's ear whispered, "Kill him. Finish it."

Gallen shouted at them, "You're a morbid mob." And he turned, advanced on the Golden. The small white royal larvae skittered away from beneath her legs.

She raised her battle arms, crossed them in surrender, and put her head to the ground. Behind him, Gallen heard clattering, glanced back. Xim toppled to the grass.

Gallen went to the Golden Queen. She kept her battle arms crossed in token of surrender.

"Under the rules for conquest, you may choose only to maim me," the Golden said. "If you so choose, I will not fight you."

Gallen stopped in front of her. She raised her head to look up at him. "Why should I spare you?" Gallen asked. "So you can continue to breed? So your children can challenge me?"

Her mouthfingers clicked over her voice drum. "I have already given birth to many Lord Escorts. My children will hunt you down. You cannot escape your fate."

Gallen stared at her distantly. He stepped forward and removed Semarritte's mantle from her head, thought that she really did have a nice golden color.

He slammed a fist into her face.

He discovered that his wrists must have been stronger than Veriasse's, for instead of merely gouging her, his blow cracked her head open.

All around him, the dronon raised their battle arms and clattered them together, crying, "Behold the Golden! Behold the Lords of the Swarm!"

Gallen raised his hands for silence, looked out over the assembly. The room fell quiet. "You tell them, Maggie. You're the queen now."

Maggie glared at the dronon and shouted, "All of you: get off our worlds!"

Gallen turned away from the carnage, wiped the sweat from his forehead with the back of his left hand. Around the arena, the dronons' carapaces scraped and rattled as they evacuated the dome.

Maggie hunched over Orick. The bear was badly cut, and he breathed shallowly. Blood soaked much of his fur from groin to chin. Yet her mantle whispered to her that the nanodocs in her pack might still save him, so she forced the seven pills down his throat and waited.

Everynne was lying in a pool of blood, too, but she already had nanodocs working on her. The tiny machines were closing her wounds, had slowed the bleeding. There was nothing more that Maggie could do.

Gallen came and threw Semarritte's mantle down at Maggie's feet, then sat and petted Orick's snout. Maggie picked up the mantle, held it under her arm. All around them the room rustled as dronon fled the premises, and within five minutes, they sat alone on the grass. The sun was setting out on the horizon, and shadows lengthened. From here, she could not see the vast sea of molten glass on the omni-mind's surface, only the other domes nearby. Overhead the stars shone more fiercely than any she had ever seen.

Gallen went to Veriasse's pack, got some water and gave drinks first to Everynne, then to Orick. He bandaged his own leg, and had Maggie pop his shoulder back into its socket. Then he sat beside Maggie and held her hand for a long time, neither of them speaking, except once when Gallen said, "Oh, my, look at that!"

She looked up just in time to see a falling star. A moment later, dronon ships began streaming away in a solid convoy.

After an hour, both Everynne and Orick were still breathing deeply. The nanodocs had closed their wounds, and Maggie's mantle whispered to her that it was a good sign. Both of them would probably survive.

Maggie sat still for a long time, then began crying. Gallen held her for awhile, and said, "I'm really tired. Do you think it gets cold here at night? Should we get some blankets for these two? Build a fire?"

"Och, you're kidding me, aren't you Gallen?" Maggie said. "You know this place has to have heaters in it. I'm sure it won't get cold."

"Heaters?" Gallen asked. "What's a heater?"

Maggie slapped him, thinking he must surely be joking, but then she looked deeper into his eyes, and she wasn't sure. Could he have learned so much in the past week and still never have heard of a heater?

He laughed at her confusion. "So, are you going to put that mantle on, or aren't you?"

"I don't know, come to think of it," Maggie said. "There's no one here making me wear it. To tell the truth, I sort of like learning slow. I could put it on and learn everything there is to know at once, but it seems to me that that would be sort of like eating all the desserts you would ever want in your life all in one day—if you take my meaning."

"Aye," Gallen said. "It does sound nasty."

"Besides," Maggie said, "it belongs to Everynne."

"That it does." Gallen sighed. "Even if she doesn't want it."

He got up, walked away in the darkness, and Maggie thought he'd gone to get his bedroll, but a moment later she heard him digging in the dirt.

Gallen had a wavy-bladed dagger, and he used it to scrape a long, shallow hole in the ground. Then he put Veriasse in, covered him with clumps of grass and a bit of dirt. Maggie went and stood beside Gallen. He gazed down at the grave for a long time and asked, "Do you think there's a heaven?"

Maggie sighed. "It's damned possible."

Gallen said. "If there's a heaven, I think Veriasse will find himself guarding the gates. You know, keeping out the rabble."

"Aye, he'd like that job," Maggie agreed.

Gallen walked over to a good spot of grass, then lay on his back, his hands folded behind his head, and stared up at the stars through the dome. The last of the dronon ships had left.

Gallen looked like some country boy back in Tihrglas.

"Gallen," Maggie said, "what are you going to do when you get home?" She didn't ask him to include her in his plans. She didn't intend to go back, and even though they'd spoken of finding a world together, she didn't know what he might be thinking now. She wanted him to come with her voluntarily.

"I've been thinking. It's been a long time since I've gone fishing, and I've got a craving for salmon. I think that first I'll go fishing in Forrest's Creek. Then I'm going to travel for a bit, see the world."

"And when you're done?"

"Well, I don't know. Tihrglas is sort of a quiet place. I could grow old there, sit in a rocker . . ." He looked up into her eyes. "But I don't think I could be happy for more than a day or two, lazing about like that. Besides, there's this woman I know, and life would be . . . dreary without her."

Maggie smiled, lay down beside him, felt the warmth of his chest against her breasts. He took her face in his hand, kissed her long and deeply.

When he finished, he whispered, "You've got no family left back in Clere, but I've got my mother to take care of. I need to go home, say good-bye, hire someone to watch after her at the very least. And I'll need to make trips home from time to time, to be sure she's okay."

"Of course, you couldn't leave her there forever alone," Maggie said. "You can just tell her that you're working, guarding ships for some merchant. Then you can stop back and see her once in awhile."

Gallen nodded, closed his eyes. Maggie lay with him for a long time, and he fell asleep. Part of her was angry with him for sleeping, but the more sensible part said, "Ah, poor boy, he needs his sleep. It's been a long week, and he's exhausted."

Yet Maggie could not rest. She checked on Orick and Everynne. Both were resting peacefully, and she washed them off a bit, then sat on the grass, looked at the silver mantle. It had thousands of tiny silver disks woven together in the chain mail. They were smaller than the disks she had seen on any other mantle, and she realized that they were made using a higher technology.

At long last, she could stand the temptation no more, and she put on the mantle, felt the cool weight of the chains running down the length of her back, over her shoulders, and between her breasts.

For an endless moment, she waited, expecting the mantle to take her, ravage her with light as the Guide had. Yet at the same time, she waited in stark terror.

She tried to clear her mind, wipe away that fear, but the knowledge never came. Nothing happened.

At last, when she was ready to throw the mantle away in disgust, a woman came to her in a vision. She had long dark hair and skin as smooth as cream. Every line of her form was perfect. Maggie did not have to beg her name.

"Your brain waves do not match mine," Semarritte said. "I can bond with you, and you will gain some use of the omni-mind, but like the dronon before you, your ability to control the device will be impaired. Still, I am loath to take you, if you fear me so. What do you want of me?"

"I want a home," Maggie said. "You know everything about ten thousand worlds. I thought, perhaps I could learn of them."

Semarritte reached out a finger, touched Maggie between the eyes. She felt a strange dizziness, and Semarritte pulled her finger away. Her demeanor changed. She looked at Maggie with a new understanding. "You would not be satisfied if I taught you all that I know about every world. You will only be happy if you go to each world and learn about it for yourself."

"That's right," Maggie said.

"So you are not searching for a world for yourself. You are searching for a world where you can be happy with your love, Gallen. I am not sure that such a world exists."

"But where should I start?"

"Tremonthin." Semarritte laughed softly. "There you can learn much, and Gallen will find his abilities sorely tested."

"Thank you," Maggie said, and she removed the mantle. Almost immediately, the vision seemed odd to her, like a dream that is forgotten upon waking, and she wondered if she had imagined it. She went to sleep beside Gallen, and he threw his arm over her protectively.

Twenty-two

For ten days, Gallen and Maggie nursed Orick and Everynne, watching them recover. In that time, many people began to arrive from distant worlds, ambassadors and powerful lords who celebrated the end of dronon rule. The first to come were Tharrin, delegates from distant parts of three galaxies who simply appeared the next morning on the road in front of the palace. They had come through their own gates. There were dozens of them—men and women with an eerie presence, a sense of light and peace that filled the air around them.

Gallen asked several of them to help clean up Everynne and Orick and move them to beds in the palace. Several Tharrin gingerly carried the two inside, and the physicians ministered to their wounds behind closed doors, then said that both would be up and about soon.

Afterward, the Tharrin came before Gallen and Maggie, requesting audience. They retired to a quiet chamber of the palace, and a powerful man named Lord Meron spoke with Maggie soberly. He was a tall man, with a barrel for a chest, long, flowing brown hair, and penetrating green eyes. He took Maggie's hand, looked into her face.

"You know," he reasoned, "it is not in the best interests of your people for you to try to claim the omni-mind."

"I know," Maggie answered. "I never wanted the thing in the first place. Gallen and I only won it by accident."

Meron patted her hand. "Still, you won it, and the dronon will hold you accountable."

"Can't I just give it away?" Maggie asked. "Give it back to Everynne?"

"The omni-mind you can give to Everynne," Meron said, "but the burden of ruling the dronon now belongs to you. They perceive you as their Great Queen, and they will seek counsel from you. If they do not receive guidance, their swarm will be overwhelmed by others."

Meron did not say it, so Maggie said it for him. "Still, they'll try to kill me, won't they?"

Meron nodded slightly in assent. "We can set barriers between them and you, protect you. We've already begun moving the omni-mind from orbit, and we'll hide it so they can't easily regain control of it. But you, you will need to hide yourself, keep moving from world to world, as Semarritte did."

"How am I supposed to hide from the dronon and lead them at the same time?" Maggie asked.

"You can appoint a regent, someone to rule in your stead."

"Everynne?" Maggie asked.

Meron nodded. "She'll do. In a way, you will be doing her a great favor. The dronon will not perceive her as a target, and she will be free to reign without fear."

Maggie nodded thoughtfully, and Gallen saw that they had won a mixed bag of goods. Gallen patted Maggie's shoulder, whispered, "It will be all right. We can make the best of it."

"Och, sure," she said. "I wanted to visit other worlds anyway. This will just keep a fire under my toes, give me a little more incentive."

By that evening, Maggie and Orick were both able to sit up and take a bit of food, and Everynne began directing the withdrawal of dronon hives from the occupied worlds.

Over the next few days, delegates from many worlds continued to gather.

The omni-mind soon began to fill with joyous people, and it became as crowded as any inn during the Autumn Fair at Baile Sean.

And in that time, Everynne grieved for Veriasse, and put on Semarritte's mantle for the first time.

It was on the fourth evening, just after sunset. The dronon had all left, and a few hundred dignitaries had arrived on the omni-mind. But Everynne did not invite them to her investiture. She planned a public ceremony for later, but for the moment she met with Orick, Gallen, and Maggie in private. "You three battled for me across the worlds. You helped me win this moment, and I owe you my life. I want you to come with me now, to witness the death of Everynne and the rebirth of Semarritte."

They were in the throne room in the palace. The room had no ceiling, just a vast chair covered in red cloth, where one could sit and gaze out at the stars through the clear dome. Maggie, Orick, and Gallen sat around her feet in a semicircle.

"Do you have to wear this thing?" Orick asked. "The dronon left without it."

Everynne smiled at him. "The Tharrin are preparing another to take my place, but his training will take many years. In the meantime, there are ten thousand worlds that must be governed. I do not rejoice in this task, but yes, I must put the mantle on. In your time, Orick, I suspect that you too will have to accept responsibilities. You will go home and become a great and wise leader among bears."

Gallen said good-bye, kissed Everynne one last time. Everynne cried and hugged him, then hugged Maggie. Last of all, she hugged Orick for a long moment and wept in his arms.

When she was ready, Everynne sat back in the chair and placed the mantle on her head. She was shaking, and Gallen took her left hand while Orick held her right.

At first, she sat regally with the silver chains cascading down her neck, and nothing seem to happen. After a moment, she got a faraway look in her eye, then stared off into eternity.

"It's so beautiful!" she cried. Tears streamed from her eyes freely. Gallen squeezed her shaking hand, then looked up into her eyes. And in that moment, Everynne was transformed. She smiled so beatifically that she seemed to radiate light.

She breathed deeply and gave a rapid succession of sighs, crying out in wonder. At last it became too much for her, and she fainted.

Gallen watched it all and realized that part of him felt jealous. She had left him behind, traveled to a far place he could never reach.

And Gallen suddenly remembered being a child, running under the trees as his father rode away on a dark horse into the mountains. Gallen recalled how desperately he had wanted to follow. He felt the same now.

After Everynne fainted, Gallen and the others waited silently with her for nearly two hours. Orick simply held her hand, did not move from her side. But Gallen got up, walked around the dome, staring out at the stars. He wondered at them. He'd stood on worlds that orbited five of those stars. Maggie came and put her arm around his back, watched the sky with him.

A few minutes later, Orick said, "She's waking up!"

Gallen and Maggie went back to Everynne's side. Everynne stirred a bit and opened her eyes. She smiled at them, and she looked as if she had gained some contentment she had never before achieved. Her eyes were filled with a terrible light.

"Semarritte?" Gallen asked.

Everynne shook her head. "Semarritte is dead," she said. "Her consciousness was stored in the omni-mind until I put it on. But she knew I feared her, so she welcomed me, and then she died."

"How could she know that you feared her?" Orick asked.

"Maggie told her," Everynne said. She leaned forward, patted Maggie's hand, and did not explain herself. Gallen was left to stare at the two women, mystified.

That night, Everynne was invested publicly with the omni-mind before a multitude of Tharrin counselors and ambassadors from many worlds. And on that night, Maggie, the new Golden Queen, publicly named Everynne as her regent to the dronon, leaving her with that undesirable burden.

In a sense, that was almost the last that Gallen saw of Everynne.

Over the next few days, he tried to speak to Everynne again on several occasions, but found it difficult. In each conversation, she anticipated his words. She would answer questions without being asked, tell him more about himself than he wanted to know. And always there was that terrible light in her eyes, frightening in its intensity. In those days, he lost his desire to travel to Gort Ard and look upon the statue that Saint Kelly had carved. Gallen had only to gaze at Everynne to see the face of God.

On the morning of the ninth day, so many dignitaries began arriving that Everynne was constantly being pulled in several directions by those who sought her ear. Each night for the past five days, the lords of the worlds had thrown parties to celebrate, and Gallen saw the way that things would go. These parties would be held every night for years, and though at each party the dignitaries were eager to bestow honors upon him as Lord Escort, Gallen felt somewhat embarrassed by the whole affair, and he wanted only to get away.

So he went to Everynne and said, "I'm thinking of leaving. I can't stand it here any longer."

"You know you are welcome to stay as long as you like," Everynne said. "And you are free to leave."

"It's my mother," Gallen said. "She's getting old and sickly, and I'm worried about her."

Everynne nodded, smiled at him. "And there is something you want from me. You have more than earned any reward that I could give you. Is that what you have come for?"

"Yes," he said. He expected her to ask what he wanted as payment for saving her life, for defeating the Lords of the Swarm. Among the things that she could offer there were many great treasures, but only one he desired. He feared that his price was excessive. He'd prepared all kinds of arguments for the occasion, but before he could ask, she said, "Yes, you may have a key to the Maze of Worlds, but only on one condition: you must put on your mantle often, and if I call for your aid, you must come."

"Of course," he said, grateful that she had agreed. But she touched his cheek, turned his face so that he had to look up into her eyes.

"Don't make that promise lightly," she warned. "You don't know what I have in mind."

And in her eyes he saw that terrible light, and fear struck him to the core of his soul. She reached into her pocket and pulled out a new medallion to wear in his mantle, a receiver that would let him hear her call, and she gave it to him along with the key. It appeared that she had only been waiting for him to ask for these things.

That evening, they went to a gathering in a large dome, where four thousand lords celebrated in a great throng. Gallen had seldom seen so many people in one place, and Orick stared across the crowd in wonder. All of the lords were dressed in their finery in a rainbow of colors. Hundreds of robotic servants had prepared vast sumptuous meals, and all evening long, people crowded around them, thanking and congratulating Gallen, Orick, and Maggie. Everynne was on the far side of the room, and at the end of the evening, Orick seemed worn.

Gallen escorted him out into the hall, and Orick said, "I've got to get out of here, Gallen. I'm feeling well enough to travel. I planned to stay for Everynne's sake, not wanting to leave her alone. But she's got so many of those Tharrin counselors around her now, I don't think she needs me."

"Perhaps," Gallen said. "Why don't you ask Everynne what she wants? She has many people at her ear, and all of them admire her, but you're her friend."

Orick grunted, went back into the great dome and pushed his way to Everynne. A moment later, the two of them got up and escaped to a side room together.

Late that night, Orick came to Gallen's room, and the bear seemed ecstatic. "Do you know that those pills Maggie gave me will keep me alive for at least five hundred years?"

"No, I didn't know that," Gallen lied.

"And I talked to Everynne. She's not going to stay here forever," Orick said. "In ten years, another Tharrin will come take her place as regent, and she's going to come back to Tihrglas to live for awhile. I promised to show her around."

"Good," Gallen said.

"So are you ready to go home?" Orick asked.

"Yes."

"Good," Orick said. "I'll go tell Maggie. Everynne is going to lead us to a gate in a few minutes."

Gallen bundled up his belongings—his outfit and weapons, along with the mantle and weapons that Veriasse had worn—and together the three went to meet Everynne one last time.

Everynne was dressed in her blue traveling robe, as if she might come with them. She said, "Next time you see me, I'll be wearing this." She led them down through unexplored passageways of the omni-mind, down to deep caverns that Everynne said even the dronon had never been told of. Behind a hidden door, they found an ancient gate the color of brass, covered with dust. It was marvelously decorated with images of people and creatures from many worlds, and Everynne told them, "This is the gate that leads to all worlds, all destinations. Enter, and I shall send you home."

A pale green light shone under the arch. Gallen, Orick, and Maggie each hugged Everynne, said their last good-byes.

Then together they stepped through the cold mist between worlds.

They found themselves on a forest road, beneath large pine trees in the mountains. The morning sun was just breaking over the mountains, a radiant pink ball. Kiss-me-quick birds called from the edge of the roadside, and in the distance an owl hooted. The air tasted as sweet to Gallen as Maggie's kisses, and he breathed in deeply.

They walked along the road for most of the day until they reached a small town called Gort Iseal and learned that they were in the north of County Obhiann, many miles away from home.

At the inn that night, people looked at them oddly, and Gallen found himself apologizing for his strange attire and hid his mantle in his pack.

Maggie and Gallen sat at a table near a roaring fire and had a large dinner. Afterward, they sat and talked softly. Some bears came to the door of the inn, begging for leftovers. Orick went outside to talk to one young female. Afterward, he came up to Gallen and Maggie all excited. "That young she-bear has invited me to the Salmon Fest. Can you believe it? We've been gone all that time, and we still didn't miss it!"

Gallen nodded, studied Orick's face. He was eager, that seemed sure. "So why don't you go? What's stopping you?"

"Well," Orick said, "I took this vow a while back. I promised God that I'd only make jolly with one she-bear in my life."

Gallen looked deep into Orick's eyes for a moment, then said, "Orick, there are as many ways to serve God as there are men who serve God. In the past few days, you helped saved every person on this planet, not to mention everyone on ten thousand other worlds. And now this she-bear wants you to serve her, and you're only feeling guilty because you'll get a little pleasure out of it in the process. Why don't you help her out? Why don't you make it two?"

"Yes," Maggie said. "I'm sure you'll be the thrill of her life."

Orick frowned. "All right, you talked me into it." Orick hung around a bit, promised to come back soon for Gallen and Maggie's wedding, then left with the she-bear.

The next morning, Gallen sold an oxygen exchanger to a sailor and used the money to buy a brace of horses. He and Maggie began to ride home in style.

But that night, they were almost in County Morgan when a bad storm tore up the sky. They took refuge at an inn, and Gallen and Maggie sat discussing their wedding plans. With Father Heany dead, no one would block their marriage. Gallen would have his cousin in An Cochan perform the ceremony. As they talked of their plans, one of the locals at another table said, "Och, what a nasty storm we have a blowing outside—and it not even yet mid-September!"

Maggie turned to Gallen and whispered, "What day was it when we left here?"

"September fifteenth," Gallen said.

Maggie turned to the stranger. "What's the date today?"

"Why, the fourteenth," the man answered.

And Gallen sat there, stunned. That trickster Everynne had sent them back in time again. He suddenly recalled that later on tonight, he would meet several robbers and a sidhe on the road to An Cochan, some twelve miles distant.

"Maggie, my love," Gallen said, "would you excuse me for a few hours, darling? There's something I have to do. I promise, I'll be back for you early in the morning."

"I suppose—if it's important," she said.

"It's not a big job," Gallen said. "But I think I need to save a man's life."

He went up to his room and dug through his clothes, put on his mantle. In one corner of his pack, he found the mask of lavender starlight he had picked up on Fale. In Veriasse's pack, he found the wavy-bladed dagger the sidhe had been carrying.

Gallen dressed himself all in black, like the Lord Protector he was, then strapped on his sword and rode out in the rain and darkness to meet his destiny.